SILENCE ON COLD RIVER

SILENCE

ON COLD

RIVER

CASEY DUNN

PEGASUS CRIME
NEW YORK LONDON

Silence on Cold River

Pegasus Crime is an imprint of
Pegasus Books, Ltd.
West 37th Street, 13th Floor
New York, NY 10018

First Pegasus Books hardcover edition May 2020

Interior design by Sabrina Plomitallo-González, Pegasus Books

ISBN: 978-1-64313-408-6

10 9 8 7 6 5 4 3 2 1

Printed in the United States of America
Distributed by Simon & Schuster

To Katelyn
The last chapter is for you, because of you. I hope you like it.

MICHAEL

THE FOREMAN LISTS THE CHARGES FOR WHICH I STAND ACCUSED. THE air in the courtroom is cold and thick. It reminds me of a lightning storm in the dead of winter, the kind that makes people look out their windows, smiling and shivering, watching for the next forked strike, counting until the next big boom.

No one is smiling now.

My attorney, Ama Shoemaker, shifts her weight off her toes for half a second and resettles. The tap of her heels against the sealed concrete floor travels the length of the courtroom. I imagine the vibrations climbing the khaki-colored walls, racing across the ceiling, weaving between fluorescent lights, and fading into oblivion.

I turn my head to stare full-faced at Ama. The side of her cheek slides between her teeth. Her eyes remain fixed on the jury. I'm not sure which aspect makes her more nervous: the fact that my trial is her first big case as a court-appointed defense attorney, or me.

Because I'm guilty as sin, and she knows it.

The foreman finishes the list of charges, and the courtroom falls silent, a string pulled taut to the point of snapping.

"Have you reached a verdict?" the judge asks. Ama doesn't glance in my direction.

The foreman clears his throat. "We have, Your Honor. In the case of the State of Georgia versus Michael Jeffery Walton, we find the defendant not guilty on all charges."

Beside me, Ama continues to hold her breath, drawing her torso unnaturally straight. I imagine her weight collecting near the front of her shoes, because by nature, humans are still prey animals, still subliminally answering when a shot of adrenaline chases a prick of fear down a spine.

The room is dismissed, clearing in haste. Ama investigates me from her peripheral vision first, shuffling needlessly through her papers before securing them in her double-buckle briefcase. She drums four fingernails on the strip of metal running across the top. Her thumb ends the run with a thump against the leather underside.

"This is when a client typically says 'thank you,' Michael," she says.

"Thank you, Michael," I reply, yet my attention is drawn to the far corner of the courtroom, next to the rows reserved for the jury, where piece after piece of evidence was offered as proof. The pictures didn't do it for me. The visual memory is hazy and far-off, a rumble of distant thunder uncommitted in its future trajectory. But the sounds. Oh, the sounds.

I close my eyes and recount the struggle note for splendid note, the shift into a ragged, exhausted tenor. There's an optimal volume for the human ear to detect a sound at perfect clarity, and most people don't realize it's quite low. At high volume, all one hears is noise. But in that perfect range, the tone comes through on a razor's edge, straight and unwavering. If only those items of proof had been captured. I would've begged for them to be admitted, to play them in this room with an audience, again and again. They'd be spellbound and breathless. Father would be proven right, dead in his grave—*all things for a reason, son*—and Mother would think there was a sliver of hope for me yet.

"Do me one courtesy," Ama says. She turns to face me, guarding her squishy, pulsing organs with her briefcase. "Make sure I never see you again."

We hold eye contact for a full second. Her pupils constrict, doubling the size of her pale gray irises.

Ama rakes her teeth across her lip and glances at her wristwatch. I follow her gaze: 3:33 PM Her mouth opens, an excuse for why she's about to leave without escorting me out probably floating somewhere in her throat. She won't need to shield my exit. Tarson is a rural town in the foothills of north Georgia and well over an hour from anywhere that matters. My work didn't even make for a sentence in the *Atlanta Journal-Constitution*. This isn't the kind of place where people picket on the courthouse steps. They'll turn over opinions in church pews and on front porches, in line at the feed store. And I'm a minor. Ama had said she'd move to have the records of this case sealed should I be found not guilty, but that was when she never thought I'd get off.

Ama reaches into the front pocket of her briefcase and extracts a handful of cash.

"I don't guess your mom is picking you up," she states.

I flinch at the mention of Mother, and my eyes travel the scale of music notes she branded into my forearm with the end of her cigarette.

CDEFGAB. Can you feel it now, Michael?

"I would guess not," I answer.

Ama sets the money down on the black tabletop. "This should be enough for a cab," she says. "I meant what I said. This is your second chance. Take it. I never want to have to cross paths again."

Ama steps out of our row and moves down the center aisle. I turn but don't follow, keeping my stare where the brown fabric meets in a seam on Ama's back as she walks to the open doors at the back of the room. Her parting words echo in my skull.

I never want to have to cross paths again.

What if we did? Not orchestrated in any way, but naturally, in a way that would almost suggest fate itself had intervened. Something random. Somewhere new. All things for a reason.

She steps through the doorway without once looking back. I imagine her steps on the polished floor, clicking and clacking down the main corridor, faster and faster as her internal chemistry demands the safety of open space and distance from threat.

If we saw each other again, it could be a coincidence, an accident. An almost. But if our paths crossed a third time . . . now that would be interesting. Three weeks, three days—the length of the trial. 3:33 PM Mother's favorite number. Her most important rule: the Rule of Three.

One time is an accident. Two times is a coincidence. Three times is mastery.

If I didn't know better, I would think Lady Fate is flirting with me.
In my mind, Ama reaches the parking lot and breaks into a run.
You run, Ama.
I can wait.

AMA

AMA CHAPLIN STEPPED OUT OF HER SEDAN, ZIPPED UP HER JACKET, AND slid her sunglasses onto the top of her head. Nearly twenty years and Tarson hadn't changed a bit. At least the crisp mountain air was clean. She couldn't say the same for anything else in the town. Ama dropped her sunglasses in place, recalling every reason she shouldn't be here and wondering how the hell she'd made the nearly two-hour drive north of the city without talking herself into turning around.

Deep down, she knew why: *that* case, that impossible case, and the wall of evidence she'd somehow managed to topple. The disemboweled cat pinned to a board like a science project found in the crawl space beneath her client's house, the other small animals in varying stages of decomposition slit into pieces and found heaped in a pile inside a hollow tree just beyond the edge of his yard. The neighbor who watched her client lure a cat with a piece of ham and tuck it inside his jacket.

Still, somehow she'd won. The rookie, the underdog, the outsider, the felon's daughter, the woman. *She'd won.*

Maybe she thought that if she came back here, breathed the air, ran the same trail she'd run every morning before heading to the courthouse, she'd rediscover that woman again—the one with barely enough cash in her bank account to fill the tank of her car and an equally empty conscience. Back then she'd had no idea how she'd won, and even now she still didn't have an answer. But maybe she would be able to unearth the reason she'd lost her case today.

She plucked a Walkman and a small can of pepper spray from under the driver's seat before slamming her door shut. The echo went far and wide. The guilty verdict had been announced with similar effect: *Ama Chaplin just lost.*

She couldn't remember the last time she'd been so unlucky in the courtroom. Denied motions, barred evidence, a star witness who never showed, and the heel on her black patent Louboutin that broke in the middle of her closing argument. She didn't want to think that had something to do with the guilty verdict, but it was impossible to be sure what affected a jury more: proof or presentation.

She knelt to thread a shoelace through the lid of the pepper spray as the memory of the foreman's voice announcing her client's guilt replayed in her mind. Of course, this latest client had been guilty. Most of them were. Ama could count on her fingers the number of innocent defendants she'd represented. Determining guilt or innocence wasn't her job. Her job was to provide the most thorough defense money could buy so if the defendant was found guilty, there would be no room or cause for an appeal. In reality, she was doing a public service. If a guilty person walked, it was on the prosecution's hands, not hers.

Failure washed over her in a wave of heat. She yanked the knot secure, then stood and brought the heels of her hands down on the hood of her car, light-headed and furious. She hadn't been sleeping as of late. The night before, she'd tried to drown her insomnia in a bottle of top-shelf gin. All she got for her efforts was a splitting headache and a forgettable night with the young executive who lived in the penthouse opposite hers. They'd exchanged casual banter in the elevator, and instead of returning to her apartment, she'd followed him to his. In hindsight, she should've opted to finish the bottle of gin. At least it would've brought some satisfaction.

Or you could always give it a go with a man your own age, Ama's assistant, Lindsey Harold, had advised whenever she recounted another lackluster evening. *At least they know their way around the bases. And they've usually learned the value of a good, long warm-up.*

Well, that would make one of us, Ama usually responded, which was followed up with Lindsey accusing her of being detached and emotionally unavailable, and naming her job the cause.

Although she wouldn't admit it, Ama had to agree with her. She welcomed the shadow of every soul with open arms, shielded it, and sent it back into the world. She'd seen some deep, dark, horrible shit in the twenty years since she'd become a defense attorney. Of course it made her reluctant to form connections. Some of the worst minds she'd ever encountered turned their wheels behind very ordinary, clean-cut faces. Preachers, teachers, Little League coaches, presidents of the PTA. Evil wore any face. So she didn't like the idea of second dates or sleeping over. Gin was her favorite company. At least she got to set the pace of how fast gin would kill her. If those were the costs of being the priciest defense attorney in the city of Atlanta, she'd take it.

She felt for her phone inside her jacket pocket. She should call Lindsey now to tell her where she was, but there was something freeing in knowing she was completely off everyone's radar. This latest loss was a big one. She knew the phone on her receptionist's desk probably wouldn't ring quite so often with calls from potential clients seeking representation in the next few days. Maybe not even until the next big win, which was months away at a minimum. The case should've been a slam dunk. What the hell had gone wrong?

Other attorneys might consider the loss the beginning of a losing streak. Most lawyers she knew practiced some kind of habit or ritual before going into a trial or carried a lucky totem with them into the courtroom. Ama wasn't one for superstition. As she clipped her Walkman to the hip of her running shorts and adjusted it to its perfect spot, it occurred to her that she had more ritualistic preparations for going on a run than she did for walking into a courtroom ahead of a closing argument. She believed in coincidence; many of her cases had been won on it. She knew she couldn't second-guess coincidence just because it wasn't stacking in her favor this time.

A decent martini and a little release usually did the trick to snap her out of a funk, but she was zero for two. Surely to God, a long drive and a hard run would do something for her mood, or, at the very least, would chase away the remnants of her hangover.

The rumble of a struggling engine approached from behind. She looked over her shoulder. An old white van pulled into the small parking lot, which was empty but for the two of them. Its rear windows were blacked out, and a pair of red bandanas served as curtains for the rear windshield.

A beat-up American-model van in the middle of nowhere.

Isn't this how most serial killer stories begin?

She stretched her arms one at a time across her chest, keeping a sidelong focus on the car. It sputtered as the engine shifted into park and then idled in a corner spot. The driver's-side window was transparent. The driver was a middle-aged black man. His cheeks were flushed like he'd either been drinking or was very upset. He gripped the top of the steering wheel with gloved hands.

Ama hesitated, eyeing her car, the keys in her hand, the tube of pepper spray tied to the front of her shoe. This trail wasn't popular. It definitely wasn't listed in any guidebooks or tourist pamphlets for north Georgia hiking. Either you knew about it or you didn't, which had once made it one of Ama's favorite places to escape. When she was here, she was small and inconsequential. She didn't impact lives here. She wasn't responsible for the grief of the victims' loved ones being made doubly worse with a not-guilty verdict.

This solitude now made her heart rate accelerate. She propped her foot on the rear bumper of her car and pretended to stretch her leg as she read the van's license tag, committing it to memory.

She switched legs, considering her options. She could get in her car right now and drive to a different, more popular trail. She could have her office run the guy's plate. If there was so much as an unpaid parking ticket, she could have them phone in a tip to the local police department. The station wasn't too far from here. He'd be picked up in thirty minutes tops. She could see the headline now: DEFENSE ATTORNEY HELPS BUST REPEAT OFFENDER. Surely that would send good karma her way. Not that she believed in that, either, unlike the guy last night. He'd asked her, *Aren't you worried helping guilty people go free is going to come back to haunt you?*

That's just not the way the universe works, she'd answered.

And she believed it.

She did.

The universe eventually took care of the guilty—like Michael Jeffery Walton drowning in Cold River a couple of years after his trial. Some say he fell. Others say he jumped. If Ama was a betting girl, she'd put her money down on someone pushing him in, vigilante justice–style. If she'd stayed in town long enough after his trial, she might've hired someone to do just that. Would she be back here, even just for a run, if he hadn't been swallowed up by that river? She wanted to believe she wasn't afraid; she'd gotten him off against impossible odds. Surely he would've wanted to keep her around in case he needed another miracle. Chances were, had he lived much longer, he would've ended up in front of a judge and jury again.

Ama opened her phone and dialed her office. The screen flashed and went blank. No signal. She'd try again once she made it to the top of the first peak. Ama cast one last glance at the van, locked her car, pocketed her keys and her phone, and jogged to the mouth of the trail.

E
D
D
I
E

EDDIE STEVENS SQUEEZED THE STEERING WHEEL UNTIL HIS KNUCKLES hurt. He released his grip and sank back against the chair. The drive had been harder than he thought. Now here he was: the last place his daughter, Hazel Rae Stevens, was ever seen alive. She walked into these woods, on this trail. He watched her do it, just like the tall blonde did now, and she never came back out.

The thought of it lit the backs of his eyes. Waiting an hour in the van had seemed like a waste of time then. He'd lucked into a string of extra work, and he was determined to save up enough money to be able to send Hazel to college without her having to take out student loans. He'd told her he had to get some work done in town and would meet her back right here.

Right here, Hazel Rae. Five PM, and not a second late, you hear? You like runnin' by yourself better anyhow.

The memory brought the burn in his eyes from back to front. They smoldered, still dry, tear ducts squeezing the way a throat does after a hot day without water. He pressed his fingers against them, trying to dull the pain and the sound of her voice in his head. She'd asked him to wait for an hour.

If only I'd waited.

He'd logged over 1,200 hours in these woods since then. He'd memorized every inch of the five-square-mile search zone. He knew where the trails were most likely to wash out during a hard rain, where the river bottom dropped after a tight bend, which rocks shifted with a person's weight. But he didn't know where Hazel was.

"Come with me," she'd pled that day. "We can just walk. It'll do you some good."

"My knee is acting up again, Hazy. I don't want to slow you down."

"You can set the pace," she'd offered.

"Not today. I got a wiring job in town. Should be quick. You and I will finish up about the same time."

"Meant to be, then," she'd said, and retracted her petite frame from the open passenger door.

"Hey, Hazel," Eddie had called through her open window.

She'd popped her head and shoulders through the opening, resting her elbows on the frame. "Yeah, Daddy?"

"I know you're eighteen and grown and all, but just be careful. Don't talk to anybody you don't know."

Hazel's expression had softened into something playful. "Daddy, I barely talk to people I do know." Then she'd walked away, her purple-streaked, frizzy hair flashing through the early scattering of trees before the woods swallowed her up.

Most people had read Hazel wrong her whole life, even more so once she hit fourteen and traded every shade of color in her closet for black. One night, he found her in the bathroom they shared, hair bleach burning her scalp. He'd steered her under the showerhead and held her there while he rinsed it clean. The bleach had been on long enough to turn her soft brown curls brittle and orange. Eddie had damn near cried.

"I'm sorry, Daddy," she'd said real soft, jade eyes downcast. "I just wanted to look like Mom."

"Me, too, Hazy. I'm sorry, too." He pressed the side of his face against her dripping head. "I'm no good at this stuff."

"You're not bad at it, either."

Eddie had told her he was going to get dinner and came back with a new box of hair dye, which the store clerk had recommended for Hazel's hair type. Hazel broke down in tears, shaking and snotty. So Eddie read the directions, pulled on the thin, clear gloves, and dyed her hair himself.

Eddie slammed his open hand on the dashboard. He shifted his gaze to the nine-millimeter sitting on his passenger seat. There were two rounds in the clip. One to fire into the air to draw the attention of anyone nearby, the second to lodge into his brain by way of his mouth. That angle of trajectory left zero chance of survival and, if he leaned toward his window, wouldn't spatter a mess on the last chance Hazel had to be found.

When she never came out of the woods that day, Eddie had gone in. He'd called her name. Waited. Listened. Only crows answered. A storm had snuck in over the ridgeline. Within minutes, the sky had opened up, and the rain came down nearly too hard to see through. Eddie had struggled up hill after hill, cursing his weight and work boots and trick knee, especially when all three hit head-on and took him to his hands in a torrent of water streaming down the narrow path.

By the time the first officers arrived, Hazel had been gone an hour and forty-seven minutes too long. The night sky was black as ink, and the lights from the patrol cars bounced off the shining walls of rain-soaked evergreens.

Runaway.

He'd heard it that first night and most days after that, usually in conjunction with the words "loner kid," "dead mother," and "goth." In the jury of public opinion, the case was closed in the first forty-eight hours. The official search ended two months later, and the disappearance of Hazel Rae Stevens moved into the cold case files by the end of winter.

Now, one year after she vanished, Eddie was determined to force his daughter's name and face back into the spotlight. There was one last way he could make them pay attention. One way he'd make them remember Hazel.

Under his nine-millimeter sat Hazel's journal and a stack of evidence Eddie had tried to give to the station months ago, with little response. Three other people had disappeared in these parts in the past ten years. There were no similarities between them, and none of them had ever been found. No bodies. No farewell notes. No scrap remnant. Just gone.

The detective assigned to take his questions and keep him updated had accepted the information like a teenage girl receiving a tacky sweater from a distant relative, complete with a pat on his shoulder, and handed it right back to him.

"She's not in those woods," the detective had said.

But she was. Eddie knew it. He also knew he wasn't a smart man. Not the kind of smart it would take to make investigators listen. And he was a transplant here, moved from Texas after his wife passed. Last year, a handful of people had baked casseroles and hung flyers and searched the forest on foot and horseback, but their commitment to Hazel evaporated in a slow, invisible way. They hadn't known her as a baby, sweet and shy. Or as an eight-year-old who could play three instruments. They knew her only as a sullen-seeming teenage girl with too much eyeliner and not enough interest in high school football or the boys who played on the team. They'd failed her. He'd failed her. There was only one way he would gain enough attention to bring her home. All he had to do was pull the trigger.

He touched the barrel of his gun with his index finger. Regret whispered through him. After two weeks with no sign of Hazel, detectives had started preparing him to find a body, coaching him on what a relief it would be to lay her to rest, to know where she was. He wanted to agree with them. He did agree. Ending his life was his last effort to find Hazel in two ways: to reignite interest in her case, and, if there was another side, some kind of place people go when they die, to maybe find her there. Everyone else was sure she was dead. He knew he'd been a fool to think anything different. So why didn't he feel it? Shouldn't a parent feel it when their child is gone, some kind of instinctive recognition? He wasn't sure either way. Aside from not knowing where she was, that unknown bothered him the most.

He pulled off his gloves and rubbed his face. What if this was a mistake? What if it had the opposite effect? He glanced at Hazel's journal, then at the clock.

"I'll sit here with you for an hour, like I should've a year ago. And if you need me to stay alive, you give me a sign," he whispered. He pulled her journal into his lap and opened the cover.

AMA TOOK THE FIRST SERIES OF RISING SWITCHBACKS TOO FAST. BY THE time she reached the peak, she was out of breath and her calves were on fire. She stopped and planted her hands on her lower back, stretching out the cramps that laced up her sides.

She hadn't heard a car door close, and the trail had split twice already. Even if the guy in the van was some nutjob sociopathic serial killer, he wouldn't find her. Plus, from what she had seen, he didn't look like he was in the best shape. She could probably outrun him.

"You're being ridiculous," she muttered. Still, she couldn't shake the tingly sensation of warning. She reached into her jacket pocket for her phone. She had a single bar of signal. "Thank you," she said on an exhale, and dialed her assistant's phone number.

"Ama? Where are you? The phone is ringing off the hook, and two reporters have come by for comments on the Hershaw case."

"I'm on a run up in the mountains. I need to clear my head," she said, steadying her breathing.

"What? Why did you—?"

"Stop talking, Lindsey. I need you to run a plate for me and call in a location if there's any kind of outstanding infraction."

"Sure, of course."

Ama recited the van's plate sequence and described the location of the parking lot.

"You're in *Tarson*? Is someone there with you?" Lindsey asked. "I don't know if you should be running in meth country by yourself, especially if you're feeling the need to call in a plate. I know you're a monster in the courtroom, but this isn't your jungle, Ama. You need to be careful."

"This is me being careful," she countered. "I will call you when I'm done. I should be off the trail by five fifteen, but the cell service up here is crap. If you don't hear back from me by five thirty, call me."

"Okay. But, Ama—"

Ama hung up her phone and stowed it in her zip pocket. Talking to Lindsey had calmed her down. Nervous people always had the opposite effect on her. Whether that was what made her a good attorney or was just a by-product of soothing guilty, agitated people she wasn't sure. Right now, she was just glad it was one of her strengths.

She flexed her feet one at a time on a tree root, excising the tension from her legs, and popped on the headphones she'd been too wary to use before, in case the music blocked out the sounds of an approaching stranger. She stopped herself from checking over her shoulder, then set off at an easy pace down the back side of the first hill.

She leaned forward into the next climbing set of switchbacks, which were steeper than the first. She felt lighter when she reached the top, the weight of pushing uphill lifted once the ground leveled briefly under her driving feet. She turned downhill again and allowed her stride to lengthen as she began the descent. The trees blurred into a palette of gray and brown. She increased her speed, thrilling at the nearly out-of-control feeling of racing down a mountain. Her arms pumped at her sides. Her pulse and the bass from her music pounded in her ears.

Ahead, the trail took a hairpin turn and leveled for about twenty yards before turning down again. She eased off her pace to save her wind for her favorite part of the trail, which was coming up quickly. The second half of the descent was steeper and cut the mountainside in switchbacks all the way to the valley floor, where Cold River, narrow and infamously deep, carved a boundary between two foothills, and marked the place where she would turn around and retrace her path back to the parking lot.

The ground dipped, and she took off, racing herself, her shadows, and the thoughts in her head until they were mostly well behind her. Only the foreman's voice from this morning kept up. She dug in, driving herself to her highest gear. Instead of quieting, his voice grew louder.

We find the defendant guilty. Guilty. Guilty. Guilty.

She gritted her teeth and pushed off the ground to leap across the tight bend. Upon landing, her left toe caught under an exposed root, but she was going too fast to control the fall. Her ankle twisted and popped. Her foot slid loose from her shoe, and she landed hard on her shoulder, then rolled down the hill until she crashed to a stop against the base of a tree.

Pain shot up her left leg and radiated across her back. She spit out dirt and debris between gasps of air. Once the world around her stopped spinning, she pulled her knees into her chest, groaning. Her ankle was fire-hot to the touch. She pulled her sock the rest of the way off. She could wiggle her toes, but the idea of bearing any weight on her foot sent shivers through her.

She sat upright and patted her head, searching for her sunglasses, but they must've flown off. Tortoiseshell frames in a blanket of leaves. They were as good as gone. Her earphones were looped around her neck like a scarf. She dug into her jacket pocket to retrieve her phone, which came out in two pieces. She squeezed the pieces in her fist and collapsed back onto the blanket of leaves and dirt.

"Really?" she asked the sky. She raised her arm above her face and looked at her watch. She'd been running about thirty minutes, which amounted to about two and a half miles with the elevation changes. She returned her focus to her ankle. Now that the sudden agony of trauma had subsided, she was able to move her foot back and forth about an inch. Hopefully, that meant nothing was broken. The area around the joint was already swelling, and the top of her foot was turning red.

Rustling leaves drew her ear. She grabbed hold of the base of a tree and worked herself to standing. A hiker was coming straight up the hill through the trees. He had a wooden walking cane in one hand and a large pack on his back, a rolled-up tent strapped to the top. His jeans were fitted but slouchy with wear. His black hair was short and tussled. Even in all the trees, his jawline was the hardest thing out there.

Ama blinked and licked her lips. If she wasn't crippled and didn't have a hundred leaves and twigs in her hair, this encounter might have gone a very different way.

"Hey!" she called out, waving. The man looked up, startled. He scanned the view in front of him a second before finding her. He picked up his pace, stowed the cane between his back and his pack, and marched the remainder of the incline.

"Is everything okay?" he asked.

"Yeah. Mostly. I'm glad you came along," she answered. She smiled, too big. Was she glad? She was alone in the woods with a strange man, and God knew what he had in that giant pack. He stopped before crossing the trail, perhaps sensing her hesitation.

"What happened to your shoe?" he asked.

Ama pointed up the hill. "I tripped on a root up the trail. The root kept my shoe."

He smiled. "Can you walk?"

"I can hobble, as long as there's a tree within an arm's reach."

"Here." He withdrew his walking cane. "This should work better than hanging on to trees."

"Thanks." The wood was warm and worn. She ran her fingers down the grain, expecting it to be smooth, but straight lines were cut into it. She rotated the cane to get a better look. Piano keys had been carved down the length of the cane. They were perfectly even. She caught herself pressing down on one, as if to test it for sound.

"This is incredible. Did you do this?" she asked.

He nodded. "After many failed attempts. Music has been a big part of my life. Carving wood didn't come so naturally."

"Well, you're obviously good at it now," she said, marveling at it. "Is it to scale?"

"That's what I tell myself."

Ama leaned into the cane. She could press the ball of her injured foot to the ground so long as she didn't let her heel come down. "This is helping. Thanks."

"Do you need water or anything?" He angled his shoulder to slide off his pack. Nervousness bloomed inside Ama. At least it wasn't the guy in the beater van, she thought to herself. Although statistically, this handsome fellow was more likely to hurt her, so long as he was over thirty-five, but she would bet he was a bit younger. The skin on his face was lineless, despite having obviously logged countless hours outside.

"This is going to sound crazy," he started, breaking through Ama's train of thought, "but have we met before? You look really familiar."

"I doubt it. I'm not from around here."

He grinned, sheepish, and ran his fingers through his hair. "Name's Jonathon."

"Ama."

"Ama? I haven't heard of many Amas." He cocked his head to the side. "Family name?"

"It's a long story," she said, irritation rekindling in the furnace of her rib cage. "The short version is that my dad was an Alabama fan, but my mother wouldn't let him name me Bama, so they agreed on Ama."

"Ama from Bama. It's cute," he offered.

"Not if you're me," she responded. "And I'm not from Alabama."

"Well, your secret is safe with me." He raised his fingers in some kind of salute. "Have you called for help, Ama?"

She nearly answered with the truth. She pressed her lips together, reconsidering in an instant. "I called a friend. He's on the way now. I'm supposed to meet him at the south trailhead," she lied.

Jonathon stared up the hill. "If you stay on the path, that's going to be over a mile to the south entrance. I know a more direct route. The first part will be tough"—he paused, motioning to her foot—"because it's almost straight down. Then it won't be so bad, and it'll be half the distance."

Ama glanced at her watch. If she stuck to the path and hobbled, it could take her two hours to get there, and she wasn't sure she had two hours of daylight left. While a direct route would cut down the distance, Ama was nervous enough at the thought of staying on the path with a complete stranger, much less wandering blindly through the woods. He seemed nice, but she'd met enough criminals to know they typically shared a charming personality.

"Actually, I'm feeling a lot better. You need to get where you're going before dark, and I can make it." She forced her left foot mostly flat against the ground, grinning to cover up the pain shooting up her ankle. "Not to be weird. The situation is just . . ."

"Weird," he finished for her. "I get it."

"Here." She tried to hand him the walking cane, but he took a step back, shaking his head.

"You need it. I can make another."

"I can't take this." She gripped the end and extended it out to him. "It's special to you. How many miles has this thing seen?"

"It's seen a lot." He smiled and gingerly took hold of the opposite end. "Well, take care, Ama. And make sure we don't meet like this again," he said with an easy laugh.

"I'll do my best. Enjoy your hike." She slid her feet forward a step, forcing herself into movement.

"I will," he called at her back. She waved over her shoulder, continuing for a solid minute before glancing behind her. He was gone. She was already exhausted, and she'd only made it thirty or forty yards. How the hell was she going to make it all the way back?

"Hey, Ama." Jonathon's voice came from close behind her. She pivoted on her good foot and grabbed a tree to keep from going down.

"God, you scared me," she said, glaring.

"Didn't mean to. I just thought you'd make it farther with both shoes," he said, producing the shoe she'd lost at the beginning of her fall. The top of the pepper spray was still attached to her laces, but the rest of the bottle was gone.

"Sorry. It's been a rough day," she said.

"We've all had those." He tilted his head to the side. "And we have met before. I remember now. It was at a martini bar in Atlanta a couple years back. It was fall. They had trees on the patio with the most yellow leaves I'd ever seen. I asked the waiter what they were. He said they were ginkgo trees. Do you remember them? Do you . . . remember me?"

Ama forced herself to swallow. How many hotel bars had she been in? How many times had she ended up in a room that wasn't hers for an hour or two?

She cleared her throat. "I'm sorry. I don't."

"It was a couple years ago. There was a piano player. He wasn't very good. You went up and talked to him."

Ama startled, stricken with recognition. "He butchered 'Stairway to Heaven.'" She laughed and shook her head. "Did you buy me a drink?"

"No." The expression on his face changed like clouds passing over a once-clear sky, blotting out the sun. "I was the piano player. You said you'd give me all the cash in your wallet if I'd take a twenty-minute intermission so you could finish your drink in peace. You said it looked like I was out past my bedtime. Your business card was mixed into the bills. That's where I remember your name from. Do you remember me now?"

"Oh, my God. I'm so sorry. I'd had a lot to drink. It was a bad night . . ." The memory came rushing back. The entire firm had gone out to dinner at Olive after the conclusion of the National Association of Criminal Defense Lawyers conference, and she'd found out she'd been passed over for partner. She'd drank her way to the bottom of a row of dirty martinis to dull the frustration. When that hadn't worked, she took it out on the mediocre piano player.

Now Jonathon wasn't just a stranger in the woods. He was little more than a stranger, with a reason to hate her. The adrenaline surging through her numbed her injured leg to a degree, but she knew she still wouldn't be able to run on it. She backed up a step, and her left ankle threatened to buckle. The trail was morgue silent, and the sudden heaviness in the air had brought a hush over the usual chatter of birds.

"You must have a lot of bad days and bad nights, Ama. And you carry a lot of cash," he mused as if he hadn't heard her. "That's not safe, Ama."

"I was a total asshole. I'm sorry. It really wasn't about you. If I could go back to that night, I'd smack myself. Is there anything I can do to make it up to you?" Her mind raced. She didn't have any cash on her, and she wasn't wearing any expensive jewelry. She had nothing to barter.

"Stop saying sorry," he barked, his calm demeanor splintering for a second. "Don't say sorry," he repeated, regaining his earlier tone. "Say thank you. This is where you say, 'Thank you, Michael.'"

Michael?

Ama swallowed hard. Familiarity washed over her. Why did that phrase hit her straight in the gut? Before she could respond, Jonathon brought his cane behind his head and swung hard. The thicker end connected with Ama's temple. The woods went bright white in front of her eyes, and a dull crunch filled her head. She was unconscious before she hit the ground.

MARTIN

DETECTIVE MARTIN LOCKLEAR SAT AT HIS DESK AT THE TARSON POLICE Department and spun a pen between his fingers, swiveling back and forth in his rotating chair like windshield wipers in slow motion. There was one critical difference: windshield wipers were useful. When he'd been considering taking the position as Tarson's only detective, he'd figured a little mountain town like this would at least have a friendly hum to it. But now, after three months on the job, he'd concluded that Tarson was more like a morgue than it was like Mayberry.

Martin's old station in Savannah, Georgia, where he'd spent a decade as a detective on the narcotics unit, was a living thing; loud as a freeway at rush hour and just as pissed-off. If there was a spell of quiet, it was understood to be an eye in an ever-present storm, a moment to prepare for battle. But the eye of the storm always passed. He'd been on edge, loaded and ready, for three long months.

He exhaled, planted his feet on the threadbare carpet, and put down the pen. Last night, Martin had pulled up to the one-bedroom brick house he rented and found himself standing in the bathroom, his hand on the medicine cabinet's mirrored door where sleeping pills and painkillers should've been—would've been, had he been standing in his old home in Savannah.

The stagnant quiet of this station, of this town, made him feel like *he* was the storm. His recent track record certainly read like the wake of one.

Martin glanced at his left hand, the fog of memories clearing for just a moment, and the stale, slow drone of the department returned. His thumb was absently gliding over his ring finger, spinning the ghost of his wedding band, his skin still faintly striped from the nine-year shadow. His marriage had almost been a casualty of his old job. Then his addiction had eaten them both, fast and whole.

His wife, Stacy, went first. He came home one night to find her gone, her closet empty. She hadn't left a note; there wasn't anything left to say that hadn't been said a thousand times before. His job had been next. They'd said it wasn't personal—budget cuts, plain and simple. They'd offered to write him a letter of recommendation anywhere he wanted to go, as long as it was somewhere else.

Martin's gaze traveled the perimeter of the main room of the Tarson Police Department, the only *somewhere else* that had even offered him an interview. Gray walls, gray carpet, a black plastic clock ticking away on the front wall, six basic desks arranged in two rows facing forward with a bigger desk by the main door for the receptionist, a woman who had an army of little fluffy dogs she knitted clothes for and absolutely no interest in answering the phone if anyone else was around to take the call. The whole setup reminded him more of an elementary school classroom than the beehive feel of his old precinct. The department chief's office loomed off to the right like an Orwellian principal.

On the back wall were doors to two incident rooms, then a short hall to a pair of interrogation rooms, a storage room, and a janitor's closet no one ever seemed to open. Just past the locked door began the second half of the building, where people under arrest were printed, processed, and detained while awaiting bail, arraignment, or transfer. Those arrests generally fell into one of three categories: drunk driving, drugs, and bored teenagers with spray paint. Sometimes an overachieving citizen managed to land in all three categories, which Martin had unofficially coined the Tarson Trifecta.

The main door swung open, lifting Martin's gaze. Eric Stanton, a baby-faced, second-generation beat cop born and raised in Tarson, walked in with two white plastic bags of Chinese takeout. Stanton dropped one bag on his own desk and then strode to the captain's office with the other bag tucked under his arm.

Captain James Barrow was visible in stripes through the open blinds that covered the large office window. He was sitting at his desk, the side of his face illuminated by a small lamp, the overhead lights turned off. One hand raked through what was left of his silver hair. The other pressed a phone to his ear. Martin watched Stanton walk into the office and set the bag on Barrow's desk. Then he retreated from the office and back to his own workstation, Captain Barrow never once looking up.

The white plastic bag slouched down, revealing a slender brown paper bag beneath, the top twisted as if wrapped around the throat of a bottle. Martin narrowed his eyes, entertaining a prick of resentment, but quickly dismissed it. What was the chief of police supposed to do, walk into the liquor store? And how could Stanton—groomed since birth to respect rank and badge—be expected to say no?

Martin had a soft spot for Stanton. The patrol officer had taken Martin out to lunch and on a tour of the jurisdiction his first day on the job, right after the captain had more or less reamed him out in place of a welcome: *I know about your record. No one else needs to. This is your second chance, so don't blow it.*

The entire tour lasted less than an hour, and Stanton's dispatch radio had remained dead. Martin had been tempted to ask him if it was on. Stanton was a talker, especially when it came to telling stories about Tarson's history. Turns out, the foothills ringing the town weren't as untouched as they looked. Beneath the earth ran a labyrinth of Cold War–era fallout shelters and abandoned gold mines. Stanton's favorite anecdote was about an evangelical group that had custom built a tiny underground village, complete with a chapel, and illegally sold sections of the subterranean real estate by the square inch.

Then the recession struck in the eighties, and it hit Tarson and places like it harder than most. What jobs there were dried up, including an old factory that had employed half the population that shuttered its doors overnight. Most of those who had the means to leave left. What remained of Tarson had been on a morphine drip for twenty years.

Martin caught himself staring at the boundary map of the Tarson jurisdiction pinned to the wall by the front door, his gaze roaming the green, unsuspecting range of foothills. Six months ago, when the posting for a detective position in Tarson had shown up on a job board the same day he got out of rehab, he'd decided to pretend that Tarson had been entirely unknown to him, that it would be new, fresh, untainted with any smudge of personal history. Telling himself an outright lie on his first day of freedom probably wasn't setting himself up for success, but here he was: three months employed, six months sober, and miserable.

The truth was Tarson was the last pushpin marker on a murder case Martin had worked that had gone cold two years prior. The final clue was at a rest stop at the edge of town, the last place a person could take a piss behind a locked door without buying something first before they reached the Tennessee state line: a garbled, seven-second message left by Toni Hargrove, a prostitute-turned-informant, from a parking lot pay phone to Martin's cell phone. Two years later, he still couldn't fall asleep without thinking of Toni, terrified and desperate, calling the one person she thought would hear her, help her, and instead of that person answering her call, he'd been adrift on a cloud of diazepam and Xanax.

When local PD arrived at the rest stop the next day, the receiver on the pay phone she'd used still dangled from the box, and two of the number keys were missing—the three and the nine—although no one who worked at the rest stop could tell investigators whether the phone had been tampered with before or after the call. It took them an hour to find Toni's body, her throat sliced from the base of her chin to the dip in her collarbones and her skin flayed open. They never did find the tip of her tongue—or any scrap of a lead on who had killed her. But Martin knew the blame was his to bear.

Martin half believed it was fate that had drawn him morbidly back to Tarson, but whether fate was shining a beacon of guidance or telling him to run like hell was a mystery. He'd wanted to shake the satellite images he'd memorized of two-lane roads crisscrossing the scar of mountains. But he saw them when he closed his eyes, a pattern seared into his mind's eye like looking too long at the sun. He did know this much: the past would always nip at his heels if he stayed in this line of work. So he took the job.

Martin bent over his computer, the burn of memories rekindling his motivation, and as he brought up the browser to check chat rooms Toni had once frequented, the department tip line chirped. It was the number citizens used to call in nonemergency situations and tips for older cases. Captain Barrow took the call from the master phone on his desk. Martin studied the older man through the glass. His expression didn't change as he jotted down a note before hanging up the phone. Then he emerged from his office, his eyes squinting with the shift in light from his dim room into the blue wash of the fluorescent lights overhead, and walked to Stanton's desk.

"Run this plate for me," he said. "Call was about some creep in a van. Digits look familiar."

Stanton took the paper. His brow lifted. "Don't have to look it up, Captain. That's Eddie Stevens's van."

"Christ." Captain massaged his temples. "Should've known. It's been a year coming up soon."

"Today, Cap. A year today," Stanton said, his voice dropping off. "Should we go check on him?"

"No. We're the last people that man wants to see today," Barrow responded, showing the first signs of softness Martin had seen since meeting him. "He can spend all day in that parking lot if it suits him," he said, and returned to his office.

Martin turned off the computer screen and strode to Stanton's desk. "Who is Eddie Stevens?" he asked.

E
D
D
I
E

EDDIE CLOSED THE BACK COVER ON HAZEL'S JOURNAL. HE COULD probably recite every entry by now. He hadn't found anything new. At least the passages about Hazel's love of music brought him bittersweet joy. When she described learning something new, her handwriting would get bigger and loopy. She'd doodled notes in the margins.

She described her devastation when her regular chorus teacher went on medical leave. Then in one entry, she'd marked the date with stars and wrote: *The vocal coach from the Music Box is our new chorus sub! He asked me to stay after class and told me I AM MORE TALENTED THAN ANYONE HE HAS EVER MET BEFORE. He said he's going to help me after school free of charge and push himself to be the teacher I need to bring out the music inside.*

Mixed emotions passed through Eddie as he remembered hearing that news. He'd initially suspected something ill-intentioned from the coach, but he was reluctant to refuse the offer. Hazel hadn't made any friends and had sunk deeper and deeper inside herself. If this was a way to bring her back out, he owed it to her to try. Eddie had sat in on their first meeting. The coach, Jonathon Walks, was calm and soft-spoken. He had immediately agreed to Eddie's request that Hazel's meetings never take place in an empty building or behind a closed door. Hazel was also a no-nonsense type of girl and would've told Eddie the moment she thought something was off with Mr. Walks.

Eddie wondered about him now. Jonathon had joined the search effort, even taking time out of work to help comb the woods and pass out flyers.

He kept looking long after the police had stopped. When he took a temp job in Dalton, he had given Eddie his phone number and asked him to please call with any news of Hazel. But there had been no news.

The patter of light rain against his windshield made Eddie look up. He glanced from the rain to his clock. It had already been an hour. If he'd done this last year, Hazel might still be with him. They could be on that hike together right now. Then again, even if he'd waited in the parking lot, whatever happened that day had happened behind the wall of trees separating the parking lot from the woods.

This is stupid. Waiting in a car isn't going to do a damn thing.

He exhaled, closing his eyes. He should've spent the time on the trail.

He drew the collar of his jacket close around his neck and pulled his hat snug against his bald scalp. It had rained that day, too. How cold had Hazel gotten? Had she been wearing enough clothes? She hated the cold. As soon as the temperature dipped below seventy, she lived in her long black coat and boots. The girl would wear three scarves at once.

Eddie pulled off his hat and shoved it in the console. It didn't seem right to strive for warmth when Hazel could be out there, cold and wet. He knew it was silly to think she was still in these woods. The only reason she'd still be there would be that she was dead. Eddie wondered if that was what he was trying to make himself see.

The dark of evening moved in with no courtship, and without warning, the world in front of him was all shadows. He gently stowed Hazel's belongings and the case file in the floor of his van and tucked his gun under his seat before turning over the ignition. The engine begrudgingly came to life. Eddie stared down the trailhead once more, then put the van in reverse. He switched on his headlights. As he made the turn, they caught on the silver sedan parked on the opposite side of the lot. He stopped the van. The lady must still be out there.

He swung his gaze back in the direction of the trail. He could tell he'd spooked her. And why wouldn't he? Since Hazel vanished, Eddie had learned how different a female's reality was than a male's. When a man walked to the store, his biggest worry was he'd forget something. A woman's biggest worry was that she might not make it home. He thought he'd understood that difference before Hazel went missing. He'd taught Hazel basic self-defense and little tricks like how to get out of zip ties. He thought it had been enough. But she was barely five feet tall and a hundred pounds soaking wet.

The blond woman was taller than Hazel but just as thin.

What if she's waiting for me to leave before she comes out?

The reasoning seemed solid to him, and he let his foot off the brake, rolling toward the two-lane road.

But what if she's not?

He braked again and put the van in park where it was, and then stepped out. Rain blew sideways in a gust of wind, pelting his exposed skin and sliding down his neck.

"Hello?" he called out, shielding his eyes. "Miss?" He waited, trying to listen through the storm. "If you're out there, I'm leaving now. Will you just shout or something so I know you're okay?"

Eddie waited. The wind wailed. He moved closer to the mouth of the trail. "Hello?" he shouted. He could barely hear himself. There was no way she'd hear him. He couldn't leave without knowing she was okay. She hadn't had on a pack of any sort. Just running clothes. Not even a bottle of water.

"Dammit," he muttered as he hustled back to his van. He pulled a flashlight out of the console and, after a moment's hesitation, plucked his gun from under the seat. He made sure the safety was on, then holstered it at his back.

Eddie crossed the parking lot and looked inside the woman's car. There was a bottle of water in the cup holder. A change of clothes was folded in the passenger seat, and a pair of shoes was tossed on the floorboard. On the back seat, paper and manila envelopes sat in uneven stacks. It looked very much like she intended to come back to her car, change into clean clothes, and head back to her normal life, not spend the night in the woods.

Eddie jogged to the tree line. He glanced behind him once more, not sure what he was looking for, then stepped onto the trail. The rain was lighter under the canopy, but between the storm and the onset of evening, the darkness was nearly complete. He swung the beam of his flashlight up the first rise. No signs of movement except for the water, which was already coming down the hill in tiny rivers.

"Hello!" he called again. His voice sounded louder here, bouncing off the trees and shielded from the roar of the wind.

Just get to the top of the first hill. I bet I'll be able to see a good piece from up there.

There were two ways up. The first and more obvious path was the hiking trail, which cut back and forth in long, slow hills across the face of the mountain. That was no doubt the way the woman had gone. The second was nearly a straight shot from the bottom to the top. It was less than a quarter the distance, but it was a hell of a climb.

His knee throbbed, stiff with the cold and from sitting in the van for over an hour, and he knew his good steps were numbered. Eddie illuminated the path once more, searching for any sign of movement, but it was empty. Before he could talk himself out of it, he stepped off the trail and headed straight up the hillside, sacrificing the easier terrain for a shorter distance. The incline quickly steepened, and he had to slow down, securing footholds against roots and rocks so the muddy earth didn't slip out from under him.

Eddie paused, panting, and glanced back, expecting to be halfway up, but he was nowhere close.

"I don't remember this damn hill being so long," he muttered. One thing was for sure, no matter how good of shape that woman was in, the going was hard for anyone. If she was still out here somewhere, which she must have been since her car was still in the lot, it wasn't on purpose.

He used the thought to power him the rest of the way to the crest of the first hill. It was the smallest in a series of three peaks, but the wind still howled a different pitch up here, sharp and nervous. The sound of it slid down his back, making him edgy. He shook off the feeling and peered over the other side. In the dark, the foothills rolled ahead of him like an ocean whipped and churning. Everything was soaking wet and reflected the beam of his light. Thousands of eyes could be looking back at him out here and he'd never see them.

What if the woman took the direct trail through to the main lot and called a friend? She'd had a cell phone and every reason to wonder why the hell he was there. He stared back down the way he came, inclined more now than ever to go back to his van and go home. But wouldn't that friend have dropped her back at her car? Maybe watched her get in and followed her out? Would they be back by now?

He swore under his breath and wiped the rain from his face. "What do I do here, Hazel?" he asked, then felt guilty. He was talking to her like he might a ghost or God; like she was gone.

Keep going, Hazel's voice shot through him. He jumped at the sound of it. He'd never heard her voice like that. Did it mean she was dead? He refused to continue the thought. He knew these woods better than anyone; probably better than Hazel by now. Whether she was dead or not, he couldn't think of a better way to honor Hazel than to search for someone else swallowed up by this trail. He trained the light on the descent and began his way deeper into the woods.

A
M
A

AMA CAME TO BY DEGREES. HER HEAD THROBBED, AND HER MIDDLE cramped with pressure. Her tongue ached with dryness, and she couldn't swallow. As her senses returned, a clammy sweat covered her skin. Dizziness set in. Bile climbed her throat, making her gag. Something was in her mouth, sour and slimy with phlegm, but she couldn't spit it out.

"Are you awake?" a man's muffled voice asked from somewhere very close.

Her mind burst into full alertness. The hiker . . . the piano player from Atlanta. Jonathon, he'd said—if that was really his name. He'd hit her with his walking stick. She was moving, being carried. The pain in her stomach was his shoulder digging into her navel. A scratchy nylon material was wrapped around her. She began desperate attempts to kick and slap, but her arms were bound in front of her at the wrists and her ankles and knees were tied together.

"Help!" she tried to scream, but between the wad in her mouth and the cover over her head, the garbled word didn't travel far.

The tarp slid apart with the stunted gait of his walk, revealing a sliver of the ground before closing again, enough for Ama to know it was dark out and they still looked to be in the woods. She grunted and heaved, trying to twist herself in any way that would allow her to bite Jonathon through his thin shirt, but the angle he held her in made it impossible for her to make contact. He stood still, waiting for her to stop struggling like a parent waiting out a toddler's temper tantrum. The scratchy fabric was bound so tight around her that she couldn't swing her legs with any real force. She let out a muffled scream of frustration.

"Save your voice," Jonathon said, and began moving again. "You'll need your breath and your strength. We have a lot of work to do."

The gag pressed down on her tongue, and she could feel the heat of stomach acid clawing at the base of her throat. She turned her head to the side and swiveled her head back and forth, trying to loosen whatever was in her mouth, but it wouldn't budge. She needed to leave a clue, some trace that she was out here.

Her watch. It was engraved with her initials. She squeezed her wrists together and contorted her fingers to try to reach it. But her arms were bare, save the binding. Either he'd taken it off or it had already fallen. No one would know where she'd been.

She examined a few inches of the material with her fingers. There was an elastic loop above her hands and what felt like a zipper pressing into her left hip. Ama surmised he'd wrapped her in his camping tent.

Ama closed her eyes, steadying her breath. She knew from statistics and history that she should fight arriving at his planned second location at all costs. Whatever he would do to her here, he'd do ten times worse once he got her somewhere he felt safe.

Ama forced herself to relax, focused on the sound of raindrops dripping from leaves, and then pissed down her legs. Jonathon shrugged her off, and she crashed to the ground in a heap. She tried to draw her knees under her so she could push off the ground, but her legs wouldn't respond, tingling with the sensation of returning blood flow.

Jonathon yanked the tarp away from her face. Ama was right. She was tangled up in his tent. He glared down at her as he peeled his shirt off his body. Even in the gray of a misty twilight, she could see tiny white marks covering his arms and chest. She wondered if they were acne scars. Was this guy some high school outcast all grown up and seeking revenge on women who reminded him of the girl who shot him down way back when? She watched him, hoping he'd be angry enough to throw the shirt aside. Her DNA on his shirt would be slam-dunk evidence. But he balled it up, pulled a Ziploc bag from his pack, and sealed it inside. Ama's heart sank.

He retrieved a new black shirt from another compartment and pulled it on. Then he bent over, picked up her feet, and began walking backward down a hill, dragging her with him. Panic raced through her. She kicked her feet against his hold, but she barely swayed him.

"You can't fight Fate, Ama. She brought us this far. She won't back out on us now," he said. Her head struck a root, sending a burst of white across her vision. The gag shifted, the knot in the back pulled up by the root, and she forced it over her teeth and to the cleft above her chin. She gulped air, spitting. Then she screamed, a sound so shrill she didn't recognize at first that it came from her, so filled with panic and instinct, so devoid of any measure of control it barely sounded human. Jonathon froze and gazed down at her, his face round, his eyes wide.

"I wish I'd been ready for that one," he whispered. "I don't want to waste anymore. If I tell you a little bit about what we're going to do together, can you promise me you won't scream again until I tell you to?" he asked.

His face was within a breath of hers. She held his gaze. Her pulse drummed in her ears.

"I promise," she said. "As long as we stay right here, I won't scream unless you tell me to."

Jonathon frowned, searching their vicinity. "There," he said, pointing down a steep ravine to a row of downed trees, which made a haphazard awning over a pile of boulders. "We can wait there. Feels like it's going to rain again soon, and I wouldn't want you to catch cold. It'll alter your range, and that just won't do."

"My range for what?" Ama demanded. Then it clicked, and her hands traveled together to her throat. He was talking about her voice.

Jonathon smiled. "I've imagined this encounter so many times. You'd think I'd know how this was going to turn out. But I don't. We'll arrive at perfection together. I have faith in us," he said.

MARTIN

Chapter 8 | 5:31 PM, December 1, 2006 | Tarson, Georgia

THE TIP LINE CHIRPED AGAIN. ON THE SECOND RING, MARTIN GLANCED up from Hazel Stevens's case file, which he'd dived into after Stanton filled him in on her disappearance. The room was empty. He hadn't noticed Stanton leave. Captain Barrow was in his office with the door closed and the shades drawn. Martin pushed his chair across the room with the balls of his feet and picked up the receiver.

"Tarson PD, Detective Locklear speaking," he said.

A woman's voice came through the earpiece, shrill and quick. "I need to report a missing person."

"What is your name?" he started.

"Lindsey Harold. My boss's name is Ama Chaplin. She's missing."

"Why do you believe she's missing?" he asked as he gathered a pen and paper.

"I don't believe she's missing. She *is* missing," she snapped.

"Tell me why you think so," he replied.

"She told me she'd be done with her run by five, and if she didn't call by five thirty, something was wrong. Did you guys run the tag I gave you?"

Martin's attention drifted back to his desk. Notes about Hazel's father, Eddie Stevens, were the only decisive pieces of information in the entire file. He had been ruled out as a suspect from the outset. He'd kept the search up on his own even after it officially ended. The only trouble he ever got into was when he called the local paper in a rage because they'd called Hazel's disappearance a vanishing act instead of an abduction.

"Neither the vehicle nor the owner came up in our system as being wanted for any reason," he answered.

"So you didn't even go look?" she shrieked.

"There was no credible reason to go check a car legally parked in a parking lot," Martin answered, losing patience.

"Well, you have one now!"

"Could she be waiting out the rain?" he reasoned.

"If she was going to wait out a damn storm, she would've called," she argued.

Captain's door opened. The smell of whisky accompanied him into the main room. Once he realized Martin was with a caller, he gave him a questioning look.

Martin covered the receiver and said, "It's the same caller from earlier."

Captain frowned and took the phone. "This is Captain Barrow. What seems to be the problem?"

Martin could hear the woman's voice, fading from irate to pleading, as she told the captain about her boss's concern and plan to call by 5:30. Captain's gaze flicked to the hanging wall clock. 5:32.

"Tell you what, I'll have an officer go check the lot. If we see her, or any reason for concern, I will call you back," he said.

He paused, listening to her rattle off a few more words. "Yes, ma'am. You're welcome. Take care." He hung up the phone and reached for his radio. "Damn city girls. Stick to running on your sidewalks," he grumbled. He pressed the call button on his radio. "Stanton, swing by the north trailhead parking lot at Tarson Woods and take a look around. I'll have Bordeaux check the south lot. Seems we might have a city girl lost on those trails. I'd like to get this wrapped up before it gets any darker."

"On my way, sir," Stanton answered.

Captain pulled his hat onto his head and moved for the door.

"Do you want me to go check anything out?" Martin asked the captain's back.

"You're a detective. You work at crime scenes. If I find one, I'll let you know," he said, and walked out.

EDDIE

THE RAIN HAD LET UP AGAIN, BUT IT WAS ALMOST WORSE WHEN IT DID because the fog rolled in, making it impossible for Eddie to see the terrain ahead. He missed another dip and slid in the mud about a foot before his trick knee gave out under his weight. He threw his hands in front of him and yelped as a jagged, skinny tree stump bit into his palm. He rolled to his back, grimacing, and clutched his hands against his stomach.

He opened his mouth and closed his eyes. Hazel was gone. That lady was gone, too. And he was just a poor old fool lying on his back in the woods. He couldn't save any of them.

Eddie pulled himself upright. It had taken him an hour to get this far, and with one good leg, it was going to take a lot longer to get back. There was an old stone single-room hutch less than a quarter mile from where he stood, marked a few years back with a plaque honoring those who lost their lives in the Evansbrite factory explosion. The little room was mostly used by local teenagers to drink and take dates or play with Ouija boards. Police had theorized Hazel had met a secret boyfriend there, supported by physical evidence Hazel had recently been inside the little structure. Eddie saw the evidence—Hazel's silver pinkie ring dropped among the blanket of rotting leaves, a token from her mother—as something different: Hazel leaving bread crumbs.

I was here. Keep looking.

He wouldn't go back to his car. He'd go to that old building and wait out the fog or the night, whichever let up first. Then he'd keep searching.

Eddie worked his way back to the trail. Between the steep grade, the exposed roots, and the standing water, every step was a balancing act. He tried to focus on his breathing as it marked time, *in-in-out*, and not the sinking familiarity washing over him, through him. Still, hesitation made a home in his chest, swelling as the distance between him and the little stone structure evaporated.

An ice storm had hit four months after Hazel vanished and taken out hundreds of trees. A group of volunteers had cleared most of them out of the traveled sections and piled them in a more remote part of the park. Eddie had joined in the efforts, certain they'd find some new clue. Or maybe even Hazel. They didn't find either. With the last tree moved, one of the more sympathetic volunteers had clasped Eddie on the shoulder with his gloved hand. "She's not out here, Mr. Stevens," he'd said.

Eddie shook the memory from his mind and trudged on. The lady was still here. He knew that for sure.

He reached the stone hutch. The metal gate stood ajar, and the floor was under water. He was grateful for a break of new rain sliding down his back, but this wouldn't afford him any kind of rest. His feet were somewhere between numb with cold and stinging from prolonged wet. His back ached with fatigue and tension. He couldn't sit down, and this room wasn't tall enough to stand up straight in.

A wink of silver caught Eddie's attention just before his flashlight burned out. He banged it against the heel of his hand, but it didn't come back on. He stuck the flashlight in his coat pocket with one hand and fished through the dark with the other. His fingers lit on a metal band along the edge of a puddle. Eddie picked it up and stepped out of the hutch, where the moonlight coming through a thinner patch of clouds washed the woods in deep silver. The band was a watch; a very nice watch, if he had to guess. That woman had glanced at her wrist when she was on the phone. Eddie closed his eyes, recalling the memory. It looked like she'd been checking the time, and in his mind, there was a strip of silver on her wrist, although he couldn't decide if he'd generated the detail here and now. He couldn't trust his thoughts anymore, or he'd see coincidences and clues everywhere. He also couldn't ignore the rhythm of the clock, ticking against his palm like a tiny heartbeat.

He tucked the watch in his other pocket and stepped out of the room. He eyed the next hill, the longest and steepest of the three. His bad leg shook beneath him, threatening to buckle, and mist began to fall. Going straight up the face of the mountain was no longer an option. If he wanted to keep going, and he did, he had no choice but to take the hiking trail. It was quadruple the distance, maybe longer. But at the top was a clearing where most of the trees had gone down last fall. He'd be able to see for a solid mile, even in the rain.

A
M
A

JONATHON TOWED HER UNDER THE COVER OF TREES JUST AS THE falling mist became rain again. He retrieved a rope from his pack, looped it around the thin metal cord binding her wrists, and tethered her to a tree trunk, giving her about a foot and a half of slack. She felt like a dog on a chain and almost wished he'd bound her fast. The tiny margin of movement was maddening.

"You get three questions," Jonathon said. He withdrew a small emergency lantern and clicked it on, washing the little shelter in a bluish glow. Shadows exaggerated the angles of Jonathon's face. Ama still couldn't remember what he looked like at the bar in Atlanta, but she had the feeling she'd seen him before somewhere else.

"Who are you?" she blurted, instantly regretting she hadn't thought out all three questions before asking.

A ghost of a smile appeared on Jonathon's lips, and he glanced down at the ground. "I'm striking that question from the record, Counselor. Try harder." He was enjoying watching her squirm. She needed to shift the focus, try to change the balance somehow.

Ama swallowed, and her temple throbbed with lingering pain and another wave of fear. She needed to remember that this man, whoever he was, was a criminal, first and foremost. She dealt with criminals all the time. She could talk them off ledges, into patience, out of the truth, and away from self-incrimination. She knew she could push this man's buttons. She just had to find them.

She forced her expression to relax. "This isn't about me, Jonathon. This is about you. I need to remember that. So why don't you start from the beginning?" she said, and leaned forward. "Tell me your story."

MICHAEL

MOTHER'S FINGERS ARE TEN HAWK TALONS IN MY SHOULDERS, CLAMPED and squeezing, and I am certain that when at last she lets me go, blood will pour from ten holes in my skin.

"Are you even trying? I have five-year-old students who try harder than you. 'Für Elise' is a beginner's song. It is *basic*. By now it should be burned in your brain, a reflex in your fingers. Why do you stumble and hunt after the refrain? What is wrong with you?" Her voice fills the room. She curls her stature over me in a cobra's arc, her fangs and tongue an inch from my ear, and yet still she yells.

"When will Father be home?" I mumble.

She releases my shoulders, snatches the neck of my shirt, and within a blink, I am slung off the piano bench and to the carpet. My face finds the floor first, and my wrist twinges underneath me.

"Get out of my sight. Go ahead. Run to your father." She glowers down at me, lips pulled back, brown eyes cut to slits. Her gaze falls on my cheek, where the rough carpet has rubbed a warm, stinging place. "You better tell him you fell."

I scramble to my feet and bolt through the front door. My feet are bare, but the ground is dry, the August sun unrelenting overhead. I do not slow down until I slide between the trees of Tarson Woods. Still, I dart from bough to bough, counting them as I pass, imagining that brick by brick I am building a wall between me and a dragon.

Cold River chatters ahead, the sound of it like tiny pieces of glass tumbling together. Father's bridge is to the right of a towering hickory tree, half the roots exposed on the sandy bank. I cross, boards creaking under-foot, then follow the narrow trail Father takes up the hill to the factory where he works. It's faster to walk straight from our backyard than to take the truck around to the access road and up and down the switch-backs to the valley floor on the other side of this rise. The higher I climb, the thinner the trees grow, and the ground turns from clay to stone, but my wall is built. Mother is not fast, and she will not come far into these woods. She believes the things they say about them and says she saw a witch in here once as a little girl. Between the two of them, I'd rather face a witch, so I take my chances.

I pass a hollowed-out tree I often hide in to wait for Father to come whistling through the woods. The path turns downhill, and I run, roots stabbing against the balls of my feet, strands of blackberry bramble nip-ping at my shins.

At last, I reach the chain-link fence. It stands twice as tall as me. Beyond it, rising from the valley floor like a gray fortress, is the factory. White trucks are parked along the wall in a tidy row. A dark gray door swings open. A man comes out, not my father, and the door hisses shut behind him. The man is staring at a box in his hand, his lips in a line. He pulls a truck door open, hops inside, and the truck roars to life. He drives away fast enough for the tires to kick up gravel. A big gate at the other end slides open, and the truck exits and disappears down the road.

I take off at a dead sprint, counting as I run. I don't know how long the gate will stay open. My father's voice is in my ear—*Never try to slide through that gate, son*—a memory from the one and only time I've been inside the factory. But there is a way in, and no one watching.

The gate clatters as it reaches the end of the track.

Nine. Ten. Eleven.

I round the corner. The gate begins its return journey. It is moving faster this way, but I am small. I will only need a little room.

Fifteen. Sixteen. Seventeen.

The metal post seems to speed up the closer it gets.

The gate is a jouster's lance, the post a competitor's body, and it is coming, coming, coming . . . I close my eyes, clench my teeth, and hurl myself through. Behind me, the gate bangs on impact as it meets the post.

I catch my hands on my knees, heaving, sweat trickling from under my hair. A group of men comes out of the door, paper lunch bags in their fists. Their voices are a storm of sounds, eyebrows knit, eyes dark. Everyone seems to speak at once, but no one looks at one another. They take turns glancing back at the building behind them. The tallest one swings his gaze ahead and catches sight of me.

"What are you doing here?" It is the voice of Mr. Bill, my father's friend from work. He brought me a deck of cards for my last birthday, and he is the only person allowed inside our house aside from Mother's students.

I freeze. I should have waited out the day in the woods, thrown rocks in Cold River, built another fort from fallen limbs where I could hide from Mother and sharpen twigs into something more useful. They make it easier to pry skin from something dead so I can see what's underneath. I have rinsed bones clean in the river. I have watched slime and maggots wash downstream, revealing the lines of muscle, chewed and pocked. I have seen guts, still warm and fresh and firmer than I thought they'd be. It is easier to split a worm than an intestine.

I wish I had a stick now. Mother has warned me that a man's rage is worse than hers, a tornado by way of comparison to a warm spring rain. I have yet to see it, but my mother has never been one to lie, save the stories she has me tell when I have a new bruise or welt. *They're to keep you safe*, she says.

Otherwise they may take you from us and put you in a group home with other boys—boys bigger than you—with a dirty kitchen and slimy dishes, with reeking toilets that don't flush, the seats covered in yellow film and streaks of brown crust, and an empty pantry, and no beds, just blankets on the floor, musty and full of holes. You think when I yell it is meanness, but it is love, Michael. You'll see. This world is hard. You must be harder. You must be ready. I am making you ready.

These rolling thoughts condense into a single, vibrating, squealing note.

"Are you okay, Michael? Is everything okay at home?"

"Yes, Mr. Bill. Is my father here?"

"Should be coming out any minute. They're having us take an early lunch. You know how your dad is, though. First one in—"

"Last one out," I finish for him. Mr. Bill eyes the factory and returns his focus to me.

"Why don't you wait by the fence?"

I back up until I feel the chain link press against my shirt.

The door swings open again, and my father lumbers out. "We got it," I hear him say to Mr. Bill.

Mr. Bill looks up at the sky for less than a second and points in my direction. "You have a visitor today," he says.

My father's gaze follows Mr. Bill's finger. He puffs up with a breath, his hands on his hips, and walks in my direction, his strides longer and more hurried than usual. I would back up farther, but there is nowhere to go. The fence is at my back, the gate locked shut, and I wonder if this is the storm, if he will brew and blow and thrash like I have never seen before.

"Come with me," my father says when he reaches me, his hand firm on one of my shoulders, and the sore places Mother made earlier throb with warning. He steers me away from the big gate, toward the back of the factory. A walk-through gate is cut into the fence at the back corner. Dad pushes a button. Something makes a clicking sound, and the gate pops open a sliver.

He is going to march me home, straight to Mother, and the two of them will be a hurricane.

Instead, we walk across the valley, over a mound, through a line of trees, and stop at a metal plate that reminds me of a sewer cap.

"I want to show you something," he says. "It's underground." He bends down, twists the cap, and casts it aside. I peer over the ledge, but all I see is darkness.

"There's a ladder. It's easy to climb. I'll go first, then you follow me," he says, and lowers himself into the hole. I sit and swing my legs over the side, feeling for the metal with my toes before turning around.

"That's good. Keep coming," Father calls from below me. I move hand-hand, foot-foot, the metal slick with a thin coat of moisture, and count the rungs as I go. There are nine, then the floor, which feels like concrete on the ball of my foot, not the cold, damp earth I expect. I hear the creak of a doorknob being twisted, the flick of a switch being moved, and the dark is overtaken by a fluorescent light. Beyond the door is a little room, not even as big as my bedroom, with a tall, square table and four chairs. Most of the walls are covered in metal cabinet doors. Two of them are painted white. The rest are silver. The floor is bare concrete.

"Where are we?" I ask.

"This is kind of like our clubhouse," Father says. "We make something powerful in the factory."

"Like magic?"

"Sort of. Yes, actually. Like magic. Magic can be good, and magic can be bad, right?"

"Sure." I nod.

"Sometimes, the magic goes badly. Like today, some magic snuck out, and it wasn't supposed to. So we all have to leave for a little bit until they figure out how it's getting loose. Mr. Bill and I made this place in case we need to be close enough to help catch the bad magic but we also need to be safe. Because magic can hurt people just as much as it helps. We're learning how to only do good. But it takes practice, and practice means mistakes."

My stomach turns to stone. Mother would not agree, and I am grateful she is not here for more reasons than one.

"What happened to your face?" Father asks, cupping my chin.

"I . . . I fell. On the way here."

He holds my head steady. "Why did you come? Is your mother having a bad day?"

"I made a lot of mistakes."

He kneels in front of me so he is looking up at me, and at this moment I feel taller than the factory outside. "You don't have to play piano if you don't want to. There are other things. Your mother . . . ever since she lost the baby, music has turned into a kind of child for her. She nurtures it, protects it. Music and that damn piano mean too much to her, but there's no convincing her of that yet. She'll come out of it. She will. But she shouldn't yell at you like she does, and I'll talk to her about that."

"Please, don't."

He exhales and looks me plainly in the eyes. "Okay. I tell you what. This weekend, we'll make you a clubhouse in the woods, too. A place you can go."

"Just like this one?"

A faint smile touches his mouth. "This one took a lot of time, a lot of money, two grown men, and a year. It's bigger than it looks. There's a door behind the ladder we came down that goes to the basement of the factory. The white cabinet doors open to a tunnel that leads to an old mine shaft. If you follow it all the way down, you'll pass a well I dug, and then you'll come out right at Cold River."

"Can I play here?"

"No, son. Now, this is important. No one else knows this is here. Just Mr. Bill and me. And now you. It's a secret. We're going to cover the top soon, so you'll have to dig it out. Memorize where it is, okay?"

I nod, then ask, "Why does it have to be a secret?"

He looks at me for a solid three seconds. "Because most bad guys have no idea they're bad," he says. "This factory is doing good for the town and for us. But that magic we're making . . . sometimes it's more like a dragon. Sometimes I worry it'll burn this whole town to the ground."

AMA

JONATHON'S CHILDHOOD STORY FILLED THE CAVE MADE BY THE STACK of trees, painting the black of night with darkness of a different kind.

"The big explosion happened a month later. I can still hear the sirens." Jonathon closed his eyes. "Just as loud in my mind as they were that day. I was at school. Fifth grade. Ms. Terry's class. She dropped the piece of chalk, and we all looked out the classroom window like we might see something. I don't know what we expected. Smoke or flames. I remember every cloud in the sky looked like it had wings and a tail."

"Was your dad there?" Ama asked. She'd heard mention of the Evansbrite plant during her brief tenure in Tarson, seen files slide across senior partners' desks and into the shredder. In her lap, her fingertips fluttered against the ends of the cables, but it was no use. Every move pulled them tighter. Still, she couldn't stop trying.

"He was a mechanic there to start, but he was the kind of person everyone turned to in a room. Bit by bit, he had a hand in most things that happened in the factory." Jonathon's eyes opened, but they were fixated on something far away. He blinked, and they cleared. "Ms. Terry had us hide under our desks for a few minutes. Then the principal came room to room and told us all to go home. The buses came early, but I walked past my bus, down the road, and into Tarson Woods."

"You went to the factory." Ama abandoned her wrists, shifted her position onto one hip, drawing her knees up to block Jonathon's view of her hands, and felt along the ground for anything sharp. Her fingers lit upon a skinny stick, but the wood was soft with moisture and rot.

"Everyone was standing outside the fence, looking at the building. There were a few people in those big hazmat-type suits. At the time I wondered if they were some kind of armor, like they were going in to slay the magic gone wrong." He looked Ama square in the face. "But no one else went in that day."

"And your dad?" She had to keep him talking, keep him distracted, hoping it would be enough to throw off whatever plan he was on just enough to make him reconsider.

"You never met him or you'd know. My dad was never one to run from a monster."

"He was still inside?"

"The explosion had destroyed the elevator that went to the basement, and there were no stairs. He was inside the processor. He had gone inside to try to disconnect everything because the control panel shorted out. They didn't get him out until the next morning."

"Was he still alive?"

"Technically. They cleared an entire floor of the hospital. We weren't allowed to see him, and the doctors who went in wore lead aprons. My mother and I sat in the hallway in plastic chairs and slept on gurneys in the maternity ward that night. Mother would hear newborn babies cry, and she would sob and scream. They sedated her more than once, but even then, tears would leak out of her eyes."

Jonathon cleared his throat, and the boyish roundness of recollection evaporated from his face, replaced with edges and shadows. "A doctor and a man in a black suit came up to us to tell us there would be no saving him. That they had no idea how he was still alive. His vitals were erratic and off the charts. They wanted to run tests, not to keep him alive but to research. My mother was horrified. She slapped the man in the suit across the face and meant to strike him again, but he caught her by the wrist and said, 'This is all going to be very, very expensive for someone. If you let us test him, we will cover his medical bills. If you don't, I am afraid the costs of all his care will fall on you.'"

"That can't be legal," Ama said.

"The factory representative said that they'd ordered an evacuation but my father refused to leave and disobeyed direct orders to try to stop the leak. Apparently, that decision alleviated the company of all responsibility for his care. That's what you'd say if it were your case, isn't it? That's what you do. You find loopholes in laws and agreements and slide a guilty person right through it." His eyes darkened under the hood of his brow.

"I . . ." Ama paused and clamped her mouth shut, reconsidering. Lying to this man would not serve her well. "I am good at what I do, yes. I can twist technicalities and mine doubt from a thousand-foot cave of evidence, yes. But I honed my craft. I sharpened my tools so I would be ready to defend a wrongly accused defendant."

Jonathon leaned back, watching her. "Tell me," he said. "Have you ever met one of those?"

MARTIN

MARTIN'S DIRECT PHONE LINE RANG, STARTLING HIM AND BRINGING HIS thoughts back inside the station walls. His mind had been attempting to turn what few pieces he had into pieces that fit into something . . . anything. He hadn't noticed how dark it'd become outside. He glanced at his watch before reaching for the phone. It was a quarter to seven.

"Tarson PD, Detective Locklear speaking," Martin said.

"It's Briggs. Captain wants you to come to the trailhead parking lot," Briggs said, his voice serious. "And to bring more flashlights and batteries."

Martin dropped the phone in its cradle and stood. Reluctance spread through him as he peered out the window. Fog surrounded the building, and what trees were still visible glistened with clinging rainwater. Searching for this woman wasn't going to be easy. She was probably lost, and lost wasn't a crime scene. Maybe he should call the captain and remind him. He was close to something in the Hazel Rae Stevens case. He could feel it. Although maybe it was the anniversary more so than an actual break.

He shook the remnants of her case from his brain, shouldered on his coat, gathered flashlights and batteries, and headed for his car.

White fog curtained anything beyond the hood of his car from sight, and the drive to the trailhead took twice as long as it should have. The blue lights from the other officers' cars finally appeared, acting like a beacon. He relaxed, releasing his grip on the steering wheel, and rolled into the parking lot. The captain headed for his car the moment he pulled in.

"What do we know?" Martin asked as he opened his door.

"We don't know shit," Captain replied.

"Okay." Martin paused. "So where should I start?"

"Did you bring the flashlights?" Captain held out his hand.

"In a box in the back seat." Martin pointed behind him.

"Well, congrats on a job well done. Go home. We'll see you in the morning," Captain said, retrieving the box from Martin's car.

Martin opened his mouth, then closed it, shaking his head. He didn't know what irritated him more: one, that they'd come to search for a woman in the woods with no flashlights, or two, that the only reason they asked him to come was to bring the flashlights they forgot.

"What are you going to do?" Martin asked.

"Have a good ol' game of flashlight tag. What do you think I'm going to do?" Captain said, glaring at Martin.

"I can help look for her. I came. I'm here. Let me do something."

"You don't know these woods," Captain responded. "They're tricky enough in the daylight. We'd just end up looking for both of you."

"Can I at least look at her vehicle?" Martin pressed.

"Be my guest. We don't have a warrant, and I already have a headache. So don't do anything stupid," he said.

"Noted," Martin answered, and headed for the city girl's car before Captain could change his mind.

He pulled a small flashlight from his pocket and shone the beam through the driver's-side window. A pair of jeans and a black sweater were folded on the passenger seat, black leather heels tossed on the floorboard. An unopened bottle of Smartwater rested against the chair back. She hadn't taken water on the trail with her. Martin's ex-wife had been a big runner. He always knew when she planned a run longer than an hour because she'd take water with her in one of those fanny packs she'd swear wasn't a fanny pack. If the run was going to be an hour or less, she'd fill a thermos with ice and leave it in the car.

He glanced into the back seat. Manila envelopes lay in a stack behind the driver's seat. The corner of a Louis Vuitton briefcase peered out from under a gray hooded sweatshirt. Her purse was visible in the opposite seat. Something about this seemed careless. He didn't know anything about this woman, but if she was a city chick, she'd know better than to leave a purse in plain sight. Something must've distracted her. Maybe a phone call or a text . . . or a man sitting in a van.

Martin glanced across the parking lot. An old white work van sat in the far corner—no doubt Eddie Stevens's van. Martin felt sure Captain would've noticed it. Maybe he was leaving it alone out of the same pitied reverence he'd shown toward the man earlier in the day. Yet here Eddie was, present at the scene of another possible abduction.

Martin switched off his flashlight and walked to Eddie's van. He circled it once, scanning the ground for anything Eddie might've dropped. Then he peered at the other officers. He wasn't sure how Captain would feel about him snooping around Eddie's vehicle. But why the hell weren't they?

Shielding his light from view, he switched it on again and stared through Eddie's driver's-side window. The seat was empty. He trained the light into the passenger seat. A pink notebook sat on top of a large binder. READ ME was scrawled in block letters with a red marker on the spine of the binder. Martin squeezed the handle on Eddie's door. It clicked open. He glanced over his shoulder to where the other officers were gathered on the other side of the lot. Only one was still fully visible. The rest had become nothing more than tiny flecks of light on the wooded hillside.

What if Eddie was in the back of the van? What if this was some kind of trap, the whole lost-city-girl thing a hoax to draw out the officers who had failed him? Or what if he was some sick bastard who had killed before and felt like killing again?

Martin slid his fingers in the narrow crack between the door and the car frame. He eased it open, stiffening as the old hinges creaked.

"Mr. Stevens? Are you in here?" he called into the back of the van. No one answered. "Mr. Stevens, my name is Martin Locklear. I'm a detective with the Tarson PD." Still, no one responded. Best-case scenario, the grieving father had drunk himself to sleep in the back of his van. Worst-case scenario, he was lying in wait only a few feet away. Or he was in those godforsaken woods . . . with her.

Martin shined his light into the back of the van. It was empty. He let out a breath.

"Martin? What the hell are you doing?" Barrow called to him from a distance. Without thinking, Martin grabbed the notebook and the binder off of Eddie's passenger seat and tucked them inside his jacket before retracting himself from the van.

"Is this Eddie's van?" Martin asked.

"You know damn well it's Eddie's van. Otherwise, you wouldn't be in it," Captain said, advancing.

"Where is he? You think he's lost out there, too?" Martin asked, attempting to sound neutral.

"He's not lost. No one knows those woods better than Eddie," Captain answered.

Martin hugged the material he'd gathered against his side. "It's likely he's one of the last people to see this woman. If she really is missing, he'd be a witness."

"Witness?" Captain narrowed his eyes. "You sure that's what you mean?"

"That's what I said," Martin countered. They fell in step as they crossed the lot.

"You leave Eddie out of this," Captain ordered. "He's got no part in it."

"How can you be sure? Two girls missing on the same day, a year apart? Eddie the last one known to have been in the proximity of both women?"

Captain spun him around by the arm. "That's his daughter you're talking about!"

"You know the statistics as well as I do. Victims in cases like this almost always know the abductor. It's very rarely the first encounter."

"I know," Captain said, sobering. "But I don't see what Eddie would have to do with a hotshot defense attorney out of Atlanta."

Martin raised an eyebrow. "That's what she does?" he asked.

Captain nodded. "Name's Ama Chaplin."

"I can dig for any information linking Eddie to Ama," Martin said, his thoughts racing ahead of him.

"You will do nothing of the sort," Captain argued.

"Captain, all due respect, but if Eddie is involved in this, and I'm not saying he is, he didn't start with killing his daughter. He started earlier, smaller, and he very well may have needed a defense attorney in the past. If it was anyone else, wouldn't you look for a connection?" Martin pressed.

Captain paused and stared at the wet asphalt at their feet. "Go ahead and do some looking," he said quietly. "But keep this between us until you find something concrete. If you find anything, you tell me immediately."

"You got it," Martin replied. He began to turn, his gaze landing on the two figures of Briggs and Stanton approaching them from across the lot. They knew Eddie, cared for him. If they were to encounter him in the woods, would they even think to protect themselves in his presence?

"All due respect, sir, if Eddie does has something to do with this, Briggs and Stanton will be in the woods with him completely unaware of what risk they might be facing," Martin cautioned.

Captain stood still, exhaling long and slow. "I'll mention something to Briggs," he said.

They parted ways, and Martin headed for his car. He glanced up at the woods, his mind racing, the lights and voices calling for Ama fading into the fog.

MICHAEL

I LEAP FROM THE TOP STAIR AND LAND IN THE GRASS. MOTHER IS CLOSE behind, the slap of her house shoes on the concrete landing, the heat of her breath urging me faster. I chance a look back. Her bathrobe sails behind her, the cape of a villain in a comic book, her cheeks red against her pale skin, her brown eyes nearly black with focus. She opens her mouth to breathe or shout, and all I see is teeth.

I swerve left and zigzag between trees. Leaves fly up in my wake. The shadows cast from boughs and branches have a dizzying effect on the path ahead. I look back again. She's farther from me now, but still coming, and she's picked up a stick.

I stare for a moment, my eyes on the stick. She's screamed herself purple. She's tied me to the piano bench for a full night, only cutting me loose come morning for fear I'd pee on the wood. She's held a metal cable to a flame before using it to burn the sheet music for *Für Elise* into the skin between my shoulder blades. But her eyes are fixed on me like a cat on a mouse, and maybe it's the shadows or the grime and grease from a week without a bath or the way her lips are pulled back, but here in these woods, I do not recognize her face at all.

I turn uphill, a steep climb—I will need to use my hands and feet near the top—and scramble for the ridge. Still she comes. I claw my fingers into the black earth and pull. She is longer and faster on the hill somehow, gaining ground, her fingers a body's length from my heel.

"Get back here, Michael!"

I crest the ridge and hear a growl, not from below but from the side.

Three dogs stand across the trail that runs to Cold River. Their bodies arch in reverse, hips above shoulders, noses tipped down, eyes staring up. But they are not watching me. They spring forward, and I jump to the side. My toe snags on a rock, and I tumble. My arms fly up, shielding my face and neck, and I bring my knees into my body. In my mind, they are already tearing through my jeans, gnawing on my bones.

The rumble of anger in a throat grows louder. I peer through the fold in my limbs. The dogs are facing away from me, pointed like three arrows down the hill. Then they hop and shuffle, bark and yap, and one goes charging down.

"Stop!" I sit up, reaching out, but the other two descend from view, and I hear a shriek and a crunch of dry leaves crushed under a sudden weight.

I climb to my feet. I do not want to walk to the ledge. I do not want to see. But maybe I do. Maybe my mother's skin has been pulled away and I can see what monster has been growing inside her since Father died.

I tiptoe to the place the terrain plummets and peer down. The bathrobe is visible on the hillside, but the dogs are nowhere to be seen. I slide down with one foot braced in front of the other. My mother is not under the robe. She's vanished like the witch in *The Wizard of Oz*, dissolved into a trail of smoke, and I wonder if my mother—my real mother—has returned.

I pick up the robe and walk home, picking bits of leaves and debris from the pilled fabric. I climb up the steps and open the door.

She's standing in the entry with a stick, one end red and slick with fresh blood.

"Come inside and close the door," she says.

MARTIN STACKED THE CASE FILE, HIS NOTES, AND THE EVIDENCE FROM Eddie's car on his living room floor and sat down cross-legged in front of it. A new case was like a puzzle with no box top as a guide. With enough Adderall in his system, Martin would thrill at the void of information, at the possibilities. Tonight his medicine cabinet was empty. His head throbbed with the sensation of reawakening withdrawal.

"Don't," he whispered to himself, and rubbed the empty place on his ring finger. He drew in a deliberate breath and let it out slowly. He didn't have to solve the case tonight. He just had to create a starting line.

He turned his attention to what he'd taken from Eddie's van, which consisted of two large binders and a spiral-bound notebook with doodles covering the front. He opened the notebook first. *Hazel's Heart* was written in big, loopy cursive at the top of the inside cover, then the date below it: October 15, 2004. Martin flipped through the pages. Some entries were brief; generally when the day was forgettable. Other entries took up five pages or more. Every now and then the writing was centered, the sentences short. Poetry, he assumed.

He reached the last page. The entry was dated a year ago yesterday. It was a short entry, relatively upbeat but otherwise typical. No mention of meeting someone, some horrible experience, suicidal thoughts, future plans, or burning excitement over some plan so secret she didn't even chance writing it down. Her handwriting looked loopy and relaxed. He thumbed back a few more pages, looking for anything new or a sudden change. Nothing. Wouldn't a teenage girl pack her journal if she'd intended to leave town?

Martin had to admit that he agreed with Eddie: Hazel hadn't run away. She hadn't walked into those woods with an ulterior plan. Something had happened to her, and Martin had a suspicion that something was Eddie. But what did this missing attorney have to do with it?

He outlined his thoughts on his pad of yellow paper, then opened Eddie's first binder. It was divided by three tabs: newspaper articles, search patterns, and maps. The second binder was divided into two categories: suspects and related cases. Martin zeroed in on the last section. Had Eddie used previous cases as inspiration? He flipped open the section and froze—the top case was *his* case: Toni Hargrove and the trail that had ended at a vandalized pay phone seventeen miles from his new front door.

"No fucking way." Had he been unknowingly hunting Eddie Stevens all along? Eddie didn't at all match the skeletal profile he'd developed while working in Savannah: a man in his late twenties or early thirties, probably white, physically fit, with a violent history. Eddie's file at the Tarson station had mentioned he was a handyman with a specialty in metal repair and car engines. Would he have had the patience and the wherewithal to remove the number buttons from a pay phone?

He grabbed both binders and his keys and headed for his car. He needed to keep connecting the possible dots while they were lining up so well, and there was no way he'd fall asleep with his brain in this high a gear. He still wasn't sure what kind of resources the office would offer, but there was a huge whiteboard, a roll of Scotch tape, a full-size computer screen, a box of markers, and spotty internet service, which was more than he had at home.

His brain began mapping what he knew as he drove to the station. The bigger unknown was Ama Chaplin, and Martin was sure he'd at least find a bio on her website. She probably had a Facebook page, too. If Eddie was the culprit, why had he picked Ama to mark the anniversary of whatever he did to Hazel? Was it convenience, pure and simple, or was the choice more personal?

He unlocked the station door. No one else was there. All for the better, Martin reasoned. He wanted to stitch up the evidence against Eddie as tightly as possible before presenting it to the captain. These guys held a soft spot for Eddie for some reason, and Martin knew his opinion of the man would be unpopular at best.

He gathered all the intel he had so far on Hazel's disappearance and what he'd retrieved from Eddie's van, pulled loose the pages of Eddie's binders, and arranged everything on his desk in chronological order. He began with the cases Eddie had saved in his binder and ended with the notes he'd taken when Ama's assistant called the second time.

He frowned, recalling the conversation. The assistant had called in a tag number. If Ama knew Eddie personally and felt threatened, wouldn't she have told her assistant to give his name? Then again, if Ama knew he was a threat, she probably wouldn't have gone into the woods with him waiting in the parking lot. Eddie's decision to target Ama was more likely one of convenience, Martin concluded. Still, he wanted to learn more about Ama. How was she likely to behave in an abduction scenario? How likely would they be to find her alive?

He turned on his computer and entered her name into Google's search bar. Several thousand hits tallied at the top. Beneath the ad for her legal advice was a strip of image results. Ama was a blonde with high cheekbones and gray eyes. Her features seemed familiar to Martin, but he surmised he'd seen her ad run during his late-night insomniac TV binges. She was also apparently quite social, as several of the top image results were from swanky nightclubs in Atlanta's Buckhead district.

He scrolled through the image results, pausing when he reached a rather unflattering picture of Ama in black and white. Beneath it was written, *V.A.A.C.: Victims Against Ama Chaplin*, and a web address. He clicked the link. The V.A.A.C. page was dedicated to victims whose perpetrators had walked free, courtesy of Ama's representation. Five major cases were highlighted on the website. There was also a public posting board where any victim could air a grievance. A couple of posts devolved into calling for a bounty on Ama's head or career. The site hosts were quick to nip the threads in the bud, but they didn't take them down.

Martin focused on the handles of the more violent posts, hoping to find whoever was responsible for the creation of the group. He wished his department had a techie who could follow HTML trails. The only person

Tarson PD had who even came close to that skill set was a deputy's kid who liked to hack into anything, if only to prove he could.

He clicked back to the list of Google results. Ama was active, albeit barely, on Facebook and LinkedIn. Her professional website listed a very brief pre-career bio and went on to detail her major wins in the courtroom. Nothing obvious linked her to Eddie, strengthening his earlier suspicion that she had been in the wrong place at the wrong time.

Martin typed Eddie's full name into the search bar and hesitated. Did he really think Eddie Stevens had a social media presence? He shrugged to himself and hit enter. Hundreds of thousands of results were listed. None of them were for his Eddie. Edmond Stevens was too common a name. He clicked back to the top, framed Eddie's name in quotations and added the word "crime." The tally reduced to under a thousand. The fourth result from the top was a six-year-old news article out of Texas about the accidental death of a woman: Raelynn Angela Stevens. "Edmond Stevens" was highlighted in the subtext summary, naming him as the grieving widower.

Martin leaned toward his computer screen and clicked on the link. A low-res image of a heavier-set black man with his hands clasped around the shoulders of a girl was framed in the top right corner. The caption read: *Raelynn leaves behind a husband and a thirteen-year-old daughter.* Martin's pulse accelerated. This was the link he'd been looking for.

He scanned the article for details of Raelynn's accident. Hazel had come home from school to find her mother in the yard and a twelve-foot ladder on its side. Raelynn broke her neck in the fall and never regained consciousness before passing away that same day.

On a hunch, Martin opened Hazel's journal. As of the first entry, they were already living in Georgia, with no mention of unpacking or settling in. He flipped open the case file on Hazel's disappearance. Someone had handwritten a lean outline of the Stevenses' life in Georgia. They'd moved here six years ago.

"Who buries his wife and then takes his daughter halfway across the country in the same year?" Martin asked the empty office. "Someone guilty, that's who."

He glanced at the clock. It was too late to phone the police department listed in the article for more information or the coroner's report. It was also probably a move Captain wouldn't appreciate him making without clearance.

He glanced back at his screen and scrolled down to the bottom to look for contact information. A picture of a blond woman at the end of the article caught his attention. She looked so much like Ama that he did a double take. He glanced at the caption.

The woman in the picture was Raelynn Stevens.

MICHAEL

IT IS STILL DARK WHEN I WALK INTO TARSON WOODS. GHOSTS DON'T show themselves in full sunlight. That's what Timmy Roberts says. He says Tarson Woods is teeming with ghosts because Tarson is cursed and if your soul was born here it will always come home. Dad was born here. If any ghost wouldn't mind haunting these trees, it would be him.

I have a flashlight in my hand, but I don't dare turn it on. I need to get to the highest place in the woods so I can see first light. Timmy said you can see them when the first rays of sun come through—you can see them chasing the last bit of dark.

I reach the peak, puffing and sweaty despite the chill in the predawn air. Coyotes yip and howl somewhere close, regathering after a hunt. I wonder what they ate. I wonder if they left any parts behind, and I think maybe I'll go look once the day breaks.

The yelping stops, and the gray air goes a thick kind of silent. The hairs on my arms stand on end. I turn 'round and 'round, searching for a wisp of gray, a flash of a checkered shirt.

"Father?" I call out. My voice sails downhill on two sides. "Father!"

Vapor rises in twists from the lower elevations, and I wonder if that's all Timmy saw, if he looks out at the steam and rising fog and sees a ghost. I nearly laugh until I think of my mother's face, all peaks and edges, and see a hungry beast.

A tangerine line breaks the horizon, and rays of sun laser through the trees. My eyes burn with light, but I cannot turn away. I see shapes in the glow, black and moving, and I hold my breath. Someone is walking toward me. Someone is calling my name.

"Father," I say. I blink against the burn in my eyes, and when I open them, I squint, shielding my view from the light. It is not my father's face. It is my mother's.

Her hands are upon me, and she is dragging me down the wrong side of the hill. She is moving so fast I nearly trip.

"Why do you keep coming into these woods?" she seethes.

"I was trying to see Father."

"Your father is dead! This place, these woods, killed him, Michael! Don't come back here!"

"You're going the wrong way," I plead. She doesn't answer. "Mother. Our house is the other way."

"We're not going home," she says between breaths.

"Where are we going?"

"We're going to the river, Michael. You said you want to see your father. If he's in these woods, I can't think of where he'd rather be," she says, slowing her steps, her voice suddenly soft.

I reach out for her hand, but she pulls it out from my fingers. I follow, my insides turning, my body light and heavy at the same time.

I have not seen this section of the river before. The banks are more rock than earth, and the drop from this point is nearly double in height, despite the darker, louder water, which rushes by, foaming and frothing as it passes.

"Is this Dad's favorite place?" I ask.

"No. It's mine," she says.

"Dad said you can't swim."

"I am not here to swim. I am here to teach you." She steps closer, and my blood runs hot. "I grew up on a very simple rule. The Rule of Three."

"Once is an accident. Twice is a coincidence. Three times is mastery," I say, reciting the rule.

"Yes. Tarson has a hold on your soul, Michael. As long as you are drawn to these woods, you will never amount to anything, do you understand me? You will never be free. This place, the factory, your father's obsession with these woods, it killed him."

"He died trying to save people," I whimper.

"Your father died because he wanted to be a hero," she says, her face curling in a sneer. "A hero for everyone but you and me. He could've come home that day, Michael. He could've been *our* hero, left when they told him to and come home. But still, these woods would've claimed him sooner rather than later." Tears bead on her lashes, and she laces her fingers through mine. "If you are meant to waste your life in this town, I would rather you not suffer it." She leans forward and stares down at the water; then her gaze slides to me. "I don't want you to suffer, Michael. I want you to be a master of your own life."

"What are you saying?" I lean away, but she squeezes my wrist and twists my hand around the wrong way. I yelp, but she doesn't seem to hear it.

"Three times is mastery. Are you going to be a master of your life, Michael? Are you going to amount to anything outside this town? The way out of Tarson is uphill on all sides. You have to be strong. You have to be willing to do whatever it takes. Pain is the best teacher for those who understand it."

"Mommy?"

Tears leak from the corners of her eyes, and for one split second, her face softens and her brown eyes glisten with something warm for me.

"This is for you," she says as she shoves both hands into my chest. I tumble backward, arms pinwheeling; then there is no ground, and the air is rushing up, up, up.

The slap of the water forces the breath from my lungs, and I plunge under. The current floods my mouth and fills my nose. I kick and claw at the water, my body spinning. My shoulder glances off an underwater stone, and I inhale water. I force my eyes open. It does little good, grays and browns sliding by at a dizzying rate.

I strike out blindly in one direction, and my knuckles drag along something solid. I reach forward with both hands, bumbling over roots and stones. At last, I grab hold. Anchoring my hand turns my body into the tail of a whip, and I slam into the bank, nearly losing my hold. I work my feet under me and claw my hands higher. My fingers feel the weightlessness of air, and I push off whatever is underneath me.

My face emerges, and I gasp for air. I grip the twists of roots that jut out from the bank and pull my head and shoulders out of the water. Shivers claim my whole body, and my hands shake so hard that it is difficult to hold on. I can't tell what side of the river I'm on, and I try to remember if it had been flowing to my left or my right when I was above the water. But Mother is not on the bank. She is in the river downstream, hip deep in the water, the ends of her hair sopping wet, her nightgown see-through and clinging to her sagging body. My father had said that she could not swim, that the river scared her. Is she so angry with me that she is no longer afraid? I could climb this bank and run somewhere—anywhere—but then I could never go home.

I let go and drift toward her. I have to press down on the river with my hands to keep my face above water. The current speeds up, but suddenly my toes drag against the riverbed. Three more seconds pass and I can stand. My mother stays where she is. She will have me walk to her. So I do.

"You are here by accident," she says.

Snot streams from my nostrils, and my limbs ache with exhaustion.

"Are you going to be a master of your fate, Michael?" she hisses.

Water and tears and mucus pool under my chin and drip off in slimy strings. It takes every ounce of strength I have to stand still in the current, which pummels my back and tugs on my legs, bending my knees. I nod, but I wonder if she can see it through how hard I'm shaking.

"I won't push you again. You need to jump. Your father said, 'All things for a reason.' He believed that things are meant to be a certain way, that we have no control over our lives, that no matter what choices we make, we will live a certain way and we will die a certain way. That's called Fate. You want to see your father, you want to remember him, this is how. Go back to the place you fell in, and jump, and Fate will save you, or she won't."

"Fate is a lady?" I ask, somehow struck by this idea that there is another woman in this river so interested in seeing whether or not I will drown.

"She must be. She might as well have been your father's mistress." She glowers, her dark eyes focusing on something other than me for a full second. "You will need to jump two times more. Surviving once more would just be a coincidence. Three times is what, Michael?"

"Mastery." I can barely hear my own voice.

"If Fate saves you, I will do everything in my power to bring greatness out of you, to make you feel the music. If you are going to leave this town, you must do something or be someone no one else has done or been before. That's the only way anyone from Tarson can go and stay gone. I will not let one more piece of me die in the shadow of that factory. Get out of the river, Michael. Go find your fate."

I walk sideways to the bank, keeping her in view until I step onto the muddy shore. I can feel her stare on my back as I pick my way up the ledge and walk to the place where she pushed me in. My toes curl over the edge. My fingers ball to fists. I suck in a breath, seal my lips, close my eyes, and leap.

I wake in the middle of the night to screaming, but it is not my voice in my ear. I try to throw my legs over my bed and to the floor, but my stomach is a knot and my sides are two bruises. I push myself to stand with my hands and hobble across my room. The screaming has turned to gasping and sobbing, and something heavy crashes to the floor.

I tiptoe down the hall, one shoulder pressed against the wall, and my mother's room comes into view. I turn on the light. She's kneeling in the center of her room, her matted hair spilled over her downturned face. Her bedside table is flung on its side and her lamp is broken in a dozen pieces on the floor.

"Michael, turn on the lights! I can't see."

"The lights are on, Mother," I whisper, hanging back in the doorframe.

"They're not!"

I flip the lights off and then turn them back on, keeping my toes behind the threshold to her room.

"They're on, Mother."

She slaps her hands against every surface within reach. She strikes out again and again, and then she waves her arms around, fingers out-stretched. She makes contact with the quilt strewn half off her bed and yanks it the rest of the way to the floor. I watch, paralyzed and fascinated, as she balls it in her hands and then pulls at it like she's preparing dough, and I wonder if she's dreaming.

Then she screams, a pure, singular note, rising in volume, consistent in clarity and pitch. The air inside me swells, and my heart begins to race. I could run to the piano keys and find that note, I could. It's just two or three keys to the right of the very middle key. Or is it four?

The sound fades, and my mind loses track of the note. I am left empty and breathless. I nearly want to stick Mother with something sharp to see if the note will come out again. I step one foot forward, disbelief flowing through me. Another step.

"You did this." She lunges in my direction, swinging out with a hand. I jump back to the threshold.

"What did I do?" I ask, nearly pleading.

"I can't see! I can't see!" She crawls on her hands and knees, panting and raging, but she can't find me. My limbs tingle, and everything inside me screams to run back to the river, to jump in one last time and let it carry me to the next town, maybe all the way to the ocean. Doesn't every river flow to the sea?

Even in my mind, though, my mother is in the river, her fingers manipulating the flow of the water, turning the current, making it flow into Tarson from both ends. Lady Fate has her by the shoulders, shaking and shaking, and if Mother truly can't see—if she's blind somehow—I can't help but wonder if Lady Fate is to blame. But when it comes to the river, when it comes to *me*, I think . . . I think Mother might win.

A burst of pain makes me gasp, and I realize my mother's nails are on my shoulders, digging for the grooves at the sockets, and she's shaking me.

"What have you done?" she shrieks, and I let her push me down to the floor, like I should have let her push me under the water at Cold River so Lady Fate would've had to go through Mother to make me live.

A
M
A

JONATHON HAD RAMBLED ABOUT HIS MOTHER FOR WHAT FELT LIKE AN hour: her demand for perfection, her gift of music, and her utter disappointment that it didn't pass to him. The more he mentioned her, the quieter he became and the faster he paced. He forgot where he was going with a story in the middle of a sentence and slammed the heel of his hand against the side of his head.

"So you have mommy issues? That's it?" Ama attacked, trying to push him over the brink while his mind teetered, hopefully far enough to get sloppy, to make a mistake. From what she could tell, a loud, aggressive woman was one thing he'd bow to. "Do I look like your mom? Did I insult your shit piano playing and so now you're taking out the years of rage on me that you never had the stones to do to Mother Dearest? I have to agree with her. You should never touch a piano again. Do you have any idea how many clients I've defended whose childhoods make yours sound like a fairy tale?"

He tore his shirt over his head and turned as he stepped into the lantern light. "Is this a fairy tale?" What Ama had thought were acne scars before looked different up close, more organized. Almost as if they were in lines. *In stanzas*, she realized, and sucked in a breath. His back read like a sheet of music.

"She wanted me to feel the rhythm. She thought this might work," Jonathon said quietly. He knelt in front of her. "But now I know it wasn't my ear that was wrong, nor my hands. I was just trying to play the wrong instrument. Now I've found it." He slowly ran the end of his thumb down the front of her throat, pausing at the base. "I can hear the music now. I can feel it, each and every note. I've started writing my own songs, and you're going to help." From his backpack, he withdrew a small black voice recorder, a frayed metal cord, and a lighter. He set the recorder to the side and flicked on the lighter, holding the end of the cord over the flame.

"It's something you have to feel to understand." Jonathon clicked on the recorder and then pushed the record button. "Ama, introduction," he said. He studied her in silence for a moment, his steady gaze probing her flickering eyes. Then he pulled the burning end of the cord out of the flame and pressed it against the inside of Ama's bare thigh. She grunted with shock and then shrieked with pain as her skin died where the cord burned it away.

"A-sharp! Did you hear it?" Jonathon asked, a note of excitement in his voice.

"Hear it?" She spat the words out between gasps. "You just branded me like a steer!"

"Emotion is music, Ama. It's human music. Here, I'll play it for you so you can hear it." He rewound the recorder and then pressed play. Ama's scream, razor-sharp and high, played between them. Ama stared at the device, heaving breaths.

Jonathon picked up the recorder and clicked it off. "The note didn't translate well, honestly. The acoustics are very poor out here, especially with the mist and the trees. There's a lot of noise interfering with your voice."

"You're insane. You are fucking insane!" She flung herself against the rope, but her bindings held fast.

"It's okay to feel angry or disappointed with yourself. That's natural. You can take it out on me. You may just feel the notes at first until you learn to interpret them. But you will. I'll help you, and we'll make music together. I've learned how to teach people—how to play them, I guess you could say. I will show you what magic you're capable of."

"That's what you're doing?" Ama cried, panting. "You're torturing people for sounds?"

"It's not torture, Ama. It's production. The three of us are going to produce music together."

Ama's entire body went still, except her heart, which galloped in her chest. "Three?"

"I'm working with another instrument. Are you prepared to be outshined by a nineteen-year-old girl? Her name is Hazel. She's brilliant, the most talented instrument I've ever held in my hands. Stubborn, though. Talent gets in the way of work ethic sometimes. I've been tuning on her for a year and still haven't been able to produce what I know she's capable of. She needs to be motivated, to be challenged. This is so perfect, you coming here, crossing paths again now. Hazel needs a mother figure. She's an old soul, but she's young, and she lost her mother several years ago. You can help her; you can be that for her. I've never played two instruments at once. The layering we could do." He blinked rapidly, his eyes staring at something far away.

"Where is Hazel now?" Ama asked quickly.

"I have to keep her where she can't hurt herself. She can stand, sit, and lie down. I'm trying to make her happy. I really am. But she won't sing for me anymore. Not a single note and not even a word—not a *sound*—going on six months, and trust me, I've tried." His expression darkened, and Ama felt sicker. "You know my path crossed with Hazel's for the third time in these woods, just like you. You'd think I'd be better prepared when I go on hikes here. Although twice is just luck, I guess. If it happens again . . ." Jonathon trailed off, a disbelieving smile on his face.

"If what happens again?"

"Three times is Fate, Ama," Jonathon said. "That's how I know who Fate is choosing for my instruments: three random meetings. I should thank you for that. You gave me the idea."

"So what, this is fate? That's why you chose me? Because by my count, we've only crossed paths twice," Ama argued, wishing she didn't sound so desperate.

"Don't you remember what you said? *I never want to have to cross paths again.* You are why this started. You are the genesis—my muse—my freedom. That moment, that day, is when this dream of mine truly began. This is when I say thank you. Not then. Now."

Then? Ama said to herself. Thoughts collided in her aching head. He'd said something similar before right before he hit her: *This is when you say, "Thank you, Michael."* Her heart skipped over a beat.

Long-forgotten pictures of an old crime scene bloomed rapid-fire in her mind, images she saw in her sleep for months after the trial, until she slowly, methodically convinced herself it hadn't been him, couldn't have been the work of a fifteen-year-old boy.

"Michael Jeffery Walton," she whispered. "But you're dead. You're supposed to be dead."

"They say these woods are haunted, you know. But I am not a ghost," he whispered back.

The hair on the back of her neck stood up as the memory of walking out of the courtroom seventeen years before, knowing he was free, washed over her. Responsibility struck her hard in the stomach: How many people had he killed since then? This girl he'd had for a year, doing God knew what to her . . . she wouldn't be his prisoner if not for Ama.

No. This is on the prosecution. The case should've been a slam dunk for them. All the evidence was there. This is on them, not me. I will not be punished for being good at my job. This is their fault. I will live through this, if only to sue their asses for every penny they're worth.

She closed her eyes, channeling resolve, then opened them to glower at Michael.

"Ama Shoemaker," he responded, his entire body settling. "So good to see you again. You know, it's absolutely critical that an instrument remembers each of the three meetings, or the sounds just aren't the same value. Worthless, really. I tried once with an instrument that didn't remember the second time we'd met. The inspiration fell flat, and I could hear it in the music. I had to throw out every note. It happened one other time—a man, a large man, big mouth, deep chest. I just knew he was going to have this great lower range that's so hard to find. But he didn't remember crossing paths, and I had to let him go. So knowing that you remember our meeting in Atlanta is a relief. Letting you go would've been the devastation of my career." He smiled, his expression practically boyish with delight. "Let's have another note, shall we?"

MICHAEL

I SIT ATOP THE PIANO BENCH, FINGERTIPS BALANCED ON THE CHERRY-wood frame, thinking at this moment of how the one-inch strip of wood is like a lip, the keys like a row of perfect teeth. I cannot touch the keys until my mother has granted permission. This is her piano, the crown jewel of the house, and when I play it, I feel like a frantic, nervous virgin bungling the bra straps of an old hooker. In my mind, it is my mother's face, and she turns to me over her bare shoulder, teeth exposed in a sneer.

Don't you know how to play anything?

I blink against the image, my spine a two-by-four, my knees squeezed together, and my weight and her expectations pressing my feet to the floor. Not for the first time, I am grateful she cannot witness my rigid posture. She'll see it, though. She's been in the dark of blindness for years, but she'll see it. She would still be able to play the piano were it not for the onset of the shakes two years later. That's when she stopped playing and teaching altogether, and her rage turned into something entirely different.

She passes behind me, her white cane held between loose, thin fingers. She's memorized this arc from corner to corner of the bench. The cane is meant for me.

"Do you think you've improved in your time away?" Her voice comes from the top of her chest, a little higher and tighter than normal. I cannot turn around or she'll strike, but I can imagine her posture, hands clasped at the small of her back, lips pursed, her shoulders pulled slightly behind the vertical of her hips.

"They didn't have a piano in juvie," I say, straining all sarcasm from my answer. This is true.

You would know that if you'd visited. Or if you'd paid bail, I could've been home practicing every minute of every day before the trial began. I don't speak any of these thoughts aloud. But they're equally true.

"Whose fault is it that you spent months awaiting trial in a detention center?" She is directly behind me now. Her breath, always cold, pricks the hair at the base of my neck.

"I was found not guilty."

"You aren't innocent. This town owed us a debt, and they knew it. You really think they'd lock you up? Your father died trying to save this town, and that factory cost me everything. My sight. My career. My . . . I will go to an early grave."

I ease my chin ten degrees, fifteen, peering at her knuckles, which are swollen with rheumatoid arthritis. It has caused her pain and instability, but I would swear it has made her stronger, her swing faster, harder. Agony will do that, I have learned. But she won't go to a doctor. Not after what happened to Father.

"This piano belongs to me," she says.

"Yes, Mother."

She brings the cane against my spine. I clamp my lips shut, trapping air.

"This piano belongs to me. It is my instrument. I ask, it sings. This instrument is the only thing in my life that has never failed me, never disappointed me." She stops again. Exhales. I squeeze my eyes shut for one second—two—three.

"Stand up," she orders.

My eyes fly open, and I stand.

"This is not your instrument. It is not fair to this piano to let you bludgeon her keys. It is not fair to call the sounds you pry from her music. You must find your instrument, Michael. But this is not it."

I step out from the bench on trembling legs.

"How will I practice?"

"That is not my problem to solve." Her eyes shudder, useless in their deep sockets. I imagine plucking them from her skull, finding new, glistening eyeballs emerging from beneath. "You may not utter a sound or eat a bite until you have found an instrument."

"I can go to the—"

She swings the cane at me like a batter at a pitch. I want to jump back, but it will be worse if she misses. The narrow end strikes between two of my ribs.

"Not a sound," she hisses.

I push my hand against my throbbing side and walk to my room. Mother is a predator. Running only serves to excite her. I close the door behind me, heaving air between my gaping jaws. *Not a sound. Not a sound. Not a sound.* I clamp my hands over my ears, the silence full and buzzing. Jail would be better than this sentence. I would be separated from a piano by bars and walls and miles, three things I could not change.

I open my closet and reach above my hanging clothes, where a silver coffee can sits in the back right corner, the only thing on the shelf. I have three dollars left.

Three.

I squeeze the bills in my sweaty hand. Three will not buy me a piano at the secondhand store on Main Street, if there's even one in stock today. But three tells me I need to try.

I grab Father's walking stick from its hiding place beneath my bed and walk to the door. Feeling Mother's eyes upon me, I turn around, my fingertips poised on the handle.

"And, Michael, even if you manage to find another instrument," she says, "we will never say another word about the trial or what you did to get you there."

Even though she can't see me, I nod before slipping through the door.

The October air is a blade in my throat, squeezing tight with the effects of lingering panic. I forgot to grab a jacket, and the front pockets of my jeans are too small to shove my hands inside. A car rolls down my street. I hunker my chin against my neck, curling to block my face as much as I can, and pretend to scan the ground. I cannot speak about the trial, and if they recognize me, they'll ask. Or they'll ask how I am. And I am not to make a sound.

No sounds. No sounds. No sounds.

I step farther off the road and slide between the trees, exhaling a vaporous breath once I'm no longer visible from the road. Leaves crunch underfoot. Squirrels chide at me from perches on branches like old women screeching from their front porches at young boys tearing across lawns: *Stay out of my yard, Michael Walton!*

"So it's true. You got off." A familiar voice spins me around. Timmy Roberts stands between two trees, his red hair cut in a bowl around his head, a single faded strap of his book bag slung over one shoulder. I remember the way his cat hissed at me, then screeched, clawing and spitting, tongue curled like a straw, and I catch myself smiling. She'd been thin and easier to cut through than the others.

Timmy sneers, and the pigment in his freckles becomes more pronounced. I stare back at him, unmoving. He must be skipping school, I realize. It's Wednesday and barely midmorning.

"What? Cat got your tongue? I heard you have a thing for tongues." He sticks his out and wags it. "You think you're too good now, is that it?" He advances, shoulders leaned toward me, his hands balled to fists. "You're still Tarson trash. Nobody's scared of you, whether you did it or not."

He scoops up a rock and hurls it at me. I twist at the hip, and it glances off my stomach.

"Say something, you piece of trash. Or did your momma sew your mouth shut? I bet she whipped you good when you got home. I bet you ain't got no skin left on your ass. She should've done us all a favor and buried you alongside your daddy." His face is red now, his dark eyes squinting. "You a ghost now? Is that it? Somebody killed you and your ghost is haunting these woods? You're just standing there like a damn ghost! Could I run right through you, you son of a bitch? Could I?" He screams the question, his voice echoing in the expanse of the still, foggy woods. He slings his book bag to the ground, and he charges me.

Maybe he doesn't see my father's walking stick.

Maybe he doesn't think I'll use it.

Maybe he doesn't think I did any of it, after all.

I sweep the stick behind my head, the way my mother has a hundred times, remembering the one September my father helped me learn how to swing a bat for the boys' church baseball team.

It's in the wrists, Michael. Step your weight forward, back to front, through the hip. Don't lift the elbow high; keep it low. A level swing makes the bat sing. Drive the elbow, then come the wrists, fast and smooth.

Timmy's face splits like a dropped melon. He falls backward, his body a cut tree, and he crashes to the mat of rotting leaves. He slaps his hands at his liquid features. His front teeth are gone. He's sputtering, sounds choking through the fluid at random. I pull off his shoes and socks. He kicks at me, unseeing, his eyes filled with blood and tears. I cover my hands with his socks and wipe his mouth out, clearing the chamber for want of cleaner sound. He screams, and the note is shocking, sharp, and true. A black key pressed down, a foot on the pedal, holding the note. I rock back on my feet, goose bumps rising on my arms, pure vibrations shimmering through every bone in my body.

Timmy stops thrashing, the initial daze and shock appearing to wane, and struggles to sit up. So I coil the stick behind my head and bring it down again.

Timmy has a hundred-dollar bill folded into a square in the toe of one shoe. If I'm Tarson trash, so is he, and I'd bet my life he stole the money. It's been at least a year since I set foot in his house, but I can't imagine it's changed much since then. His daddy is alive but gone, and his mom is here but passes each day on the couch in the smoke-filled front room of their house, a bottle of whisky always within reach. His mom got sick about the same time mine did. Sick looks different on everybody.

I pick up his ankles and drag him backward. He is shorter than me but heavier, and within a minute I am sweating despite the cool air. His hands trail behind his head. His fingers are pudgy and soft, and I imagine he would have a better feel for piano keys than I do.

I stop and kneel to examine the fat pads on each fingertips and compare them to mine, which are narrow, the bone just beneath the surface. Is this all I lack—a quarter-inch layer of flesh?

I drop his hand and stand to search the surroundings. No one comes out here anymore, but once Timmy doesn't come home, it'll be only a day or two before someone suggests searching Tarson Woods. But no one knows these woods like I do.

A stone's throw from here, Cold River cuts through Tarson Woods and bends in a teardrop shape. An old tree uprooted last fall and fell across the water. It's tempted plenty of kids across, and some come to school wet and sandy after an attempt. One boy was swept nearly a mile downstream when he plunged into the frothy current, swollen with a week's worth of rain. But we haven't had a drop in weeks. Rocks will be exposed, water slow and thin. It would be the perfect place for a boy skipping school to take off his shoes and book bag and try to walk across, arms out to the side, toes gripping the slick, bright moss, chin held up so he couldn't become fixated on how high he was, what might happen should he lose his balance.

M
I
C
H
A
E
L

TWO HOURS LATER, I STAND AT THE COUNTER OF THE SECONDHAND shop, Timmy's hundred-dollar bill in one hand, my other hand resting on an electric keyboard.

"Sixteen dollars, even," the cashier says.

I hand him the hundred.

"Do you have anything smaller? I don't have enough change to break this."

I want to tell him it's all I have, aside from the three singles in my jeans pocket, but I can't speak. Not yet. The instrument doesn't belong to me.

I stare beyond the man, blinking away a surge of heat. The man blurs, the background becoming clear. On the shelves behind the counter stands a line of wooden carvings of miniature pianos, most of them uprights, with one baby grand, scale perfect, sitting dead center.

"Is there anything else you might want?"

I point to the baby grand carving.

"Oh, that's more than . . ." He pauses, regarding my face. "That would make up the difference." He takes Tommy's hundred-dollar bill, then plucks the piano from the counter and hands it to me. It's surprisingly light, not laden with legacy and expectation and failure.

"Do you have a hobby? Baseball or hunting?"

I shake my head.

"I could teach you how to carve. If you want. You could carve a little design into your stick. Your initials or something. Make it harder for somebody else to claim as their own. Not when it's wet, mind you. You'll want to let it dry all the way out first."

As he wraps the piano in paper, I examine the stick, making sure the side with the darker streaks faces me. Cold River couldn't draw all of Timmy out of the wood, but the red has faded to brown and could be mistaken for a natural effect.

"There you go." He hands me a bag with the piano carving with one hand and the keyboard with the other, the cord wound around the body. "My name is Rick. Come back any time, okay? I'll teach you how to make those. It's more patience than anything."

"I might take you up on that," I say.

EDDIE

A HUNDRED YARDS REMAINED BETWEEN EDDIE AND THE PEAK. HE grabbed the slick trunk of a tree and stared at the place where the rise finally leveled. His knees ached. The soles of his feet were hot and tender, having soaked too long in his wet socks. His breath was labored, and the cold air stung his throat.

He leaned into the tree and let out a bitter, choking laugh.

I'm never going to make it. And what for? That woman isn't out here. I scared her out of whatever she'd come here to do. She's at a friend's house with a cup of hot tea in her hands and a blanket over her shoulders, telling about the man she was sure was going to snatch her.

Eddie squeezed his eyes shut. He slowly straightened, stretching the cramping out of his legs, when the ghost of a scream sailed over the top of the mountain and hung in the sky.

He jerked to attention, looking at the black above as if the sound he heard might emit a glow. He started to shout back, not sure if the scream had been real. He stopped. If someone was out here, screaming like that, they were in the worst kind of trouble. Shouting back would only serve to alert the possible danger of his presence. Eddie wasn't fast, and he wasn't as strong as he used to be. He'd need surprise on his side if something really was happening down the hill. If he reached the clearing and didn't see anything, he'd call out.

Adrenaline coursed through him, dimming the pain and exhaustion, and the peak seemed to rush at him. Once the ground leveled, he broke into an uneven jog. His pulse beat a rhythm against his palms and pounded in his ears. At last, the trees opened and the trail ended at a lookout point over a sharp descent, revealing foothills rolling to the south.

Eddie felt his way to the edge of the drop-off and peered over. Except for the wind, the forest was silent. He raised his hands to his mouth, preparing to shout, when a flicker of light peeked from the valley floor. He squinted and leaned forward. The glow disappeared, and then came back. Someone was down there.

A thinning patch of clouds allowed moonlight through. Eddie searched for a way down. The trail ended here for a reason. People turned around and went back the way they came in for a reason. No out-of-shape old man in his right mind would try to make this descent. But no father would turn back now.

MICHAEL

FRIDAY EVENINGS BREATHE LIFE INTO MAIN STREET'S ONE-BLOCK PROM-enade. It's the same stores, the same street, but string lights in blooming trees, turn the soundtrack up a little louder, and leave every door open, and the mood shifts from errand to event. Yet all I can think about is the keyboard Mother flung against the wall, the cracks in the plastic where it gave way under pressure.

Get out of my house! Take that piece of trash with you!

So I am on Main Street, wondering if there's an instrument I can put on layaway in the junk shop, and my keyboard is in the dumpster. At least I still have my walking stick. It feels like more of a home than the walls of our house.

The vibrant cadence of a bow on a fiddle draws my ear. I track the music into an art gallery. A petite girl sits on the ground with a fiddle in her arms and a piece of cardboard at her feet with the words DONATIONS WELCOME scrawled in purple marker. Her eyes close. The fingers on her right hand flutter from string to string as her left hand draws the bow back and forth.

She cries out a wailing note, and I am rooted to the spot, the sensation buzzing in my toes and fingers and scalp. I watch the blood pulse on the side of her neck, her chest rise and fall with each breath. I press my tongue against the roof of my mouth, suddenly dry, and I want to know if she'd hiss like a cat with my hands around her neck.

She opens her eyes and catches me staring. Her lips curl in a snarl.

"Freak," she says.

I walk away from her and tuck myself inside the doorframe of the secondhand store, and when she leaves, I follow her. Down the road, between a row of abandoned redbrick buildings, across a yard, and into Tarson Woods.

MICHAEL

THE BUZZING I FELT IN MY PALMS FROM THE GIRL'S VOCAL CORDS straining past the pressure of my hands lingers now, even though I washed my hands clean in the river. And I do feel clean—despite the crust of sweat on my face, the smell of the woods in my hair. I feel clean. I feel . . . new.

I saw the world in that girl's eyes, a flash of last light like the universe spinning around the sun, her last sound, soft and pure. I heard it over the rushing water; I hear it even still.

Maybe Mother was right. Maybe I am destined for more, saved by the river, and I must go. I must leave this town. I must find my fate.

Mother may have taught me that, but she won't let me leave if she's awake. It's the leaving that hurts her most. So I will spare her that pain and be gone come sunup.

In the dark, I stuff my backpack with clothes and all the cash I can find in the house. On my way out, I press her door two inches ajar. From her outline, I can tell she's lying on her back, rigid even in sleep.

Lady Fate requires patience, a skill Mother's never mastered. Even if she did, Lady Fate demands obedience, and Mother answers to no one. I once considered that trait an asset, a line I might possibly reach only once Mother was dead and chilly. Now I see how it limits her, and I cannot allow her limits to stifle me.

I retrieve my father's walking stick from the hall closet, slip through the front door, and lock it behind me. The night is quiet and black and still. Then a wind picks up, sudden and warm, and the trees bordering the left side of our yard and the boundary of Tarson Woods sway. Branches saw against one another, and in the grind I hear my father whisper my name.

I stumble down the three steps of our front stoop and into our narrow yard, dry grass crunching underfoot.

Michael.

I run into Tarson Woods, zigzagging between boughs and ducking under low hanging branches.

Michael.

Louder now. Cold River roars ahead, the fallen tree still balanced between two banks, sagging in the middle.

Michael.

I reach the river's edge. Timmy stands on the opposite bank, pointing at my feet with a skeleton finger, blood matted in his red hair, eye sockets empty, his left cheek peeled back from time and water and blow after blow after blow.

Something cracks, splinters; then there's a rush as the middle of the fallen oak gives way. The two halves of the rotted tree plummet to the water and are pulled downstream twenty feet before coming to a tenuous resting place. Now my breath is the only sound, the river continuing as if nothing has changed, the woods quiet, the wind and the voice and Timmy evaporating into the night.

Timmy disappeared three years ago. In retrospect, it was amazing how quickly people stopped looking, how quickly they assumed he'd fallen in, how quickly they accepted a body wouldn't be found. It took me longer to carve piano keys from his femurs.

I stare down at the fallen tree, at the gap between the two halves where the black water sails through.

I step out of my shoes and leave them on the bank.

A FLASH OF MOVEMENT HIGH ON THE HILL BEHIND MICHAEL CAUGHT her eye. She wanted to scream, but it could have been a deer, for all she knew. Michael seemed more settled now, his whole story spilled between them. She didn't want to risk agitating him again. Ama stole a glimpse over his head. The wind made the trees rock and bend. It was impossible to discern real movement from shadows.

"Why did you come back here?" Ama asked. As if it mattered. As if she could've outrun him longer in a city of five hundred thousand people instead of forty square miles of trees and hills. A month after his verdict, she took her paycheck and put a down payment on a house an hour away. She'd convinced herself it wasn't because of Michael, that she'd just have a better opportunity to make a name for herself closer to Atlanta. Somewhere along the last seventeen years, she'd bought the lie—and he'd been in Atlanta with her nearly the entire time.

"Fate told me it was time," he said.

"Fate isn't real! It's an excuse. You chose to come back here just like you chose to leave. Nothing is guiding you."

"Answer me three questions. Tell me why you took my case, why you changed your name, and why you became a defense attorney, and I'll prove to you that Fate has been guiding me, probably both of us, since the moment we met."

"I took your case because no one else would."

"That's not the whole truth, is it? You weren't even supposed to be the lead attorney on my case."

"I fought for it," she whispered.

"Why?"

"Because I knew they thought I'd lose," she answered, mentally revisiting that day in the office, their knowing stares, their not-so-discreet smiles.

"But you thought I was guilty."

"It wasn't about you. It was about me. I wanted to prove myself. I wanted to show I could win," Ama said. "Do you have any idea what it was like to be a female attorney in rural Georgia at that time? They'd just as soon send me for coffee or to make copies than hand me a case."

Michael opened his hands and brought the tips of his fingers together. "Was it worth it?"

She trembled, wondering at the notes he'd already recorded, the sounds he'd torn out of people. At the nineteen-year-old girl locked away somewhere, refusing to speak.

"That's on the prosecution. Not me," she finally said.

"Which brings me to question number two." He gave her a pointed look.

"The answers for questions two and three are linked," Ama began. "My last name isn't really Shoemaker."

Interest pricked Michael's features. "Go on," he said.

"Shoemaker is my mother's maiden name. We both changed our last names after my father was wrongly convicted for weapons trafficking. The short version is that he was the fall guy in a deal gone bad. He just routed trucks, dispatched drivers, made sure payments were picked up. Higher-ups in the company he worked for blackmailed him into being the go-between for sales. But his bosses had built a web of connections that all led back to him, and when they got caught, they all said he was the ringleader. He died in prison four years into his sentence."

"So you became a defense attorney."

"So I became a defense attorney."

"But you changed your name back to Chaplin. Why? Because of me?"

"No," she answered. "I took his name back to remember why I became an attorney. Not for people like you. For people like him."

"Why not a prosecutor? You didn't want to go after the men who framed your father?"

"It's easier to put the wrong man away than to save the innocent one. I guess I liked the challenge."

"That would explain your eagerness to prove my innocence all those years ago."

Ama arched a brow. "You weren't innocent. Discrediting the witnesses shouldn't have been enough. You had luck on your side."

"You look at my life, my father's death, my mother's hand, my scars . . . and you call it luck?"

"I'm the one here against my will." Ama glared. "You should be in prison, but you're not. What would you call it, Michael?"

"I have something on my side, it's true. But it's nothing to do with luck." Michael stood and reached behind Ama, disconnecting the chain. Then he pulled up on the cord, hauling her to her feet. Her wrists howled with fresh pain.

"Wait," Ama pled. "You still have to prove to me that fate has a hand in this."

"That's what I'm doing," he said. "But this is a story you and Hazel should both hear." He opened the Ziploc bag with his soiled shirt, tore off a strip, and fitted it between her teeth before knotting it behind her head. The smell of her urine stung her eyes and made her stomach turn.

"Bet you wish you hadn't pissed yourself right about now," he murmured, adding a second strip of fabric. He slung his pack onto his shoulder before untying the rope from the tree. He knotted it at her wrists and then looped it around her neck, then held the end of it like he was holding a dog leash. "Time to go," he ordered, pushing at the center of her back with his walking stick.

She stumbled forward, catching her weight on her bad ankle. It buckled underneath her, and she staggered to the side. She tried to throw out her hands to stop herself, but Michael held the rope taut. She spun around on her heel and fell on her butt. She drew her knees under her, panting. A choke of a sob burned a path up her windpipe, and fresh tears spilled from her eyes.

A twig snapped close by. Michael yanked on the rope.

"Don't make a sound," he hissed, and drew the hood of his sweatshirt over his head, his face shrouded in shadows, and turned off the lantern. Fear ignited inside of Ama. Then she heard labored breathing and the shuffling sound of someone walking. She tried to cry out, but the fabric pinned down her tongue, making her cough.

Her eyes adjusted. A hunched figure strode toward them. The person raised their arms, and a glint of silver shone in the moonlight. The unmistakable sound of a cocking gun hammer filled her ears.

"Let her go!" a man's voice shouted, and the sound of a gun blast filled the dark.

Ama froze. The rope went slack. Ama turned her chin in time to see Michael pivot and take a running step downhill. She swung her gaze back to the man. He followed Michael with his gun, brought his elbows in, taking aim. Relief trickled through her. Then she remembered Hazel, locked away, imagined her surrounded by petrified organs pinned to boards. Michael had inadvertently conditioned her to never respond. Even if rescuers called her by name, she wouldn't answer. They hadn't found her in a year. She highly doubted Michael's dead body would leave any remarkable clues. If Michael died, Hazel died, too, slow and silent and alone.

She tried to shout at the man to stop, but the gag garbled her voice. The man with the gun didn't turn his focus from Michael. He brought the site closer to his eye. His arm steadied to the point of motionlessness. He was going to shoot.

With a grunt, Ama sprung up from her knees and leaped sideways, hoping to distract him just enough to at least make him hesitate. A second blast of gunfire jumped into the night at nearly the same instant. Pressure and heat flooded her chest, and a crunching sound filled her. She dropped to her side. Flecks of cold mud spattered her open mouth. She tried to crawl forward but couldn't lift her body off the ground. Her left side throbbed, her left arm fire hot and limp. She moved her left hand to touch it. There was a soft place below her collar where her ribs should've been. Too soft. She pushed a finger into it, finding it wet.

Confusion spread through her brain, painting over something she'd been so sure about just a moment ago. She rolled to her back and stared up, the sensation of becoming liquid spreading through her. Above, the stars became brighter and blurred into tiny lines. They stretched until they connected, crisscrossing the dark like stitches on a patchwork quilt. She heard gurgling and rasping, but she couldn't tell from where. The sounds faded, and the darkness turned to white.

E
D
D
I
E

THE WOMAN CRUMPLED TO THE GROUND, WRITHING. EDDIE DROPPED the gun. His hands shook.

She'd jumped in front of the bullet, hadn't she? Or had she tripped? Taken off in a blind panic? It didn't matter . . . he'd shot her.

Eddie lifted his gaze. The man he'd intended to shoot looked directly back. Between the dark and the hood drawn over his head, all that was visible of the man was his nose and the outline of his chin. The woman gasped, the sound of it liquid, and broke the spell that had settled like stagnant water, too warm and glistening with oil from decay.

Eddie stepped toward her. The man reached for something in his pack. Eddie snatched the empty gun from the ground and trained it on the man's chest.

"Stay where you are!" Eddie shouted. "Help! We need help!" he screamed louder, tilting his mouth skyward in hopes the sound would carry farther. They had to be two miles from the main parking lot, maybe more. There's no way anyone would be able to hear them. The man opened his mouth, closed it, then turned and fled downhill.

Eddie rushed to the woman's side. Her breaths came in wisps. Her eyes were unfocused and glistening with panic.

"You're all right. You gonna be all right," Eddie said. He pulled the rope from around her neck and took the gag out of her mouth. She cried a little girl's cry, small and breaking. He cradled her head in one leathered hand and felt for the bullet hole with the other. Blood spurted from a hole high on her chest. He pushed his palm against it, hoping to slow it down.

If she kept bleeding this fast, she wouldn't make it to the parking lot alive. He balled up the strip of fabric he'd taken from her mouth and stuffed it into the wound. A groan emitted from deep inside her, and her torso curled away from him.

"Why did you do that?" he pled, staring over her head into the night. She tried to respond but sputtered instead, and then began to choke. Something warm and sticky pooled in the hand Eddie was using to support her head. She was bleeding from her mouth.

"No, ma'am. Don't be doin' that now," Eddie whispered. He knew he shouldn't move her, but he figured that rule only applied to people with decent odds of survival. He stuck the gun in his coat pocket, bent down, and picked her up. She was heavier than he thought she'd be. His legs shook, and his feet were on fire. How was he going to carry her up? She moaned and clutched his jacket. Her face twisted with concentration, and her lips curled around a word. Her fingers fluttered at his hip. Her mouth opened, and her eyes focused on his face for a full second.

"What are you trying to tell me?" Eddie pled, studying her.

"Aaace," came out of her mouth, ending in a hiss, and her bloody finger scratched against his chest insistently. Her eyes rolled back in their sockets, and her body went limp.

"No!" Eddie shook her. She rocked in his arms, her limbs swaying. "No!" He hugged her close and staggered to the base of the hill. He looked up, searching for the way he'd come. Beams of light shone down from the crest. He squinted in the sudden flood of light.

"I see someone!" a voice shouted from above. "Tarson PD! Who's down there?"

"Help! It's me, Eddie," he cried out. "I . . . a lady's been . . . she's hurt bad!"

"Stay right where you are, Eddie!" another voice shouted. "Don't move!"

Eddie turned and leaned against the hill, holding the woman against his chest. He wished any sign of breath or life would stir under his hand.

Scuffling sounds on the hill drew his ear. He glanced over his shoulder. Two officers descended, guns drawn. As they came closer, he recognized them as Briggs and Stanton, officers he'd spoken to over the last year in his search for Hazel.

"Let her go, Eddie," Briggs said, and aimed the barrel of his gun near Eddie's face.

"I don't think I should do that," Eddie said, distracted by the gun. He probably hurt her more when he picked her up. He couldn't very well risk putting her down again. He began to straighten, shifting the weight of her.

"I said don't move!" Briggs shouted. Eddie flinched, and confusion set in. Why was Briggs yelling at him? Static buzzed from the radio clipped on Briggs's hip, and the captain's familiar voice blared through, asking if they'd found anything.

"We got her. We've got them both," Briggs said. "Ama. Ama, can you hear me?" he said loudly.

"She's unconscious," Eddie said, rocking forward again, trying to move so they could see her face.

"Stay where you are!" Briggs growled. "Put Ama down on the ground, Eddie. Then back away."

"I can't do that!" Eddie shouted back. "What if I hurt her worse?"

"Did you hurt her, Eddie?" Briggs asked, stepping toward them.

"No . . . well, yes. But I didn't mean to."

"Put her down!" Briggs ordered.

Recognition charged through him. He was standing in the woods with a warm gun in his pocket and a dying woman in his arms. Her blood was on his hands, his coat, his shoes. The bullet lodged somewhere inside her would match his gun. His fingers had gunpowder on them from the discharge. His heart shuddered in his chest. He kneeled down and gingerly placed her on the earth.

"Hands up!" Stanton barked.

Eddie raised his hands. "Let me explain. This isn't what it looks like. A man had her," he said. "I tried to shoot him, but she jumped in the way. I . . . I shot her. I didn't mean to."

Briggs crouched down beside the woman and put his fingers on her throat. "She's still alive," he said. "But I don't know how long she's going to stay that way. It'll take us too long to carry her out. Do you think we can get a chopper?"

"Even if we had one, I don't know where it would land," Stanton responded, stepping close to Eddie, his gun trained low.

"There's a clearing not far from here. Right beside the river. It's pretty level," Eddie mumbled, watching Ama; the way her hand dangled from her wrist, her light hair spilled across the ground like milk on a dark wood floor.

"Shut up," Briggs responded. He brought the radio to his mouth. "Ama is in bad shape. GSW to the chest, lots of blood. She needs to go straight to the hospital in Dalton. We found Eddie holding her."

"This isn't what it looks like!" Eddie pled.

"You know, I prayed for you after Hazel disappeared," Stanton said, glaring. "I searched these woods for her with you. You had us all fooled. What did you do to Hazel, Eddie? Is she out here, too? What kind of man hurts his own kid?"

Eddie's head snapped back as if he'd been struck, and rage blazed a path up his spine. "I would never harm a hair on my daughter's head," he roared. "I have never hurt anybody!"

Briggs grabbed Eddie's elbows, pinning them behind him. "Do you have a weapon on you of any sort, Mr. Stevens?" Briggs cuffed his wrists.

"Brennen Briggs, you know me!" Eddie shouted, reeling.

Briggs shoved his hands into Eddie's pocket and pulled out the gun. He smelled the barrel. "Is this what you shot her with, Eddie?" he pushed.

"It wasn't supposed to be her!" Eddie shouted. "I told you, another man was here with her. He had her gagged and tied up. I was trying to stop him before he could run away. I couldn't just let him go," Eddie pleaded. "What if . . ."

What if he knew what happened to Hazel?

The train of thought didn't leave his mouth. They wouldn't believe him. Not now. They needed to get this woman to a hospital. She had to live so she could tell them Eddie didn't do this. What if she didn't remember?

Briggs searched his other pocket without answering. His hand went still, and then he slowly withdrew it. The little silver watch dangled from his fingers.

"What are you doing with a lady's watch?" he asked.

"I found it in the old stone hutch," Eddie said.

"Sure you did," he answered. "Want to know a secret?" he continued in an angry whisper. "Chief told me our new big-city detective has Hazel's file on his desk right now, Eddie, and the only person he wants to talk to is you."

Fear, cold and wet, trickled from the base of Eddie's throat, through his body, and down his limbs. This was his last chance to help Hazel. Her killer was in these woods right now; of that, Eddie was sure. And yet the likelihood of the police taking him seriously now, and being willing to comb this mountain range one last time, seemed impossible.

"Stanton, you tell the captain to get a chopper here no matter what it takes. We need Ms. Ama to wake up long enough to tell us Eddie shot her. Eddie"—Briggs turned his attention to him—"you're coming with us."

Briggs began to recite the Miranda warning. The sound of Eddie's breathing decelerated in his ears. He stared at the woman, blinking slowly, his eyelids like lead. Her jaw was slack. Her eyes weren't open or closed. Briggs was right. If she died without regaining consciousness first, he'd never be able to clear his name, and any hope of Hazel being found would be locked up with him.

MARTIN

MARTIN STOOD IN FRONT OF THE ONE-WAY GLASS, PEERING AT EDDIE Stevens. Eddie had been sitting alone in an interrogation room for the past couple of hours while Martin gathered as much evidence as possible and decided how he wanted to approach the interview. He preferred to let a suspect simmer. The truth spilled out easier and faster that way.

Eddie looked older than Martin had imagined, even noticeably older from the picture in Hazel's file. A year of unrelenting stress did that to the body. His hair had silvered around his temples, and the lines around his eyes were deeper and had doubled. Plus it was nearly two in the morning. Stanton had told him it took almost two hours to walk Eddie out of the woods, and then another hour spent on travel to the station and processing. Every person still left in the precinct looked as though they'd aged a decade.

Martin wondered if he'd see the telltale hollowness in Eddie's eyes he often noted when he'd finally caught a criminal long on the run, but Eddie hadn't yet raised his head high enough for Martin to be able to tell. He hadn't touched the cup of water they'd left for him, either.

Eddie lifted his arms and pressed the heels of his hands into his eye sockets. The chain connecting his handcuffs to the floor clanked against the side of the table. The cuffs slid down his wrist until the width of his forearms caught them. Eddie was a solid man. His knuckles were leathered and oversize, evidence of a life of labor. They hadn't cleaned the blood off his skin, although they'd stripped him and put his bloodied clothes in evidence bags, then had him dress in a gray prison jumpsuit.

Martin opened the file. At the very top was Ama's silver watch in a plastic bag. This was as open-and-shut as a case could get, whether Ama woke up or not. Yet while he'd waited for Eddie to be brought to the station, a thought had surfaced in his mind that he couldn't shake. How could Eddie have been so careful about the murders of his wife and daughter yet been so messy with Ama? Raelynn Stevens hadn't been shot, and what details he'd dug up in the disappearance of Hazel didn't point toward a quick end by a bullet. What had gone wrong when Eddie tried to take Ama? He drew in a breath and held it while he organized his thoughts. Then he exhaled and shouldered open the door.

"Mr. Stevens, I'm Detective Martin Locklear. Thanks for your patience." He slid into his seat and scooted himself closer to the table. Eddie showed no reaction. Martin tapped the file on the tabletop. "Mr. Stevens, do you know why you're here?"

"Is she dead?" Eddie murmured without looking up.

"Ms. Chaplin is in surgery, last I heard."

"Is she going to die?" Eddie's brow lifted.

"I don't know. Would it matter to you?"

"Of course it matters!"

"What's she going to tell us if she wakes up, Eddie?" Martin asked as he propped his elbows on the table.

"I shot her, but I didn't mean to. A man had her in a bad way. I aimed at him, and I pulled the trigger. But I swear on my life, she jumped in front of the gun, or she jumped thinking she was moving out of the way. I didn't shoot her on purpose. I was aiming for him."

"Why shoot either one?"

"I just wanted to stop him. I wanted to ask him . . ." Eddie trailed off and shook his head.

"Ask him what?"

"If he had Hazel," Eddie answered in a whisper.

"Why would he have Hazel?" Martin pressed.

"Somebody does. You think it's me. You think I did it." Eddie looked up. Tears ran freely down both sides of his face. "You and everybody in this building think I killed my own little girl." Eddie's voice faded into a strangled rasp. "She was my light. She was my *life*."

"She *is* your light. She *is* your life," Martin replied carefully, and narrowed his eyes.

"What?"

"You seem to think she's out there somewhere to be found, kidnapped by a man in the woods. Yet you referred to her in the past tense, like you know she's dead."

"She ain't been home in a year. I don't want to believe she's dead, but I swear she talked to me today. She told me to go look for that lady. I've been sitting here for Lord knows how long, thinking about Hazel, about the woods, about that woman. I messed up." His face twisted, and a sob of grief escaped his mouth.

"What do you mean, she told you to go look for that lady?" Martin asked, and his drumming fingers fell still.

"It's been a year today since Hazel disappeared. I'd dropped her off at that trail. I didn't go with her." He squeezed his eyes shut, and fresh tears spilled out. "I went in to look for that lady, and I nearly turned back, but Hazel told me to keep looking. I swear she did. So I kept going because I would've wanted someone to keep looking for Hazel. She didn't run away from me."

"But they organized searches for Hazel," Martin argued as he flipped through her file. "The official search lasted months. It sounds like they looked pretty hard for her."

"You're new here, right?" Eddie said. "Maybe they haven't told you how people vanish in those woods. They fade away like smoke in the wind and nobody says anything too loud or for too long. It doesn't make the paper or the nightly news. They're just gone. Hazel got more attention than most. Uniforms came from all over the state. She was still in school. She made pretty good grades, except for math. But she got that from me. That's not her fault. So people noticed when she didn't come home . . . for a while, anyway. Then people forgot. They talked about her, like you said, in past tense. They didn't think she was dead. They just didn't think she'd be back."

"So what were you doing in that parking lot?"

"She wanted me to hike that trail with her last year." Eddie's features slide lower on his face. "I didn't go. Had a job in town. One hour. I couldn't give her an hour." He shielded his open mouth in the crook of his elbow as a new round of sobs escaped him. "I was gonna kill myself today," Eddie whispered. "The gun was for me. One bullet to draw attention to me. One bullet to draw attention to her."

"How would that have helped Hazel?" Martin asked. His mind sorted through what he remembered finding in Eddie's van.

"I tried to give the police the evidence I told you about. They didn't see the links. But I do, Detective. I see them all over the place, like threads of a spiderweb. Hazel is in that web. I figured . . . if I died with all that information sitting beside me, maybe they'd look one more time."

"You were going to kill yourself to make them look?"

Eddie nodded. His chin quivered. "I couldn't even get that right."

Martin pushed back from the table. Nothing about the conversation was going at all like he thought it might. Eddie hadn't glanced once at Ama's watch, the trinket the officers were convinced he'd taken as a trophy. He also seemed genuinely hopeful Ama would live, which didn't make a damn bit of sense. Still, the case files, the timing, the death of his wife. Martin didn't believe in coincidences.

"Why haven't you asked for a lawyer?" Martin asked, narrowing his eyes.

"I'm innocent."

"Innocent people need lawyers even more than guilty ones."

"I ask for a lawyer, you and every cop in this place is going to start looking at each other like you got me red-handed."

"We do have you red-handed." Martin pointed at Eddie's crusty hands.

"I didn't mean to shoot her!" Eddie balled his bloodstained fingers into a fist and slammed it down on the tabletop.

"Right. You were aiming at a man. And she jumped in front of it?"

"I don't know what she did! I had a shot, I took it, and she got in front of the bullet. Maybe it was an accident. Maybe it was on purpose. I don't know."

"Why would she jump in front of a bullet meant for someone you claim was hurting her?" Martin pressed.

"You're the detective. You tell me."

They stared at each other, the silence between them charged.

"Let's take a break. I'll see if there are any updates, on Ama or otherwise." Martin stood and moved to the door. "You're not asking if you can leave?"

Eddie looked up then, and his gaze locked on Martin. "Are you going to keep looking into Hazel's case?"

"Yes."

"Then there's no other place I need to be."

"Was that what this was all for?" Martin mused, turning to face him again. "You couldn't pull the trigger on yourself, so you shot the first person you saw?"

Eddie sat back. A storm of emotions changed the slope of his features. He licked his lips. "I got a bad knee. Don't you think if I wanted to shoot that lady to get your attention, I just would've done it in the parking lot when I first saw her? Saved us all a lot of trouble?" he answered quietly.

"Maybe." Martin stood still for a second longer, then walked out of the room.

MARTIN

MARTIN HEADED FOR THE CAPTAIN'S OFFICE. IF ANYONE IN THE DEPART-ment knew Ama's current condition, it would be him. Through the half-drawn blinds covering the captain's office window, Martin could see him sitting at his desk, propping himself up on both elbows. His lights were on, but his eyes were closed, his fingers in a steeple in front of his nose. Martin kept his face in view and tapped twice on the door, which was open a sliver. Captain waved him in without speaking. Under the glare of fluorescent lighting and the weight of what would surely become a high-profile case, Captain's face was sinking. Martin eased the door shut behind himself. He didn't venture deeper into the office.

"You know, if you'd told me yesterday Eddie Stevens would be in police custody and had admitted to shooting someone, I would've given you a Breathalyzer. But the more I sit here and think about it . . ." He stopped talking and shook his head. "It makes more sense than I wish it did."

"Honestly, the more I think about it, the less sense it makes," Martin responded.

"You seemed pretty damn sure of yourself in that parking lot."

"Do you honestly think Hazel ran away?" Martin asked point-blank.

"No. But it was a popular opinion. People disappear around here, Martin. That's a fact. Every month somebody new is missing. Most of the time, honestly, it's some kid leaving a bad home for an even worse situation and they just don't know it yet. I don't have to tell you there's a drug problem here. Anybody with one good eye who stays here for twenty-four hours could tell you that."

"So what do you think happened to Hazel?'" Martin asked.

"That trail she was on isn't easy or safe. Any number of things could've happened. She could've fallen in an old mine shaft or gotten lost or fallen into Cold River. We had three days of hard rain after she went missing. That kind of water can move and cover up a lot of things."

"So you think it was just some tragic accident?" Martin narrowed his eyes.

"Yes. It's not something I ever said straight out to Eddie, but in my heart, until about four hours ago, that's what I thought happened to Hazel Stevens. The woods swallowed her up. It's happened before. It'll happen again."

"And now?"

"Now I don't know. I can't see Eddie doing something to Hazel. But I can't imagine him shooting a lady, either," Captain answered.

"What about the man Eddie says was there with her? Do you think there's any truth in it?"

"I want to believe it. But let's say it is true. He tries to shoot the man holding Ama and instead of just saying he missed, he says Ama jumped in front of the bullet. What abduction victim would take a bullet for the assailant? Especially with the shape she was in. The doc in the ER said she has burns all over her legs like somebody tried to brand her. What would make her save his life?"

"That's what I keep asking myself," Martin said. "How is Ama? Any news?"

"Still in surgery as far as I know. Is Eddie saying anything new in there?" Captain asked.

"His story is the same. He mentioned trying to bring outside case information to your attention. He thought it was related to Hazel."

"I remember that." Captain blinked, his focus traveling somewhere unseen. "He was sure there was a connection. He called it . . ."

"A spiderweb," Martin finished for him.

"That's it. Anyways, I glanced through it, but I didn't see much. The cases he picked, there was no common victimology. The missing people ranged from fifteen years old to well over fifty. I remember there was an

Asian woman and a migrant worker from El Savador with false identi-fication, but most of the other victims were white. There wasn't another black person in his file." Captain paused and rubbed his face. "Eddie's name can't be released to the public on this yet, and do not discuss the link between Hazel and Ama with anyone outside of this building. Not until we're sure. I don't want to set Eddie's world on fire if he didn't do this."

"But he did shoot a woman in the woods. His name is going to be hard to keep out of the press."

Captain glared at Martin. "Accidental shooting is a lot different than attempted murder and killing his daughter. Let's know what we're accusing him of, first."

"I'll call the hospital and make sure no one speaks to any media and that this stays off the public scanners as much as possible," Martin offered.

The phone on Captain's desk rang. He plucked the receiver from the base. "Captain," he said. His eyes tracked the shape of the ceiling as he listened, then he squeezed them shut. "What's the prognosis?" The quiet in the room was as still and tight as a violin string, as though any move-ment could make all the walls vibrate. "Keep us posted of any further change. I'll let the DA know."

Captain replaced the receiver and rested his hand on it. His jaw shifted from side to side. "Ama's out of surgery. They said no major organs were damaged, but the bullet nicked her axillary artery and she lost a lot of blood. She was hypothermic when she came in, which they said is the only reason she didn't bleed to death out there. But she is taking longer to wake up than they expected. A lot longer."

"Is she *going* to wake up?" Martin asked.

"Only time will tell. But the longer she goes . . ." Captain broke off and shook his head. "I think with the evidence we have, finding him guilty wouldn't be hard even without her."

"I really need her to wake up," Martin said. "Do you have a second, Captain? I want you on the other side of the glass when I tell him Ama may not wake up. I want you to read his face. You know him better than I do."

"Maybe I do, and maybe I don't," Captain answered, pushing up from his chair.

Captain followed Martin back to the interrogation room. Martin felt strange with Captain behind him. He'd felt superior to this man from the moment he met him until about two minutes ago. Captain's new faith in him was a heavy thing. Now that he had it, he wasn't sure he wanted it.

Captain stepped to the side as Martin walked through the door and closed it. Martin stopped at the corner of the table, making sure the entire window behind him was exposed for Captain to watch Eddie through. Eddie looked up at Martin. His eyes went wide with knowing, and he slouched in his chair.

"She's dead, isn't she?" Only his mouth moved.

"Technically, no. But there's a very good chance she's never going to wake up," Martin said.

Eddie threaded his weathered fingers, pressed his thumbs into his eyes, and let out a big, jagged sob. His forearms gave way, and his head came down to the tabletop. Tears streamed down his lined face.

Martin studied him, watched his heavy breaths make circles of vapor on the brown laminate. This reaction was completely at odds with how a compulsive killer following a ritual would behave. The only angle that would make sense was if he was mourning the fact that she was still alive at all.

"I lied, Eddie. Ama is awake," Martin lied. He wondered what Captain's expression looked like on the other side of the one-way mirror.

"She's awake?" Eddie jerked upright. "I need to talk to her. Is she talking? What did she say? Did she tell you the man was there? That he was hurting her?"

Martin closed his eyes.

He might be wrong.

He might be completely wrong.

MARTIN

MARTIN POURED A CUP OF TEPID, DAY-OLD COFFEE AND SWALLOWED IT in two gulps. He made a face as bitter grounds trapped themselves in every corner and crevice in his mouth. He could've made a new pot; it was morning somewhere. In Tarson, the sun was still hours from the horizon, and he didn't have the patience to stand by and listen to something drip, not when his case was both revealing itself and imploding at the same time.

Five minutes later, he stepped inside an empty incident room and closed the door with his hip, his arms loaded with the tub containing evidence from the time of Eddie's arrest and the files Martin had collected on Hazel's disappearance, including the information from Eddie. He was no longer convinced there was a connection, but for the next hour, or as long as the caffeine lasted, he was determined to pretend there was and see what links this belief might conjure.

On one corner of the table, he placed a picture of Ama he'd printed from her online bio. In the opposite corner, he placed Hazel's senior picture. On immediate assessment, the only three things these women had in common were gender, the trail, and Eddie. A call to the hospital confirmed Ama had no signs of sexual assault, although in Martin's opinion, the burns on her thigh seemed suspect of intent. He grimaced, wondering, if this man-in-the-woods theory was true, what Hazel might have endured while she was still alive.

"We need a body," he muttered to himself. Otherwise it would be almost impossible to tie these two together without implicating Eddie. No matter what he felt in his gut, he couldn't reclassify Hazel from runaway to homicide without evidence. Without a body or a confession, he couldn't even really call her dead. His mind returned to Eddie's face when he'd prompted the tense change; the weight around his eyes, the way his cheeks sagged. He had become the picture of a sail with no wind.

Stanton's head appeared through the door. Martin hadn't even heard it open. "You wanted a list of names of everyone from the anti-Ama site?" he asked.

"Yeah, thanks." Martin stretched out a hand without standing.

"So you don't think Eddie did it now?" Stanton tried to maintain a neutral tone, but his concern lined his forehead.

"I don't know," Martin mused.

"I hope he didn't. But finding him like that, with that lady . . ." Stanton trailed off and shook his head. Without another word, he backed out of the room.

Martin set the list aside. If he was going to pinpoint a connection between Ama and Hazel, a group of vigilante victims' families wasn't the place to start. Hazel had never been in trouble with the law. She'd never seen the inside of a courtroom. She didn't have a Facebook page, and he hadn't discovered any handles for any chat rooms. She was quiet, low risk. Ama was all over the internet. She was neither high risk nor low risk.

Martin rubbed his face. The only thing that made any sense was that both grabs, if this was a man in the woods, were rooted in opportunity, not in victimology. So why had Ama's injuries seemed so . . . personal?

He pulled out a map of the mountain range and highlighted the trail. He hadn't even known it existed until yesterday. It wasn't listed in any guidebooks as far as he could tell. Ama must've known it because she'd lived here at some point or knew someone who did. And if there was a man in the woods, he had to be local, or at least well versed in the area.

From what Martin had heard, this trail was lucky to see a hiker a day, and more or less remained empty once colder weather hit. How would his suspect know anyone was coming? His suspect would have to be fit enough to grab and drag another adult across mountain grades. There were elements of opportunity and elements of planning. It was like he was dealing with two completely different people.

What if Captain was right and Hazel had fallen victim to the mountain, while Ama had been snatched by a pissed-off vigilante? Trying to force a link between Hazel and Ama might botch this whole thing.

Either Ama needed to wake up, or Hazel's body needed to show up. Otherwise, he would need to put Hazel's box back on the shelf and focus on Ama. Except he wouldn't be able to do that, he knew. This whole thing had a feel about it, a bigness. Whoever took Hazel, if she had been taken, hadn't left a trace, not a single hint, and there had been no sign of her in a year. This couldn't have been a first crime for whoever had done it, Eddie or otherwise. There had to be a beginning, and this wasn't it.

He stared at the wall, bringing his fingers together against his lips, imagining Eddie sitting at the same table in the room opposite his. No wonder Eddie brought that gun, why he thought it would make the brass pay attention. Ama would win over Hazel, and Hazel would slide back into the shadows of the unknown once more.

Sighing, Martin reached inside the tub and pulled out the first bagged evidence, which contained the clothes Eddie had been wearing at the time of his arrest. The bag was heavier than it should've been, his clothes still soaked through with rainwater. He imagined they probably already stunk of mildew. He unsealed the bag, and a wet smell filled the room. Martin hung the jacket over the back of the spare chair and draped Eddie's jeans across the seat. Ama's watch was in a separate bag, tucked into a corner. He plucked it from the rest and watched the light catch on the silver. He'd read that Eddie had sworn he'd picked it up while he was looking for Ama.

Martin paused, recalling a detail he'd read in Hazel's file: a little ring they'd found somewhere on the search. He rifled through Hazel's official file, hoping for a picture, but the only evidence regarding the ring was a scrawled note about finding it on a search and that they believed it was her way of saying goodbye. Martin sealed the watch inside the plastic bag, pocketed it, and headed to the interrogation room where Eddie still sat alone.

Eddie glanced up. His eyes were bloodshot. Martin sat down across from him and put the watch on the table between them.

"How did you find this?" he asked.

"It was in the stone memorial hutch close to the old factory. Whenever I'd look for Hazel, I would go look there."

"Why?" Martin leaned forward.

"That's where I found her ring."

"What made you go in there the first time?"

"It started to rain. The gate wasn't locked, so I stepped inside to wait out the storm. I found her ring in there."

"Where is it now?"

Eddie bent down so that his chest was nearly resting on his hands. He worked his fingers under his shirt and pulled out a gold chain. A little silver band with a small amethyst stone was strung on it.

"They gave it back to me when they called off the search for Hazel," he said softly. "It was like a consolation or something. A piece of her, I guess. I know they think I did it now. That I killed Hazel. That I shot that lady—Ama—on purpose. But when they took my clothes, they didn't take this. I don't know why. Maybe somebody still believes me."

"And you found the watch in the same place?" Martin asked.

"I think that's why I couldn't just leave it there," Eddie said. "I thought if I picked it up, maybe it would help me find her."

"But the ring didn't help you find Hazel."

Eddie slipped Hazel's ring back under his shirt. "We don't know that yet," he said.

"I need to check on a couple things." Martin stood, studying him. He needed to go back through the evidence. "Do you want to call a lawyer yet?"

"Are you charging me yet?"

"Not yet. DA wants to see if the charges will include murder or attempted murder."

"Then I guess I don't need one yet," Eddie said.

Martin nodded, his mind already back in the woods, and walked out of the room.

M
A
R
T
I
N

MARTIN SAT DOWN AT HIS TABLE. HE GLANCED FROM AMA'S PICTURE to Hazel's. He couldn't help fixating on how small her ring was, especially in comparison to Eddie's fingers. Even his palm had looked oversize beneath the little band. Her file had her listed at five foot one and a hundred pounds. They'd also noted that she couldn't swim. Whether she fell into the river or into this hypothetical man's hands, she'd never stood a chance.

Martin stared at Eddie's jacket, deeply tired. He began to stand when his gaze caught on a brown line near the hem of the jacket's front. He turned his head, studying it, and moved closer. That line was intersected at a perpendicular angle by a second line that linked to another, which ran nearly parallel to the first one he'd noticed.

"What the hell?" he murmured. He rounded the table and pulled the front of the jacket straight. Next appeared to be an upside-down V. Another line began almost immediately after in a continuous zigzag, which dipped off the end of the jacket. A quick inspection confirmed that these lines were limited to only this place on Eddie's jacket. It was unlikely a muddy branch had swiped across Eddie's left hip repeatedly and left such a clear pattern. This also had to have happened close to the time of his arrest, or the rain would've washed it away.

Martin gently swiped one gloved index finger down a stripe. He'd seen enough blood on blue latex to know it when he saw it, and that was exactly what was on Eddie's jacket. Blood spatter wouldn't be any surprise. He'd held a bleeding woman in his lap. But this looked organized, purposeful.

Martin took a picture of the pattern to preserve the integrity of the finding. He needed to send the jacket to the lab for testing to confirm his suspicion that the lines were drawn in blood. First, he wanted to take a crack at discerning the meaning of the pattern.

He turned to a blank piece of paper and sat on the table, allowing his eyes to wander the lines. Sometimes patterns appeared easier on their own, when they didn't think they were being hunted. The first group of three lines jumped out at him.

"I," he whispered as he jotted it down. He moved to the second group, committed to writing down whatever first came to mind. "V." He looked at the zigzag. "N." He looked down at his letters and wrote them congruently: IVN. Were they someone's initials? Did that mean Ama knew her attacker? Maybe she was trying to spell "Ivan"? He wrote down the name with a question mark and circled it.

He kept pushing for possibilities, flipping the puzzle pieces around in his mind.

What if the V *is an* N? *Which could make the zigzag a* Z.

He wrote: INZ. "That doesn't make a damn bit of sense." He stood, needing a break and to send the jacket back to the lab. He also wanted to get the search for "Ivan" underway, just in case anything popped from the name. He eyeballed the jacket from his peripheral as he passed, and then stopped cold. From the opposite angle, the lines on the *I* turned it into an *H*. Using the new angle, he reevaluated the letters.

"Holy shit," he said on an exhale, and bolted from the room.

MARTIN

WITHIN MINUTES, MARTIN HAD SHUTTLED CAPTAIN BARROW INTO THE incident room without telling him why. Martin dipped his chin low, studying his superior officer from under his brow, his thumb pressed against his lips to keep him from blurting out his theory. Captain planted a hand on either side of Eddie's blood-streaked jacket. Martin noticed how Captain's fingers quivered. Withdrawal, he'd wager. They'd barely slept since Ama had been found, much less had time for a vice. Martin was grateful. If he'd had a free hour, he'd have driven to the nearest pharmacy and done his best to convince somebody behind the counter to refill a prescription—anything he had—one more time. Hell, one more pill would do.

It would do a lot, Martin told himself. *None of it good.*

He exhaled through his nose.

"Am I boring you, Detective?" Captain asked.

"No, sir."

"Why don't you just tell me what you see so we can move on with our lives?"

"I don't want to color your judgment, Captain. I may be wrong about Eddie Stevens. I don't want to lead you here, too."

"Well, I don't see shit. So spit it out or I'm leaving. I have a press conference in thirty minutes at the hospital for the six AM news cycle and a date with a shower and my bed after that."

"I see 'Hazel,' sir. The first three letters, anyway."

Captain narrowed his lids and craned his neck. He traced above the fading lines with his pointer finger, and his lips morphed as he mouthed each letter.

"I don't see it."

"If you look from this angle—"

"No, Martin. I see what you're trying to see. But it's not there. You're reading too much into this. Ama Chaplin's hands were covered in blood. She was probably clawing at his jacket or trying to sit up."

"Then why isn't there a handprint?"

"Martin. Drop it."

"Ama must have come into contact with Hazel. Or at the very least, she knew about her. These cases are related, whether Eddie is the real perp here or not."

Captain rounded the table and marched toward Martin, stopping only when the toes of his dress shoes were inches from Martin's sneakers. "You leave this alone, Martin. Hazel's gone. If Eddie is the reason why, he already knows she's gone. If he isn't, then let that poor man believe his daughter was swallowed up by Cold River. If you tell him Ama was writing 'Hazel' in blood on his jacket and that the sick fuck who burned lines into that woman's thigh was the last thing his daughter ever knew or saw or felt, you think that's going to bring him peace? We need to bring in bigger brass. You jumped on your first instinct, and now you think you were wrong. Every path after this is dirty, and you know it. We need fresh eyes, more resources, and people who have worked this kind of case before."

"All due respect, but we're not even a full day out. And I *have* worked this kind of case before. This is what I'm good at."

Captain paused. His cheeks sucked inward, pulling at the bags swelling under his eyes. "Not good enough," he said.

M
I
C
H
A
E
L

Chapter 30 | June 1993 | Atlanta, Georgia

WIND HOWLS DOWN DEKALB AVENUE, THROWING RAIN SIDEWAYS. Raindrops assault windowpanes and passing cars, pound themselves against the asphalt in a frenzy of mist. I duck under the awning of a pay-by-the-hour motel.

A woman steps out the door. Boots encase her calves nearly to her knees, and a corset binds her torso, flesh squeezing out both ends. The only thing free is her auburn hair, which tumbles down her back and sails with the wind.

She glances at me and catches me staring.

"I know what you're thinking," she says. It's the first full sentence anyone has spoken to me since I stepped off the Greyhound bus that brought me to Atlanta. She lights a cigarette and brings it to her lips. A silver crescent moon on her ring finger catches my eye, the red stone in the middle the color of dried blood. "I'm a singer." She exhales a stream of gray smoke. "We're all just trying to make it, you know what I mean?"

I have no idea what she means.

"How old are you, boy?" she asks, and I imagine her vocal cords vibrating in her throat.

I stare at her without answering.

"You got a place to stay?"

I shake my head.

She watches me for three seconds more, something between contempt and concern in her gaze, and in this moment, in her brown eyes, I see my mother in the year before my sister died, hear her voice in my head. *Get*

out of my house, Michael. I can't stand the sight of you. Put on your
jacket before you go or you'll catch a cold.

"Look, you can't stay here. Not unless you're paying for a room or my time," the woman says, bringing my mind back to the motel stoop. Her eyes are darker now, shifting to their corners. "I said it's time for you to leave."

There's agitation brimming at her edges, like fish panicking just under the surface of water. It draws alarm out of me, and I step back.

She exhales two jets of smoke through her nose before dropping her cigarette on the ground and stamping it out. "If you need somewhere dry to stand, there are some down-luck fellas three blocks from here. They keep a fire going, and there are a couple of empty buildings on the alley. Three blocks," she repeats, and points a long finger down the street. "Tell them Garnet sent you."

Three. Without further hesitation, I hunch my shoulders to my ears and hurry through the rain. I reach the corner of the third block and cast my gaze down the alley. Tucked behind a dumpster near the end of the street, three people huddle around a burning barrel. I silently count cracks in the asphalt as I walk down the center of the alley.

My fingers squeeze the end of my father's stick, and I see one pair of eyes take notice. I back away, the flesh between my shoulder blades tensing. All at once, the three pairs of eyes ringing the burning barrel lift to stare beyond me.

I turn in time to see the end of the swinging pipe six inches from my face. Then there is a sound like a dropped egg, the flood of iron on my tongue, and iridescent bursts in front of my eyes. I am spitting and writhing. Hands clutch and pull and yank. I roll to my back, clawing upward, my vision doubled and blurring, and watch the pipe come down once more.

My eyelids crack open. My head throbs, pushing at the backs of my eyeballs, drawing bile from my stomach like the tide to the moon. I roll to my side and dry heave. A chill sets in, plunging deep the moment it touches me, and I realize my coat and backpack are gone. My shoes and socks have been removed.

One man is standing alone by the burning barrel. He is wearing my coat.

Where is my father's walking stick?

I haul to my feet, steadying myself on the dumpster.

"I just want my walking stick," I say.

He glances at me and pokes at the fire with a piece of rebar, conjuring sparks. I don't see my father's walking stick, but he has it. I know he does.

"You keep on wanting, then," he says.

"Garnet sent me," I say, and it comes out like a plea. The man pauses his stirring.

"I threw that stick in the dumpster," he says after a few seconds. "It's got bad juju on it. I think you best leave it behind. You leave it in the trash, then you can stay, and you won't have any more trouble. If you take it out, you best get on out of my alley and not ever come back," he says.

I lean into the dumpster, retrieve my father's stick, wondering at the vibration I feel when I touch the wood, if that's the juju he's talking about. I glance at the man, who watches me from under a hood of lowered eyelids, hands still and clasped at his front like he's standing over a casket, listening to a preacher talk to God about someone who's neither in the ground nor in heaven. The hum from my father's stick grows stronger, tunneling from my palm, up my arm, and into my chest. I want shelter. I want security. But this feeling, this electricity, is akin to a heartbeat, to breathing, and I cannot imagine waking up tomorrow without it within reach.

I pulse my grip, turn around, and limp away.

MARTIN

MARTIN WAS STOOPED OVER HIS NOTEPAD, STUDYING THE DETAILS OF Ama's external injuries despite the explicit instructions Captain had given him to cease all work on the case, when the main door to the station swung open. A heavy-set, middle-aged woman blew in like a storm come ashore, her graying hair pulled back, face flushed, features severe with intent. Sunlight glared in after her, and Martin was nearly afraid to look at the clock, although he could tell by smelling himself that he'd been in the same clothes for at least twenty-four hours.

"Who's in charge here?" she blustered to no one in particular.

"In charge of what, ma'am?" Martin asked, swiping at the wrinkles on his shirt as he pushed back from his desk.

"The case! Ama Chaplin's case!" She glared harder.

Martin stole a glimpse of the captain's office to verify that he hadn't yet returned from his meeting at the Georgia Bureau of Investigation, at which he was planning to hand them the damn reins to Ama's case. Save Martin and this woman, this section of the station was empty.

He stood. "I'm Detective Martin Locklear. How can I help you?"

"Why haven't charges been filed yet? Why isn't anyone telling me anything?"

"What is your relationship with Ama Chaplin?" Martin asked. He drew his pad of paper closer to him with a finger.

"I'm her assistant."

"Lindsey Harold?" Martin recalled. Her name had appeared on the call log multiple times. They'd tried to question her formally over the phone twice, but she had been so adamant to do the questioning herself that they'd gotten absolutely nowhere.

"That's correct." Lindsey exhaled through her slender nose, nostrils flaring, and crossed her arms at her front. "If anyone at your station had done their job the first time I called, she might never have been taken by that man. I tried to give you information before all this started and no one would listen."

"The first time you called, you asked us to run a plate on a van legally parked in a parking lot. The second time you called it was after 5:30 PM Whatever happened to Ama had very likely already begun. This isn't on you."

Her expression turned to stone. "It's on you."

"It's on the man who did this." Martin leveled his gaze at her, sizing her up in a matter of seconds: highly anxious, usually right, underestimated, and overlooked. He'd worked this personality type more times than he could count.

He started again. "I've really needed your help, actually."

"Clearly."

"Tell me about your role as Ama's assistant. What do you do for her?"

"I make and take phone calls. I do research. I grab her lunch or coffee."

"She called you when she felt unsafe, Lindsey. I think you're more to her than a gopher."

Lindsey blinked, and she shifted foot to foot. "We spend a lot of time together. It's part of the job."

He gestured to the chair next to him, inviting her to sit. She perched on the front of the chair, her back rigid, both feet flat on the floor.

"Right now, I need the help of someone who knows Ama well. Some pieces of this case are not adding up. I need to understand more of who Ama is and who might want to hurt her. This looks very personal, and we can't find any evidence that she knows the man from the parking lot. Whoever did this to your friend knew her before today."

"Ama doesn't really have friends."

"None?" Martin leaned back, watching her closely.

"None who would do this, and none who would talk to you."

"You're a smart woman who works for a criminal defense attorney. I'm sure you have a head full of statistics about how many victims know their attacker and how seldom it's a random event," he pressed.

"I'm telling you, it's the wrong tree."

Martin nodded, making a note to dig deeper into Ama's personal life. Lindsey would probably be more cooperative if he had specific details. She might be good at stonewalling, but she didn't strike him as a liar. "What about enemies?" he asked.

"She doesn't have a lot of enemies, either. Not like that. Prosecutors don't like her because she's good at tearing apart their cases, but they respect her, too. She's not dirty. She plays by the rules. Most of the time. As much as any of them do."

"Sure." Martin nodded.

"Sometimes victims' families will send her nasty letters. I think her car was spray-painted once, but that was a couple years ago. There hasn't been anything recent. And she just lost a huge case. No angry families there."

"What kind of case?"

"Vehicular homicide. It's been all over the news."

"I'm new in town. And I don't have cable."

"Pro athlete was involved in an auto crash. There was a fatality in the other car. Six-month-old infant. He's looking at fifteen years in prison. He wasn't even driving."

Her gaze briefly sought the window. Martin would've bet the bank the athlete was absolutely in the driver's seat.

"You don't think her client would come after her?" he asked. "Or maybe a teammate? A fan?"

"She didn't tell anyone she was coming up here. We got the verdict, she grabbed her gym bag out of her office closet, and she split. She didn't even tell me where she was until after she got there. No one knew. I even called . . . around. She hadn't told anyone."

"Do you know why she became a defense attorney? It's a cold line of work," Martin asked, shifting tactics. He starred the earlier note he'd made about Ama's alleged lack of friends. He wished he could subpoena Lindsey's phone records, but he had no cause.

"It's a necessary line of work," Lindsey countered.

"Your day was undone by someone being held responsible for the death of an infant."

"That's not fair."

Martin shrugged.

"Innocent people are wrongfully convicted more than anyone wants to believe. Ama knows that better than anyone," Lindsey replied.

"Because of her job?" Martin pressed.

"You wouldn't believe some of the things she's seen."

Lindsey's throat and ears turned pink, and Martin wondered at the details she was clearly keeping from him, at the way they damn near set her face on fire just by holding on to them. Why was everything regarding Ama Chaplin's life beyond the courtroom so categorically off-limits? Lindsey shifted, preparing to stand.

Martin fished in his drawer and extracted his card. "Call me if you think of anything. Do you know of any family I might be able to contact?"

"No family. She was an only child, and her parents are deceased."

"Aunts, uncles . . . ?" Martin stayed seated. Lindsey seemed more relaxed with height on her side.

After a pause, she answered, "None that I know of. Ama keeps her private life private, and she certainly doesn't bring it to work."

As she tucked his card into her purse, his direct line rang. He held up a finger, motioning for Lindsey to wait, but she was already backing away. She gave him one last look, her lips pressed together in a line, before spinning on her heel and heading for the door.

"Detective Locklear," he said into the phone. He covered the receiver with his hand, preparing to call out to Lindsey.

"This is Cathy Richards. I'm a nurse at Dalton Medical, Ama Chaplin's nurse. She woke up," she said, her pitch high with excitement, and Martin forgot all about Lindsey Harold and her blushing face. "Just for a few seconds. She's back out now. But she woke up."

Martin nearly leaped up from his chair, but he couldn't very well bolt down to the hospital. This kind of update should have gone straight to the GBI.

"Did she say anything?" he asked quietly.

"Maybe. But I don't know if it's going to help you any."

"Why? What did she say?" Martin pressed the speaker harder against his ear.

"It sounded like she was saying 'Hazel.' She said it a couple times. Then she was back out."

Martin covered his mouth with his hand, his mind racing with what that tiny word could mean to the case, to Eddie. Until he was sure of what Ama knew, he couldn't risk anyone else finding out.

"Do me a favor," he finally said. "Do not tell anyone else what you just told me."

MARTIN BOLTED FROM HIS DESK FOR THE INTERVIEW ROOM WHERE Eddie was still waiting. He sat down across from Eddie, the other man's daughter's name circling his head, marking time with his pulse in two beats. *Ha-zel. Ha-zel.* He wanted to blurt it out, to take Eddie by his big, stooped shoulders and shake him, shout that a break in his daughter's case was on the horizon and watch for the change on the surface of his eyes. Dependent upon what he saw in that moment, he would be sure—irrefutably sure—about Eddie Stevens.

"Ama Chaplin woke up," he finally said, staring directly at Eddie. Eddie broke into a grin before covering his mouth with both hands. As Martin watched, Eddie's entire upper half folded onto the table, damn near melted, and he wept into the laminate, tears and mucus painting four shiny lines on his face.

"What did she say?" Eddie asked between gulps of air, righting himself.

"You get one chance to change your story. One." Martin held up a finger. "Then I'll tell you what she said."

"It happened like I told you it happened," Eddie said, and his brows came down, casting shadows over his eyes. "I don't got anything to hide from you. Every word I've said in here has been the God's honest truth."

Martin pushed up from his chair, frustration squalling in his chest.

"What did Ama say?" Eddie asked, and confusion lit upon his features.

If Martin stayed in here any longer, he knew he would tell Eddie about how half his daughter's name was written in blood on his jacket, that the same name had sailed out of the mouth of the woman he shot the moment she regained consciousness. Martin moved for the door.

"Detective!" Eddie shouted at his back, but Martin didn't turn around. He swept down the hall and rounded the corner, nearly colliding with the captain. Captain's eyes glistened with drink, and his face was cleanly shaved, probably both effects of his meeting with the GBI.

"Ama woke up," Martin blurted out. "She said 'Hazel,' sir. She woke up for five seconds and said 'Hazel.' We can't give Ama's case to the GBI. Ama knew about Hazel. She even wrote it on Eddie's jacket. Ama *knew*—I'm not wrong about that. I'm not done with this case." Martin was halfway between pleading and barking at his superior officer. "Get the case back."

Martin stared at the captain, marveling at his relaxed composure—his hands in his pockets, his chin nodding gently—and felt insane in comparison.

"I didn't give the case away," Captain said. "Not yet. You have twenty-four hours to prove to me that you should remain the lead on this case. After that, it goes up the chain. I'm delaying this for Eddie, not for you. So don't be wrong again." He paused to glare at Martin, then added, "Are you lying about Ama saying 'Hazel'?"

"No, sir."

Martin's mind was reeling, the sudden weight of the case passed back into his hands so quickly throwing him off-kilter. He felt unprepared, as if he hadn't closed his hands in time to catch it, and now it was like a stone dropped on a pane of glass. "Nurse called while you were gone," Martin said. "She said Ama was only lucid for a few seconds. She's back out now."

"Make sure that information does not leave the hospital," Captain cautioned. "Not until we know what it means. And do not under any circumstance say the name 'Hazel' to Eddie until you are surer about what happened to that girl than anything you've ever been sure about in your life."

"What about that list Eddie had of people gone missing from this area? It probably goes back a decade or more. You said it yourself—people vanish in Tarson. What if Hazel isn't the linchpin? What if she's the tip of the iceberg?" Martin asked.

"Don't say shit like that in here." Captain rubbed his face, and weariness returned to his weather-beaten features.

"Still, it might be worth a look."

"You can't even find out what happened to one woman when we got the man admitting he shot her sitting down the hall. You want to try to link every person who's gone missing in those woods in the last ten years?"

"It could be a forest-for-the-trees situation here, Captain."

"I said don't say shit like that."

"I just need to broaden the lens."

"Jesus. Your twenty-four hours started the second I told you that you had it. You waste it however you want. But just remember, Eddie's fate is in your hands."

"It's his work I want to look at. But I need your help. I don't know this town or these people like you do. I need you to give me the CliffsNotes on these cases, especially where a body was never found. Please, Captain. For Eddie."

Captain looked down the hall to the room where Eddie was detained. He pressed his lips together, then glanced back at Martin.

"Convince Eddie to stay of his own free will. That way we can help delay formal charges and keep his face out of the public eye for a little longer. Set him up in the spare office."

"There's a spare office?" Martin asked, swinging his gaze over his shoulder.

Captain pointed past Martin at the door no one ever opened. "The detective we had a while back was set up in there. Liked to keep all his boxes with him instead of in storage. Crowded the whole damn main room, so we stuck him and all his stuff in there. In hindsight I think that was his goal all along."

"You told me that was the janitor's closet," Martin responded.

"Have you ever seen a janitor around here? And you call yourself a detective." Sarcasm turned the captain's voice nearly playful. Then he shook his head. "There's a desk and a couch in there, probably still covered in boxes. Guy was a hoarder. Get it cleaned out for me and move all the boxes into storage. Eddie will at least have somewhere to sleep. There's a mini fridge you can stock with water and food for him, and it has its own little bathroom with the world's smallest shower. There's no window or door to the outside, and the interior door locks. Better than a cell, but it should still get the point across that he's not off the hook for this yet. We're going to keep his phone for now, too. See if anyone calls. Once you get all that squared away, bring Eddie's research and the evidence from Ama's shooting, and meet me in room two."

Martin stared back at him, speechless and altogether irritated. His blood throbbed with stress and fatigue, and he tasted the bitter trail of swallowing a pill dry. He'd wanted this case back—begged for it.

"Oh, and, Detective," Captain continued as he began walking away, "if you want your name on that office door, you've got to earn it."

Martin watched him disappear into the filing room, but all he could think about was the mental image of that stone sailing through a sheet of paper-thin glass, and at his feet were broken shards scattered in all directions.

A
M
A

EVERYTHING HURT. HER HAIR HURT. HER TOENAILS. AMA TWISTED from her left to her right. She sandwiched her head between two flimsy pillows and stared at the mist condensing in beads on the outside of the windowpane. A cart clattered by her closed door, and she made a mental note to suggest that ICU rooms be made soundproof. Unless those carts could bring her a few shots and a decent chaser. Then she would welcome their arrival on the hour, every hour.

She picked up the button for her morphine drip and put it down again. She needed to remember what had happened. She'd been shot—it was hard to argue with a bullet hole. She knew victims oftentimes didn't remember much after the initial blow of a violent attack, a phenomenon called barrel focus, where the survivor can't remember anything visual past the end of the gun. It was easy to discredit witnesses with shaky descriptions to start. By the time Ama was done with them, they weren't usually sure if they'd been attacked by her client or their own mother.

This side of it—the not-knowing, the darkness, the void in her brain—was utter hell. It was as spongy and thick as the swelling on her sprained ankle, too crowded yet undefined, and when she prodded the space for reaction, it hurt just as bad as a hard jab to the injured joint.

She stared at the window and watched a morning storm thrash the world outside. Beads of rain gathered on the glass, forming streaks, then trailed down the pane and pooled on the sill. She stared and stared and stared, but nothing came. A gust of wind sent rain pattering against the pane, blowing the streaks sideways. Stray light from outside refracted in the beads and lines as they blurred and bent. Pain stabbed straight through her eyes and into her brain. Ama breathed in and out through her mouth, trying to slow her pounding heart, the rush of blood in her veins like someone had opened an internal floodgate.

The beads turned to a haze, drawing her eye past them, and in the gray bloomed the whites of two eyes and the silver nose of a gun. She could see it, short and gleaming, pointed at an angle just beyond her.

Another cart hit an uneven lip of tile outside and something must've fallen out, striking the floor with a sharp and sudden sound. Ama jumped in her bed, her fingers strangling the pilling bedsheet. A flash of light played on in her mind's eye, a platinum starburst of discharged gunpowder, and she felt herself move into it, lurch toward the explosion.

"Hazel." The name whistled between her teeth.

Hazel. Hazel. Hazel.

She jerked upright and swung her gaze from side to side in search of a phone, pulling at every tether with her fingers. Then her blood ran cold and she froze, her hand suspended midair, her lips ajar with an inhale.

Michael Jeffery Walton.

In an instant, she remembered jumping in front of the bullet, the need to set something right, to tell someone Hazel was alive, somehow greater than the need to save herself. She alone knew who had Hazel. But she also had a very good idea of what he was capable of, of how obsessed he could be, how careful. If she knew where to send police, she'd be screaming his location from the rooftops. But she had no idea where he was, only that he'd never been found or found out. If Michael got wind she was sending the law after him, he'd either kill Hazel and disappear, or run and take her with him.

Seventeen years ago, she knew as she walked out of that courtroom that Michael would kill again, that he would escalate to humans. But she also knew she couldn't look back. She'd defended other patterned killers since then, studied two or three times as many as that. Nearly all of them shared one trait in common: they would not have stopped on their own. They had to be stopped. Once their need was triggered and the ritual began, completion was the driving goal.

Ama was Michael's trigger, ritual, and completion. There was a very good chance he knew she was alive. Ama could only hope he didn't know she was awake and talking. Michael was unique in that he didn't live for the hunt, didn't stalk, didn't chase. He allowed. He waited. And he remembered.

But what if Ama didn't remember? He needed to cross paths at random three times, isn't that what he'd said? That it was critical—necessary, even—for an instrument to remember all three encounters? He'd even let one go because he didn't remember. That man went home never knowing how close he'd come to never going home again.

What if she didn't remember the attack, Hazel . . . how far back could she pretend to forget? Would people buy it? Would it buy Hazel more time? Could Ama survive Michael then? And if she did, could she live with what she'd done?

Her thoughts turned to the man who'd fired the gun. She'd pull what strings she could to reduce or dismiss whatever charges he was facing. But what the hell was a grown man doing in the woods at night in the pouring rain with a gun, anyway? He might not have meant to shoot her, but Ama doubted he was up to any good.

MARTIN

CLEANING OUT THE OLD DETECTIVE'S OFFICE HAD TAKEN THE ENTIRE morning. An hour into the project, Martin was furious, cursing the detective for leaving so much shit behind and the captain for making him clean it up. He was already behind on the case, and several hours of his twenty-four-hour time were spent in a dark, musty room, cleaning up another man's trash. He couldn't afford to lose a morning to a housekeeping assignment, but he didn't have a choice.

While his body stretched and worked, Martin surrendered to the task, and his brain slid into a resting state. With each box identified and moved, his thoughts began to slide into place, too. He trusted Eddie more than he wanted to, he realized, especially after convincing him to remain at the precinct of his own free will proved far easier than the task of readying the old office for Eddie's stay.

Martin left Eddie, swallowed the remainder of his lunch—a Pop-Tart from the vending machine—and walked into incident room two. He found Captain staring at an empty whiteboard. Eddie's jacket had been resealed in its plastic bag and now sat neatly on the far side of the rectangular table. Manila envelopes were stacked to the left of it. Captain had another one in his hands.

"Did Eddie give you any trouble?" Captain asked.

"I think the trouble would've been asking him to leave. He said he isn't going anywhere until we find out what happened to Hazel. I told him we'd be working in here and to knock loud on his door if he needs anything." Martin nodded at the files, spying the names labeled on the tabs. "Let's get started. I want to go interview Ama as soon as I get a feel for how big this might be."

"Now hold on a second. I'll walk you through what I remember from these old cases, but there's something you need to keep in the front of that mind of yours: sometimes people die and didn't nobody do anything to them. Accidents happen. So does bad luck. A kid tries to run away or gets lost in thirty square miles of untouched terrain like Tarson Woods, and those odds go up a lot. Then there's Cold River. It's a monster when it's full. I remember one boy fell in my first year with the department. Looked like he'd tried to cross a fallen tree and slipped. We took his backpack to his mother. She didn't even get off the couch. Barely looked at us. Just stared at the TV set, laying there in a tank top and underwear. There was a little girl toddling around the living room, kind of whimpering, and it's like she didn't even hear her.

"The mother passed not long after. Was diagnosed with leukemia and died within a week, daughter wound up in the system. Maybe that's why, when people go missing, others don't look too hard. We just hope they made it where they were trying to go."

Martin stared at nothing, his mind adrift, his memory traveling on the captain's words, racing thousands of miles northwest to the small, frigid Alaskan village he'd grown up in, to the kids who walked away from that cluster of squat, cold homes, and the mix of emotions it stirred inside his fifteen-year-old chest when a week passed without them being found. *They got out* . . . he would think to himself, and in his slumber he would dream of hot, noisy, fast, crowded places.

"Tarson Woods wasn't always a state park," Captain continued. "About thirty years ago it was the site of a nuclear plant. Owned by an outfit called Evansbrite. Most people in Tarson and the surrounding areas worked there somehow—janitors, receptionists, assistants, secretaries, mechanics. They had to get security clearances, but those came with a little bonus. Made people in this town feel like we were a part of something, that good things were coming—growth, money, the future. Families could buy cars they never would've dreamed of before. A man could take his family out to dinner on a Friday night—and there was actually a place or two to go."

"What happened?"

"The plant started having trouble. There was a small explosion, contained in one section, and they said it was taken care of. Then there was a bigger one, which caused a major mechanical failure, and a few people died. People started getting bad sick. Women lost pregnancies, or babies were born not . . . right . . ." He cleared his throat. "People weren't just angry anymore. The mayor called for a town hall meeting with the plant higher-ups. They didn't show. When employees went to work the next day, the gates were locked, razor wire curled all around the fences, and there was a letter on the main gate telling employees that Evansbrite had gone under and would be sending them all a two months' severance in the mail."

"Did anyone ever pursue Evansbrite for damages?" Martin asked.

"Plenty of people have tried, but it's like the company was everywhere and nowhere. They had friends in DC—lobbyists, congressmen—but no brick-and-mortar address. Ownership had changed a dozen times and was split into so many fractions and offshoots you couldn't tell where it all started. The buck was passed from hand to hand to hand. It was always 'under investigation' or 'in review.' Honestly, I think it still is. Companies with money in pursuit of even more money take advantage of towns like this. Desperate, hungry, hardworking towns. You look at us, and you think we're less than. I can see it in your eyes." His gaze fell to the manila folder in his hands.

"I don't think you or anyone else here is less than," Martin said quietly. "I think your resources are less than. Your infrastructure. I know what that does to a town. To its people. The morale. In many ways, the simple life is a hell of a lot more complicated."

Captain looked up, a wisp of a smile lifting one corner of his mouth. "That's a good way to put it," he said. "Suffice it to say, Tarson Woods has become as close to a ghost story as this town has. I don't have to tell you what kind of draw that can have on a bored teenager."

"But it's not just bored teenagers disappearing," Martin pressed, refocusing the conversation. In his opinion, a pattern there would actually point more to the captain's theory, but he kept the thought to himself.

"They range from fifteen to seventy years old, male and female, low risk, high risk. Less than half of them were local at the time they vanished. One had never been here before in his life that we could find." Captain began plucking snapshots from each folder and taped them in a line across the top of the whiteboard.

"First vic, Timmy Roberts, 1989. That's the boy I just told you about, who looks to have drowned. Second, homeless girl, 1992. People knew her for playing the fiddle on street corners and shoplifting cosmetics and snack food from the general store. She called herself Sabrina but was never formally IDed. She was last seen leaving the square and was known to frequent the woods. Michael Walton was reported missing a couple months later. In 2004, Thomas Eads, a bartender from Chattanooga. Told his girlfriend he was going on a run in a state park, and his credit card puts him at the Shell station at our exit off State Route 411. He's got a record, and we don't have proof he was in Tarson long, but the girlfriend never heard from him again, and that gas station charge was the last activity on his card."

Captain paused for a moment, staring at the next picture, an old man. "Bill Blassing, 2005," he started again. "He's a local. Born and raised here. Missing for a little more than a year. We searched all over for that man. We found his car in the parking lot at the cemetery where his wife was buried, and there was a note inside saying he was leaving his future up to fate. Then we found out he had terminal cancer and had kept the diagnosis secret, and that seemed to make enough sense at the time. Maybe he'd wanted to go off the grid or travel with what time he had left. It was something he would've done."

"All due respect, Bill Blassing didn't disappear in the woods," Martin said carefully.

"No. But he worked at the factory, and he hiked in those woods almost every weekend while he was still able. He led volunteer groups to clean up the trails after storms, and he loved the river. Took his lunch along the bank more days than he didn't. During the search we combed them on horseback but never saw any sign he'd been there. You wanted to widen the lens, and it didn't feel right leaving him out," Captain said.

"And six . . . Hazel Rae Stevens." He carefully taped Hazel's picture to the end of the line, his eyes lingering on her for several seconds, and Martin wondered what regrets might be whispering through him now.

"Bill Blassing and Hazel Stevens disappeared within two months of each other." Martin glanced at Captain over his shoulder. "That didn't raise a red flag?"

"Honestly, it's the only reason Hazel's active search lasted as long as it did. We kept the fire burning under that case for twice as long as we normally would and even brought in bigger brass. Then the case for a runaway kept getting stronger, we had a plausible explanation for Bill's disappearance, and Hazel and Bill are about as different in victimology as two people can be—age, race, gender, social circles, location. I tried to connect those two, I really did. But there was no connection to be found other than proximity of time."

"I have someone to add," Martin said. "Be right back."

Martin walked to his desk, grabbed the file he'd taken with him from Savannah, and came back. He pulled the snapshot of Toni Hargrove from the folder. It was a mug shot from one of her first arrests. She couldn't have been more than twenty years old in the picture, and her freckles and flame-red hair made her look even younger. Her red-brown eyes were another story, already ancient, propped up with thick eyeliner and puffy bags. When he'd seen her body at the morgue, she'd been nearly thirty years old. He hadn't seen her in person in years by then. She'd left Savannah for Atlanta several years before, convinced she was going to make it big in the rising music scene. Six months later, when she was busted for prostitution, she gave the Atlanta PD Martin's name and contact information, along with a story about working undercover.

In the morgue, he'd touched her hand when no one else was looking. He'd been checking for her ring—a little silver crescent moon cradling a garnet stone. It was the one thing she'd ever been sentimental about. But her hand was bare, and for a second or two, he convinced himself it wasn't Toni on the slab, just someone who looked a lot like her. Someone else who knew his phone number by heart. Someone else who called him in their most desperate hour. But standing there, even as high as he had been, he knew no one else relied on him like that anymore. The only person who still thought he was good and trustworthy was now mutilated on a metal table.

The ring. Jesus Christ, her missing ring. The thought shot through Martin like he'd stuck a key in a light socket. *Hazel's ring, Ama's watch, Toni's ring.*

He swallowed hard, trying to keep the connection from bursting out of his mouth. Unless the ring had turned up inside the stone hutch where the other two pieces were found, he doubted the captain would entertain the link, especially since he couldn't prove she'd been wearing it at the time of her murder. But in the spiderweb of possible evidence, Martin silently connected the strands as he positioned Toni's picture to the left of Bill's.

"She was found murdered at the rest stop just south of Tarson," he narrated. "Half her tongue was removed."

"I remember that." Captain's gaze shifted from the photo to Toni's folder. "Do I want to know how a case file from your old precinct came to be in my station?"

"No, sir."

"Your vic's body was found. I don't know that she belongs up there," Captain said, apparently deciding to listen to Martin, and pointed to the first three pictures in the timeline, all young and sullen-faced. "They didn't find those boys, either. Timmy looked like an accident. There were signs he'd fallen off a downed tree and into the water. Michael Walton looked more like a suicide."

"Department is sure about a suicide without a body?"

"Michael left his shoes on the bank and carved 'I'm not sorry' into a tree. His dad died in the plant explosion. His mother is a hard woman. She had been a secretary at the plant until she got pregnant again, then taught piano lessons out of their house for extra money. Her baby was born without a brain stem. Lived a matter of hours. Mother lost her sight a couple years later. Became a recluse. She didn't even report Michael missing. A friend of Michael's hadn't seen him for a while. I guess they used to meet up pretty regularly. He went by Michael's house and he wasn't there. About a week later, a teacher from the high school went looking for him in the woods and found his shoes by Cold River. They'd been there long enough to be covered in leaves and moss." Captain stared at the boy's picture. "He went to trial for an animal cruelty case when he was a kid. They tried him as an adult."

"For animal cruelty?" Martin arched a brow.

"You didn't see the animals."

"So how did he end up jumping into Cold River if he went away for animal cruelty?"

"The jury found him not guilty."

Martin studied him, saw the shifting of his jaw, the twitch at the corner of his mouth, then asked, "What do you think?"

Captain shrugged. "Doesn't matter what I think. He got a fair trial, and his records are sealed. And he's dead."

"Right." Martin's attention returned to the boy peering out from beneath a veil of greasy, chin-length hair. *I'm not sorry.* His eyes didn't look menacing or scared or sad or guilty. They were empty. All color and no depth. Two locked doors.

"Martin, no one has seen that kid in fifteen years. If he isn't in that river, he definitely isn't here. I never thought I'd have to beg you to focus on Ama and Hazel. Ticktock. Iceberg or not, you've got twenty hours to prove it."

"Sorry," Martin murmured as he angled his body to Hazel's picture at the far end of the board. But as Captain began rattling off details of the day she disappeared, Martin couldn't help glancing back at Michael one more time.

Stanton's head and shoulders appeared in the door, his face lit up like Christmas morning. "Captain, the hospital called. Ama Chaplin's awake and talking."

Martin went stone-still except for his eyes, which swung to meet Captain's shell-shocked gaze. Ama could connect every thread. If all these cases were somehow related, Ama could very well solve multiple murders.

"Go," Captain said, and the single word sent Martin into motion. He swept several photographs and papers into a file, tucked them under his arm, and bolted for the door.

Four hours later, Martin stood in front of the closed door to the investigation room, the interview with Ama replaying in his mind. Through the narrow windowpane, he could see Captain still studying the board of pictures and notes. The older man planted his hands on his hips, his shirt wrinkled and partially untucked at his waist. Captain heaved a sigh and glanced at his wristwatch, no doubt wondering where Martin was and what he'd learned from Ama. Neither one of them had slept since the day before, and in that moment, Martin felt the full weight of utter exhaustion and the captain's expectations crushing down on him. He put his hand on the doorknob, closed his eyes briefly, and walked into the room.

"What did Ama say?" Captain's blue eyes were bright, and Martin was struck by the hope in them.

"She doesn't remember, Captain."

"Doesn't remember what? Hazel?" Captain capped a pen, and his brow descended, casting shadows on his eyes.

"Anything. Ama Chaplin doesn't remember anything."

IT'S NEARING TWO IN THE AFTERNOON ON A SUNDAY. DUMPSTERS should be heaped with new scraps in the coming hour. I can't bring myself to linger like a stray dog, but I will walk by and lift my nose, sampling the air like I might be strolling once again through Tarson Woods, the end of my father's walking stick marking a leisurely cadence on the asphalt.

"Didn't think I'd see you again," a woman's voice calls out. Garnet is standing in the frame of the back door to a bar, old grease emanating from behind her. She has a lacy apron tied around her waist and a full trash bag in her hand, red hair piled on top of her head. "I heard what happened. You should've said my name straightaway," she says.

I tighten my grip on the walking stick and stare at her. Her advice nearly cost me everything, but the mention of her name saved me the stick. "I can't feed you, but I know someone you might want to talk to. He has a recording studio, and he's looking for somebody to clean after hours. He's good, honest. That's harder to find than a free meal around here. If you want, I can introduce you."

"He makes music?" I ask, interest sparking a sharp and sudden feeling in my chest like the first note struck in a silent, waiting concert hall.

"So you do talk." Garnet smiles. She pulls a little notepad and a pen from her apron front and jots down something on a piece of paper before handing it to me. It's a name and an address. "Do you have a name so I can tell him who I'm sending?"

I don't answer.

"Just tell him Garnet sent you. But this time, it better come out of your mouth the second you get there. None of this scared, quiet-mouse nonsense. You can *be* scared. We're all scared. But you can't let it show. Not if you want to survive." She tosses the trash into the dumpster and wipes her hands. "I think for now I'll call you Sticks," she says. "I gave myself a new name when I came here. You could do the same. No harm in that."

AMA

AMA RAISED THE HEAD OF HER NEW BED. NOW THAT SHE WAS STABLE, they'd moved her to the maternity ward on the police department's order, to better shield her from press and public access. The added security was a bonus, but a baby was constantly squalling, and in the hallway, visitors and siblings and new grandparents squealed and whispered.

Her mind was louder. Every time she let her focus wander, her mind's eye ran to the picture of Eddie Stevens, not his cloaked face peering at her through the dark and rain but the mug shot of him from the Tarson Police Department, his face full and empty at the same time.

"They are going to lock him up and throw away the key," Detective Martin had said. "He admits to shooting you. The gun was registered to him. He was covered in gunpowder and your blood. You're a defense attorney. This is as slam dunk as it gets. There is only one way this man gets off."

Witness testimony. They both knew it.

Martin had gripped the railing on her bed, his skin drawn tight over scarred knuckles.

"If you can't remember what happened, Eddie Stevens's life is over, and from the way he tells it, he shot at someone to try to save you. He just hit the wrong target."

She'd stared at him, remaining blank. He'd pushed back and turned away from her, the soles of his shoes squeaking on the tile.

"What did he say he was doing out there?" Ama had called out as he left.

Martin had paused near the door, his chin over his shoulder, but he wouldn't meet her gaze.

"He said he went in looking for you."

"Why?" She'd leaned forward. Baited, she realized, but didn't care.

Martin's eyes flicked to her for the briefest of moments, and then he'd walked out.

She watched the doorway now, imagining him there even though the conversation had taken place in the ICU hours before. She had a feeling Martin was really the one behind her move to the maternity ward instead of a general floor. He must feel pretty certain there was another man in the woods aside from Eddie Stevens.

A new nurse walked in and scrawled his name on the board—Nathan—before he checked her blood pressure and took her temperature. Ama realized she'd never asked Michael his name. Not when he was butchering that song in the hotel bar and not when she'd seen him on the path in Tarson. He'd just offered it. And she was annoyed. She didn't ask—hadn't cared. She'd spent entire nights with men whose name she never learned. Names weren't important—a string of letters like beads on a necklace, so we know when to turn around when someone behind us calls.

Ama was worried about only one voice at her back. Even all these years later, she could still feel Michael's frigid stare penetrating the seam of her jacket and burrowing under her skin as she did her best not to run from that dumpy little courthouse. She remembered the relief she'd felt when she'd heard Michael was dead, the exhale, the little laugh that followed. She'd giggled, for Christ's sake, went out for drinks with an old friend, paid for the rounds, and didn't tell him why.

But Michael wasn't dead.

And now there was a girl locked up somewhere in those godforsaken woods, and even if Ama told someone about Hazel, no one would find her. Michael might just be an even bigger mystery than that evergreen labyrinth. No one knew *him*. His mother was blind and had been well around the bend even seventeen years ago. If she was still alive, she'd be little help. The only person who had any idea how Michael ticked was Ama, and he'd had two decades to sharpen his tools since using a paring knife to slice neighborhood pets and peel back their throats and lungs to look like butterfly wings.

The only tools she'd sharpened in those same years were weapons meant to fight back against those who would hold Michael accountable for what he'd done. She'd positioned herself between defendants and their accusers for so long that she wasn't sure if others saw any difference between the people who committed these crimes and what her role was in the aftermath. She knew she wasn't an accessory after the fact. So why now, with a bullet wound in her chest, a brace on her foot, and a nurse checking her vital signs every three hours, did it suddenly feel like it?

MICHAEL

Chapter 37 | October 2004 | Atlanta, Georgia

I SIT AT A CORNER BOOTH IN A WAFFLE HOUSE, MY THIRD CUP OF BLACK coffee steaming between my hands, the entrance ramp to the interstate a quarter mile away, and Ama Chaplin's business card on the table.

Chaplin.

She must've married. I close my eyes and recall her hand as she shoved a wad of cash in my face at the hotel bar. She wasn't wearing a ring. Then again, she doesn't seem the type. She was different than I remember. Something about her was equal parts emptier and more weighted down, worn dull and yet sharp enough to slice through bone in a single stroke. But it was her, striding away to the cadence of an imaginary snare drum, right between the two trees that framed the doorway to the patio, their leaves impossibly yellow.

Ama and I have found each other once more in a city of half a million people, in a landscape made of concrete, and I realize in this moment that Fate still managed to show me Ama walking through trees as if she might be on a trail in Tarson Woods.

Tarson is calling me home. I can hear it, just like I can hear the music when people make notes of unchecked emotion. Music is just like Fate— you have to allow it to unravel to understand the ending. You must learn to play with soft fingers. A loose grip yields a stronger swing. My hands are still. My pulse roars. Ama is *here*, so I must go *there*. And when Fate is ready, Ama will come to me. I cannot leave anything to chance now. There is only Fate.

I finish my coffee, leave a five-dollar bill from Ama's cash on the table, and walk out the door. Once in the car, I pull up to the road and pause. The interstate is to the left, but nothing will be open in Tarson by the time I get there, and I don't know how to walk back into my old house, if it even still belongs to me.

I turn away from the interstate and drive until I find a motel that charges by the hour. There are only a few cars in the lot, and a single lamp is visible in the lobby. Someone is sitting on the wooden bench just outside the door. As I pass by, I see a tendril of red hair peeking out from under a gray hood. I pause, and the fingers on the ivory hands—slender and long, like my mother's—squeeze tighter. Her knuckles are scraped, and a couple of nails are broken. On her ring finger is a silver crescent moon, a round, dark red stone nestled in the curve.

"Garnet?" I whisper.

She looks up, surprise stretching out the angles on her face. Recognition lights upon her eyes.

"Sticks? What are you doing here?" she asks.

"I'm going to stay the night, then I'm going to head out of town for a while."

"Where are you going?" she asks.

"Home," I say. "What happened to your hands?" I study the wounds, wondering if she cried out when her nails broke.

"Professional hazards," she says.

"What are you doing out here?"

"I'm waiting until I'm tired."

"You look tired."

"Thanks. Asshole." A downturned smile elongates her mouth. "I'm glad to see you made it, by the way. I wasn't so sure you would. Now here you are, all grown up and polished. Professional. Heard you were the best hire at the studio. Never missed a day. Climbed on up that ladder, didn't you? You're doing all right for yourself. I barely recognize you. I'm glad our paths crossed again so I could see it. Gives me faith."

"Three times." I look her dead in the eyes, and the sensation of electricity courses through every fiber of my body. "Our paths have crossed three times, haven't they?"

"In front of that hotel in the rain, in the alley behind the restaurant, and here," she lists, and her expression becomes wistful. "Did you ever pick a name?" she asks.

"Jonathon Walks." I show her the Oregon driver's license I bought off a Georgia Tech student once my work responsibilities included runs to the liquor store to retrieve liquid courage for new artists.

"I guess he does kind of look like you." She shakes her head. "But you'll always be Sticks to me." She bites her lip and looks me up and down. "Maybe our paths keep crossing for a reason. Do you believe in stuff like that? Meant to be?"

"Yes," I say. The night, the hotel, the roar of the interstate, blurs to nothing, and all I see is Garnet. All I hear is Lady Fate whispering, whispering, whispering.

"Why don't you save your money?" she says. "I already got a room. We can share."

With my eyes, I trace the length of her slender throat, imagine the shape of her tongue resting in a bed of yellow teeth. My pulse is a bass drum in my car—boom, boom, boom—and my fingers tingle with anticipation.

"Sure," I say.

I follow Garnet to her room. The bed is unmade, the cover strewn over one corner, the sheets rumpled. I will wait until she falls asleep, I decide. Wait, and then slide a pillowcase off a pillow, spin it into something useful, twist it around her throat, and listen to her whispers of sounds as long as she can keep them up. I imagine she has decent stamina.

In front of me, Garnet shoulders out of her jacket and lets it fall to the floor, revealing a corset and a miniskirt and flesh. She slowly sits on the edge of the bed and spreads her pale legs, her skirt hitching over her hips. She slides her hands behind her on the comforter and curves her back in an arch. She isn't wearing any underwear.

I stare at the dark place at her center. "How many men have been inside you?"

Her knees slam shut, and she sits up. "Do you think you're too good for this? You're the same as me, Sticks. We survive how we can. You climbed up a ladder I propped up for you, boy. You'd think that would mean something for me, but a man's rise never benefits a woman. You're in a room I paid for. I saved you, Sticks. You made it because of me. Without me, you'd still be street trash!"

Her last word strikes me center. Her red hair is autumn leaves blanketing the floor of Tarson Woods.

Her bottom lip trembles. "Jesus, Sticks. You?"

"No. I didn't mean to upset you. I was only asking because I have never been with a woman."

"Seriously?" She smiles, shuddering with emotion, and turns her face down, shaking her head. "Never?"

"No."

"Some men like to go pro their first time." She curves to her side, softening the angles of her body. "I can make you feel like you're earning it." Tears are still beaded in her eyelashes.

"Can we go somewhere . . . special?" I ask.

"This isn't classy enough for you?" She glides her finger over the swell of her breasts. "Trust me. You won't remember where you are."

"What if I want to? I'll . . . pay you."

"What did you have in mind?"

"Have you ever seen moonlight on water?" I ask.

"Not in a long, long time," she says, and then studies me for two seconds, three. "Okay. Just promise me you aren't going to want to run off and get married or something afterward. That's happened to me before, you know."

"No, nothing like that." I manage a little laugh and peer at her from the corners of my eyes. "But I would love to hear you sing."

E
D
D
I
E

EDDIE STARED AT THE DOOR. IT WAS LOCKED, BUT HE COULD COME AND go with a knock. He could use the facilities, make phone calls. He wasn't detained. Not exactly. But he didn't have a key to the world outside and had no idea what time it was, what day. So then again, maybe he *was* detained.

But they were listening to him. Things were moving. He left the room more often than he needed to so he could see if the board in the room across the hall, visible through a rectangular glass pane in the door, had changed again. Change was good—that much he knew. Something was ruled out or something was ruled in.

They had not mentioned moving him back to a holding cell. Eddie wondered if they'd moved him to the musty office just because they needed his cell, but he'd seen only two people walked down the hall leading to those beds, and one had walked back out not long after. Probably drug busts or DUIs. Maybe they were being taken to court, or for processing through to longer stay prisons.

Eddie knew that walk, those steps, the circle. In and out, doors and chains. Van doors slamming shut. Metal doors rolling closed. He'd stolen more than a few cars before he even had a license to drive, with no parent around to notice he wasn't in bed. When he was in group homes, they rotated kids through quickly, and often even the well-meaning fosters couldn't keep up with their names. Bigger boys started calling him Boost. He could make anything start. But he couldn't lie to save his life. Then he got caught. At fourteen, he was looking at a two-year sentence in juvie.

Mr. Flemmons, a science teacher he barely knew from the school he rarely attended, had approached Eddie and his lawyer before the hearing. Eddie remembered never having felt so small before, sitting on that wooden bench, men in pressed suits and polished shoes passing behind Mr. Flemmons as he knelt on the floor in front of Eddie.

"Why do you like stealing cars?" he'd asked.

"I don't like stealing them," Eddie answered.

"So what do you like about it?"

"I like making them start."

"Why?"

"Because I'm good at it."

"I can teach you to be even better at it," Mr. Flemmons said. "If starting the cars is the part you really like."

Eddie had nodded, his eyes down, pimpled chin still stinging from a fresh shave with a disposable razor. Mr. Flemmons stepped aside, spoke to the lawyer, and strode down the hall a ways. Out of the corner of his eye, Eddie saw Mr. Flemmons knock on a big wooden door. It swung open, and he stepped inside.

The hearing was moved to the judge's chambers. Eddie sat down at the nicest table he'd ever seen, and he imagined it was the same kind of table knights sat around and did whatever knights did when they came together. Eddie had wished the faces staring at him then were hidden behind armor— his lawyer, Mr. Flemmons, the judge, the prosecuting attorney, and the man whose car he'd been caught stealing. Eddie had touched his forehead to the mahogany tabletop, feeling how cool it was, how damp it immediately became with his sweat, the glossy table foggy with the heat of his drowning heart.

Eddie's sentence became longer and shorter at the same time. He had to provide a list of all the cars he had stolen and where he'd taken them, then write a letter of apology to each of the owners as they were identified.

"I don't know how to write too good," he'd said.

Mr. Flemmons spoke up. "I'll teach you. I can teach you everything you want to know about motors and electricity and batteries, too. But first, you have to agree to let me help you improve your reading and writing. You will not miss a day of school, and you will spend every afternoon in my classroom until your guardian picks you up."

"And you will perform oil changes on my client's car every three months until the day you graduate," the other attorney had interjected, "and you will wash and vacuum it once a month."

"Is he going to let me touch his car again?" Eddie had asked Mr. Flemmons. He heard the man turn away.

"Any slipups and this offer expires immediately and the original sentence will apply," the man's attorney answered for him.

Eddie remembered how he couldn't speak, couldn't make a single sound come out. So he nodded. The attorney and his client leaped from their chairs like the table had caught fire. The judge, his lawyer, and Mr. Flemmons stared back at him—two dark faces sandwiching an old white man with whiter hair. They had reminded Eddie of an Oreo cookie.

"This is your shot, Eddie," the judge had said. "Don't blow it."

At first, the owner of the car would stay inside his brick house when Mr. Flemmons brought Eddie to service or wash the car. Then one day, about six months after the hearing, he was standing in the driveway in plain clothes and asked Mr. Flemmons to teach him, too. Mr. Flemmons stepped aside and asked Eddie to walk him through the steps. Then Eddie, his face and pants streaked in oil, had whispered, "Do you want me to show you how I started your car?"

Eddie smiled to himself as he sat on the old couch, remembering the curiosity like fishhooks that pulled up the man's eyebrows. "Hell yeah," he'd said.

The flicker of joy within him sunk, tethered, always tethered, to Hazel. His relationship with Stan Flemmons was one of the reasons Eddie had been supportive of Jonathon Walks taking her under his wing. Not that she was a troubled kid in need of a shot—Hazel was a saint. But she was also alone. Eddie might sing along to a favorite song on the radio in the car, but music was background noise to him, something to regard, like the temperature or the season. It could set a tone, sure. That's why they used it in movies. Even tone-deaf folks like Eddie could take the hint.

Still, he was grateful for Jonathon. Even if Hazel was dead, and maybe she was . . . maybe she was . . . that man had brought the life back to her eyes for just a little while.

M
I
C
H
A
E
L

Chapter 39 | October 2004 | Tarson, Georgia

I PASS THE TARSON CITY LIMIT POPULATION SIGN. IT HASN'T CHANGED, save the longer streaks of moss and the deeper pocks of corrosion. I wander aimlessly down Main Street. Perhaps my time in Atlanta has colored my perspective, but I swear the buildings look shorter, the road narrower, the lights slower.

An old Toyota Tacoma in front of me slows, approaching a green light at an empty intersection. Wiry gray hair crowns the driver's peach-colored scalp in a crescent, and I nearly prompt him with my horn. I sit back and rest the heel of my hand against the six-o'clock position on the steering wheel of my Jeep.

One honk and everyone would think I'm not from around here.

I press my palm flat against the center of the wheel. The horn blares for a second and a half. The truck jumps ahead, then the brake lights flash. An older man hangs out the window far enough to look back at me. I roll my window down and stick my hand out, gesturing the opposite of an apology, emulating what I've seen a hundred drivers do on Atlanta's streets.

The driver waves me off, his frown visible in the side-view mirror, and drives ahead. I turn at the intersection. I wasn't planning to, but I don't have any plan, really. Fate told me to come back, that she's ready, that I'm ready. So here I am.

I am relieved to find that the antiques shop is still here, an open sign in the door. With any luck, Rick is still here, too, and I'll be able to gauge the community's reaction to my potential return without inciting a riot. I try to peer inside as I drive past, but the windows are dusty, and although I'm sure the store is stuffed from wall to wall with trinkets and junk, from the outside I see only brown. Even the plants in the window planters are curled and dying. I imagine they would snap between my fingers.

Bones don't snap, by the way. They're not brittle, not unless someone is really old and calcium depleted, or if the bones have been cooked. Raw bones are quite hard and remain so long after exposure.

I pull into a spot, one of three marked for the store, but the whole row in front of the sleepy strip of stores is completely empty. I leave my stick and my pack on the floor behind my seat and step out of the car. My shoes are the shiniest thing in this town, and I nearly consider changing them before walking farther onto the sidewalk. The sound of another car approaching spurs me along, and I push through the door to the antiques shop, a little bell above my head jingling to announce my arrival.

The inside of the antiques shop is exactly as I left it. Boxes piled in a corner, shelves laden with musty, forgotten castoffs. But the little engraved instruments are not sitting on the shelf behind the counter. In their place stand a row of old Beatles records and a poster of Marilyn Monroe.

A man steps out of the employee office, and he is not the same, either. He steps into the light, and I see that if he is a man, he is just barely—probably eighteen or nineteen at the oldest. His hair is oil black and pulled up in a Mohawk.

"Can I help you?" he asks.

"I'm just passing through. Something in the window caught my eye."

"What was it?"

"A little wooden piano," I lie.

His face knits with doubt, but he rounds the counter all the same and hustles to the window display. "I can't remember seeing one of those recently, but to be honest, some of this stuff has been here since before I started working here."

"How long have you worked here?" I let my gaze roam, remembering how tall the shelves once felt, how strong the walls. This place was like a fortress for me. Now the ceiling, its exposed pipes and beams peeking from squares where tiles have been removed, feels like it might cave in with a hard rain.

"About a year. A little over. Yeah, sorry. I don't see anything like that up here. Are you sure you saw it?"

"I heard this store used to carry miniature instrument carvings. Must have been the power of suggestion," I say.

"Rick carved them back when he managed the store. He was my neighbor. That's how I got the job. I'm not exactly marketable, as my mom says." He grins. "They might still sell them at the Music Box, though. It's right across the street."

"Is Rick still in town? I do a little carving myself. I'd love to pick his brain."

"He doesn't live in Tarson anymore. A friend of his killed himself in Cold River a long time ago. My mom said he never could get over it."

My finger pauses on the spine of the book. Could Timmy, that pudgy, redheaded shit, have been a friend of Rick's? I recall the hours Rick spent with me, teaching me how to guide the blade of a knife for precision, depth, line versus slope. And patience, always patience.

You can only make one stroke at a time, Michael.

I am filled with the desire to hold the walking stick, to trace each key under my thumb. I move for the door, calling out a polite farewell.

"Hey, wait," the boy says, and I turn on my heel. "He left a number so I can call him if I have any trouble. I don't know if it's still his number, but it might be worth a try. Maybe you can buy something over the phone." He hands me a scrap of paper. "Don't tell him I mentioned the suicide. He gets pretty locked up about it. He was the only friend in town the kid had. I think he feels like he failed him."

I take the paper and stow it in a pocket. Timmy had plenty of friends. Even now I can see their faces circled around me, mouths open with shouts, spit flying.

"It wasn't a popular thing, the friendship," the boy said.

"Age difference?" I speculate.

"No. I mean, maybe, if the kid was normal. But this kid. Monster."

He smiles and shudders at the same time, and the hair on my arm raises, sensing a coming lightning strike, an approaching storm. "His name was Michael Walton. You should look him up. Closest thing this town has to an urban legend."

AMA

Chapter 40 | 11:00 PM, December 2, 2006 | Dalton, Georgia

AMA WOKE GASPING FOR BREATH, EVERY INCH OF HER BEADED IN chilly perspiration. The bullet wound ached with fresh pain as if she'd just been shot, and she realized she was pressing the undersides of both wrists together, bound once again in her dream. She slapped at the button for the bedside light. If getting out of bed wasn't such a production, she'd turn on the overhead light, too, but the switch was by the door. Between her sprained ankle and the sedative they'd given her to help her sleep, she wasn't sure she could make it without falling.

She was panting and furious, scared enough to sweat and shake in a hospital room where more security and more doors would separate her from Michael than at any point in the future, unless by some miracle he was caught. She wondered if Michael would own space in her brain, a sliver of every shadow, every bump in the night, for the rest of her life. By letting him go, she gave him that. And she gave him Hazel. If only that man hadn't had a gun, hadn't tried to shoot Michael. Maybe he would've run off and left Ama standing there in the rain.

But Michael would've come back.

She recalled the crime scenes in the case she defended for him. The cat that had been dissected piece by piece, layer by layer. A small dog with its ribs broken open with a hammer, its lungs cut open with a pair of gardening sheers. Michael Jeffery Walton finished what he started.

She pulled her legs into her body and rested her forehead on her knees. Would he see this as a negotiation on her part—a plea deal? She would leave him alone if he would leave her out of it. But could she do that?

Really? He'd already had Hazel for an entire year. She'd been with him for a matter of hours and hadn't thought she'd survive.

She opened the laptop Lindsey had brought up for her earlier in the day, along with a change of clothes and a bottle of Zinfandel. The only thing stopping her from opening the wine was that Lindsey had forgotten to bring a corkscrew. Reading comments about herself on the V.A.A.C. site was like some kind of purgatory, or whatever it was called when Catholics punished themselves. One of the comments mentioned Eddie by name and said they would be paying him conjugal visits in prison as a way to say thank-you.

"Christ Almighty," Ama muttered.

Someone tapped on the door before pushing it open. A nurse walked in, petite and lithe, a cable-knit sweater draped from her shoulders like it was sliding off a hanger, and Ama wondered if she had to buy her clothes in the kids' sections at department stores.

"Hi, Ama," she said. "Trouble sleeping?"

"I'm just ready to be in my own bed," Ama replied, closing her laptop and casting it aside.

"Nothing is better than your own bed," the woman agreed. "Your own pillows."

"No offense, but it's criminal to call these flimsy things pillows," Ama said. "And don't get me started on the sheets."

The woman laughed, an easy sound, like they might be trading stories at a bar about crap dates or ridiculous pickup lines, and Ama wondered at the sense of relief bleeding from her heart.

"If you drink enough of that wine, the bed will be more comfortable," the woman offered, eyeing the bottle, and Ama smiled in spite of herself.

"If I could get it open, I would."

"I can help you with that. Just don't tell the supervisor." The woman arched a brow and reached in the oversize pocket of her sweater, producing a set of keys held together with the loop end of a Leatherman keychain.

"You are my hero," Ama said, feeling as light as she had since waking.

"My name is Kim," the woman said as she removed the cork and passed Ama the open bottle. Ama realized this relief, this coolness flowing through her, was a response to the sheer normalcy of this moment—of these ninety seconds not discussing vitals or reliving flashbacks.

Ama poured wine into a plastic cup and offered it to Kim.

"No, thank you. I'm working," she said. "But I can hang out here for a minute if you want company. It's no fun to drink alone."

Ama swallowed a sip of wine and a smartass remark about drinking alone, and nodded a response.

"So how are you doing, Ama?" Kim asked, and slid her hands in her giant pockets. "How are you *really* doing?"

"I don't even know." Ama brought up the head of her bed and sank back against it.

"I'm sure it's hard to answer that when there's still so much unknown." Kim frowned. "I think random evil is so much scarier than if there's a reason. It's like something truly terrible—like what happened to you—can happen to anyone at any point, and there's nothing you can do to see it coming. Nothing you can do to stop it."

"I'd never met that man before in my life," Ama said.

"I thought you didn't remember what happened. Have you had a breakthrough?" Kim leaned forward, her expression too eager.

"No." Ama swallowed hard. "A detective came to question me. He brought his picture by. I'm sure I've never met him before."

"You said 'Hazel' when you first woke up, didn't you? A nurse is telling everyone about it."

"Who knows what I said. I was waking up from surgery." Ama's hands began to shake. She put her cup down to keep from spilling.

"Did you mean Hazel Stevens, the girl who disappeared in Tarson Woods last year, the same woods where you were found? That was the shooter's daughter. Did they tell you that? Do they suspect Eddie Stevens for her disappearance now? Why did you say her name? Did he tell you something?" Kim asked the questions in such rapid succession that Ama could barely keep up.

"What is this, an interrogation? This is highly inappropriate. I'm going to report you to your supervisor." Ama glanced at the whiteboard where every nurse had written their name the first time they came in the room. Kim, Ama realized, hadn't done that.

"Who are you?" Ama growled.

The woman stood and withdrew her hands from her pockets. She was holding a press badge and her cell phone, blinking with an ongoing recording. Ama thumbed the call button on the side of her bed. "I need security! Someone's in here!"

The woman bolted through the door in one fluid movement. Ama sank back against the raised head of her bed. She'd just been had by a reporter and she'd nearly sung like a damn bird, because why? Because they had laughed about shitty pillows together and she'd opened a bottle of wine? She blinked back a sting of tears, feeling utterly betrayed by herself.

Two nurses rushed in, looking over the room from corner to corner.

"Are you okay?" one of them asked.

"No." Ama glowered, needing a place to aim her disgust other than herself. "A reporter was just in my room. I want to know who to speak with about nurses disclosing patient information to the media." The nurses looked from Ama to each other. "Now!" she barked, and they scurried from her room. Her heart thudded in her chest—something the reporter had said still bleated in her mind.

Ama grabbed her laptop again and typed "Hazel Stevens" into a search engine. She clicked on the first link, an article from a year ago about Hazel Rae Stevens, vanished in Tarson Woods on December 1, 2005, and a picture of her distraught father: Edmond "Eddie" Stevens.

And who, one year later, would come into Tarson Woods looking for Ama.

Ama slid from the hospital bed, hobbled to the bathroom, and vomited into the toilet. She rested her cheek on the cool seat, heaving and spitting. It made sense now. It all made sudden, undeniable sense. Eddie Stevens was the man crying in the van. He'd realized Ama hadn't come back out of the woods, and he'd gone in after her.

Ama stood up, rinsed her mouth, and, gripping the edge of the sink with both hands, stared at herself in the mirror. If she stayed silent, people wouldn't think Eddie had just tried to kill Ama; they'd think he did away with his own daughter, too, especially once the media began promoting the connection. At the very least, she needed to say she remembered something—something that would clear Eddie's name. Maybe the gun accidently went off. Maybe she remembered being grabbed by someone other than Eddie but didn't remember who or what he looked like, and Eddie really was a hero.

Michael would know, though. He would know she couldn't remember what happened without remembering who . . . without remembering why. She had to figure out how to let Eddie off the hook without spooking Michael. If the media broke a story that turned up the heat on Hazel or Tarson Woods, he would see it as Fate telling him to leave, to find safer, calmer water, that the time wasn't right. He'd left Tarson before. He'd leave again, and he'd take Hazel with him, or he'd leave her wherever he'd locked her up and she would die.

If she didn't say a word, kept to her story of amnesia, Eddie Stevens would be labeled the killer of his own daughter for the rest of his life.

If she told the truth, Eddie Stevens would very likely never see his daughter alive again.

Ama couldn't be sure if or when Kim planned to break the story tying Hazel to Ama's shooting, but she doubted Kim would sit on it for long. She needed a way to keep Michael in Tarson long enough to draw him out and snare him. To do that, she would need bait, and the only thing he valued at this point was her voice. She wanted to be back in Atlanta so bad she was tempted to walk there, but if she wanted Michael to stay in Tarson, she couldn't leave, either.

How could she tempt him to her, and where, with any hope of escaping the meeting? And, maybe the larger hurdle, how would she get the message to him alone? She had to figure out how to write an invitation in the proverbial sky that only he would see, only he would truly understand.

I'M DEAD.

I sit back in my chair at the library and reread the archived article about my suicide in Cold River. I stare at the photograph they used, one of those school pictures with the blue backgrounds that makes it look like you're underwater or in the sky. Either way, it's a touch morbid.

I was small for my age, undernourished and constantly in motion. In this picture, my younger self is drowning in fabric. Once my clothes were too small, I had only my father's to wear. There was no in-between, save the random jacket or pair of shoes some woman from the church would drop off when the weather turned each year. I was covered in acne and ghostly pale. My hair was lighter then, too, mousy brown, stringy and long, and constantly covering my face. I remember the photographer coming around the camera to tuck the curtains of it behind my ears when I refused to do it myself. I'd shaken my head just before the picture, and greasy clumps of hair had framed my cheeks like prison bars.

The school never did ask when I planned to reenroll, and the women from the church, who once brought over fresh-baked casseroles and pies every Sunday and Wednesday for years after my father's funeral, shifted to dropping off nonperishables once a month following the verdict. The bags were more like donations to a food pantry, and I remember wondering what ate at them so much that they were bound and determined to keep us just enough alive.

My father's death.

My mother's sight.

Me.

Maybe Mother was right. They saw the bruises and burns on my limbs. They watched my pants become too loose and too short, the fronts cut out of my shoes to keep from rubbing sores on the tops of my toes. They explained away the time Ms. Nichols caught me with her cat tucked inside my jacket in the dead heat of summer, limp and foaming red spittle. This town had taken enough from me and my mother, they'd decided, so they would not take my future, too.

All this time, Ama thought she'd won, when really she was never going to lose.

A card catalog slams shut, and my mind returns to the library, my eyes to my reflection on my computer screen, my face parallel to the image of my teenage self. Even side by side, I wouldn't consider these two faces one in the same. Similar . . . a relative familiarity, maybe. But in coming home, I have been born anew. I will have to claw out from neither Mother's shadow nor her thumb. I am not of her any longer. I am born of Lady Fate, and she has named me Jonathon Walks.

I leave the library and drive to my old street. My childhood home comes into view, a brick corner peeking out from behind a magnolia tree. The squat house seems even smaller now, quieter. The windows are dark, but I can see the same checkered curtains on the other side of the bay window off to the right side of the front door, so chances are my mother still owns it.

I should've searched for her obituary. In retrospect, her health had been in a tailspin since before my baby sister was born. It just didn't become obvious until her sight failed and her hair grayed and began falling out by the handful. Even then, though, I didn't think she was sick, just that she was poisoned with regret of me.

I spy a potted flower on the stoop, and my toe pushes down on the brake pedal. I idle in the road, staring. Pink blossoms are visible even from this distance. The plant is thriving under my mother's care. This is perhaps a larger surprise than finding out this town thinks I'm dead.

I let off the brake and roll past my house. If everyone thinks I'm dead, I can't very well walk up the three steps to Janie Walton's house and knock on the door. There is only one place I can go, one place I can stay out of sight until I figure out how Fate means for me to complete our song.

I have to think about how to drive to the factory; I have only ever walked there. I pull down the dirt road and leave the Jeep in a cluster of trees. The factory looms ahead. I imagined it would be covered in kudzu or moss, nature slowly slaying the concrete beast. But it is just as stark as the day I last saw it. The wind picks up and sends dust spinning in the empty lot. Even though I am alone, I swear I hear boots on gravel, the laughter of men grateful for a break in the day. I turn, feeling like a child, too small in my clothes, the air too big in my lungs, but no one is there.

I raise my shoulders around my face, turn from the factory, and stride for the entrance to my father's underground shelter. The grass grows taller and thicker the farther back I walk, and I have to trace several circles before I find the metal cap, which I do with my toe—it's a sudden rise in the ground, a change in tone underfoot.

Kneeling, I wipe away the dust and dirt, and the cap appears. More dirt and small pebbles have filled the gap between the cap and the frame, and I have to scrape it out with my pinkie finger. At last I pry the cap loose and set it aside. The tunnel down is shallower than I remember. I don't even need the ladder. I just hop down. With my feet flat on the dirt floor, I can reach back out and touch the grass. I don't remember my father's head being quite so near the surface. Am I now taller than he was then? I can't imagine the possibility.

The hatch door to the shelter is located ninety degrees from the ladder. Indirect light spills down the hole and across the door in a diagonal slice. I turn the dial, pull the door open, and step through.

I let my eyes adjust in what dim light filters in from the hatch door. The square table is still in the middle of the room, one chair pulled out like someone got up for a glass of water and hasn't come back yet. I struggle to remember the last time I was here. Had I left a chair out? I can't imagine being so careless, but my head was spinning, my hands trembling at the idea of leaving my home, my song, behind. I had only just discovered my instrument. I had nearly bolted up the ladder, my father's stick knocking against the rungs as I ascended.

The cabinet doors are all closed. I open the closest one. Cans of beans and bags of rice, years expired, are stacked in rows. I will need to throw these out. I make a note to add trash bags to my shopping list, the black kind that stretch no matter what you put in them. I'll need to do my shopping elsewhere, somewhere bigger; box stores, younger employees, higher turnover. Somewhere that I am but a face among thousands.

I bypass the next few doors and open the next-to-last one. It's shallower than the others, but the back wall is false, a place my father once hid a handgun and where now my first bone carvings are stored. I remember Timmy's radius breaking when I cut down too hard and deep. His ribs were better for me to learn on, flatter and denser. I carved a conductor's wand out of one. I pick it up now, noting the rough, uneven surface. I smile, remembering my pride, my wonder. Now, I see a rudimentary effort, a beginner's work.

I crouch to open the lower cabinet. Timmy's lungs and throat are still pinned to a board. More mess, jagged edges and places the tissue tore. Everything is shriveled now, brown, dry, and cracking. I'd sprayed them with a sealant I'd found in my father's tools. Considering the chemicals I'd used and the time that had elapsed, I'm surprised there's anything left at all. Perhaps it's a gift from Fate, a reminder of how far we've come.

One day my compositions will be worth millions. I could put them on eBay and watch the price skyrocket. I won't have to hide my work anymore. People will understand. The masterpiece will be reason enough. People will line up. *Take me*, they'll cry. *I want to be part of your song. I want to be remembered for all of time.*

The vision fades and the bunker returns, dark and quiet. In the back corner, a generator sits under a blue tarp. My father showed me how to start it, made sure I committed every step to memory, and as I walk to it and pull off the tarp, I wonder if he hadn't made this shelter for himself . . . if all along he had made it for me. Why would he have shown me how everything worked, how to connect each appliance to the generator, made me memorize a list of priority uses for the limited electricity supply, revealed where every tunnel led to, where his weapons were stowed, if he had planned on being here, too?

Father must have made this for me.

MARTIN

GO HOME, MARTIN.

Captain's orders chased Martin out of the office and into the night. The same three words followed him down the two-lane roads between the station and his street, up the porch stairs, and through his front door. He slammed it shut, and the sudden disturbance in the stale air made the stack of paper he'd left on the ground light a few inches above the carpet. He tossed Ama's file into the room ahead of him, feeling brief satisfaction as her picture and his notes scattered across the floor.

How could Captain send him home with Eddie sleeping on a damn couch in an office, with six faces staring out from their investigation board and absolutely zero in terms of leads?

Ama's voice slipped into his head—*I don't remember anything*. She was lying, he knew. It was the way she said it, so sure about not being sure. He wanted to take her by her shoulders and shake her, to show her a picture of Hazel and Eddie and make her understand what she was costing them. If this woman had been willing to tell the truth, this case could be cracked wide-open. Hell, it could be solved and done. What could a stranger in the woods have said to her in a matter of hours that would spook her—a defense attorney, who had no doubt seen some shit in her career—so bad?

His ears rang. The floor beneath him began to tilt. He walked unsteadily to the bathroom and opened the medicine cabinet. It was empty. Of course it was. There was no pill fairy that would magically conjure a prescription and fill it. Martin shut the mirrored door and took stock of his reflection.

His eyes were bloodshot, his skin sallow and hanging from the peaks of his cheekbones. It had been two days since he'd eaten something that hadn't come out of a vending machine.

He didn't want to eat. He wanted to work. He turned his back on the mirror and took out his cell phone. No service. He tilted his chin to the ceiling and closed his eyes. Did he have any prescriptions with refills left?

Stop it.

He needed something. A meeting, maybe. But he hadn't looked into NA since arriving, and to look it up he'd have to drive back to the station. If he got in his car, it wouldn't be a meeting he'd go looking for. It would be a fix. And even though he didn't yet know much about Tarson, he knew the usual places to start asking. Push came to shove, he could always go drown himself in a case of cheap beer.

Get it together, Martin.

He returned to the living room, and his eyes caught on the picture of Ama he'd printed out at the station—her gray eyes, her tight-mouthed smile. He growled down at her, then moved out the door, down the steps, past his car, to the end of his driveway, and into the middle of the road, his breath and footsteps punctuating the quiet of the night. He pulled his phone from his pocket and selected the only number left on his speed-dial list.

"Hello?" his ex-wife's voice was groggy with sleep.

"Don't hang up," he said.

The line went dead.

Martin pressed the phone to his middle and doubled over, hunger and desperation churning in his stomach. He wanted to scream or throw the phone or run into the darkness and not stop. He was chasing a ghost—a theory. Was it any wonder he couldn't catch it?

Martin stared at the ground, his hands in fists. He'd have a better chance sleeping at the station than he would here, and at least if he locked himself inside, he'd have to think a little longer before going to hunt down some kid with a backpack pharmacy.

He climbed in his car and cranked the ignition. His phone rang. He fished it out of his pocket and answered it without looking.

"This is Martin."

"What did you take?" his ex-wife, Stacy, asked.

"Nothing." A tremble began inside him. "I'm clean, I swear. I didn't want to be. I'm still . . . I'm fighting it."

"What's wrong?"

The burn of tears came to Martin's eyes, and he had to stifle a laugh of relief at the sound of her. Someone who knew him. Someone who had once loved him.

"It's . . . it's a case," he started.

"Go ahead," she said, and he could hear her settling into her favorite chair, the creak of leather, the shift of a heavy blanket. Only his wife was cold year-round in Savannah.

Ex-wife, he reminded himself; then he relayed everything he knew about the case.

"Go to sleep, Martin," she said once he was finished. "It's three thirty in the morning. You sound delirious. Go to sleep, and when you wake up, tell Eddie what Ama said. He's known all this time what no one else has seen."

"Or he killed his daughter and shot Ama in cold blood," Martin countered, Stacy's sudden certainty somehow having the opposite effect on his own.

"He didn't. At least, you don't think he did," she said.

"You don't know that."

"Yes, I do. I know you, Marty. I still know you. Can you imagine how upset he'd be if he found out from anyone else that you have evidence Hazel might still be alive?"

Martin breathed out, weighted down and buoyant at the same time. "Okay. So I tell him. Then what?"

"I don't know," she answered, her voice soft and far away. Martin caught himself pressing the speaker tighter against his ear, closing his fingers around the phone. "You'll just have to wait and see," she said. "Go get some rest."

"Okay," he answered, knowing full well he wouldn't.

"I mean it. Eddie is going to have questions, and maybe good information you'll miss if you're tired when you hear it. He deserves to have you at your best."

Martin breathed in, out, remembering all the times she'd tried to save him from himself, tried to save what they had. How she deserved to have him at his best and how he had let her down.

"Okay," he said again. This time, he meant it.

MICHAEL

SOMEONE HAS LAID FLOWERS AT THE FOOT OF MY TOMBSTONE, WHICH relays only my name and the dates of my birth and death. I cannot imagine who might have brought these here. My father's and sister's graves each have a single flower propped up on their markers. Mine is different, a cluster of blossoms tied with a ribbon. There's no fourth tombstone for my mother. I'm not yet sure whether she's still living in my old house, but it would seem she's still alive.

My gaze lingers on my sister's grave, and I can still imagine the boundary line of where they pulled the earth up, how short it was compared to all the other visible graves. By way of comparison, my father's grave seemed impossibly long, the mound of dirt behind it a mountain. How would he claw his way through all of that when at last he woke up and came home?

I know now that he was working to prepare me. Mother, too, in her own way.

"You were wrong, Mother. The third time isn't mastery. We don't master. Not in this life. The very best we can hope for is to understand how to allow Fate to work her plan, to forfeit control. Three isn't mastery. Three is Fate."

I find myself wishing I was speaking to her grave.

A gust of hot air sails across the cemetery, and in it I hear echoes of my mother's wail the day we put my sister in the ground, her hands and forehead pressed to the wet earth, her black dress hunching around hips still wide with recent pregnancy.

G. My mother grieves in G.

MARTIN

MARTIN AWOKE FACEDOWN ON HIS MATTRESS, STILL WEARING HIS WORK clothes, his shoes dropped on the floor at the foot of his bed, the heavy curtains drawn across his window shrouding the room in darkness. He felt around for his phone and, squinting, brought it to his face. The screen was black, the battery dead.

"Shit." He struggled to sit up. Even though he'd spent most of the past couple of days sitting down or standing still, he felt as though he'd lost a boxing match and then been hit by a truck on the way home. He slid out of bed, plugged his phone into the charger, and shuffled into the kitchen to check the time. The clock on the microwave read seven thirty. Martin stared at it, then swung his gaze to the window, where morning sunlight should be streaming through, but it was black as night outside.

"Shit," he repeated, louder this time. He'd slept all day. He cursed a blue streak under his breath as he littered a trail of musty clothes from the kitchen to the shower. He stepped under the spray of water the second he turned it on. It was so cold it snatched his breath, and in his mind he could imagine Hazel running her guts out through torrential, frigid rain, heaving breaths, too scared to chance a look over her shoulder as she tried in vain to escape whoever had hunted her down in Tarson Woods.

Within fifteen minutes he was dressed and jogging out the door, his hair wet, the papers and pictures from Ama's file jammed back inside the folder and hugged to his chest. He'd missed more than a dozen phone calls before his phone died, half of them from the precinct, several from an Atlanta phone number he didn't recognize, and one from

...

his ex-wife. She hadn't left a message, but she had called. It was message enough.

The voicemails that had been left could wait until he got to the station. He was sure the captain was plenty pissed he'd been MIA, and Martin knew he'd plead his case for forgiveness more successfully in person.

He recited his speech in his head as he pulled into the parking lot. The heart of it came from what Stacy had said: *Eddie deserves me at my best, sir. Hazel and Ama, too. I'm fresh now. Just give me one more day.*

He pushed through the doors, determined to show how alert he was, how fresh, but no one else was there. His desk phone immediately rang. He hurried across the floor and snatched the receiver.

"Detective Locklear," he said.

"Detective, I've been trying to reach you," an unfamiliar woman's voice said. "I spoke with Ama Chaplin last night about her attempted murder."

"Formal charges haven't been filed," Martin responded, but uncertainty flared inside him. Anything could've happened in the past seventeen hours. "Who am I speaking to?"

"What's the delay on that?" the voice continued. "Are you trying to decide if you're also going to charge Eddie Stevens with the murder of Hazel Stevens?"

Martin's blood ran cold. "Who am I speaking to?" he repeated through his teeth.

"Esther Kim, reporter for the *Atlanta Journal-Constitution*."

"Well, Esther, no recovered body makes a hard case for a murder," he said, throwing her a bone. A hungry reporter was often more compliant than a starving one.

"So there are no leads for Hazel's whereabouts at this point?"

"Hazel's disappearance is not an active investigation," he responded.

"But you know about her disappearance and you've been on the job . . . three months, is that correct?"

"It's still fresh in people's minds up here."

"And Ama said 'Hazel,' upon waking after surgery, is that correct?"

"I wouldn't know. I wasn't there."

"I have a source who confirms that this occurred."

"I'm sure you do." *Damn that nurse.* He plunked down in his office chair and pulled Hazel's case file from his drawer. He flipped through it. No one had added any notes or updates.

Esther paused, and the silence was a magnet for Martin's thoughts, drawing everything he didn't want to say dangerously close to the surface. It wouldn't do any good to link the seven cases in the media when all they had was speculation and a couple of coincidences. The tip line would flood with nosy neighbors and phony psychics, bored teenagers and old women who watched too much true crime TV.

"I know these incidents are linked, Detective. I've been researching Hazel's case since the day her disappearance was made public. Two women disappear on the same trail exactly one year apart, and one man, the last to admit to seeing them both, was arrested in connection to Ama Chaplin's shooting. This is textbook. Unless it really, really isn't. And my money is on option number two."

"And why's that?"

"Because if you thought Eddie was responsible for both incidents, he'd be formally charged by now. There has to be something of significant value to be gained by holding off, and I want to know what it is."

"Is that all?" Martin said, releasing irritation into his voice.

"I have my own theory."

"Is it a theory you're sharing?" He swiveled his chair 180 degrees and connected dots on the ceiling with his gaze, and he realized he was making an "H."

"Hazel Stevens is still alive."

"What evidence do you have?" he asked. "Because from where I sit, with her file on my desk, it would be a pretty short article. One, maybe two sentences at most. Something like this: 'I think Hazel Stevens is still alive because her body hasn't been found and a gunshot victim might have said her name. The end.' I don't know, Esther. I'm no literary critic, but I don't think that's a winner."

"So the Hazel Stevens's file is on your desk?" Esther said more than asked, and Martin grimaced. "There's more to this, and we both know it."

"Well, if you write something useful, let me know. I might even buy a copy," he said, and hung up.

Martin's attention shifted over his shoulder in the direction of the office where Eddie was waiting. He checked his cell phone's call history once more, confirming his ex-wife had called him once more while he slept. He wore this truth like armor, and, before he could talk himself out of it, he headed for Eddie's room. To his surprise, the door was unlocked. He cracked it open. Eddie was sitting in the center of the couch, his shoes still on and his feet on the floor. His eyes were closed, but they opened as Martin approached.

"Can I come in?" Martin asked.

"It's your office," Eddie said.

"It's not, actually." Martin walked in and leaned against the wall. He was fairly convinced Eddie hadn't shot Ama on purpose, but that didn't mean Eddie wasn't a threat. He was a big man, twice Martin's size. He was also, if his story was to be believed, willing to fire a gun at someone running away, and if he was completely blameless in this mess, he had reason to be really, really pissed-off.

Eddie sat back and crossed his arms. "You look like you have something to say, though. So why don't you just go ahead and say it."

"I don't know whether to call it good or bad," Martin started, "and honestly, most of it is just theory at this point."

"I'm listening. If you're actually going to tell me something this time, that is."

"I am, but what I'm about to tell you is between you and me. Nobody else. Understood?"

Eddie nodded, his eyelids narrowing.

"When Ama woke up the first time, she said one word before knocking out again. I wasn't lying to you about that."

Eddie watched him without responding. Martin inhaled and let it out slowly. There would be no going back after this. He would have to answer every question, field every emotion, and he would be committing his investigation on a path shaped by Eddie's innocence. It was a high price to pay, especially if he was wrong.

"Hazel."

"What?" Eddie sat upright, and his brow crushed down on his dark eyes.

"Hazel. Ama said 'Hazel.'"

"You're sure?"

"That's what her nurse reported."

Eddie leaped to his feet, and his face lit up with a smile. "That's good, right? That's better than good. She might know something."

"That's what I thought, Mr. Stevens. But when I went to question Ama, she said she didn't remember anything."

"Well, that's okay. It's in there. It'll come out. When people go through that kind of thing, sometimes they forget, right?"

"That could be."

Eddie went still, but Martin could see the wheels of his mind turning behind his weary eyes.

"You don't think so. You think it's something else," Eddie said.

"I think she's remembering a lot more than she lets on."

"Why do you say that?"

"Because it wasn't the first time she'd tried to tell someone about Hazel. I think she tried to tell you, too."

"She didn't say a word to me. She was . . . she was dying."

"She didn't say it." Martin paused and stared blankly at the ground as he considered what to say, how to tell him about his daughter's name written in blood. "Come with me," he said.

Eddie followed at a distance, nearly tiptoeing at first. Martin led him to room two. He wondered how Eddie would react to seeing his daughter's picture in a line of others. No doubt his mind would jump to the worst conclusion. Sometimes the worst conclusion suited. Martin's gut told him this was one of those times.

"Mr. Stevens, if I show you this, if I bring you in on this investigation, it is off-the-record. Do you understand that? We do this after hours. Me and you. Nobody else knows. Business hours come and you go back to the office for the time being. Deal?"

"Deal."

Martin opened a manila folder and retrieved the picture of Eddie's jacket. He pinched it hard between his fingers, waiting as Eddie took in each photo on the board.

"What is all this?" Eddie asked.

"These are people who walked into Tarson Woods or have a strong association with the area, and have disappeared without a trace." Martin scanned the line. "Except her. Her body was found." He pointed to the redhead. "She's related to an old case of mine."

"So why is she up there?"

"I'm not quite sure why I put her up there, to be honest with you. I just feel like . . ." Martin's voice dropped off. *Like I was more interested in sailing away on a cloud of diazepam when she called for help from a rest stop twenty miles from here.* "Like she belongs," he finally said.

"So if she didn't disappear in Tarson Woods, why does she belong?" Eddie pressed.

Martin glanced at his profile. "You had her case in your notebook. So why don't you tell me why she's up there?"

"There's a footpath that ends at that rest stop and goes all the way to the edge of Tarson Woods. A little overgrown, but it's there. I found it when I was looking for Hazel. I think transients use it, mostly. A woman getting cut up and killed like that a few feet from a trail nobody knows about . . . it just felt like she belonged," Eddie echoed.

"You know, that folder and the fact that you had that case in it is one of the reasons I thought you were guilty."

"Well, damn." Eddie shook his head. "Thought?"

"You shot Ama, no question there. But I don't think you hit her on the head, bound her wrists, and burned lines into her legs."

"I didn't even see anything like that on her. There was so much blood," Eddie said softly. "It was dark. And I swear to God, I didn't aim for her. I tried to shoot the man who had her, and she jumped in front of him."

"You realize what a stretch that is to believe, don't you?"

"Yes."

"I'm going out on a limb for you, though. In all fairness, you had a folder full of information about other murders and missing people in your van. You couldn't have made yourself look more like a serial killer if you'd tried."

"That wasn't my intention." Eddie sat on the table. He wiped his face, but the heaviness remained. "I wanted someone to remember Hazel, to look for her, someone to believe that she didn't run off and leave me. Hazel wouldn't leave me like that, not by choice."

"Mr. Stevens, all due respect, but had you killed yourself at the trailhead where your daughter disappeared and had a stack of unsolved cases in your possession when you did it, best case, it would look like a grieving father who couldn't live life without his runaway daughter. Worst case, it would look like a confession. The case would have stayed closed forever. I know it hasn't all gone like you thought it would, but it's a really good thing for Hazel that you went in after Ama. Whether we're looking for her or her body, now at least we know to look."

Martin's own words tunneled through his brain and into his ears. When a victim was missing this long, bodies were often found only if a killer led police to where they'd taken them. Hazel had been missing for a year. Dead or alive, they weren't going to find her without help. If Eddie had shot the man who had taken Hazel, they may never have found her. Eddie's story, then, might be absolutely true: Ama may have jumped in front of the bullet in hopes that Hazel would be found.

But why? She didn't know Hazel beyond her name, as far as Martin could find, and Eddie swore he'd never met her before that night. A parent would take a bullet for a child, a spouse for a spouse, a friend for a friend . . . but one stranger for another when an escape option is already presented? Recognition washed over Martin, and hope clawed from the depths of his racing heart, made buoyant by the sudden current. All of these scenarios had one thing in common: one person was saving another living soul.

"Are you absolutely sure your daughter has never met Ama Chaplin? Has she spent any time in Atlanta?" Martin pressed.

"We went to Atlanta a couple times a year—go see the World of Coke, maybe catch a Braves game—but she never went without me. Hazel doesn't have many friends. She isn't social." Eddie glanced down. "Wasn't."

"She's not a body yet, Mr. Stevens."

"I know the statistics. I could quote them in my sleep."

"Then answer me this. Let's say Ama jumped in front of the bullet like you say. Why would she do that?" Martin's voice sped up.

"I don't know."

Martin handed Eddie the picture of his jacket, the HAZ circled in black ink. "Why would a woman take a bullet for her captor and then try to write a name in blood if the only thing out there to find is a dead body?"

EDDIE WAS ALL MOTION, NONE OF HIS LIMBS SATISFIED TO REST FOR longer than a full second. Even if he stopped to stare at a photograph or a page of notes, his fingers would tap the closest solid surface. Martin's attention was divided between Eddie and his notes. He felt more useless by the second, especially in the presence of Eddie's renewed sense of hope, which was a palpable thing. It spurred Martin to dig deeper. It made it hard to breathe.

"It's someone they all knew," Eddie said suddenly. Martin looked up from his case notes.

"What makes you say that?"

"Hazel wouldn't walk off with a stranger. Like I said, she didn't have a big social life. She barely spoke to people she did know. I even told her . . ." Eddie pressed two fingers against his closed eyes. "I warned her not to talk to anyone she didn't know. I said that to her, Detective."

"Call me Martin," he corrected quietly.

"Martin. I told my daughter that." He shook his head and cleared his throat. "She wasn't wearing headphones. No one could've snuck up on her. She knew the world isn't all nice. I tried to be real honest with her about the good and the bad. She wasn't sheltered. And she could run, Martin. She could run faster than all the boys on our old street when she was nine years old. If she got a split-second head start, there's no way anyone could've beat her off that trail. My wife used to say she was built like a greyhound."

Martin's focus tripped on Eddie's mention of his wife. He could barely bring himself to look at the widower, revisiting how sure he'd been that Eddie was responsible for not just one crime but three: Ama, Hazel, and Raelynn. Even last night, swallowed by the pit of desperation and dead ends, he'd reached back for that conclusion just like he'd reached into the medicine cabinet for want of a fix.

"Martin?" Eddie's voice reached Martin in the internal maze he was building.

Martin cleared his throat and blinked the haze of recent memories clear from his mind. He wanted to ask Eddie about his wife's death, but now was not the time.

"Were teachers interviewed at the time of her disappearance?" he asked instead. "Did they ask if she seemed to be close to anyone new? Did any new students enroll midyear?"

"Officers went to the school a couple times. The captain did, too. We didn't have a detective back then."

"Okay." Martin dropped his elbows down on the table and stared point-blank at Hazel's photo. "We need to start the investigation into Hazel's disappearance from scratch, like you woke up this morning and she was gone. If she's still alive, there's a reason. You say her circle was small, and that's a good thing, especially since we both believe she knew whoever took her. She's how we solve this case—hell, maybe all of these cases. She's how we find her."

Eddie lifted up on his toes several times and shook his hands loose at his sides.

"There's just one thing, Eddie. We have to solve this without letting anyone know that we're looking for her. We cannot let anyone know we believe she's tied to the Ama Chaplin case."

"Why?" Eddie came down on his heels.

"If whoever has Hazel realizes we know she's alive, he will do one of two things—neither of them good."

"Leave town, or . . ." Eddie planted his hands on his hips and dropped his chin to his chest.

"Shit." Martin closed his eyes. The reporter from the *AJC*. She may not have enough of a scoop for a story, but she also may not have been showing all her cards. If she ran a story connecting Ama and Hazel, implicating Eddie Stevens in the murder of his own daughter, it would follow him for the rest of his life. If Esther instead took the angle about Hazel being alive, Tarson Woods would be crawling with do-gooders and the morbidly curious. Whether they meant well or not, they'd likely do more harm than good, and either way, they'd put a dangerous kind of pressure on whoever had taken her.

"Hang tight, Eddie. I gotta make a phone call."

Back at his desk, Martin recovered the number Esther Kim used to call him and dialed her back. He glanced at the clock. It was past ten.

"Change your mind?" Esther answered, sounding very much awake.

"You can't run your story," he said.

"Because I'm right?"

"I don't know that yet," he answered.

"I'm running the story."

"You can't even have enough of a story to run!" Martin pled, exasperated.

Esther threw Martin's words back at him. "You don't know that yet."

Martin drummed his fingers on his desk. He couldn't ask her what she knew without revealing there was something *to* know. He needed something to point her to, something to keep her busy, in case she agreed and her word wasn't as good as her pride.

"I don't know what you know and what you don't, but I am positive you don't have the *whole* story," he offered.

"I'm listening," she answered.

"I don't just have Hazel's file on my desk. I have seven files."

"Would the name on one of those files happen to be Toni Hargrove?" Esther asked, her voice sickeningly sweet. "I find it interesting, you coming to Tarson. Could you not get a job anywhere else after your little habit ruined your career and flushed your solve rate down the toilet?"

Martin went utterly still, his lips ajar, his mind racing. She'd dug into his history, his life. Here he'd thought he'd start over in Tarson, bring only the pieces of his old life with him that he wanted to, and she was going to unpack his entire past, spinning it whichever way made for a more compelling story.

Martin heard the sounds of paper rustling over the phone.

"Your wife—sorry, ex-wife—didn't have much to say about you or Ms. Hargrove's murder. She's pretty frigid, honestly. Guess you have to learn how to be cold when you're married to a detective. Or maybe that's just her nature. She's only quoted once in the article so far. I worry for her, though. You know how readers respond when a woman says 'no comment' to crimes against other women."

"That's low. And honestly, it's the easy way out. It's beneath you. Or it should be."

"So give me something I can use," Esther countered.

Martin managed a terse laugh, but inside he was in full panic. Stacy didn't deserve this. Neither did Eddie or Hazel. "You're right. This is a high-profile situation, and it deserves to be on the front page of every paper. It's also much, much bigger than you realize. Eddie Stevens is a piece of it, but just a piece. You wait to run your story, and I'll bring you into the station and tell you everything I know. You'll have plenty of information, I assure you. Way too much to fit in a filler line from a washed-up detective's ex-wife."

"It's tempting, really. But there's just one thing. The space for my story has already been committed—front page of the Sunday paper. I've been working on this story for months, and it'll be my first front-page Sunday byline, and I'm not giving that up. And if seven files are on your desk, and Eddie Stevens isn't charged with anything yet, it sounds like you're either tallying up a body count before filing, or you're looking at someone else—someone who isn't in custody. The public has a right to know, don't they?"

"Just wait, please. I'm begging you. One life might be actively at stake, and if you run this story, you'll increase the risk that we don't find this person alive."

"You're not using pronouns on purpose, Detective Locklear. Thank you for your official comments and confirming my theory about Hazel. Good night," she said, and hung up.

Martin slammed the phone down. He could only hope the reporter was bluffing and would phone back once she made sure she'd have a front-page Sunday byline with a story including the additional information. But for now, he needed to act as though the whole world would know Hazel was out there to be found come Sunday morning and that whoever had her would feel the squeeze.

Martin returned to Eddie's room and nearly shoved a piece of paper and a pen in his direction. "Write out every person in this town you think Hazel would willingly have had a conversation with."

"Everything okay?" Eddie asked, taking the pen too slowly between his fingers.

"I just got off the phone with a writer at the *AJC* who's put the Ama and Hazel connection together. She's running the story Sunday. I couldn't stop it. I believe Hazel is still in Tarson, Eddie. But after Sunday, there's no telling where whoever has her might take her once the spotlight turns back on these woods."

Eddie nodded, blinking rapidly, working his lips around a thought. "I . . . I don't know that we need a list of who Hazel would've talked to," he stammered, obviously feeling the sudden shifts in control and pressure. "There was a freshman girl she ate lunch with. Vivian? Violet? Something with a V. And one girl in the school chorus she would study with sometimes."

"Anybody else?" Martin pressed.

"Well, there was the substitute music teacher. She adored him. He's going to sound suspect the way I sounded suspect," Eddie cautioned. "They were close, but nothing inappropriate, I can promise you that."

"Why is he going to sound suspect?" Martin flipped his notebook to a clean sheet and grabbed another pen.

"Don't let this sidetrack you again."

"All I'm going to do is listen."

"The music teacher's name is Jonathon Walks," Eddie started slowly. "He took Hazel under his wing, worked with her after class—always out in the open. He asked my permission. He saw her talent, recognized that she wasn't using it to her full potential, and really brought it out of her. I don't even think she knew what her voice was capable of until he showed her it was in there."

"You're protective of him. Why?"

"He brought Hazel back to life, Martin. After her mother died and we moved here, I felt like Hazel had slipped down this deep hole, and I was throwing everything I could in there to help her back out, but it wasn't working. That teacher . . . he made the light come back on inside of her."

"Just playing devil's advocate here," Martin started. "Manipulators generally target potential victims like Hazel—outsiders, kind hearts, loners . . ." He hesitated. "Broken homes."

"Our home wasn't broken," Eddie said, and his jaw set.

"You know what I mean. Don't take it personally. This is investigating. We're digging. Building. Shifting pieces. It's hard. It's messy. It's why we don't usually involve the family on this side."

Eddie closed his eyes and seemed to center himself. "It's just, Jonathon seemed a little bit like a kindhearted loner, too. He kept to himself. He joined the search for Hazel. He walked every inch of Tarson Woods with me, even did some of the harder terrain on his own for me." Eddie tapped his right leg. "I have a bum knee. Going up isn't so bad. It's the coming back down that gets me."

"Okay, so hear me out." Martin stood and wrote *Jonathon Walks* on the board. "We have a teacher—a temporary teacher—who takes a special interest in Hazel. Spends extra time with her. That's often called 'grooming.'"

"I know what it's called."

"Then Hazel disappears and Jonathon interjects himself into the investigation."

"He just helped look for her. Hung flyers."

"He saw everywhere police were looking. He'd know if they were close," Martin countered.

"I hear you. But you think all these people might be connected to one person. What would he have to do with Ama or those two teenage boys from twenty years ago? He cared about my daughter. He looked for her because he cared. Is it so hard to believe someone else cared about Hazel besides me?"

"That's fair. And, Mr. Stevens, a lot of people care about Hazel." Martin frowned. "Here's what I think we know. We are looking for a white man, someone who would blend in easily around here. Probably pushing forty, but not younger than thirty, if he's connected to those boys. Physically fit; he'd have to be. Local. Each of these people knew the attacker."

"Jonathon isn't local. He moved here from Atlanta a couple years ago."

"I'd still like to talk to him," Martin said.

"He doesn't work at the school anymore. The regular teacher, Mrs. Anderson, came back. He said he had a good temp job offer over in Dalton."

"Did he move away?"

"I'm not sure where he was living. I never went to his house. Neither did Hazel."

"Was it shortly after the investigation ended?"

"Maybe six months after Hazel disappeared. Jobs don't come easy here, Martin. He had to go where the money was."

"Sure," Martin said absently as he wrote Jonathon's name at the top of the paper, along with a note to check into his credentials and his last known address.

His gut was a seesaw on the possible lead. Jonathon Walks had all the markers for someone grooming a victim. But Eddie was right—he had nothing to do, that they knew of, with the early people on this list, and the only obvious connection to Ama was that they both lived in Atlanta at some point, a city with nearly half a million people.

Martin's eyes flitted back to Toni Hargrove. Was he wrong to put her on this list? Was her presence throwing off his judgment? No, he decided. If nothing else, she would be a constant reminder to stay focused . . . and to stay sober.

"He gave me his number, though," Eddie said. "If you want to talk to him, I can call."

"Write it down for me," Martin said, and spun the pad of paper to face Eddie. He wasn't about to call Jonathon until he was absolutely sure of two things: if Jonathon was who he was looking for, and where he could be found.

If nothing else, Jonathon Walks was as solid a lead as he could expect—somewhere between a person of interest and a suspect—which also meant he had a place to start and something of value to report to Captain. Martin could only hope it was worth enough to buy him a little more time.

MICHAEL

"CLASS, THIS IS MR. WALKS. HE'S A VOCAL COACH AT THE MUSIC BOX. Some of you may remember him from Career Day. He'll be stepping in for Mrs. Anderson through the end of the year while she's on medical leave. I expect you to give him the same courtesy and effort you give any member of our staff," Mrs. Brownlow, the school's principal, instructs the group of teenagers.

I look out over them, unconcerned. Chorus is an elective music class. Students want to be here. The only trouble I may have would be from the two muscle heads in the back row—probably athletes who took this class thinking it would be an easy A.

Nothing about music is easy.

One of them catches me staring and locks eyes. I don't look away. He blinks once. Twice. Three times. Then slouches down in his seat and drops his gaze to the cell phone he's hidden in his lap. I watch him long enough to be there when his glance flicks up at me once more. He shifts in his seat, pretending it was an accident.

"Hazel, are you listening?" Mrs. Brownlow asks, the tone in her voice breaking from the melody.

Next to the window, a girl sits up and closes her notebook. She nods.

"We listen with our eyes, too," she instructs, bringing her finger to the bridge of her nose.

That's not your eye, I have to resist telling her.

Hazel watches Mrs. Brownlow for a few seconds before attention begins to leave her face a degree at a time. As the principal turns control of the class over to me, Hazel flips her notebook to the back cover and draws with a purple-ink pen. Her gold eyes are rimmed in charcoal black. She reminds me of a cobra, and although she is, at a glance, the smallest person in the room, her every movement triggers my nerve endings. A shot of adrenaline races down every limb, and I feel as alive as the moment I burst above the surface of Cold River when I had every reason to sink into the dark.

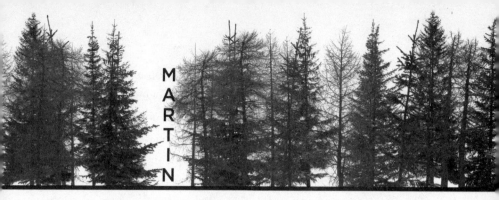

MORNING CAME, BRIGHT AND UNFORGIVING. IT HAD ONLY BEEN NINE hours since he'd botched the phone call with Esther Kim, but with the sun up and his back throbbing from a three-hour nap at his desk, it felt like he'd already lost a whole day to her deadline. He had to hope Esther was bluffing and didn't have anything sensational to report. Maybe the phone call had been purely a proverbial fishing trip, the anniversary of Hazel's disappearance making for good emotional fodder, in which case he'd given her a ten-pound bass. He had half a mind to get a subpoena for her notes, but he didn't want to give her the satisfaction.

He stared across the table at Eddie, who was leafing through Martin's case file from Toni Hargrove's murder.

"How do you see this kind of thing all day, every day, and not go crazy?" Eddie asked.

"Pain pills. Sleeping pills. Uppers, downers, whatever I could get my hands on." Martin leaned back in his chair and pointed at Toni's picture. "That woman died because of me. She called me from a pay phone not fifteen miles from here, and she had to leave a message because I had taken enough sedatives to down a horse. Never heard the call come in."

"She should've called nine-one-one," Eddie countered.

"The nine key on the pay phone didn't work and the number three key was missing. I think my number must've been the only one she could think of with no nines or threes."

"How did you know her?"

"I'd used her a few times as an informant. She turned tricks in Savannah.

I kept her out of the pen. She kept me in the loop on a couple of her clients' whereabouts, guys with ties to drug trafficking. Then one day, she was in the wind. I think she might've run her mouth to somebody, or someone found out she was relaying information. I hadn't heard from her in years. I knew she'd been picked up a couple times in Atlanta for solicitation. I talked to her once when she was at the Fulton County station. She gave them my name and tried to tell them she was undercover. During that phone call she told me she was leaving corners behind and was going to be a singer. You know, she actually sounded genuine."

"She said what now?" Eddie asked, and his expression turned to stone. "You said she wanted to be a singer?"

Martin swung his gaze across the line of faces again. Maybe Toni wasn't the piece that was throwing off the picture. Maybe the first two—boys who Captain said didn't even really fit up there—were coloring the line with the wrong tint.

"From what I know, it's a fifty-fifty split up there as far as music is concerned," Martin said. "And that's being generous. Still, I think it's worth a trip to the school, see what I can find out about your teacher friend. Don't tell him I'm looking for him yet, just in case it turns out I need to be. We need to get you back in the 'holding cell' before anyone clocks in."

"Okay," Eddie said, and Martin could tell Eddie was less sure about Hazel's teacher than he had been hours ago. Maybe it was the music link. Maybe it was the pictures of Toni's body. Maybe tiny details in his subconscious were beginning to stick together, forming something not so small, not so easy to overlook.

THE LID TO THE SHELTER IS NOT HOW I LEFT IT. I LEAVE MY BACKPACK aboveground, grip my cane in my right hand, pull the lid back, and hop down. The hatch door is wide-open. An old man sits at the table, his pale skin paper-thin and sagging, his scalp rung in short-cropped silver hair. His hands are clasped on the tabletop, and he's spinning something between them.

"I knew it was you the second I seen you at the cemetery," he says, and his voice registers his name: Mr. Bill. "You got gone. Why didn't you stay gone?"

"Felt like the right time to come home," I answer carefully.

"Your momma know?"

"You of all people should understand why I didn't feel compelled to go knock on that door," I say as I walk into the room.

"She's better now, you know. Still can't see much, of course. But better. She has regrets, Michael."

"Regrets." I nod. "I don't believe regrets exist. Not really. I believe in Fate, Mr. Bill. Fate guides. Fate clears the path at our feet. Fate always brings us back to where we ought to be. So how can we have regrets? Mother taught me that, you know. She showed me how powerful Fate can be."

"She told me," Bill says quietly.

"She doesn't understand Fate, Bill. Not even a little bit. And you . . . you shouldn't be here."

"I helped your father build this. I helped dig both tunnels. I helped

install every cabinet. I know what should be here and what shouldn't be."
He opens his hands, and the skeletal remains of Timmy's fingertips appear
in his palm.

"You shouldn't be here," I repeat, regarding him, the prickly sensation
of being too warm spreading through me. Lady Fate is a raven in my
chest, cawing and flapping, driving my blood ever faster. "But now you
can't leave," I say, and I close the door.

AMA SHIFTED IN THE PASSENGER SEAT OF LINDSEY'S HONDA ACCORD, unable to find a tolerable position. She grunted, twisting again, and her mind turned to Hazel—underground. Hazel—chained to a wall. Hazel—another day spent in utter silence, despite Michael's best efforts.

"I don't think you should've signed yourself out of the hospital before they thought you were ready," Lindsey said.

"I'm fine. My vitals are stable. They were planning to discharge me tomorrow if nothing changed, anyway," Ama answered.

"I still don't understand the rush to leave just to come stay here." She pulled the car into the parking lot of a motel near the state route exit for Tarson. Ama could feel Lindsey's gaze shift from the squat L-shaped building to Ama's chest, no doubt eyeing where the bullet had gone in.

"Let me take you home," Lindsey said softly, the car idling, her hand clutching the gear shift.

"No. I need to stay in Tarson."

"Why?" Lindsey pressed.

If she was being honest with herself, Ama knew part of why she wanted to stay in Tarson was because Michael wouldn't expect it. He'd peg her for someone who would throw herself back into her life and her work, determined to prove he hadn't affected her. The last thing he'd think she'd do would be to stay in a run-down motel within walking distance of Tarson Woods. She also knew she couldn't draw Michael to her from her penthouse apartment overlooking Piedmont Avenue. That wasn't how he operated. She knew she needed something so big, so tempting, his curiosity would override his rule about the organic crossing of paths.

"Ama?" Lindsey prompted, and Ama's focus returned to the present. "What's going on?" she asked. Lindsey knew how Ama liked her sandwiches, her coffee, her drinks, her men. She knew instinctively when to cancel unnecessary appointments and kick Ama out of the office for an hour or two. And she would know if Ama was lying, so Ama had to tell at least a fragment of the truth.

Lindsey turned off the engine and stared full faced at Ama, waiting.

"I want to give back," Ama said, which was partially true. "You said it yourself: my image needs damage control. Getting shot doesn't make me nearly as sympathetic as you might think."

Ama's thoughts returned to the V.A.A.C. page, to the things people had said about her. A lot of those things held partial truths, too.

"You don't owe anyone anything," Lindsey said firmly.

"No, I do. And I need your help to do it. If you wanted to draw a big crowd for a good cause, how would you do it?"

"Like a fundraiser?" Lindsey suggested.

"A fundraiser would be perfect," Ama said, her thoughts taking off at a sprint. "A silent auction, with live music, catered food, a dance floor . . ."

"What are you raising funds for, exactly?" Lindsey asked.

"Maybe for the Tarson Police Department, as a way to say thank-you. Maybe they can buy some new equipment or safety gear or something," she heard herself answer, but her mind wasn't on the police station. She could already see the auction bursting to life, people talking, swarming the open bar, placing bids, talking plenty of shit about Ama, no doubt. The most important piece was silent and empty: a baby grand piano spotlighted alone on a stage. Michael wouldn't be able to resist, would he? Then again, if uniforms were everywhere, he may not chance it. She bit down on her lip, suddenly flooded with doubt.

"If you really want to make yourself sympathetic and have a bigger impact, you have to think smaller," Lindsey said, and a curious expression came over her face. "Younger."

"The school. That's perfect," Ama answered on an exhale. "We'll hold a fundraiser for the high school, for the music department."

"Okay," Lindsey said slowly. "Why music?"

"The holiday," Ama answered quickly. "Music makes people festive, makes them generous."

"That's a good point. How soon are you thinking? And where? It's going to be hard to pull something off this close to Christmas. Would you rather have it in Atlanta?"

"No, it has to be here, and it has to be soon, very soon," Ama said, her tone harder than she intended. She paused and tried again. "If anyone can make the right people say yes, it's you. I think holding it here will make the effort seem more genuine. And maybe people will be willing to give more money if I'm still bandaged and limping." She forced herself to smile.

"That's not a bad thought," Lindsey mused. "Does this town even have a venue nice enough to set the kind of tone that opens wallets?"

"It has exactly one: the courthouse."

The old, Southern-style building was rung with giant porches and nestled between two groves of magnolia trees. In the back, a carpet of tidy grass rolled for half an acre before butting up to the edge of Tarson Woods. Ama hadn't seen it or set foot near it in seventeen years. When she'd lived here, it had been the crown jewel of the city. If there was anything small-town people believed in, it was justice. With any luck, both those things still rang true.

"I have an idea. Give me the morning to get settled in and make some plans. Can you meet me here this afternoon? Maybe bring some of my clothes and some lunch for us? I'm going to need someone to help me pull this off, and the only person I trust to help me is you," Ama admitted.

"I . . ." Lindsey trailed off, visibly flustered. "I'll be here," she said.

"Good." Ama reached over and squeezed her hand, and she realized in all the years they'd known each other, that may have been the first time she'd touched Lindsey on purpose.

There was no way she'd be able to pull together a large-scale event on her own, bullet wound or not. This was Lindsey's territory. She'd planned weddings start to finish for a handful of paralegals in their office. The firm called on her any time a venue had double-booked something they needed, and she'd always walked away from such conversations victorious.

After the opening arguments in the most recent case, Lindsey had warned Ama that she didn't think they had the right jury to win for the driver in the vehicular homicide, and she had been right. Ama understood how to work the legal system and how to work criminals, and she alone understood how to work Michael. Figuring out how to draw him out, how to leave bread crumbs tempting enough for him to find and follow, would be a big enough undertaking. Thankfully, Lindsey understood how to work everyone else.

Ama could admit to herself that manipulating Lindsey wasn't new, but this feeling—this niggle of worry that Lindsey would be hurt should she find out—was a first.

M
I
C
H
A
E
L

THE JOCKS FROM CHORUS DON'T RECOGNIZE ME HERE IN THE GAS STA-
tion: sunglasses, unkempt hair, and two days' worth of stubble on my face.
I've captured two quick glances from Jake, the ringleader, as if maybe he
knows me, but he's not sure from where.

They're dressed for a run. Want creeps though me, and a flat note
echoes in my head. This is the second place I've seen them, our paths
crossing in front of the refrigerated beverages section. That's the way Fate
can be; sometimes laughably simple.

"Let's go somewhere different," Jake says, and I watch him tuck a
Snickers bar into his palm before sliding it into the pocket of his sweatshirt. "I'm sick of the regular route."

"What about the Timberline trail?" a smaller boy answers. He's wiry,
one coiled muscle from the base of his throat to his ankles. I imagine he
lets Jake win, even though he could probably beat him at any distance.

I wander to the other side of the store and pretend to look through
various snacks until the boys leave, falling into a fantasy about what vocal
range Jake might have if he were pushed into discovery. Those kinds of
kids always do best with a tough-love approach.

"Sir?" the cashier's voice breaks through my haze. I'm standing at the
checkout counter empty-handed. "Did you want to buy anything?" he
asks.

I glance at the cooler where the Gatorade is stocked. I must've put mine
back, but I can't remember doing so.

"I, uh. I think they may have stolen something from you," I say.

"Really?" He slides off his stool. "I'll check the security tape. Thanks."

"Anytime," I say, and leave the store.

I cross the road and head straight into the trees. I won't take the Timberline trail, won't set a single foot on it. If I run into Jake again, would it count as a third time, or am I tempting Fate, playing God?

No, I decide. I'll head into the woods and see where it takes me. If our paths cross, so be it.

I don't see a soul for the first forty minutes. Then, ahead, a flash of red catches my eye. Jake had been wearing a red shirt. I increase my speed, turning uphill when I come across a trail marker. I force myself to slow down. I can't hunt Jake. That wouldn't be authentic, and Lady Fate is easily offended.

"Mr. Walks! What are you doing out here?" an unmistakable voice calls from behind me.

It's Hazel.

"This is the last place I'd expect to see you," she says.

The taste of metal floods my mouth. A third crossing has presented itself. Fate has led me here, no doubt as a test. Hazel is as close to a friend as I've had. How could I not have seen this before? Her range will be unmatched, her tones clearer than any other contributor.

Hazel is no test. Hazel is a gift.

I turn, smiling. "This is the last place I'd expect to see you, too, Hazel. Want to walk a ways with me?" I ask.

"Sure," she says, and we walk up the rise toward the peak overlooking Cold River together.

In the dark of the underground room, I feel for the second screw head joining the two metal panels of the kennel. The first screw is in my pocket, and my left thumb is raw. When I stick it in my mouth, I taste blood and I can feel where my nail is cracked.

That's why you have two, Hazy. I imagine my father's voice in my head, and it drives me on.

I twist and pry at the screw with the nails of my thumb and pointer finger. Something rattles to my right, a dull sound coming through the locking cabinet door I see Mr. Walks crawl through sometimes, and I freeze. He doesn't usually come in that way unless he used it to leave. He says it goes to the river. I wonder if the water is rising, pushing debris up the chute. I wonder if the door will cave and water will rush in, washing everything else in this tiny room back out, so all that will be left for him is me.

Between my still fingers, the screw moves. It isn't much, maybe a quarter of an interval. But it moves. I dry the sweat from my fingers and try again. It spins all the way around, looser now. I wiggle and pull, wiggle and pull. It comes out in my hands, and the burn of relief floods my eyes.

I put a hand on each panel and push out. They give, but barely, still held in place where they join the ceiling and the floor. Desperation swells inside. I cannot be found with a half-finished escape. If there is the slightest gap, he'll see it. I don't want him to see this hole until it is giant and I have slipped through and have run far from here.

He'll see my nails, I realize. He'll put me somewhere different, somewhere smooth. He only wants me to experience pain if he's present to hear it. I have to force my way out now.

I heave against the cage. I grunt, biting back any other sound, and push harder still. My shoulders burn. My hands throb and shake. I hear metal pop loose above my head. The top panel has given way. I go still for less than a second, disbelieving, but I press my fingers on the ceiling of the cage and it moves.

I smile in the dark, my breath coming fast. The ceiling is still held down in three places, but with this corner blown and the adjacent wall undone, I can squeeze through. The joints bite into my skin, and the pressure of the panels longing to rejoin is tremendous, but the pain is nearly euphoric—it is freedom. I am forcing my way out. I am a goddam butterfly.

I tip blindly over the panel, my hips still caught, and throw my hands out for balance. I am too far from the floor still to touch it. I sink as much weight into my feet as I can, and then dive sideways. The crate rocks, and then resettles. I leap again and again, faster and faster, and at last the cage tips over, and I crash to the side. The corner digs into my navel and the ceiling pushes on my spine. I kick and writhe and fight. I am free to my thighs. The metal scrapes along my skin. It is a meter of progress. Knees, calves, my feet are through, and I am free.

I stand and nearly topple back over.

How long has it been since I stood all the way up?

Between the rush of blood and the utter darkness, I have no sense of balance. I reach my fingers out and feel the counter, which runs along the left arc of the room and to the main door, I know.

The sound of my breathing fills the little room, hammers in my ears. Then the dial to the door is in my fingers. I turn it clockwise as I have seen Mr. Walks do. I feel the clicks coming through the metal. When it stops, I try to push it open, but it doesn't budge. It must be some kind of combination lock. I spin again, listening to see if there's any change in the sounds, feeling for any tension in the dial, but there's nothing. I try again and again. I spin the dial counterclockwise, then back to the right, like we do on our lockers at school. In my fingers, I swear I feel a new resistance. I must be close. The second the dial feels like it wants to stop, I let it and shove my shoulder against the door. I pound on it with my fists. I feel around for the seam of the doorway. The crack is so narrow, the sides so smooth, there's no way to gain leverage.

I am all at once too heavy for my legs, this defeat a stone in my belly. I sink to the floor. My sweaty skin grips the cool metal, and my descent makes a squeaking, screeching sound. Tears pour down. My heart shudders in my chest, and every piece of my skin I sacrificed to wriggle out of the cage now flares with acknowledgment. Every inch of me hurts—every ounce. But it is better than feeling numb.

I work my way to standing and feel out into the dark, searching for a light switch, when my fingertips graze the stiff, thin, curled edge of what Mr. Walks has called his instruments—pairs of lungs slit down their middles and pinned open, something thin and yellow and hard strung across the widest part, and I recoil, my hand trembling as if I've been shocked, my gasps echoing in the dark.

I stumble back and collide with the cool plastic of a fold-out chair. I lower myself into it. The sound of the dial turning fills the black air. Mr. Walks is back.

I could bolt for the door, which he will block, try to climb the ladder, which he'll yank me down from, shimmy through the sewer lid, which is secured with a padlock, and try to sprint across the field on legs too weak to stand.

I close my eyes and imagine the day on the Tarson Woods trail when Mr. Walks approached me, a smile on his face and despair in his eyes. As we walked along the highest bank of Cold River, I asked him what was wrong. In my mind, I rewrite the moment, and as he begins to answer, I shove him off the cliff.

MARTIN WALKED DOWN THE HALL OF TARSON HIGH SCHOOL, TWO steps behind an armed school resource officer. Tangerine lockers lined both walls, and Martin wondered if everyone here felt like a hamster in one of those plastic tunnels, or if it was just him.

In the past six hours, he'd lost almost every piece of the puzzle, and he damn near lost the case, again. If not for the lead on Jonathon Walks and confirming the existence of the little footpath that led from the rest stop where Toni was found to the edge of Tarson Woods, Captain would have pulled the plug.

Ama had checked herself out of the hospital against medical advice and hadn't yet shown back up at her apartment in Atlanta. No one they contacted admitted to knowing where she was, although Martin would've bet money Lindsey, who had yet to answer her phone, had a pretty good idea where she'd gone.

Martin also hadn't been able to track down a single address listed for a Jonathon Walks that matched Eddie's description of the teacher. He was almost glad Eddie was still semi-detained at the station. Otherwise he might vanish, too. Did a case exist if every person involved evaporated into thin air?

The officer stopped outside the door to the main office. Martin stepped past him and approached the desk.

"I'm Detective Martin Locklear. I called earlier," he said to the receptionist.

The receptionist stared at Martin as if he ought to have a name tag on. "Mrs. Brownlow is in her office." She pointed to the closed door behind her.

Martin rapped his knuckles against the wood and let himself in. Mrs. Brownlow sat at her desk, her face bathed in the light of a computer screen.

"Detective, take a seat." She scooted herself closer to her desk and turned off her monitor. "I understand you want to ask some questions about Hazel Stevens. What would you like to know?"

"Hazel began working with a vocal coach she met through a career day here," he started, straining all accusation from his tone. "Do you have records of the people who come to talk to the students during the event?"

"There's a flyer that goes out about a month beforehand—we send it home with students and post it at all the businesses in town. The school counselor lists his email as the contact, and if a professional is interested in attending, they sign up via email. Then there is a sign-in sheet the day of."

"Do you conduct any kind of checks on the people who come?"

"Mr. Locklear, I understand you're new in town, but for the most part around here, I see a name, I know the background."

"What can you tell me about Jonathon Walks?"

"He's quiet, polite, all-business type. He moved here a couple years ago. He's a vocal coach at a music shop in town, and he also volunteered as a teacher's aide for our chorus teacher for almost a year. The teacher has been battling some health issues for quite some time. Mr. Walks was a godsend, really. Very dedicated, very good with the students."

"So if he subbed, you have records for him."

"He wasn't technically a substitute. He was an aide; a volunteer."

"But he had access to your students," Martin stated.

"I'm sure he filled out the necessary paperwork, if that's what you're asking. He knows how to play every instrument we have, and he has ten years' professional experience in a recording studio. He exceeded every job qualification and then some, and while he was in the classroom he was consistently monitored by a school employee."

"Do you know where he lives?"

"Well, here, I imagine."

Martin dropped his pencil on his pad of paper, exasperated. "Do you know his address?"

"I would need to look through last year's archives. We haven't used him this year."

"I have time," Martin offered, leaning back.

"I don't, unfortunately. I'm actually running late for an important meeting. Now, on the phone I believe you said you wanted to speak to Hazel's teachers. This isn't really a good time, since students are present. Perhaps if you came back after school hours are over?"

"Perhaps I'll find the teachers on my own," Martin said, standing. "Thanks for all your help." He strode for the door.

"Mr. Locklear, you can't just wander school halls!"

"I have a badge and a gun. Looks like I have all the necessary qualifications to sub for your resource officer," Martin replied. "I'll stop back by on my way out. Do you think you can put your hands on that paperwork between now and then?"

Martin walked out of her office without waiting for a response, Mrs. Brownlow barking his name at his back.

Martin tucked his pad of paper, still blank, under his arm and walked down the main corridor, checking names on doors. Eddie had provided him a list of all of Hazel's teachers he could remember. Classes were in session, and a distracted teacher wasn't worth an interview, but he at least wanted to make initial contact. When he saw a name matched from the list, he waved to get the teacher's attention and handed them his card. On the back of each he'd already written: *Please call ASAP. Re: Hazel Stevens.*

Before returning to the parking lot, Martin swung through the main office. All Mrs. Brownlow had left was a handwritten note with the name and address of the music shop where Mr. Walks once worked, which Eddie had already given him.

Martin glared at the note as he shouldered through the door. For a man who'd been in Tarson for roughly two years, people didn't seem to know anything about him. The night-shift cashier at the grocery store already knew Martin on sight and knew to tell him when cashews were on sale if she saw he hadn't put any on the belt. How could a man fly under the radar so successfully, and, more important, why?

He was halfway across the lot when a flash of movement caught his eye—a woman walking slowly and gingerly from the side door of the school to the drive-through pickup area. She stopped at the curb and wrapped one hand around her side, fingers pressed into her back. He stopped in his tracks. A black car pulled up in front of her. Lindsey Harold hustled around the front of the car and opened the passenger door. The other woman turned, as if feeling Martin staring. It was Ama.

"Ama! Wait!" He started for the car. "Ama Chaplin!"

She slammed the door shut. Her profile disappeared behind a tinted window. The car pulled off and turned onto the two-lane road. Martin stopped jogging, but his mind began to race. The only reason Ama Chaplin would appear at Tarson High School was Hazel Stevens.

Within minutes, Martin was once again standing in the main office, nearly out of breath.

The secretary stared at him, her face the definition of underwhelmed. "Mrs. Brownlow has left campus for the rest of the day," she said.

"That's fine. That's not who I want to talk to. You just had another visitor. Name's Ama Chaplin. Who did she ask to speak with?"

"I don't think that's any of your business."

"You can tell me, or I can get a warrant to search your records. I have questions about a lack of proper credentialing for your volunteers and substitutes, so that would actually help me out *a lot*." He leaned over the counter. "Do you want to help me out a lot?"

"She spoke with Mrs. Brownlow and Mrs. Anderson, the chorus director."

Martin rocked back on his heels. "Is Mrs. Anderson with a class now?"

"No. She's probably on her way out, if she hasn't left already."

Martin whipped out of the office, mentally mapping where the chorus room had been when he'd given out cards earlier. He jogged the length of the hall and nearly collided with the teacher as he pivoted inside the open door. Mrs. Anderson hopped backward, clutching her chest.

"Oh, you scared me," she said, managing a laugh.

"I'm sorry," Martin said. "I came by earlier. I'm Martin Locklear with the Tarson PD."

"Yes, and here about Hazel Stevens. How can I help?"

"I heard Ama Chaplin came by to meet with you. Would you mind telling me what you two talked about?"

"Well, you probably already know. Ama Chaplin came by to discuss putting on a fundraiser to help the school. She was so grateful to the Tarson Police for saving her life and wanted to give back to the community. She said she spoke with the department about what she could do, and they said the school could use the help the most with the budget shortfall we're facing this year. Thank you for that, by the way." She smiled, catching her breath. "You know the arts are always the first to go when the money isn't there."

"You're welcome," Martin replied, managing to sound genuine despite knowing full well Ama hadn't once called the police department of her own volition since regaining consciousness. "Has she ironed out any details yet?"

"She wants to have a holiday silent auction on the courthouse lawn, right here in Tarson. They're going to string up lights and garland, bring in tents, a piano player, and a dance floor. She said she and her friends can donate some items and services that should bring in good money. Some businesses in Atlanta are on board, too, upscale restaurants, a day spa. It should be a lot of fun."

"So why did she bring this to you? Why not run it by Mrs. Brownlow?"

"She secured Mrs. Brownlow's approval first. But she came to speak to me because she wants to have the chorus perform. I suggested they sing the solo Hazel never got to sing last year, and she was moved to tears. She also wanted recommendations for local piano players."

Martin's thoughts turned immediately to Jonathon Walks. "Did she have any opinions about what kind of music or a performer? Did she ask if anyone specifically from the school other than the chorus could sing?"

"She didn't mention anyone from the school. She was adamant about having a live pianist and time for anyone from the audience to play. Get this—she even offered to sing. She said she's going to make sure the

Atlanta Journal-Constitution puts something in the paper about the auction, drum up some buzz."

"How soon is she thinking?"

"Well, she really wants to use the media attention around what happened to her and the generosity of the holiday season. She even mentioned she didn't mind some people coming who were just curious about the incident. She's hoping to get everything organized for some time before Christmas, if the courthouse will let her rent their lawn on such short notice. She's all business, that one."

"It would seem so."

"She's really pulling out all the stops. It sounds like the event is going to be beautiful and meaningful, definitely in the true spirit of the season. I'm just so glad to hear Mr. Stevens didn't shoot her on purpose."

"Did she tell you that?" Martin crossed his arms at his chest. So much for Ama not remembering anything. What the hell kind of game was she playing here?

Mrs. Anderson nodded. "I can't imagine how upset he must be. First Hazel, now this, with his gun accidently going off as he's trying to help Ms. Chaplin to her feet. They say lightning doesn't strike twice, but it sure seems to for Eddie. I'm just glad she lived to clear his name. Is he all right, Detective?"

"He's doing as well as could be expected," Martin answered, processing the information for any possible clues to Ama's motive. Was her goal simply to help clear Eddie's name? "Keep me in the loop with this," Martin continued. "I'd like to help with anything I can."

"I'll be happy to."

Martin started for the door, then turned, one more question on his mind. "Did she say what song she was going to sing?"

"'Stairway to Heaven,'" Mrs. Anderson replied.

MICHAEL

I TAKE A SEAT ACROSS THE TABLE FROM HAZEL. SHE GLARES AT ME, EYES black and white with no color between. Long, deep scrapes travel her legs, almost as though she outran a pack of wild dogs, but not without a tussle. She smells like a chase—sweat and earth and adrenaline.

"You don't understand what I'm trying to do," I say softly. "We will make music together. You are an instrument, Hazel. Fate chose you."

"We can make music anywhere," she pleads. "We can go back to the Music Box. I won't tell anyone."

"We can't make this kind of music in the public eye, not yet. You don't even understand it, and you *are* music, Hazel. What would your father think? Your teachers, other kids? As a culture, we're so afraid of pain. We shun it. We forbid it. But it sets us free. It brings out the best, Hazel. The purest pieces of our hearts, desires of our souls, notes of our songs. You can't sit around and plan this. You have to evoke it one beat at a time."

"Why do you want to hurt me?" Her expression melts, erasing all angles of maturation, and in front of me is a child, tears and mucus and confusion.

"I don't want to hurt you, Hazel. I want to set you free to follow Fate's path. She chose you. Once the world understands our music, we can let them see how we make it, but no one will let Fate write her song if they see the process before the product. It's like anything else. Bacon, cheese-burgers, sheepskin boots. If people had to see the process, most of them would never endorse the product."

"I didn't choose this," she whispers.

"You didn't have to. Fate chose you."

"Why does Fate get the final say?"

"She is the conductor, Hazel. We're here for her."

"Prove it." Sharpness returns to her features.

"I told you. Our paths crossed three times at random and—"

"No." She cuts me off. "This is a small town. People run into each other. Prove to me that Fate wants me to do this."

"You don't want Fate to prove herself," I say, suddenly feeling small, hearing the roar of the river. "It's a cruel experience."

"I won't believe in Fate until you show me the process," she says.

I pause, then stand and hold out my hand. "Remember when you are in her grip and she is squeezing you and saving you at the same time that you asked for this."

Hazel rises but doesn't accept my hand. She follows me to the pair of cabinet doors leading to the river. To the right is the escape tunnel my father and Bill dug and proofed two decades ago. To the left is my addition: a branch that tunnels not so far from the main chamber, but twice the depth. This tube doesn't end at the river—it ends in the water table.

I pry open the lid. Bill's eyes are two reflective circles in a swirling dark pool in the pit. The water is low, lapping around his waist. His arms tremble—whether it's from the cold or the fatigue of being suspended above his head with a chain, I can't guess. Maybe both. When the water table rises, pushing him up, at least his shoulders will be offered a reprieve.

"Oh, my God," Hazel says from beside me. "Sir? Sir!"

Bill's lips move and sounds come, but his words are chopped to syllables and single letters.

"Why are you doing this?" she demands of me. "What does Fate have to do with this man?"

"Fate didn't choose him. He came here on his own. He interfered. He chose this. I won't kill him. I keep him fed and watered. Fate keeps him alive, or she doesn't. His life is in her hands now. If you want to see if you are chosen by Fate, you can see whether or not she keeps you alive."

"How long are you going to make him stay in there?"

"Until my song is finished. If he lives that long, then he is meant to live. If he doesn't, then his life's purpose has already been fulfilled."

"You're crazy!"

I smile at her, doing my best to remember she's basically still a child. "I am trying to spare you the fight of discovery. Fate has picked your path, and I am sweeping it clean for you, Hazel."

She looks at me, our eyes meeting for a long moment. Then she turns back toward the pit, and she jumps.

MARTIN

MARTIN STEPPED OUT OF HIS CAR AND ONTO MAIN STREET, WHERE wind whipped between the two rows of buildings. He stuffed his hands in his jacket pockets, having left his notebook in the passenger seat, and walked into the Music Box.

An older man stood to greet him from behind a desk. He was wearing wire-rim glasses, a button-down shirt, and a V-neck sweater vest. This man, Martin thought, couldn't look more like a music nerd if he tried.

"Welcome," the man said. An accent made his word rise at a faster clip. German or Swedish, if Martin had to guess.

"Thank you. I'm Detective Locklear." He paused long enough to flash his badge. "Do you own this store?"

"Yes. I'm Bjorn Fleiss. I opened this store twelve years ago. I can show you my business license," he answered, fumbling with a drawer.

"That won't be necessary. I'm here to ask about Hazel Stevens," Martin started. He wanted to shout Jonathon's name, to search every photograph hanging in the building in hopes of finding his face, but Jonathon was clearly adept at hiding in plain sight, and if he felt any kind of pressure, he was likely to run far and long.

"Oh, that poor girl. Did they find her? I saw something on the news about her father."

"Don't believe everything you see," Martin summarized. "I'm new to the Tarson PD. The captain has asked me to give a few cold cases a once-over with fresh eyes. I'm starting with this one."

"She's worth every effort," Bjorn said.

"What can you tell me about the time she spent here?" Martin asked.

"She worked mostly on vocal training with my assistant, Jonathon Walks. She was very committed, very responsible."

"I don't remember reading anything about a Jonathon Walks in the original file. What can you tell me about him?" Martin asked, trying to sound as casual as possible.

"He worked at a recording studio in Atlanta for nearly a decade. He came in looking for a miniature piano and found a job instead." The old man smiled to himself, smitten with the memory.

"Is Mr. Walks here now?"

"No, he's taken a job in Dalton. He fills in for me when he can."

"Do you think he would be willing to speak with me about his time with Hazel, give me any insight into her mental state?" Martin asked carefully.

"I'm sure he would. He took time off after her abduction. He helped with the search."

"You called it an abduction," Martin interjected. "She was ruled a runaway."

"That girl would never run away. I don't know how anyone who spent any time with her could think that was a possibility. Jonathon felt the same way. He was sure someone had taken her."

"Is that so?" Martin tried not to look too interested.

"He would rant about it, fall to pieces. I had to send him home a couple of times."

"Does he still live in town? I think he could really help me understand Hazel better," Martin pressed.

The man shrugged. "He never mentioned moving."

"Do you happen to have an address or a contact number?"

"I have his number," the man said as he flipped through the pages of a three-ring binder. "I'll write it down for you."

"Do you also happen to have a picture of them together?" Martin asked, leaning over the counter to see if he could put eyes on a mailing address. But the ledger only had a phone number, a tally of hours worked, and corresponding payments—all even dollar amounts in increments of ten. Martin was almost sure from this information and its arrangement that Jonathon was paid in cash under the table.

"I don't. I tried once, but Jonathon was uncomfortable with the idea. He said Mr. Stevens was already apprehensive of how close the two had become and that a picture may be misunderstood. I am certain there was no inappropriate behavior between the two of them, though. They were never together behind closed doors. I never even saw him touch her. Not once. If he wanted her to adjust her position, he would demonstrate the change on himself and have her copy him."

"That's good to know," Martin said, handing him his card.

"If you're looking at Jonathon for this, you're wrong. I've never seen a man as devastated as he was after Hazel was taken—aside from her father, of course. I never would have guessed Mr. Stevens would shoot anyone, especially a woman. Everyone thought they had a happy little home, he and Hazel. But now . . . well, I don't know what to think. Is that why you're asking? Are the incidents related?"

"If we decide to connect them, I'm sure I'll be back to speak to you about that aspect of the case. But right now, I'm more interested in any relationships Hazel Stevens had outside the home."

"Yes, all right." The shop owner blinked rapidly behind his glasses. "After Hazel was taken, Jonathon didn't eat for weeks. It looked like he wasn't sleeping, either—bags under his eyes. The new job has helped him, though. The last time I saw him, he seemed back to his old self. Maybe . . . maybe don't bother him with this unless you have to," the man said.

"That's probably a good idea," Martin said, backing toward the door. "Why don't we keep the conversation between us?"

"Yes, I think that's for the best."

H
A
Z
E
L

MICHAEL DROPS THE LID IN PLACE. THE DARKNESS FEELS THICKER THAN the water, and my sense of balance tilts. I flail my hands out, searching for the wall. I splash more than I want to and have to remind myself that there aren't sharks circling my feet and that the only teeth to worry about are above me.

At last I touch a wall. It's bumpy under my fingers, and I find a hold on what feels like a notch on a tree.

The man's voice floods the black: "Grab . . . the chain . . . when the water . . . goes up."

"How long have you been here?" I ask, wondering how it could already feel like an hour since I jumped. I doubt it's been longer than a minute.

"I . . . don't know. What-day-is-it?"

"I don't know."

We stand in the silence.

"Sometimes the water goes almost to the top, about six inches of air to spare. Sometimes it all drains out. You'll want to take off your socks and shoes." He pants with the effort it's taken to deliver such a long message. "The skin on your feet will stay wet and rot if you keep them on."

I reach down and pull off my socks and shoes. I stuff the socks inside the toe of a shoe and hold them out of the water.

"Just let them go, honey. Save your strength. He only drops food down every couple days, and to drink . . . well, you're looking at it. Hold your bowels if you can. He'll drop a bucket once in the morning and once at night."

"He kept me in a cage before this and I got out of it. I just couldn't open the main door. I'm going to get out of here, and I'm going to need to run."

"Then you save them shoes. 'Cause you know what, you find a way through that main door, I can tell you the combination to the little cubby door behind the ladder. And when you get out . . ." His voice becomes weaker and is then overtaken by a cough. "You tell them that man's name is Michael Walton and that he didn't die at Cold River all those years ago. You got that?"

"You tell them," I say. "You tell them when you get out of here."

"Oncologist told me I had six months to live when I climbed that ladder into this shelter—only reason it was worth the risk. I'm not getting out of here alive. But what I will tell you is the story of Michael. He's stronger than you. He might be smarter, too. But the more you know about him, the more buttons you'll have to push."

I nod, waiting.

"When I met Michael, he was seven years old," the man begins.

I stare in the direction of his voice, but it's Mr. Walks's—Michael's— words in my head, his belief in Fate, that Fate would show me I'm meant to be here. In these first few minutes with this man in this hole, I have been shown one thing: I am not meant to be here at all.

MARTIN STOOD AT THE RECORDS DESK OF THE COUNTY COURTHOUSE, waiting for the clerk to review the log to see if Ama had booked space for her event yet. He watched handfuls of people walk down the long, wide hall that ran across the front of the building. He marveled at how much busier it seemed than the precinct. He'd been so focused on Ama, Hazel, and Eddie that he'd nearly forgotten that other crimes were being committed, that anyone had anything else to think about.

"Yes, here it is. The fundraiser is on the books for Saturday, December sixteenth," the court clerk told Martin.

Martin squeezed his hand to a fist—that wouldn't be soon enough. The *AJC* would beat them to it, and Hazel would be as good as gone.

"Looks like she convinced them to move a party they'd already committed. I guess it's hard to turn down someone with a gunshot wound, huh?" He flashed a grin.

Martin tried to wipe all judgment from his face. "I guess so," he replied, if only to keep the conversation going.

"She's supposed to email me a flyer to print out," the clerk said. "She definitely knew her way around. I guess all courthouses are set up mostly the same."

"What makes you think she knew her way around?"

"She was very specific about where and how she wanted everything set up, what parts of the building she wanted guests to have access to. She even knew where the bathrooms were and which doors would need to be left unlocked. She didn't ask where anything was."

Martin tapped a finger on the countertop. "Would you mind looking to see if she's tried a case here?"

"Sure." The clerk typed something on the keyboard, and his eyes flickered back and forth across the screen. "Nope, Anna Chaplin never tried a case here."

"Okay, thanks." Martin turned on his heel to leave and then stopped, keeping his hand on the counter. "Did you say 'Anna'?"

"Yes. Anna Chaplin?"

"Ama. Her first name is Ama with an 'm.'" Martin held his breath.

"Nope. No Ama Chaplin. There were a few old listings for an Ama Shoemaker," he said, his brow lifting.

"What are the specifics on the more recent cases?" Martin worked his lip under his teeth, a sudden craving rising in his blood.

"She's listed on a few trials in the late eighties." He trailed off, reading. "Her last listing is a criminal case back in 1989."

"What info can you give me on the last case?" Martin pressed.

"The defendant was Michael Jeffery Walton." The clerk dragged out the "n" sound as he moved the computer mouse around on the pad, clicking feverishly. Faster still was Martin's pulse, his mind painting the row of pictures taped to the whiteboard in room two. "Records are sealed on that one. Sorry I can't give you more."

"Thanks." Propelled by the new connection, Martin had to stop himself from bolting for the door. The two Amas were one and the same, no doubt, and this seventeen-year-old case was no coincidence. He needed to go back to the beginning of Ama's career, to the time when she was Ama Shoemaker. Had she married and divorced? The new attack didn't read as simple as a spurned ex-lover, but the lead certainly pointed to her past.

Was it someone who was angry Michael had walked away with a chance to start over? Was his death not of his own doing? Did someone push him into Cold River? The words found carved into a tree nearby would make more sense for a homicide: *I'm not sorry*. Ama would be a likely second target, having been the reason Michael went free. But where did Hazel fit?

Martin's thoughts traveled back to Jonathon Walks, a man who was known to have hiked every inch of Tarson Woods. Could Jonathon have been in the woods fourteen years ago and shoved Michael off a cliff? If that was true, Jonathon wasn't an outsider—Jonathon had returned.

AMA

AMA HUNG UP AND WROTE DOWN A FEW MORE ITEMS A COLLEAGUE HAD been willing to donate: a Prada handbag, a Chanel belt, and a sterling bangle from Tiffany's. Even if her plan didn't draw Michael out, she would definitely raise money for Hazel's school and try to clear all the mud off Eddie's name.

A cramp laced up her ribs and pulled tight, and she had to concentrate to breathe through it. She was pushing too hard, she knew, but she also knew it still might not be enough. She didn't know where Michael was, only that he'd been carrying her in the direction of the factory. She'd had rain and darkness on her side, no doubt slowing him down. She'd learned a police officer had been parked on the access road to the factory that night, too, in case she came out of the woods on that side, and she wondered if Michael had gotten close enough to see him, if that was a reason he had been so willing to wait when she had asked.

Overnight, she'd scoured maps of Tarson Woods and circled where she had fallen on the trail, the factory, and where the police had found her and Eddie Stevens. There were a few houses on the other side of the woods, too, including Michael's childhood home, but she doubted he was headed back there. Wherever he was, she needed to make sure he knew about the concert.

She looked again at her media checklist. She'd contacted every local news station in the state and emailed the news editor of the *AJC*, promising an exclusive interview after the event—and to forgive the misconduct of the reporter who'd snuck into her hospital room—if they'd run a full-page ad for the fundraiser, but she hadn't heard back yet. She needed to hit a few radio stations with advertising requests, too. Top 40 stations for the nameless, faceless crowd she hoped to draw beyond the perimeter of Atlanta for a philanthropic day in Small Town, USA, and classical and jazz stations for Michael.

Even still, there was a very real possibility Michael would see all of this for what it was and run in the other direction. Ama wasn't sure what would happen if she was able to draw him out, and she was glad to have a couple of weeks to figure it out. She hated to think of Hazel spending more time as his prisoner, but if Ama rushed in with a half-cooked plan, Hazel could be lost forever. At least now Lindsey could take over all the party logistics while Ama figured out how to set her trap.

Her phone rang. The screen flashed a number and the location it was tied to: Savannah, Georgia. Detective Martin was calling again. She looked away and out her motel window, watching cars sail down the state route. Someone moved in front of her view. Detective Martin Locklear peered back at her from the other side of the glass, his phone pressed to the side of his head.

"You have got to be kidding me." She dropped the curtain.

Her phone beeped. Martin had left a message. Ama punched in her passcode and listened: "Ama *Shoemaker*, this is Detective Martin."

She startled at the use of her old name, paused the message, and started it over again. It hadn't been a figment of her imagination; he'd called her by her old name. She'd known leaving her name on the reservation for the courthouse was a risk, but she had to use any detail that would tempt Michael to come out.

The only way to get Hazel out was to get someone in—and if Ama was right, there was only one person Michael needed for his song, one person he'd risk himself to catch. If the cost was a pill-popping, washed-up detective finding out she'd changed her name, so be it.

Martin tapped the glass on her window, and her phone rang again. She picked it up and accepted the call.

"You found my old name. Congratulations," she nearly spat.

"That's not what I'm calling about, at least not yet. I need to speak with you about Michael Jeffery Walton."

Ama's fingers went slack, and the phone slid through, thudding against the thin carpet. Martin must have linked her old name with the old case, but to what end? She limped to the door, drew herself as straight as she could stand, and let him in.

"Surprised you're staying in town," Martin said. "But then again, you do have a big event to plan. Thank you for the kind words you said about the PD and Eddie Stevens to Mrs. Anderson, by the way. Hate it when a guy goes away for attempted murder when he doesn't have to."

"What can I do for you, Detective?" She had to remind herself not to touch her side, not to press her hand against the dull ache that throbbed every time she breathed.

"Actually, I'm not here to ask about you. I need to ask you a few questions about a former client."

"You know that violates attorney-client privilege."

"The client in question is dead."

Ama looked down and touched the tip of her tongue to the roof of her mouth in an attempt to freeze her expression. She could not let the police know Michael was still alive. She could not let them in on her plan. They would take over, make it too big, too loud. She would lose all control over it and the entire situation, and Michael would see it coming from a mile away.

"That doesn't negate attorney-client privilege, and you know it," she finally answered.

"His face is on my board, and I know nothing about him. Seems like nobody does," Martin said.

"What board?" Ama's curiosity was piqued. "*My* investigation board? Why?"

"I have a row of pictures of people who walked into Tarson Woods and never came out. I think we have a serial killer on our hands, and I don't think it's Eddie Stevens. You're on that board. Maybe you shouldn't be. Maybe you are the factor that's throwing this whole thing out of whack. I've thought about this over and over, and I am going to level with you, Ama. I think something really fucking terrifying happened in those woods, so scary that you do not under any circumstance want to draw the attention of whoever grabbed you off that trail."

Ama sucked her cheeks in. The truth was right there, screaming in her brain, knocking on her teeth.

"Let's pretend you're right," she started. "What does that have to do with Michael Walton?"

"That's what I'm trying to figure out." He leaned forward, and a pen clicked in his hand. "I don't think he jumped into Cold River."

Ama felt all at once exposed and on the cusp of falling, plunging from somewhere impossibly high.

"What do you think happened?" she asked.

"I think he was pushed. And standing here now, watching you fidget, I'm wondering if you knew. I'm wondering if you know who did it."

Ama snorted then, too on edge to control herself.

"That's funny to you? Interesting. I'm obviously getting warm here. Hell, maybe it was you. Maybe you carved those words in the tree after you shoved Michael off the highest point. I wasn't going to bring up your past, which I spent my entire night researching, by the way. Shit childhoods aren't generally targets I take aim at, but you did just laugh about a dead kid.

"Did you have a hand in Michael's death, Ama? Did your father teach you how to cover stuff up? He was good at making some truly heinous, soulless shit look and smell like a garden of roses. That's what he was known for, what he was hired to do, right? People who are dealing illegal weapons, trading them for ten-year-old girls and bricks of cocaine, they generally want the best when it comes to creating a smoke screen to cover up what they're doing." Martin finally paused, shrugged. "I mean, we're all good at something."

"He didn't know," was all Ama could say, gasping for breath, pain ripping through her as if she'd been shot all over again.

"Of course he didn't. What father would cover up a trade of other men's daughters?" Sarcasm turned his voice to venom, and Ama immediately felt paralyzed. "They had him by the throat, blinders on his eyes, right? He was just doing his job. He didn't know. He wasn't involved. He was just keeping a completely separate log for all those vans and didn't ask any questions because he was a naïve, innocent, *good* man, right?"

In her mind, Martin fades away, and Ama saw her mother screaming at her father in their yellow kitchen, air sliding under the cracked window behind the sink, ruffling the sheer curtains. *Is that how we can afford this house on a dispatcher's salary, Paul?*

Her father had reached over and slammed the window shut. It was the only time she'd ever seen him use force on anything. He'd pointed his finger in her mother's face then, whispering so loud Ama could feel his voice in her bones: *We'll pack up, cash out our accounts, leave here. Start over. I just need a week, Grace. Give me a week. Then everything will be okay.*

Ama could still imagine her nine-year-old self, corn silk hair and freckled cheeks framed with two white balusters, tears sliding down as she watched them from the top of the stairs. Her best friend, Durante, had sat beside her as she listened to her parents yell. He'd threaded his fingers through hers, leaned his head on her shoulder. She'd pressed her forehead to their hands and noticed how his fingers smelled like tree bark and books.

Now, thirty-five years later, with twenty of them spent in the justice system, there were still pieces of her father's case and alleged crimes she didn't wholly understand. He dispatched trucks, plotted routes, and handled payments. He answered to higher-ups, did what they told him to do. He didn't decide, couldn't have known, what was actually in the cargo loads. But then he found out. A driver lost control of the truck, and, as per strict company guidelines, called dispatch instead of 911. Her father, Paul Chaplin, had answered. The driver reported hearing strange noises coming from his cargo. Paul had driven out to meet him, and they'd discovered two girls in wooden crates crammed near the front of the closed cargo compartment.

He wouldn't have gone if he'd known what they'd find. If he was guilty, he would have sent someone else. This was the one truth that had kept Ama's faith in her father afloat in a sea of doubt and accusations.

He wouldn't have gone.

Now Ama was a woman who knew a girl was in danger, in the hands of a monster, her life and body being traded for sound, and Ama wasn't going to the police, wasn't following the rules. What if she died between now and the auction? What if her plan didn't work and Michael didn't come?

"Ama, I am begging you here," Martin said, and the sound of his voice wrestled her from her haze of memories. "I know you know more than you are saying. You of all people know firsthand what kind of damage covering up the truth can do, the innocent people who get hurt as collateral damage. I can help you, but you have to help me."

"Get out," she said. Her wound throbbed. She pushed a hand against it and leaned into the pressure.

"Ama," he said, and reached a hand for her.

"Do not touch me. Get out of my room," she said through her teeth. "This conversation is over until you have a court order to continue it."

"Just tell me one thing," Martin said quickly. "One thing and I will leave."

"No."

"Is Hazel still alive?" he asked anyway.

The question hung between them, and the air was just as still inside Ama's lungs. She didn't dare breathe in case her mouth shaped the exhale into the truth.

"The *AJC* is running a story outlining a theory that Hazel's still alive, based largely on the fact that you said her name when you woke up from surgery," Martin said. "I'm sure you have an idea of what that kind of pressure might do in a captive situation. I know you have some kind of plan here. I'd like to help you, and help Hazel. Please."

Ama stayed silent, concentrating on breathing past the pain swelling in her chest. She squeezed her fingers together to keep her hands from shaking, tried to ignore the sensation of sinking through the floor.

"You have my number," he continued. "It's in your call history about a dozen times. If you decide you want to help Hazel, you know how to reach me."

Martin put a hand on the door and paused a final time. "The story is running in the Sunday paper, front page," he said, his voice soft. "If this auction is meant to help find Hazel, December sixteenth will be too late." He let himself out of her room without closing the door behind him.

Ama slid to the floor, everything inside her, every moment, every memory, dissolving into a pool of doubt. What if she couldn't pull this off? What if Hazel was already dead? What if Michael got to Ama first and no one cared enough to look, the families of victims rejoicing in their online chat rooms and websites?

Above all of it, though, one question rose like a ghost from the fog, hung in the air, stole her breath, stilled her heart: What if her father hadn't been innocent?

She hugged her knees, weeping and shaking, her father's voice in her head and the heart of a nine-year-old girl cracking wide-open in her chest.

MARTIN

MARTIN SAT IN HIS CAR OUTSIDE JANIE WALTON'S HOUSE, WATCHING her feel for a flowerpot with a cane, a golden retriever with a service harness perched on the stoop. His thoughts were still in Ama's motel room. He replayed the conversation in his head, closing his eyes the moment he saw her come unglued—the moment he reminded himself of his own father. Martin had to admit to himself he would've responded the same way Ama had: shutting down, closing him out. He could only hope he hadn't lost her for good.

He exhaled, refocusing, and pushed his door open, then gently closed it after climbing out. He was acutely aware of every sound and every move he made. He walked up, nearly waving in greeting, and clasped his hands behind his back. The dog let out a quiet bark. Mrs. Walton stood upright and cocked her head a bit.

"Who's there?" she called out.

"Mrs. Walton, I'm Detective Martin with the Tarson Police Department. Would you mind if I take a few minutes of your time?"

"What's this about?" she asked.

"Your son."

Mrs. Walton deflated. "Come on in."

Martin trailed Mrs. Walton and her dog inside, the going slow, the cane tapping in front of her.

"Please sit," she said, feeling her way toward a wingback chair.

Martin sat down on an old velour couch. There were no pictures in the parlor room—not on the wall, not on a table surface. It felt more like the waiting room at a doctor's office than a home.

"Mrs. Walton, I am sure this is a difficult subject for you, but I need to ask you some questions about Michael. What was he like? What were his interests? Those sorts of things."

"Are you referring to his interests in animals?"

"Anything, ma'am."

"To talk about Michael, we need to talk about me. I was a firm mother. Expected a lot. After my daughter died, and then my husband passed, my world became very dark, and Michael—" Her voice broke. "Michael was where I put all that darkness. I remember I would be so angry." Her fingers squeezed so hard into fists that her knuckles blanched. "Rage. Just . . . rage." She reached for the back of her head and needled a finger into her scalp.

"A few years ago, a clinic in Atlanta started testing anyone who worked at the factory for cancer, free of charge," she continued. "Bill, a friend of my husband's, insisted I go. He took me, and we were tested together. *Tumors* had stolen my sight—not my grief, not my son, not the river. Cancer, and that damn factory. For Bill, it stole the end of his life. His cancer was terminal; his tumors were inoperable. A year or so ago he left town. I imagine he was checking off a bucket list of sorts. Most of us in Tarson don't leave much, if ever. My tumors were operable—a cluster in my brain and one on my kidney. It makes sense now, things I thought I'd seen, the way an emotion would spark and then grow and roar. And Michael, God forgive me. Michael was the only target I had."

"What are you saying, exactly, Mrs. Walton? Do you feel you mistreated your son?"

"Oh, yes. I blame myself for everything."

"Are you referring to the trial?" Martin asked carefully. "Or your son's suicide?"

A smile broke over Mrs. Walton's wrinkled face. "My son didn't jump to his death in that river," she said. "I know people think so. I let them think so. But I can tell you that river would not see my son dead. I tried, Detective."

"You tried what, exactly?" Martin reached for his pad and pen.

"Early one morning, when Michael was twelve, I heard him open the refrigerator then leave the house. I watched him from my window. He went to our neighbor's property, stood behind a tree, and lured her cat to him with a piece of sandwich meat. I wasn't seeing well—my peripheral vision was all but gone, and what was left had double imaging. But then later that week I found a dead cat in the yard, eyes plucked out, heart in a Dixie cup, belly split open. The next morning, I heard him leave again, earlier this time, and I followed him. He went into Tarson Woods. I caught up with him. I took him to the river, and I pushed him in."

"Mrs. Walton, it's my understanding that Michael died in Cold River when he was eighteen."

"I didn't say he drowned. I pushed him in. I chased him downstream, waiting for him to go under and stay under, but the river spat him out. I told him . . . I told him he had to prove his life was destined for something great to keep it, that I wouldn't let him suffer this town for no reason, and I made him jump two more times. But the river wouldn't keep him. And come dawn, what was left of my vision had gone dark. You see, it doesn't matter how many times he jumped into Cold River. He could've tied cinder blocks to both feet, and the river would still have found a way to save him. And I swear, it punished me for trying to keep him in it."

"I thought you said the tumors affected your sight."

"They were part of it, to be sure. But you aren't from around here, are you, sir? You don't know the way this town works, the way it holds on to people. For a few months after my diagnosis, I thought all of it was tumors. But now my tumors are gone and the light treatments I do have helped me regain minimal sight. But I still hear the river. I still feel nervous every time I get close to the county line."

Martin smiled, nearly disregarding her suspicions, but then he remembered the pull of the Tarson police station, the little job post on a message board, the way he couldn't stop staring at it. But his obsession with this town had everything to do with Toni Hargrove . . . didn't it?

"So if you don't think Michael drowned in the river, what do you think happened to him? Why would he carve *I'm not sorry* into a tree?"

"I used to teach piano, and I thought I could make him better than I had been, find him a ticket out of this town if he could just play well enough. But he had no ear for music. Utterly talentless, and to hear it would just rile my blood. He would cry and snot and say he was sorry, and I would bark at him, 'Don't be sorry, be better. Sorry doesn't do anything for me!'" She was yelling by the end of the recollection, her face distorted.

Martin sat back. If this was a cancer-free Mrs. Walton, Martin couldn't fathom spending time with her *and* her tumors.

"The message was for me," she concluded. "I believe he was telling me goodbye. He was leaving . . . to be better."

"So why let people believe he's dead if you think he's still alive?"

"I owe him that much. After what I did, what he did, the trial, the way his father died . . . there was no life for him here."

"What do you think Michael would mean by 'better'? What would his dream be?"

"A doctor, maybe. Or a coroner." A bitter smile pulled at her face. "He liked to understand how things worked. I really think that's what he was doing with those animals. Maybe he found them dead."

"You don't really believe that," Martin pressed.

"I don't know what to believe anymore. But I do know he wanted to be great. I could feel it in him. He got that from me. He just didn't get the talent to back it up." She held up her hands and stretched her spindly fingers wide. "I was made for the piano. Michael had the deck stacked against him—a short reach, no ear, no feel for the keys. He just needed to find his instrument.

"Before I lost my sight, I found a few blank pages of composition paper in his room. He was going to try to write a song. He'd titled it 'Molly's Song.' Molly was his sister's name. She lived a matter of minutes. The silence in the house, in the nursery, when there should have been coos and squeals and cries, it was the loudest thing I've ever heard. I think he wanted to fill that silence for me."

Martin jotted down some notes, until a thought struck him between the eyes and he put his pen down.

"Mrs. Walton, do you think there's any chance your son would ever come back to Tarson?"

"Not of his own free will," she started. "But Tarson has a way of drawing people back, and that river . . . I swear that water runs in his veins. Detective, can I ask you something?"

"Sure," Martin answered.

"Do you believe in Fate?"

AMA SAT ON THE FLOOR OF HER MOTEL ROOM. BESIDE HER WAS A nearly empty suitcase. Before today, she hadn't opened it in over a decade. It was hard to imagine that ten years had passed since the day she organized all the evidence and information she'd ever found on her father's case and filed it inside this piece of luggage. Five hours ago, Lindsey had brought it to her motel room on her request, along with a takeout container of chicken soup Ama hadn't asked for. Now, the soup sat untouched where Lindsey had left it, and most of the contents of the suitcase were arranged around Ama in a circle, organized in chronological order.

The room was silent, a Do Not Disturb tag hung on the outside doorknob, the motel phone unplugged from the wall, and Ama's cell phone switched off. Her mind roared. She jotted down thoughts as they came, typed fragments of information into a search engine, and wrote down anything that stuck out, desperate for a linchpin, a foundation stone: the beginning of this thirty-year-old crime, something neither attorney had ever been capable of providing at trial.

She wanted to believe now like she had then that her father hadn't known what was going on, that all he took in that deal gone bad was the fall. But she also remembered the two-story house they'd moved into, the four-poster canopy bed she'd slept in, the gleaming new car her father had driven home one Friday evening and the look on her mother's face when he'd pulled into the driveway and said he was taking them out to eat. If he hadn't known, hadn't suspected, had he at least wondered why he was being paid so much to route freight trucks?

She wished her mother were alive to sit on this floor with her and sort these pieces of her father's life. She had only been nine when he was arrested, eleven when he was convicted, fifteen when he died. As an adult looking back, she knew she was remembering only the very best and very worst moments—that there were days' and months' and years' worth of moments that had faded from her memory. But from a young age she'd known her father was innocent, good, wrongly put away, and this truth had made her who she was, what she was, had steered every step of her path.

Ama worked through the night, sifting pieces, turning over proverbial stones. She wasn't sure what she was looking for, what grain of evidence would be heavy enough to tip the scales one way or the other. The weight of uncertainty pushed down hardest of all, locked her to her spot on the floor. Her legs cramped beneath her, and her shoulder ached from propping herself up on her hand. Her eyes were so tired from reading in low light that she had to squint to keep the small letters from blurring. At last, she curled up like a cat and drifted into a fitful sleep within the circle of her father's past.

H
A
Z
E
L

Chapter 60 | December 31, 2005 | Tarson, Georgia

THROUGH THE GRATE, I HEAR THE CABINET DOOR OPEN, AND MICHAEL'S footsteps echo down into the hole. For once I don't mind the distraction. For the last untold number of hours, I've only been able to hear the memory of Bill's yawning, last breath. I swear it's still echoing even now.

The cable is pulled taut by his weight. His forehead is resting on my knees, and I don't dare to kick out for fear of dislodging him. The vision of him knocking against the wall is not one I am willing to let become reality if I can help it.

The lid slides open, pulling Bill's hands and wrists above water. Michael lords above me, backlit from light spilling in from the main room. His expression becomes elated the moment he realizes it's just my face staring back at him.

"You see, Hazel. You see. Fate chose you."

"You put me in here with a cancer-stricken old man who had been in here for God knows how much longer than me," I spit back at him. "It would only be Fate if the fight had been fair. There was nothing fair about that."

"Who said fair had anything to do with Fate?" Michael cocks his head to the side. "I find it's actually quite the opposite."

"Then yeah, sure. Call it whatever you want."

Michael plucks the ladder from the wall. I tremble with weakness and the constant exposure to cold and water. My shorts sag on my hips, heavy with water and now two sizes too big. Yet my mind remains strong, steel forged in fire, and I conjure an image of reaching the top rung, grabbing his ankles, and yanking his legs from beneath him, watching him disappear in the black water before dragging the grate over the hole and locking it shut. But this plan can only exist in my mind, keeping me warm from within. There are two other things tending to that internal fire, two secrets Bill told me before he died: the code to the door behind the main ladder, and how to find the gun he'd hidden beneath the false floor of his locker in the basement of the factory. But there is one door I can't open between me and that gun. One door I can't open between me and the rest of the world.

I grip the ladder. My arms shake harder. My legs wobble, feeling loose and disconnected at the knees. I drag myself up the rungs, colder with every step.

"I need my shoes," I say, bending to retrieve them from where they're tied.

"First, you need a bath," he says as he slips a cord around my neck like a choke collar for a dog.

We walk into the main bunker, me ahead of him, and take an immediate left through another pair of cabinet doors. We have to duck to fit under the counter, and the grade immediately turns downhill. My back and core are too sore and weak to carry my body at the angle, and I am forced to crawl. The floor of the tunnel is dry and clean, as if it's been swept. Michael's feet fall behind me. He doesn't apply pressure on the leash, keeping the distance between us the same, and I resent the twinge of unbidden gratitude.

The slope levels off, and I feel cold sand under my palms. I strike the crown of my head as the tunnel narrows and I hear Michael drop to all fours, his knees scuffle, and the collar jerks at odd intervals with the disunion in our movement. He pulls on the wire, and it bites so hard into my throat that I cry out and rock back, desperate to loosen it. I imagine the cord cutting into my skin, blood running down, and I start to thrash.

"Stop." Michael feels around my shoulders for the wire and loosens the pressure. "I will have to keep this drill in mind. That was a nice sound, high octave. You gave me chills."

"I'm not going to sing for you," I rasp. "Never again. Not another note."

"You will. Everyone does."

Ahead, the utter blackness gives way to a crescent of moonlit dark and a burst of fresh air. I hear moving water and can smell the pine-sap-and-rotting-leaves scent of the forest. Michael holds me still with the leash and wriggles past me, leaving the tunnel first, where the top and bottom thirds of his body disappear from view. He stands still, waiting. I do not want him to pull the leash again.

I hoist myself out with my hands and immediately have to duck so I don't hit my head on a tangled overhang of roots from a fallen tree, which all but conceals the tunnel. When the water is high, it would be completely submerged. I will not allow him to drag me up that tunnel again. I draw in a breath, flooding my lungs to bursting, and scream.

The collar snaps tight around my neck, and then I am flung backward so fast and hard that I land on my back before I even think about throwing my hands down to catch my weight. The collar draws tighter still. I can gasp in tiny breaths, but exhaling past the pressure is nearly impossible.

"No," he scolds. I struggle to my feet, desperate for slack, but the knot doesn't slide back. It takes every ounce of willpower left in me to not lean away as he reaches for the knot and draws the loop toward him. "Not a sound," he says.

I plant my hands on my knees, heaving air, and wonder if even this is too loud.

His fingertips press into my back between my shoulder blades and steer me to the water's edge. We walk out together, each of us submerged to our armpits. The current tugs me downstream, and I have to lean against it to keep from drifting. He cups water and spills it into my hair. I shake so hard my breaths become choppy, and my teeth clatter together.

Michael hovers over me and samples the air. "That's better," he says. "Once you're dry, we'll get to work."

"I won't sing for you," I whisper.

"You will."

"I won't." I clamp my teeth together to keep them from chattering.

Michael walks back to me until our faces are inches apart. "If I can't make you sing, I will make you speak. You'll see," he says.

AMA

Chapter 61 | 7:30 AM, December 6, 2006 | Tarson, Georgia

AMA WOKE TO POUNDING ON THE DOOR AND LINDSEY'S VOICE CALLING her name. The numbness of sleep slipped from her like a blanket sliding away, and instantly she was chilly and sore from half a night spent on hard ground. She pushed herself to standing, teetering on bare feet, then limped to the door and cracked it open. Morning light burned her tired eyes, and she shielded her face with her hand.

"Lord have mercy, Ama. Are you okay?" Lindsey asked, taking stock of Ama. "Did you . . . are you hungover?"

"I'm fine. Why are you here? I don't need you. I didn't call you."

"I called *you*. About twenty times." Lindsey peered past Ama, probably trying to see if Ama had anyone else in the room with her.

"Just me. Sorry to disappoint you."

"What the hell is going on?" Lindsey asked, and her expression hardened.

"I'm working on something. You talk too much, and I can't think with all that blabbing," she snapped.

Lindsey frowned at her, and for a second Ama wondered if Lindsey was about to cry, wondered, too, at the guilt stirring under her ribs. Then Lindsey planted a hand on the door and shoved it completely open. Ama nearly stumbled in her effort to get out of the way. Light flooded the room and illuminated the ring of paper, the unopened dinner, the empty suitcase.

"What is all this?" Lindsey asked as she strode inside.

"It's not your business." She moved in front of Lindsey, but Lindsey walked around her.

"This is all from your father's trial." Lindsey glanced back at her. Then her gaze shifted to the empty suitcase. "Is that what you had me bring up here last night?" She walked the circle of information, two chronological arcs meeting at top and bottom, the left half for innocence, the right side for guilt. "What are you looking for?" Lindsey asked softly.

"The beginning." The confession fell from Ama, heavy and barbed, and it took pieces of her with it as it left her body.

"Why?"

"What if he was guilty?" She can barely speak the words.

"What if he was?" Lindsey echoed.

"I've built my whole life around knowing he was innocent, knowing beyond a shadow of a doubt they'd put an innocent man away. I have been determined to put the system on trial ever since. But what if they weren't wrong? What if, all this time, I've been wrong, and the system worked?"

"Having faith in your father doesn't make *you* wrong, no matter what he did or didn't do."

"Doesn't it, though?" Ama turned away from the pressure of Lindsey's attention and caught herself staring at a photograph she'd tucked into the netting of the suitcase. Her and her father, at a park for her eighth birthday.

"You were a little girl with a father who adored you. You weren't on trial then, and you're not on trial now."

"It feels like I am," Ama said. She leaned back against the wall and ran her fingers over the textured surface, anchoring herself to the present.

"Why does it all matter right now?" Lindsey asked, her voice suddenly firm. "Is it because of what happened to you? You think you got shot by a stranger because you defend guilty people?"

"I don't know."

"The Ama Chaplin I know doesn't think the world works that way," Lindsey said.

"I'm not sure I even know who I am anymore. I know how that sounds. God, I know how that sounds." Ama tsked at herself. "I set out to put the system on trial, to force it to be better, to shine a light on all the trapdoors innocent people can fall through. And for all these years, I've felt like whatever hurt I've caused other people along the way was just the price of doing business, the cost of revealing a larger truth. What if, all this time, I've been dead fucking wrong?"

Lindsey watched her for a minute. "I've seen you lose cases. I've seen you put the fear of God in the minds of monsters. I've seen you pull out that newspaper article in your bottom desk drawer from the day your father was convicted and stare at it for your entire lunch break. But I have never seen you question yourself or why you do what you do.

"Because you are good, better than good, which means you force prosecutors to work harder, you force the system to honor our most basic foundational principal in a court of law: *innocent until proven guilty. That* is the beginning, Ama. That's the only thing that matters. I don't know what you're going through, but I know you well enough to see that whatever this is, it isn't just about you and it isn't just about your dad. I think it has something to do with whatever really happened in Tarson Woods. I know you won't tell me everything, and that's okay. You don't have to. But if you want me to help you, you do have to tell me what you actually need."

Ama looked at the circle of evidence as if seeing it for the first time. *Innocent until proven guilty.* She of all people understood how sometimes evidence lied, how every single finger and test and lead could point to someone innocent. She couldn't change the outcome of her father's trial from the floor of this motel, and even if she stumbled upon irrefutable proof her father had been innocent, he was dead. There was no changing that.

Had she launched herself into his trial because it seemed easier, less overwhelming, than finding Michael and Hazel? Their case—her case—was over her head and out of her league, no question. But then whose league did it belong in? The justice system had failed to convict Michael, and this town had been staring at his face for two years and had no idea. She couldn't hand off the one chance to bring him down and bring Hazel back alive to the department that kept fucking it up.

With a start, the simplest of truths presented itself to Ama: *she* was putting herself, her life, her work, on trial. But Lindsey was right—Ama knew exactly *who* she was, and that value wasn't something she was willing to put on trial for anyone. Guilty people didn't go free because the defense was too good; they walked because the prosecution hadn't been good enough.

"Lindsey . . ." Ama trailed off and clamped her teeth briefly down on her lip, organizing her thoughts, focusing them ahead instead of in the past. The fundraiser was still the best option she could think of to draw Michael out of hiding and into the public eye; her instincts hadn't been wrong there. But if Martin was right about the timing of the news article, he was also right about the event being too late for Hazel. Even if the *AJC* agreed to delay the story, she couldn't be sure they wouldn't tease it somewhere. The date of the event would have to be moved to this Saturday. At least she hadn't sent off the press releases yet. She could only hope that with more money, the promise of press, Lindsey's ability to talk people into anything, and the opportunity to look like good Samaritans, everyone would be willing to accelerate the logistics.

"I'm not going to tell you everything," Ama began again.

"That's okay," Lindsey said. "I'm used to it. Just tell me enough."

MICHAEL

I SPRINT DOWN ONE LAST HILL, DARTING BETWEEN TREES, AND BURST into the field surrounding the factory. Overhead, the clouds part and I am spotlighted by the moon, which washes the wet, dead grass in a silver glow. Mist rises from the damp earth, swallowing me from all sides, hiding me from anyone peering down from higher ground.

I have lost Ama for now, but it would appear I have not lost all favor with Lady Fate. *Protect yourself, protect our work*, she seems to say.

When Eddie appeared in the dark, I thought I was seeing things the way I saw Timmy's ghost on the bank of Cold River. Then Eddie spoke, fired the gun, the blast tearing apart the dark, echoing in the chambers of my ears. How could I not have foreseen that this piece would be the most challenging, that Lady Fate would make sure I earned it?

I laugh in spite of myself as I pry open the cap to the underground bunker. The harder this becomes, the more opposition we face, the closer we must be to the most perfect song.

I steal down the ladder and crack open the main door. Hazel sleeps huddled in the corner between the concrete wall and the metal shelving unit. Her forehead rests on her knees. Her elbows frame the sides of her face, and her shackled wrists swing back in forth in tiny movements, pitched and dangling ahead of her like a diver leaning over the side of a pool.

I creep across the floor to retrieve Hazel's recorder from the counter. Then I walk back out of the bunker, leaving the door open a hair. I climb up the ladder just high enough to peer aboveground and make sure no one has ventured this way. I am still alone, cloaked in fog and night. I rewind

Hazel's tape to the very beginning, then move my thumb over the play button. This is a risk, but it is one I need to take. If I play this and Hazel—the real Hazel underground, chained to my wall—makes a sound, we will have to leave here, and I will have to trust that Ama will come back to me another way, another time. But if I play this and Hazel remains silent, then we are meant to stay, and Lady Fate will take care of the rest.

I draw a breath, hold it, and press play.

"Hazel!" Eddie's recorded voice sails across the field, spills down the tunnel, slides through the crack I left in the door. I notch the volume louder. "Hazel! Ha-zy?"

Eddie's voice pleads with her absence. I remember the day I recorded it, as we searched the same area where he'd caught Ama and I just now, how I hoped he wouldn't realize I wasn't calling out for Hazel, too.

From inside the bunker, I hear the chain knock against the metal pipe frame of the shelving unit, the scuffle of Hazel's feet drawing under her.

"Hazel! Can you hear me? Hazel!"

I lean into the hole, ear turned and straining to detect the smallest whisper, but Hazel remains true to her vow of silence. If Eddie really was up here, treading across this field, crying out for his daughter, she wouldn't answer.

All things for a reason.

Lady Fate was right to condition Hazel to silence. When will I stop second-guessing the process just because it isn't happening on my schedule?

We can stay, and Ama's time is now. All I have to do is wait for Fate to shine her light. I shake my head at myself, relief spreading through me cool and tingling, and lower myself back into the earth.

EDDIE

EDDIE WAS NEARLY ASLEEP ON THE COUCH WHEN MARTIN SWUNG OPEN his door. Since they'd begun investigating the case, Eddie had taken to sleeping during the morning. He'd worked nights before and was well practiced at snatching sleep when he could, but between the sleeping arrangements and Hazel's case on the forefront of his mind of every waking minute, sleep seemed as evasive as the criminal they were hunting. He couldn't turn it off, and even if he tried, he'd be so overridden with guilt that he'd never be able to get comfortable enough to doze off.

After he'd gone the first two days there without a wink of sleep, he'd finally found a way to make his mind hold Hazel close and let go of consciousness at the same time. He would close his eyes and conjure the trail along Cold River in his mind. He imagined her walking behind him, where he could hear but not see her, and he counted her footsteps, one-two, one-two. At last, the office fell away and he walked through dreams with his daughter.

If only he could see her. But even in his dreams, he couldn't turn around, couldn't find her face or feel her breath, and when he woke, he would realize it was his own heartbeat he had been listening to. Waking up began to feel like dying anew.

Eddie sat up, alarm coursing through him. "What happened?" he asked, and in the split second it took Martin to answer, Eddie's mind filled with the two worst possibilities: they'd found Hazel's body, or they'd found proof that whoever had her had left Tarson.

"Absolutely nothing," Martin said, and his face sagged. Eddie noticed how tired he looked, how gray, and he wondered if that was Martin's worst possibility: that nothing would ever be found. "But I want to go look for something in Tarson Woods, and I'll need your help to find it."

Eddie practically leaped from his seat on the couch. He hadn't been out of the station since he'd been processed, hadn't seen the sun or breathed fresh air. He wondered if it would feel different outside the same way the confirmed possibility of Hazel still being alive changed everything inside, and he realized he felt alive again, too.

"Put this on," Martin said, and tossed Eddie a navy blue hoodie with an emblem from the Savannah Police Department. "It'll be too small, but this way you aren't walking around the woods in prison scrubs. Plus it frosted overnight. You're going to want an extra layer."

Eddie's heart sank, his elation with it. Hazel would be out in this cold somewhere. He doubted she was being held somewhere soft and warm. Someone who would abduct and keep another person probably wasn't too concerned with their comfort, especially if Martin's contact out of Savannah had ended up in the same hands as whoever had Hazel. He flinched at the thought, closed his eyes against the pictures resurfacing in his mind of Toni Hargrove's crime scene.

"You okay? We don't have to go anywhere," Martin said.

"No, it's not that. This . . . this whole thing gets harder, the closer it feels. Even though you think she could still be alive after a year, every minute that passes I feel like I'm running out of time," Eddie admitted.

"I think that's true for every case, every time. The closer I feel, the closer an inevitable collapse feels."

"Do they usually collapse?"

Martin studied Eddie for ten seconds before answering. "There's nothing usual about this case," he finally said. Then he quickly turned away, leaving Eddie to wonder if there was something in his expression Martin didn't want Eddie to see.

Eddie followed Martin through the precinct to the parking lot. He wasn't in handcuffs, but he was still wearing his jailhouse grays under Martin's sweatshirt. He felt freer than he had in a year, but he still didn't feel comfortable deviating left or right without asking. When they reached Martin's car, he waited by the back door, unsure whether he could touch it.

"What are you doing?" Martin asked, then recognition washed over his face. "Hop in the front."

"Are you sure this is a good idea?" Eddie looked around the empty parking lot, feeling exposed, vulnerable. What if they got separated and Eddie was found in the woods by someone who didn't believe him?

"I need you to tell me the best way to get to that stone hutch where you found Hazel's ring. I don't know how to get there, and I don't want a bunch of uniformed cops crawling all over the woods for various reasons."

"What are you looking for?" Eddie asked.

"Toni's ring. But that stays between you and me," he said, and disappeared inside the car and started the engine. Eddie hesitated, mind reeling, pulse soaring, and then he slipped into the passenger seat and locked the door behind him.

They drove in silence, Eddie pointing whenever Martin needed to make a turn. They pulled off the paved road onto a gravel road, brush overgrowing the edges. Martin glanced over at him, his face a question mark.

"This goes to the old factory. The little hutch is still about a mile in, and we're going to have to cross Cold River, but there's a big tree that fell across in one spot, or we can just walk across where it's about hip-deep, if you don't mind getting wet," Eddie explained.

"And this is the best way?" Martin raised a brow.

"We could drive to the other side, and it'd be about a six-mile walk. Up to you."

Eddie had a pretty good idea of what Martin would choose, knowing Martin wouldn't want to draw a lot of attention or spend more time than necessary on the trail. Eddie also wasn't about to tell Martin about the little footpath they could've accessed from the county courthouse, which would've been just a half-mile walk from the courthouse parking lot across fairly flat terrain to the little hutch. Eddie had picked this way because he wanted to get a good look at the factory in daylight. The big, silent building made the hair on the back of his neck rise every time he came near its shadow, and even though it had been searched top to bottom twice when Hazel disappeared, Eddie always felt her there, swore she'd be right behind him when he turned around.

"I'll get wet," Martin said, and Eddie was clotheslined with both relief and reawakened nervousness. He remembered how spooked the officers seemed every time they stepped inside the concrete walls, as if they were disturbing an ancient graveyard. Eddie was more nervous about the living. What if whoever had Hazel was watching from the factory, saw Eddie traipsing across the field, then took Hazel, and vanished?

Eddie realized, with a sinking, gasping feeling, that he assumed whoever had Hazel would know Eddie on sight, would have known him before, and one name kept surfacing in his mind: Jonathon Walks. For the first time, he was grateful that Martin hadn't given him back his phone, or he may have called Jonathon, just to see if he got a feeling one way or the other. If Martin was right, one little phone call could tip him off and send him and Hazel out of Tarson.

They parked the car alongside the chain-link fence. Eddie pulled the hood over his head before stepping out of the car. It felt colder here than at the station, the sun blocked by elevation and trees, the wind sliding down the mountain, but his skin felt like it was on fire, his blood nearly boiling in his veins. Without a word, he walked into the woods, this time with Martin trailing behind.

They climbed the first rise, weaving between trees.

"We're not on a path," Martin said.

"Didn't think you'd want to run into anyone," Eddie answered. "And didn't you ever hear that the shortest path between two points is a straight line?"

Martin, save his labored breathing, stayed quiet the rest of the way.

It felt strange to be in these woods without calling out for someone. The only sounds were the rustling leaves under their feet and birds chirping overhead.

They reached the little stone hutch, the door propped open, and for a moment Eddie froze. What if a new piece of jewelry sat waiting for them atop the earth? What would it mean for Hazel? He wondered if Ama escaping gave Hazel a better chance, that whoever had her—not Jonathon, he wouldn't commit to that yet—would keep her alive longer having lost his next victim. He would be enraged, Eddie realized. The reality of what Hazel might be facing struck him square in the chest, and he doubled over, catching his hands on his knees.

Martin's feet appeared next to his, and Eddie felt his hand on his back, light and unsure.

"Go sit," Martin said. "I can take it from here."

Eddie propped himself against the outside of the hutch as the spinning sensation faded, and he watched Martin maneuver through the door. He listened to Martin push aside leaves with his foot, then the sounds turned softer, and Eddie imagined he was prying at the earth with his fingers.

"Find anything?" he called to Martin.

"No. Wishing I brought a shovel right about now."

"How far down are you going to dig?" Eddie asked.

"Until I find something."

Eddie peered into the hutch, saw Martin's streaked face, brown fingers. He saw himself in Martin's eyes, the desperation, the need, the regret.

"Let's take turns, then," Eddie said.

They dug all morning, layer after layer of earth coming out of the hutch. The sweat and exertion made Eddie drive harder, grateful for the feeling of doing something, watching the hole grow. Martin, on the other hand, seemed to grow more agitated and less committed with every turn. As the sun began its slide toward the west horizon, Martin emerged from the hutch with defeat hanging off his face, pulling on his shoulders.

"Nothing," he said. He planted his knuckles at his waist and tilted his head to the sky.

Eddie wondered if he was having a few choice words with whatever higher power he believed in. He knew that look, knew that talk. He'd had them both out here at least a hundred times.

"Let me have one last go," Eddie said, and was squeezing through the propped door before Martin could disagree. He dug like a man possessed, chipping away at harder ground with the sharp end of a rock. A chunk of dirt broke off, and he pulled it away. Beneath it, something silver caught his eye. He reached into the soil, not daring to hope, unwilling to alert Martin until he was sure. The first object was a silver spoon, the kind used to ladle soup or punch. He set it in his lap, then felt around the fresh hole with numb fingers, unearthing several silver coins. He brushed the dirt off of one well enough to read the year: 1980. Old, but not remarkably so.

He breathed out a sigh and rocked back on his heels, his bad knee throbbing for want to stand. One more go, he told himself, and reached inside again, tilling the earth with his hands. Something round and hard passed between his fingers, and he plucked it from the dirt. The piece of silver was like the threaded end of a screw, but on its head was a dished, metal plate. He'd seen these before, a decade before, when Hazel started learning how to play a violin. It was a tuning peg she used to change the tension on the string. Nine years old, and she'd had to teach Eddie how to do it.

There, inside the hutch, Eddie could remember the way his wife and his daughter belly laughed at his utter inability to hear the difference in the string as he twisted the knob back and forth, loose and tight. It had all sounded the same, like how all shades of blue were just blue. For Hazel and Raelynn, sounds were a spectrum of the color. Looking down at the tuning pegs, Eddie nearly cried, blindsided by a memory he hadn't thought of in years. It was a gift, a painful, heartbreaking gift to remember something again, as if seeing it for the first time.

Blinking back tears, he felt around in the loose earth, and found another one, and then a third. Next, he pulled a steel string from the ground, coiled like a little gray snake, and he jerked back with recognition as if the wire had struck out to bite him. The girl from the board, who panhandled and played a fiddle on the town square, who walked away from the promenade one night in the direction of Tarson Woods and was never seen again.

Eddie lumbered out of the hutch, his spine howling from being hunched over, his nails filled with dirt, and his eyes wide with speculation. He held out his hand for Martin to see what he'd found. Martin went still, then reached a finger for Eddie's palm, and his gaze leaped to Eddie's face.

Without saying a word, they each peered behind each other, searching the woods like two lost kids with night coming and proof a monster was somewhere close.

The girl with the fiddle.

Hazel.

Ama.

Proof someone had left a memento of each behind.

"Put it all back," Martin said.

Eddie closed his fist around it. "Why?"

"Whoever is out here, whoever has your daughter, he is methodical, obsessive. He may be able to tell that someone's been in here digging around, but I'm damn sure he knows what's buried here, and if he sees it's still here, he may not be as concerned. But if his ritual ground is dug up and things are missing, we will lose him," Martin said carefully.

"We'd be breaking the law, wouldn't we? Tampering with evidence?" Desperation hummed in Eddie's chest, his hands.

"Do you remember when I said nothing about this case is usual? This falls into that category."

Eddie exhaled, his palms breaking out with new sweat. Then he ducked back inside the cave and replaced the spoon, the coins, the pegs, and the string exactly where he'd found them. He hated himself, and he hoped like hell all at the same time.

Wordlessly, Martin and Eddie buried the evidence of the dead, stamped the earth flat, and covered it in a blanket of fallen leaves.

A
M
A

AMA PACED HER ROOM. HER PATH FROM THE WINDOW TO THE BATH-room door felt shorter with every loop. A cramp knotted her side, but she kept moving. She had to do something to feel like she was preparing for the auction in some kind of way or she would go absolutely insane.

Lindsey, with the help of Ama's bank account and humanitarian angle, had managed to bump up the auction date to the coming Saturday and had convinced the caterers and the musicians to follow suit. She was now ensuring every media outlet in the greater metro area would be pushing the event to their audiences.

Meanwhile, Ama was stuck in this cramped, dark motel room, wearing a trail in the carpet and spinning her mental wheels.

She exhaled slowly and rubbed her thumb against her aching shoulder socket as she mentally went over what she knew of her plan so far: the fundraiser would open with a performance by Tarson High School's choir, singing the solo Hazel was supposed to have sung at the winter festival the year before. Then the piano player would begin his set, and they would open the silent auction to bidding. Ama would stay on the platform and read descriptions of the donated items so she could watch the crowd from above for any sign of Michael. Then they would have a thirty-minute window for the open piano while dessert was served. After that, and before the winners were announced, Ama would sing "Stairway to Heaven." She would have Lindsey take over as MC so she would be free to follow Michael, should she spot him in the crowd. Ama felt sure he wouldn't leave before her song. He would be there to record her voice. But there would be no reason for him to stay afterward.

Then she would have a choice to make. She would be standing there onstage with a microphone. She could call him by his real name, let people know there was a monster in their midst. Maybe they'd tackle him.

There was one big flaw in her plan, one she hadn't yet been able to bring herself to face. The only way to find Hazel was to be led there by Michael himself. If he was caught away from where Hazel was, he would never tell them where she was being held. They would have no chance of finding her alive. Ama had to be taken to Hazel purposefully by Michael, and then hatch a plan of attack and escape from the inside.

But how the hell was she supposed to plan an escape against a psychopath who had gone completely undetected for seventeen years? She didn't have the first clue where he was keeping Hazel or how it was safeguarded. Who in their right mind would take that kind of gamble?

Her thoughts went back to where they always did: Eddie Stevens, standing there in the mist, the barrel of his gun looming so big and yet so small. He'd walked into Tarson Woods in the black of night through sheets of rain just to try to find Ama.

The weight of needing to repay him pushed down on her, and she nearly wished he'd never gotten out of his van, when a thought struck her: If Michael took her again, maybe she didn't need to escape. Maybe she just needed to be found.

She stared at the circle of evidence from her father's trial still sitting in piles on the floor. Someone had known where the wreck had occurred— someone who wasn't on the scene, who didn't have access to her father's logs or his drivers' routes. The jackknifed truck had been the bait, not the hook. Someone had to have known when to pull. Someone had known he was there.

Rocking back on her heels, the truth hit her full force: someone had planted a locator on the rig and on her father. Someone he trusted. It's the only way they would've known when he had reached the truck. Someone else, somewhere else, knew the exact moment *he* needed to be found.

Ama leaped for her phone, ignoring the bite of pain that clamped down on her side, and dialed Lindsey's number. Lindsey answered on the second ring.

"Come pick me up," Ama said.

Three hours later, Lindsey drove Ama through a gate in a chain-link fence where little storefronts sat in a squat row, their doors and windows barred.

"There," Ama said, and pointed to Happ's Hot Spot, a gaming and electronics shop. Lindsey did a double take, her stare rebounding between Ama's face and the storefront, which was covered in fantasy characters and computer game logos.

"I'm going in for you," Lindsey said, shifting the car into park.

Ama shook her head. "I need you to wait here," she said.

"Ama, God knows who's in there."

"I know exactly who's in there. That's why I came," Ama said, and lifted herself out of the car.

She did her best not to limp as she walked inside the shop. The front of the little building was checkered with collapsible tables and chairs, where people played Dungeons & Dragons or chess. In the back there was a glass counter, about eight feet in length, and a familiar face behind it: Durante Happ, the boy from her childhood staircase, now the owner of the shop, and the best tech guru in Atlanta.

"Ama," he said, grinning, and dropped his glasses in place. "It's good to put eyes on you in person. I seen you on the news. I tried to call, but you didn't pick up."

"I needed to disappear for a minute," she said.

"I get that," he replied, and she knew he did. Ama smiled at Durante, remembering when he was the only person who showed up to her birthday party the year her father was convicted, the only kid who would play with her at recess. He'd grown up slow in an accelerating world, raised by a single dad who worked at a tech development company by day and wrote romance novels under a woman's name by night. Durante spent his afternoons perched in tree branches reading books, wandering through the woods in search of magical creatures, or scouring the neighborhood creek for discarded trinkets and jewelry.

Their friendship became a fortress, and their skin grew leather tough against insults and accusations hurled their way so long as they withstood them together. They would go on to withstand lonely weekends together, homecoming dances, and proms. They called each other after first dates, first kisses, first breakups, Ama's first car accident, and Durante's first college acceptance letter.

After graduation, invisible power still enchanted Durante, but his interests turned the way of his father's—technology—and he went on to Georgia Tech while Ama went out of state to Auburn University, hoping a state line could somehow strain her past and her father's infamous legacy from her future. It wasn't lost on Ama she'd attended the school rival to her father's alma mater. Maybe even then she'd been angry with him and just hadn't known it yet, silently, blindly furious for everything she'd lost.

Somewhere along the way, Ama had lost Durante, too. It hadn't been intentional or acute. It had been slow and quiet, time between calls growing longer, conversations—when they did happen—shorter. She stopped going home for summers and holidays, stopped tending the past, her hometown, and anything and anyone to do with it. She had become Ama Shoemaker, top of her class, heading to Auburn's law school.

After the Michael Walton case, she'd moved to Atlanta, and within a year, she'd needed a resource for wires and discreet recording devices. A colleague had pointed her in the direction of Happ's Hot Spot, a little gaming spot in the middle of one of Atlanta's more dangerous areas. Ama had nearly run through the door of the building, not daring to hope, and there he was, his smile all teeth, hair stacked a foot high on his head. He'd wrapped her up in a hug, and she'd nearly come apart at the seams.

This time, he came around the counter and held her gently. "I can't believe you're up and out already."

"I'm up against an evil wizard. There's no time to rest," she said into the divot beneath his collarbone.

"How can I help?"

She pulled back so she could look at him. "I need a GPS tracker. I need it small. And I need it to be able to send a location, or have some kind of frequency on it that can be sent to a second party remotely and easily."

"Why don't you tell me the situation you need it for and I can tailor to suit." He squeezed her hands before returning to his position behind the counter.

"I need to go somewhere I shouldn't be, and I need to be found, but no one can know I'm going until I get there."

"Okay." Durante narrowed his eyes, studying her. "This sounds like some risky business you're getting into. You need company?"

"No company, just your expertise. Can you do it?"

"It's going to have limits as far as range and how many numbers it'll access. It'll have to be limited to one-way communication, too."

"That's fine. One more thing." Ama leaned over the counter. "Can you make it waterproof and able to fit inside a tampon applicator?"

"Are you questioning my skills or the security of my masculinity?" Durante pulled a box of Tampax tampons out from under the counter.

"I'll need it delivered to me in person. I'm up in Tarson at the Sleep Inn Motel. How fast can you have it to me?"

"Twenty-four hours. I'll bring it to you myself. Leave the phone numbers you want it to be able to communicate with and I should have everything else I need, or I'll call you."

"Do you want me to leave a deposit?"

Durante pursed his lips. "Ama, how long we go back?"

"All the way back," she said. She kissed him on the cheek, breathing him in. He was nearly forty-four years old in the middle of a city made of brick and stone and noise, and yet he still smelled like trees and the pages of a new book.

MARTIN WAS SEARCHING SURROUNDING STATES' DMV DATABASES FOR any registrations for Jonathon Walks when Captain's face appeared above his screen.

"Look, Martin, the DA is on my ass. We either need to charge Eddie or turn him loose," he said.

"I don't like either of those options. What about protective custody? We'll tell the DA he's a witness to a major crime and we'll have more for them ASAP."

"That might work. But I am not keeping that man locked up in that office anymore. You're here, he's here. You're home, he's home—at *your* home. We don't let anyone else know where he's staying. Now go home, and take Eddie with you. And take a shower. You smell."

An hour later, Martin was sitting in his living room staring at his notes, wishing Mrs. Walton had been able to locate just one picture of Michael from the year he allegedly died, when his cell phone rang.

"Martin," he answered.

"Lindsey drove Ama to Atlanta. She stopped by a storefront off Bankhead, like an electronics pawnshop or something," explained the deputy he'd assigned to tail her. "We went in after she left, but nobody was really handing out information. Some people were playing games. They had some old computer parts and gaming systems for sale."

"What the hell is she doing?" Martin muttered, more to himself than to the deputy on the other end of the line. Between speculation about Ama, Michael Walton, Janie Walton, and Jonathon Walks, the only solution

Martin's mind kept rolling back to was an Ambien and a Valium. He was too wired to sleep, too tired to think.

Another call beeped on the line. Martin looked down. It was Ama. "Shit," he muttered.

"Everything okay?" Eddie asked from where he was sitting on the floor in the corner, a box of cheese pizza in front of him. He'd gone so long without saying something that Martin had forgotten he was there.

Martin nodded, then told the deputy on the phone, "I gotta go," and clicked over to Ama's call.

"Detective Locklear," he said.

"You know who this is. Don't play pro with me."

"What can I do for you?"

"I need Eddie Stevens's phone number."

"Can I ask why?"

"To invite him to the fundraiser, personally, and to apologize for the hardship this incident has created for him. I plan to publicly clear his name, so I want to make sure he's there."

"I'm going to have to get back to you on that," Martin said in order to stall, eyeing Eddie.

"Well, I've changed the date to this Saturday, so get back to me quickly."

Martin froze. What kind of strings did Ama have to yank to move the event? He couldn't imagine the money she was putting up in rush fees. The event was going to cost more than it made. Martin was right—this auction was a smoke screen for Hazel.

"I can help you here," he said. "Whatever it is you're trying to do. I won't involve the department. It'll be just me and you. No other brass. I swear."

Ama went silent, but the line was still there, a faint buzz in his ear.

"Ama, please." He wanted to tell her he was figuring it out, pieces of it, anyway, but he didn't want to push. She was sitting dead center on the fence of indecision, and he knew the more he said, the faster she'd jump back to her own side and keep the boundary between them.

"Saturday, during the auction, Eddie is going to get a message from an unknown number. Tell him to expect it. When he gets it, help him figure out what it means, and then go with him. Don't bring anything or anyone but a gun. Maybe two. Yes, bring two. And give one to Eddie. He's a good shot."

"I need more than this."

"That's all I can tell you," she said quickly.

"Here's his number—are you ready?" Martin asked, keeping his words slow and calm, trying to draw her off whatever mental ledge she was standing on. He relayed the number twice through, confirming she'd heard it right.

"Ama, let me help you," he whispered. He knew he sounded like he was begging, but he didn't care. He *was* begging.

"I think event planning is probably out of your job description," Ama replied, and Martin could tell she was pulling her face away from the phone, ready to hang up.

"Ama!"

The line went dead.

"Dammit." Martin scowled, furious with himself for burning the bridge with Ama in her motel room, for throwing her father's past in her face. It had been an unfair shot to take, and he knew it.

He's a good shot. Ama's words bloomed inside his mind, drawing all focus. Eddie was right—Ama had jumped in front of that bullet, and now she was aiming for her abductor or Hazel, or maybe both. He had to admire her. She was pulling off a socialite extravaganza in a matter of days, all to cover up a bigger, more important move. There was no way the department could've moved as fast.

He also hated her guts. It was very likely that she was going to get very close to a serial killer's location, and Martin didn't want to come with just an old, limping man and two guns. He wanted to bring down the fires of the GBI and a SWAT team so they had every chance to take the perp into custody and survive doing it.

"Damn that woman," he said. He wondered how she would react when he told her he'd interviewed Mrs. Walton . . . when he told her Mrs. Walton was very sure Michael was still very alive.

"Who was it? And why'd they want my number?" Eddie asked.

Martin nearly lied, but he couldn't bring himself to mislead the poor man again. "It was Ama Chaplin. She wanted your phone number so she could invite you to the fundraiser personally."

"Can I go? Are you going?"

"Eddie, you're not a prisoner. This isn't house arrest. It's just an arrangement, for now. We're trying to limit the outside world's access to you, and we promised the DA we'd keep you under supervision. It's the only way they'd delay charges." A drop of sauce from Eddie's slice of pizza landed on the floor. Eddie dabbed his napkin into his water cup and scrubbed it clean before it could stain.

"Sorry about the lack of furniture. I picked up an air mattress for you, but honestly, it's probably less comfortable than the sofa at the station. My ex-wife was more the decorator than me. The house needs a woman's touch," Martin said. He felt a pang of guilt in his chest, remembering how sure he'd been that Eddie was cold and calculating, manipulative of the entire justice system and every heart in two towns.

Eddie snorted. "Between me and my wife, I was the decorator. But the yard was her territory. She'd tend a garden like most women fawn over a baby. Had the greenest thumb in Texas. I'm a homebody, though. I want to like the way my house looks, and she said if I liked it so much, it was my responsibility to keep it that way. Heck of a woman." Eddie's eyes shone with emotion, and he cleared his throat. "I know people thought me moving right after she died was bad, bad for Hazel especially. But I realized my wife is what made that house a home. Not the furniture, not the paint or the pictures. Her voice, her laughter, her dirt all over my clean floor. I couldn't walk through the front door of that house anymore without her in it."

"Why was she up on a ladder?" Martin asked.

"It was my fault. She'd asked me to hang flower boxes under the bedroom windows, had been after me for weeks about it. The windows were on the second story, but there was a little pitch roof under them that shielded the front porch. Best I can figure she'd made it up to the roof. I never told her how slick the shingles are when they're wet, and it was springtime, dewy in the morning. Hazel got home from school, found her in the yard, ladder on its side." His voice broke, and he stopped, shook his head. "That's the other reason we left. Hazel was so scared to come home and find something bad again that she stopped leaving the house. We pulled out a map and tried to find somewhere as far and as different as we could. We just needed . . . we needed to start over."

"That makes plenty of sense to me," Martin said, remembering how he'd fit what he could of his old life in two boxes and a duffel bag and left the rest behind. His thoughts returned to Ama. When he'd mentioned Michael's name on the phone outside her motel room, he would've sworn she dropped the phone. Maybe she'd just hung up on him. He'd never know. But either way, she'd let him in. If in her mind Michael was a closed book, a dead body, would she have been as affected by the mention of his name?

Martin knew she did have to uphold confidentiality even after death, but she'd shut down completely. He thought back to how she'd reacted when he asked about what she remembered from her attack. She'd given him the same stonewall. She was protecting someone. Whether it was herself or someone else, Martin wasn't sure. Ama would no doubt be faster to hide the identity of someone she knew. Someone she had feared not for just a matter of hours but for years.

Maybe Michael Walton wasn't a victim at all.

M
A
R
T
I
N

IT WAS DAWN WHEN MARTIN PULLED UP TO THE SCHOOL, HOPING TO FIT in an interview before classes started. Eddie sat in the passenger seat. He was reading Hazel's journal again. It had spent the previous night tucked under his arm.

"It's probably best if I go in alone," Martin said. "I don't want anyone seeing you in police presence and making the wrong assumption."

"Okay." Eddie's voice was distant, and he didn't look up.

There were two teachers currently employed by Tarson High School who had also been there when Michael Walton was a student, and only one, Mrs. Jacobs, had had Michael in her classroom. Martin went inside and found her room, tapping on the doorframe.

"Mrs. Jacobs, Detective Locklear. Thanks for meeting me so early."

"Yes." She sat up and swiped her blond bangs to the side, smiling. "Please, sit in any of the desks."

Mrs. Jacobs had an obvious warmth about her, a softness evident from twenty feet away, and Martin half expected to see a plate of chocolate chip cookies and a glass of warm milk on her desk.

"You're here about Michael," she said.

"Yes, ma'am. Anything you can tell me about him. Nothing is irrelevant or too small a detail."

"Well, I had him for biology. He liked my class, I could tell. He was always reading his textbook, even when he was supposed to be listening to me. He did well on his tests. But his semester grades were average at best. He seldom turned in homework, didn't participate in class except for during labs. I don't know that I ever heard him say more than three or four words at a time, but to read his essays, you'd think you were reading the work of a college student. His vocabulary was well beyond his years— well beyond Tarson, to be frank. And he had a memory like a steel trap, incredible mind for details."

"What about his personality? Did he talk much? Did he have a friend? A hobby?"

"He wrote music notes in the margins of his textbook, even though they aren't supposed to mark inside the books at all." Her expression changed, becoming heavier. "I tried not to get after him too much, though. You could tell a raised voice meant something to him."

"Can you explain that to me?"

"I . . . I don't want to speak ill of someone who isn't here to defend herself."

"You mean his mother," Martin prompted.

Mrs. Jacobs nodded. "Nowadays I'm sure a student in his condition would be reported. But back then, it just wasn't something we did, especially after everything his family had been through. I tried to bring him a little extra food, send him home with a new pencil. He'd wear these oversize long-sleeve shirts, even in August. He would tell me he was wearing them because they belonged to his father, but one time one of the sleeves was pushed up, and I saw burn marks in a line up his arm."

"You seem to have a memory for details, too."

"Michael was special. He was one who grabbed your attention, even if he never made a sound. And seeing that kind of thing . . . well it's not something I'd easily forget."

"What did you think about the trial?"

Mrs. Jacobs let out a sigh. "I remember that I was the only person who sat on his side of the courtroom. Maybe he killed those animals, and maybe he didn't. But I know him enough to know it wasn't out of meanness. We had begun dissecting animals in class—frogs, fetal pigs. His precision was . . . remarkable. He had the right feel for it. He handled each part of each animal so carefully. If he cut open neighborhood animals in the same manner, well, he shouldn't have done it, but it's nothing to lock a kid up and throw away the key for. And he certainly didn't deserve what happened after the trial."

"What was that?" Martin asked.

"Some roughneck senior boys pushed him into that river. I know they did. And then what they carved on that tree." She shook her head. "If anyone should have their names dragged through the mud and face a trial, it should be bullies like that."

"Mrs. Jacobs, do you know of anyone who might have a picture of Michael? I visited his mother, but she didn't have any."

Mrs. Jacobs tsked and slid open a desk drawer. "I keep a photo album of my favorite students. Michael didn't care to have his picture taken, but I got a good one of him one day. It was the last day of school for the year, and he was the only student who didn't seem happy about it. I tried to cheer him up, make him feel special, so I told him I took pictures of all my favorite students. You should also check the library for that year's annual—1988 or '89, I believe."

She handed Martin the photograph. A ray of sunlight had streamed through the window and spotlighted Michael at his desk. He looked five years younger than anyone else in the class, but his eyes were ancient and ringed with exhaustion. Shoulder-length, greasy hair fell across half his face. His hands were in two fists under his chin, and the corners of his mouth were pulled up in the faintest smile.

"Thank you, Mrs. Jacobs," Martin said. "Can I keep this photograph for a little while?"

"Sure. May I ask what this is about?"

"Off the record," Martin said, and Mrs. Jacobs nodded. "Off the record, we are looking into what really happened that day at the river. I'll be in touch."

M
A
R
T
I
N

MARTIN WAS NEARLY TO THE STATION WHEN HE GLANCED OVER AT Eddie. His forehead was pressed against the window. His gaze was fixed on the trees blurring by, but Martin had the feeling he wasn't seeing them at all. Eddie hadn't said a word for the entire drive.

"You okay, Eddie?" he asked quietly.

"It's been months since I've seen the school," Eddie said. "Got to where I couldn't even drive by it. I'd look too hard for her, or feel like the worst person on earth if I drove by without at least a glance." Eddie let out a shuddering breath. "All this time, I knew she was out there to be found, and now she *is* out there—we know she is—and it feels like she's farther away than ever before."

Martin didn't know how to answer. He couldn't promise that they'd find her, and it seemed trite to say they'd try. Six days into this investigation, and Martin was struggling. Eddie had been fighting this battle mostly alone for months. Reading a face and asking questions was Martin's job, and he had no idea what to say.

"Martin, can I go home? Just for a bit?" Eddie asked, breaking the silence. "I just need to be where I feel her."

"For as long as you want," Martin said.

Eddie steered Martin north, then down several little roads. His property was on a cul-de-sac, and the front was mostly shielded with trees. The driveway curved left, and then a little white house appeared, one story, trimmed in gray, with a porch extending across the front. There were two rocking chairs framing a bay window, and Martin wondered if Eddie could bring himself to sit in one with the other empty, rocking with the slightest breeze.

Martin trailed Eddie up the steps and through the front door. Everywhere Martin looked, he saw places where two people should sit: two chairs in the living room, an old wood table with two mismatched chairs in an open space beside the kitchen. Martin was accustomed to the quiet in his own home; no one had ever lived there with him. He wondered at the shadows Hazel's memory cast in every room, and he thought about what Michael's mother had said about filling the silence.

They walked down a narrow hall, and Eddie paused by a door to the right, his fingers frozen on the knob, and even before he finally nudged it open, Martin knew this must be Hazel's room. Daylight streamed through two big windows, shining on a wooden desk. The bedframe was made from whole boughs of slender trees, and her bedspread, still tossed to the side like Hazel had climbed out that morning, was a patchwork quilt.

Eddie pointed to it.

"Hazel made her bedspread from her mother's dresses the summer after we moved here," he said, flicking a finger near the corner of his eye.

A lump rose in Martin's throat as he remembered who he'd thought Eddie was—what he thought he'd done.

"Look around, if you want to," Eddie offered. "You want to know about Hazel, this is where she spent most of her time."

Eddie pulled open a desk drawer and withdrew a black recorder. "She wrote her own songs, covered others. Those last few months, she was always singing. She was working on a song, got real private and silly about it. That's what makes me know it was good." He smiled then. "I haven't been able to play this. Hey, you think . . . you think they'd play it at the fundraiser? That way, no matter what happens, she'll be heard one more time. She'll sing to a crowd."

We're going to get her back, Martin wanted to say, but standing in her room, the possibility she'd one day walk around in it again seemed far away and improbable. Martin had seen too many people *nearly* rescued alive to believe the odds were in Hazel's favor. When he finally spoke, he said: "There won't be a dry eye in the house."

Martin opened the second drawer in the desk. There was a stack of notebooks, a handful of CDs, and a couple of pencils. He put the notebooks on the desktop, then flipped open the first one. There were more doodles than words, then a few short poems and several sketches of a girl with her eyes turned down, shoulders slumped. Self-portraits, if Martin had to guess, and he checked to make sure Eddie wasn't looking over his shoulder. Eddie was standing by Hazel's bed, his fingers on her pillow. Martin turned away, feeling like an intruder, and continued flipping through the notebook. Finding nothing, he leafed through the rest of the stack.

The corner edge of a picture stuck out of the bottom notebook. He slid it from between the pages. It was a candid shot of Hazel, her head thrown back, mouth open in a carefree grin. In front of her, a man pumped his arms as if in some kind of victory.

"Who's this?" Martin asked, flashing the photo at Eddie.

"That's Jonathon Walks," he said, confirming Martin's suspicion.

Martin looked closer. One corner of his shirt had pulled loose from the waist of his pants, and the sleeves of his shirt had fallen down his arms, where a row of circular scars was visible.

Michael Jeffery Walton.

Martin panicked in silence. If he brought this to the captain, Michael's face could be splashed across every major network and social media site within the hour. Ama would be safe—for now. But Hazel . . . they wouldn't find Hazel. Ama's silence and secrets instantly made sense. He watched out of the corners of his eyes as Eddie picked up Hazel's pillow and brought it to his face, his shoulders quivering.

Ama, you better be right, and you better be good.

He slipped the picture into his pocket. If her fundraiser didn't bring Michael out of hiding, he would have no choice but to bring the department into the investigation first thing Sunday morning.

MICHAEL

THE GAS STATION TWO EXITS SOUTH OF TARSON IS QUIET FOR RUSH hour on a Friday morning. I grab two sausage biscuits from under the heat lamps and a newspaper from the wire stand, plunk down a five-dollar bill on the counter for my customary $4.79 bill, and leave with a wave. I have not wanted to come back here since Ama was taken from me, but not appearing would arouse suspicion, so here I am.

A cold mist hangs in the air. I sit in the front seat of the Jeep and open the paper, scanning for any mention of Ama or my real name splashed across the headlines. I flip to the next page. My name is nowhere to be seen, but Ama's is there with a picture of her face, gray eyes steady and defiant. I read the caption: *A-list defense attorney to hold silent auction and sing for Tarson High School at courthouse.*

The paper rattles in my hands, and the page begins to tear at the center fold. Ama is going to sing. I do not have one usable note recorded from Ama. Not one. And she knows it. I read the article. A pianist will give a concert; then the piano will be open for anyone interested, and Ama will sing "Stairway to Heaven." Adrenaline blooms in a fiery flower at my center.

This is for me, absolutely and undeniably. She will sing the song from our second meeting at the place of our first—the place where she told me to never let our paths cross again, the birthplace of this endeavor, of my song, of my Fate. Now she is building every road back to her. I imagine she's hoping to contribute her notes in her own way. That would be very Ama, after all. But it won't do. Not for Fate, not for our song.

A lesser man might think she's setting a trap, that plainclothes police officers will be mingling with the partygoers, waiting for me to appear, but I know better. She didn't tell anyone about what happened between us in the woods, or about my song and what I've done to create it. The entire county police force would be looking for me by now were that the case. This is more than that—much more.

Ama is either calling Fate to the dance floor or declaring war. Either way, I will be there to watch them collide.

H
A
Z
E
L

MICHAEL IS MOVING FASTER THAN USUAL, MORE CARELESS, SNATCHING instead of plucking. He grabs his little knife and begins to whittle a long ivory stick. It's knobby at both ends and more slender at the center. It's a bone—from the length of it, either a femur or a humerus. No one has been here in the last year besides Bill and me.

Nausea rolls through my stomach, and a sour taste lands on my tongue.

"You're going to have a roommate soon," Michael says without looking at me. "I should've thought of this a long time ago. You can keep quiet during our drills together, but what about watching someone else's pain—or causing it? I imagine that might evoke a little more commitment from you."

I stare at the back of his head. My gaze travels the length of metal pipe I'm bound to by a chain. It's a support rail for the metal shelves lining the wall opposite the cabinets. I imagine pulling over the whole unit, crushing him beneath like the end of a superhero comic book—Batman or Spider-Man. The bad guys always come back out, though, stronger, meaner than before.

"A duet," he continues, then begins humming. He stands, retrieves his walking stick, and leaves without another word. The door clicks shut behind him.

Michael is right. I cannot stay silent when someone else is suffering. I heard Bill die in the dark. It was slow, quiet, and yet I knew what it was. I felt the water around my calves warm as his body voided postmortem urine he'd been holding all day. I heard water win the fight for space in his mouth and throat.

But I also heard every word when Bill explained how to access the tunnel to the factory, where his locker was inside the building, how to retrieve his gun from the false floor, how to fire it.

I look up at the pipe where my constant walking back and forth, pull, loosen, pull, loosen, has pried a screw from the wall. I won't make the same mistake. I won't show my hand while the main door is closed and locked. But with two of us soon to control, he'll make mistakes, he'll get sloppy or distracted, and that door will be left open just a sliver, just once, and I'll be gone.

A
M
A

THE STRETCH OF GRASS BEHIND THE COUNTY COURTHOUSE WAS FRAMED with white tents, which had sheltered the auction items from an early-afternoon thunderstorm. Mercifully, the storm had delivered more sound than rain.

When Ama had woken up that morning, she'd wondered if she would not wake up the next day. It was an unsettling thought, stirring again in her middle as she recalled it now. She tried not to revisit the seventeen-year-old courtroom memory, or the way Michael had stared at her profile while they waited for the verdict to be read, but in the shadow of the building, the memory felt as present as the ground beneath her feet.

It all started here. It would begin to end here, if all went according to plan. There was beauty in that, if not nearly enough justice.

As the five o'clock start time drew closer, two caterers scurried inside a food truck at the back of the lawn, and several servers and a bartender prepped the open bar under another tent. A small stage and a set of risers had been arranged on the courthouse terrace. Even though the area was well protected from weather, the podium and the piano they'd brought in for the event were covered in a sheet of plastic and would stay that way until right before the event began. From the podium, Ama memorized the layout, paying extra attention to places someone could stand and watch without drawing much attention from the crowd.

The sound technician arrived with two box speakers, and soon after him, the Tarson High School chorus filed out of a big van and headed up the steps. A gaggle of gray-haired women holding two giant flower arrangements better suited for a wake or a funeral came tromping up the wet sidewalk, voices tittering, faces angled in. A couple of them appeared to be holding casserole dishes. They began sliding couture auction items to the back of the table to make room for the food they'd brought, and Ama shook her head, wondering if she'd even survive the event long enough to be abducted by Michael.

The pianist appeared onstage, hands clasped at his back, his eyes on Ama, waiting for her cue to begin. *It's showtime,* she told herself, repeating the only thing she told herself before walking into a courtroom for opening and closing arguments. She held lives in her hands all the time. This was exactly the same.

It was a lie, she knew. But sometimes people needed to be lied to, herself included. She wondered how many lies Hazel had told herself, how many days she'd woken up and swore to herself she wouldn't end the day as Michael's captive. The thought steeled her nerves. She pulled the covers off the podium and piano, plastered a smile on her face, and hobbled off the stage and into the fray.

The notes of the piano floated in the atmosphere and partygoers strolled down the rows of items up for bid. Ama lost count of how many people approached her, touched her arm or her shoulder. How many times she had to tell Lindsey she was fine before sending her on a useless errand, and why didn't she grab herself another drink on her way? How many times she repeated what happened in the woods: *I'd sprained my ankle and he found me, bent down to help me up. I heard a bang, and the next thing I knew I woke up in a hospital.* Ama wasn't sure what she liked least, the looks of pity some gave her or the smirks other people didn't fail to hide. But as long as they bid on something, they could wear whatever face they wanted.

Nearly an hour into the auction, she excused herself from a group of perfect strangers who had spent the last few minutes peppering her with questions about the Hershaw verdict and carefully wove her way through the crowd. She kept her face turned down, letting her hair curtain her profile, and returned to the corner of the stage. Tucking herself behind a pillar, she strangled the stem of a champagne glass filled with sparkling water and studied each man in the crowd. The piano would be open soon, but Michael was nowhere to be seen.

Two men crossed the lawn. Ama recognized Detective Martin immediately. With him was Eddie Stevens, who had already adjusted his tie twice since she'd taken notice of him. She thought she'd feel better with the event under way, the tracking device in place, and Eddie and Martin in sight, but she was instead laden with doubt. This was stupid. She was aching and exhausted, and the piano player was just finishing his playlist. The night was still very young, the plan at step one, and she was damn near dead.

Panic erupted inside her. She moved away from the party, seeking a moment of quiet in the empty courthouse. It was funny how calm these halls could make her feel when almost everyone else who walked them was rife with nerves. She fingered the dainty silver chain that hung around her neck, which was more than just for looks: the thin loop of metal was a complete circuit and would send a signal from the locator between her legs to Eddie's phone the moment she broke it.

Her grand plan was feeling equally as fragile, and in that moment she realized she was wrong to keep Martin out. She needed backup. She'd looked into his history enough to know that he'd solved his fair share of cases. She was lucky Michael hadn't shown up yet. She would find Martin, tell him her entire scheme, and let him follow her at a distance, and he could grab Michael when he got the chance. Hazel had to be somewhere in this town. They could go door to door, search every basement, every inch of the woods.

Outside, a girl's voice rose over the noise of the party, an incredible, piercing note sailing through an open window and flooding the hallway. Ama moved to the window, craning for a view, when a thought shot through her: Why was the window open?

She spun on her heel, terror blazing down her limbs, and collided with Michael.

M
I
C
H
A
E
L

AMA'S LIPS OPEN; HER EYES GLISTEN WITH EMOTION.

"You get it now, don't you? You understand," I murmur.

A tear leaks out of one of her eyes, and she blinks it away, nodding.

"We will have to sneak away. You're the guest of honor at two events. Are you choosing me?"

"Yes," she says softly, and I feel a quiver in my chest.

"We can't get back out through the window. You'll tear your dress," I say. She's worn a gauzy, long number, ethereal and feminine, and I am touched by the respect she's showing Lady Fate.

"There's a door that will let us out on the side exit, closest to the trees. Do you remember it?" she asks. Her pulse flickers on the slope of her neck.

"Yes. You'll have to leave your purse."

"Should I drop it out the window?"

"That'll be fine," I answer. "I need to check you to make sure you're not bringing anyone with us."

"We're alone," Ama offers quietly, and steps her feet apart.

I reach under her dress and feel up one leg. Her skin is warm and smooth, and she doesn't flinch beneath my touch. I trace between her legs and down the other side. "I need to take off your ankle brace."

"Okay. I'll need help walking," she replies.

I watch her face, mystified, and peel off the brace before dropping it out the window. Then I stand and lift her hair away from her neck, checking the back of her dress for a weapon or a wire, but all I see is pale, sloping skin and the satin edge of her underwear.

I am suddenly overcome, bewildered by a burning sensation in my eyes. "No one has ever done anything like this for me. What made you change your mind?"

"When that man tried to shoot you, it made me realize . . . it made me realize what's really important, and that I needed to do what I could. That's why I haven't told anyone what really happened or who you are." She smiles and brushes her hand down my arm. "You'll tell the world when you're ready."

"Thank you."

I take her hand in mine, keeping the rhythm slow as not to rush her until we're safe from prying eyes, and we walk out of the courthouse together.

HAZEL'S SONG ENDED. THE APPLAUSE WAS LOUD AS THUNDER, PUNCTU-ated with whistles and calls for an encore. Eddie hadn't moved from the moment his daughter's voice came through the speakers until the last note had faded into the night. The next track began, and Hazel's voice rose above them all, covering an up-tempo song. Some guests started dancing on the square of empty lawn close to the stage. Martin clapped Eddie on the back, and they watched the crowd come to life.

"This is unreal," Eddie said, grinning and dazed. "I need to thank Ama."

"Let's find her," Martin said, and peered across the lawn. The tents made it difficult to see anyone from the waist up, and this crowd was a gathering of fashionable, fit city women. They were swimming in a sea of Amas.

Martin and Eddie made a loop around the auction tents, but Ama wasn't there. They swung by the bar and the buffet, then searched the parking lot, but Ama was nowhere to be seen.

Martin glanced up at the stage, where the pianist had begun playing along with Hazel's voice, and spotted Ama's assistant. She took a couple of clumsy steps and then steadied herself on a pillar.

"Come on," Martin said to Eddie, and moved in the direction of the stage. As the crowd thinned, Martin caught sight of Captain standing at the foot of the stairs, his hand like an arcade claw on a drink. Martin changed direction, hoping to avoid an interaction with him until Eddie received the message Ama had told him to expect.

"Detective Martin," Lindsey said, her voice cutting through the noise. He looked up and forced a closed-mouth smile. Captain spotted him, too, and waved him over.

Martin shoved his hands in his pockets and made his way to the captain, Eddie following behind. To his surprise, Lindsey hurried down the stairs, catching her balance on the captain's shoulder.

"Have you seen Ama?" she asked. "I can't find her anywhere."

"She was on the stage when we first got here. I haven't seen her since," Martin said, straining urgency from his voice. Something in Ama's plan could have gone wrong, very wrong, or this disappearing act could all be part of it. *Dammit, Ama.*

"Let's look for her inside," he suggested. He pulled on the first door within reach and found it locked. "Do you know if any of the doors are open?"

"Just the service entrance, as far as I know," Lindsey said. "It's on the far side of the building."

"Thanks."

Martin wheeled away from her and hustled across the terrace. He knew walking this fast might draw unwanted attention, but the sense of alarm flooding his bloodstream was overriding his sense of caution. Eddie's uneven footsteps sounded behind him, and he heard the captain catching up, too.

"We need to get inside," Martin said. "Eddie, did you check your phone?"

"Nothing yet."

"Call her," Martin ordered as they reached the service entrance. They waited outside as Eddie pressed his phone to his ear. The seconds passed maddeningly slow, and finally Eddie shook his head.

"Dammit. Call her again. Keep calling her." Martin swung the door open and headed inside. Most of the interior doors were locked, save the doors to the bathrooms. He pushed each door open and called inside, but the bathrooms were empty. He jogged the length of the corridor, peering out every window and around each corner. There was no sign of Ama.

He returned to the center window and stared across the parking lot, his eyes following a group of laughing women, desperate for one of them to be Ama. But she wasn't among them, and immediately he felt the weight of another body on his conscious. He cast his gaze down, sick with himself, and there in the bush bordering the front of the courthouse he spied a little white purse, the kind women carry in their hands, like what his ex-wife would take to parties and then make him hold once she'd had a second drink.

He unlocked the window and lifted it up, then leaned across the sill to retrieve the little purse. Inside were Ama's wallet and a phone, and on the ground was a black ankle brace.

"Shit," he hissed under his breath.

"What did you find?" Captain asked.

"It's Ama's purse." He turned to face the other man. "We have a major problem."

EDDIE

MARTIN STOPPED TALKING, AND CAPTAIN BEGAN ROARING. EDDIE stood still, his phone still ringing Ama's.

"Turn that thing off!" Captain shouted, and Eddie snapped back to the present. "Do you have any idea how many random people are here today, how light the security? What were you thinking? We could've had plain-clothes officers valeting cars or serving drinks. We could have had a picture of his face to every unit in the entire state. What were you thinking?" he repeated.

"I was thinking your department didn't have those kinds of resources or knowledge of how to do that, and good luck finding a picture of his face," Martin replied. "I tried."

"We don't find *Ama* tonight, it's your badge," the captain said, pointing a finger in his face.

"If we don't find her, you won't even have to ask for it. It'll be on your desk Monday morning."

"Goddammit, Eddie. You were in on this? How could you, with Hazel potentially at stake here?"

"She's been at stake for a year, sir," Eddie answered. "A year in this man's hands, a man you thought was dead. You thought she ran away, and you thought I'd killed my own daughter." Eddie's eyes welled up.

"*Martin* thought it was you. Martin convinced us it was you, so don't put this on me." Captain raked his fingers through his hair. "Christ Almighty. Where do we even start?"

"Tarson Woods," Eddie said. "That's where he had her. That's where

he faked his death. That's where he took them both. That's not a coincidence. That's where he feels safest, where it's quietest in his head. That's
his home."

"That is also thirty square miles of terrain," the captain countered.

"Then we better hurry. Make an announcement, see if everyone at the
party will help us search. Call every police department you can think of,"
Martin said.

"Wait!" Eddie looked at his phone. "I just got a text message, like you
said I would." He showed the screen to Martin. It was a long series of
numbers and letters and what looked to be a phone number.

"That's Ama waving the flag," Martin said. "I don't know how much
time that means we have, but I do know we don't have time to call anyone
except for whoever that number belongs to."

Martin took Eddie's phone, dialed the number, and put the phone on
speaker.

"Hot Spot," a man's voice answered.

"Do you know Ama Chaplin?" Martin asked.

"She said you'd be calling sometime today. The number she sent to you
is a tracking number. There's an app to read it. I'll send the link to this
phone; then you can see where she is. Any troubles, you call me back."
The line went dead.

"Jesus," Martin whispered. "That woman is in the wrong line of
work."

A
M
A

AMA WATCHED MICHAEL DROP HER NECKLACE TO THE GROUND IN THE little stone hutch, hoping that the broken chain had sent the text message to Eddie's phone. She hoped they could figure out to call the second set of numbers and that Martin wouldn't be a complete asshole to Durante. She looked at Michael's scarred hands and, above all else, hoped she would survive the worst decision she'd ever made in her life.

Michael knelt and trailed his fingers over the ground, rubbing a streak of topsoil between his fingers before standing.

"Why do you drop jewelry here? You left my watch here, too. It has some significance to you," she asked, partly to slow him down and partly out of genuine curiosity.

"When they opened the factory, my dad and a few of his friends gathered here and they each buried a piece of silver. Apparently someone said their grandmother swore it would bring them money."

"It didn't, though. So why continue it?"

"They sacrificed themselves for magic." Michael's face turns down, and the corner of his mouth curls in a boyish expression. "My father used to call it that—what they produced at the factory. Magic and money were produced, just not for them. You will produce magic, and it will probably yield money for someone, just not for you."

Ama masked a shudder as Michael steered her deeper into Tarson Woods. The dark of night and her staggered gait forced every step to be deliberate and slow. She had no idea if she'd been out here for five minutes or five hours, and despite the blinding pain of each movement, Ama felt

weightless and adrift, sailing on a steady stream of panic borne adrenaline. Nausea washed hard over her, and she crumpled, trying not to dry
heave. Michael hauled her up by her elbow.

"I'm glad it happened this way, walking through the woods together.
Not to mention it'll be a lot faster than me carrying you. You're heavier
than you look. I had to stick to the trails as much as possible before. Took
way longer than it should have." He let out a boyish laugh.

"I'm all muscle," Ama said through chattering teeth.

"It's time to use those muscles, my lady. Let's pick up the pace," he
said, becoming serious. "We need to get underground before anyone
misses you." He yanked her arm and she stumbled forward.

Underground. Fresh terror slithered through her. Would the tracker
work underground? Durante had said it would carry up to five miles. But
could it do all of that from under the earth?

M
A
R
T
I
N

A TWENTY-MINUTE SEARCH OF THE WOODS BEHIND THE COURTHOUSE lawn yielded no sign of Ama, and her location had yet to come up on the map. Martin stood in the middle of a grove of trees and laced his fingers together before pressing his hands down on top of his head. The pressure did nothing to slow his spinning mind. He'd lost Ama, and in losing her, he'd lost Hazel, too. He closed his eyes, wondering how he would ever be able to look Eddie in the face again, how he would be able to look at himself.

There were more people in this section of woods than Martin could count, but as the voices rang out, Martin realized he hadn't once heard Eddie call out for Ama. He opened his eyes and turned in a circle, but Eddie wasn't just quiet, he was gone.

"Eddie!" Martin cupped his hands, projecting his name into the night. He walked deeper into the woods. "Eddie!"

"I'm here," Eddie answered, and his form solidified in the shadows as he appeared on a skinny trail. He was out of breath, walking faster than Martin knew he was capable of moving.

"Has her location come up yet?" Martin asked, Eddie's urgency spurring on his own.

"No. But she's out there somewhere," he said, and opened his big hand, which he'd been holding in a fist. The little silver necklace Ama had been wearing at the fundraiser pooled in his palm.

"Where did you find that?" Martin demanded.

"The stone hutch."

"Why didn't you tell me where you were going? We could have gone together, been on their trail this whole time. Now they're half an hour ahead of us at minimum, Eddie!"

"The hutch is half a mile from the courthouse. I didn't tell you because if I was wrong, we'd both have wasted all that time. And Jonathon doesn't stick to trails, Martin. He could have gone anywhere after dropping off that necklace. He could've even double-backed here and hopped in a car while the rest of us were walking into the woods."

Desperation shook Martin from within. "Jesus Christ. How the hell are we going to find her? Are you sure there's no sign of her on your phone?"

"Nothing," Eddie said, and showed him the phone. Martin glared at the screen, tempted to snatch the phone and hurl it into the dark. A sense of utter failure struck him dead center, and it was all he could do to keep breathing, to keep pretending like he was someone who knew what to do next. But he had no idea what to do.

The impending collapse he and Eddie had talked about in Martin's living room floor loomed high over them now, and Martin inhaled long and deep as if preparing for the moment it all came crashing down. He'd been caught up in this wave of defeat before. Maybe he'd never really left it.

"What if Ama's location never comes up?" Eddie's voice brought him out of the dark of his mind and back into the woods. "We can't just stand here and wait."

Martin cast his eyes down, unable to admit this truth while looking at Eddie. "I don't know," he said.

"Don't give me that. I know these woods, but I don't know how to hunt for a criminal. According to you, I walked all over these hills with that monster right by my side. You tell me where we should go, tell me how to find him, and I'll get you there."

Martin blinked, his mind falling quiet. Eddie knew how Michael would behave out here better than anyone. He also knew every inch of the woods.

"Was there an area Jonathon kept you from in the woods? Anywhere he always volunteered to look or told you not to bother with?"

"No," Eddie answered, but now he sounded unsure.

"There had to be," Martin said, his thoughts gaining traction. "We know he's in these woods. He has been all along. He either tried to keep you from a certain location, or he made damn sure he was with you when you were going to search close to his safe place. Where is it?"

"No, no, it's the opposite," Eddie said, his entire body taut. "He didn't like going near the old factory. He never said anything, but whenever I said I was searching that area, he never came to help."

"Then we start there," Martin said. Immediately, he called the captain and told him to send all available units and anyone willing to search to the Evansbrite plant, then began striding deeper into Tarson woods, committing his entire self to this choice.

"Hold on, Martin. I know how wrong it feels to leave right now, but driving is going to be a whole lot faster," Eddie called at his back. By the time Martin turned around, Eddie was already hurrying in the direction of the courthouse lawn.

Martin caught up to him before they reached the edge of the grass, and they matched strides all the way to the parking lot.

When they reached the car, Martin tossed Eddie his keys. "You drive. You know where we're going. I know who to call for help."

They climbed into their seats and slammed the doors shut. Eddie cranked the engine and floored the gas, the tires spitting out gravel and kicking up dust. Martin braced a hand on the ceiling and began scrolling through his phone until he found the number for Mrs. Walton.

She answered on the third ring.

"Mrs. Walton, this is Detective Martin. I need your help." He spoke as calmly as he could as he relayed his suspicions, and then he hung up and turned to Eddie. "I know it sounds insane, and I trust your instincts about the factory, but we need to pick up a woman named Janie Walton first." He gave her address.

Eddie glanced at him, reluctance plain on his face, his fingers clamped around the steering wheel. Eddie didn't have to say anything for Martin to know he didn't want to go anywhere but the factory. "Tell me how to get there," Eddie said at last.

Martin knew it was a gamble, and what the delay of even a minute might cost them all, but he was absolutely sure of one thing: if they found Michael with Ama or Hazel held hostage, his mother was the only person on earth who stood a chance of stopping him.

AMA ARRIVED AT MICHAEL'S BUNKER PANTING AND SWEATY. SHE WAS almost grateful to step inside, if only for the break in movement. But seeing Hazel in the flesh didn't bring near the flood of relief Ama had anticipated.

Hazel sat in the far corner, barely eight feet away, both hands chained to the brackets on the metal shelving unit bolted to the bunker wall. Her shirt hung on her like it was pinned to a clothesline, and the slope of her face dove off her cheekbones. Her hair was knotted. She was missing several fingernails, and Ama spotted burn scars up both arms. Hazel's eyes were open but barely tracking Ama's presence.

In that moment, Ama knew she couldn't stay here and bide her time until Eddie and Martin found them. Each day she would be weaker. Minutes from now she would probably be chained to the shelves alongside Hazel. If they wanted out, they would need to act now—together—with absolutely zero communication and even less of a plan.

Michael's footsteps approached from behind, and the door swung shut, trapping them inside. Even though nothing in front of her had changed, the underground bunker felt smaller with the exit closed and Michael's breath close enough to warm her bare shoulder.

She and Hazel needed something, anything, to gain the upper hand on Michael. Neither of them were as physically strong as he was. Could they outrun him once free, Ama on one good ankle and Hazel half dead?

Michael reached past her and set his walking stick on the table, just out of reach of her and Hazel. Behind her, she heard the click of a lighter igniting.

"I've been waiting a long time," Michael said softly in her ear. "I have learned that the first sounds are the purest. The rest are tainted with fatigue. The pain becomes dulled over time. You'll get breaks when the tone weakens; then we'll start again. It's art, yes. But I have studied how people respond to stimulus, how the notes devolve in a session. I have this down to a science."

Ama's limbs tingled with adrenaline. Michael was a planner, methodical, tidy. The way to throw him off, the way to get ahead, was to make a mess. A big, loud fucking mess. And to do it sooner rather than later. She couldn't let herself get locked up; she couldn't trust that the tracker was transmitting, that Martin and Eddie were on their way here. She had to assume it was her versus Michael. Right here, right now.

Ama felt the presence of heat at her back, intense enough to make her instinctively flinch away. She would be like Hazel—she wouldn't make a sound. She wouldn't give him that. She stared at Hazel, desperate to channel her, to not end up like her, a skin-covered skeleton chained to a wall, and mouthed the words circling her mind as she tensed for the first burn: *Scream, Hazel. Scream!*

The sharp, heated end of a wire buried into Ama's back, scorching the skin covering her spine. She slammed her teeth together. Her arms shot straight out. She wouldn't make a sound, she wouldn't, but there was a scream in her ears, so loud it drowned out every thought—just pure rage and pain and fuck-you.

But it wasn't Ama's voice. It was Hazel, her mouth open, her dark eyes blazing like two lit coals. Ama heard the wire hit the ground and Michael began muttering notes. She flattened out her hands, pressing palm to palm, spun on her heel, and struck Michael directly in his Adam's apple. He gasped and coughed, but his hands came forward. Ama ducked under his reach and stumbled across the room. Michael barreled toward her and suddenly was sprawled face-first on the ground, one foot caught over the twiggy shape of Hazel's leg.

Ama grabbed the table and flipped it over. His walking stick flew across the room and clattered against the concrete. She slung a chair in the direction of his head. Hazel screamed again, a different pitch, high and shrill.

"No! Wait. Hazel, wait," Michael sputtered, and began crawling in her direction. Ama let out a roar, and Michael swung his gaze to her, lips opening, eyes bright. Hazel shrieked, notes flying from her mouth like a flute in a centrifuge.

Ama jerked open the other drawer. Sheet music was stacked inside. She snatched the paper out first, tore it down the center, threw it in the air.

"What are you doing?" Michael yelled.

Ama yanked open the cabinets and began flinging everything out of them, hurling canned goods and bottles of water in his direction, and then leaped across the room as he swung out at her. Michael followed, nostrils flaring, head lowered, teeth bared, when Ama saw Hazel climb on a chair, reach up, and slip the length of her chain through a gap in the wall and loose metal. She jumped down, snatched up the wooden stick, and swung.

Ama heard a crunch, and Michael's legs went out from under him. He struck the side of his head on the corner of the overturned table and slumped to the ground.

A
M
A

MICHAEL'S BREATHS CAME SHALLOW AND WET. BLOOD LEAKED FROM his nose, mouth, and ears.

"It's okay," Ama said. She reached out for Hazel, who jerked away.

No, it is not okay. Not by a long shot.

Ama's gaze turned to the door. "My name is Ama. Your dad is on his way. Your dad and a detective. They're coming."

"They won't find us. Not down here. Everything is locked. We have to get aboveground." Hazel's shoulders shuddered, and her tiny frame began to shake. "If we can get this door open, I can get us all the way out." She staggered to the door and began pounding it with her fists.

"What kind of lock is it? Combination?"

"Yeah. Bill . . . Bill said it's a four-number code, but Michael had changed it."

"What's the biggest number on the dial?"

"One hundred," Hazel answered.

Ama sat quietly, remembering the day she walked out of that courthouse following Michael's verdict, knowing immediately she was leaving there for the last time. How for years she would do her best to convince herself she didn't remember the date, didn't care that Michael was free.

"Try ten, ten, nineteen, eighty-nine," Ama said quietly. "You'll need to spin four intervals to the left on the first one, then it's just like a high school locker."

"We don't have time to be wrong," Hazel cautioned.

"Ten, ten, nineteen, eighty-nine," Ama repeated.

Hazel heaved a jagged breath, and then spun the dial as directed. The hatch popped open, and she let out a child's laugh, swinging her gaze at Ama.

"No!" Hazel shouted suddenly. Ama turned in time to see Michael swing the walking stick at her injured leg. The cane cracked the outside of her knee, and she dropped, smacking the side of her face on the floor.

"Run!" Ama sputtered, gasping, nearly blind with pain as starbursts clouded her vision. She kicked out and slapped her hands in the space above her. She was able to flick her eyes briefly to the open door—it was empty. Hazel was gone.

Michael gripped her wrists and dragged her to her feet. Heat and anger rolled off him, and his face was the portrait of rage. She would have one shot to survive the next sixty seconds. One. And it was going to take everything she had.

MICHAEL

AMA STOPS FIGHTING. I STARE AT THE BACK OF HER HEAD, BEWILDERED and panting, my brain pounding in my skull. She raises her hands to the welt blooming on her face. The door is open, but she isn't lunging for it, isn't screaming. She doesn't want to run with Hazel . . . she wanted to drive her away.

"You remember," I say, the pieces clicking together. "You remember the day this began. You remember what you said about our paths crossing. It was a test, wasn't it? You wanted to see how committed I was. Fate used you to test me." I nearly laugh. "You want this to be your song. And you're right, Ama. The two of you together, the voices didn't work; they competed instead of complemented. Hazel was throwing you off. The notes weren't clear at all. You've been a part of this from the beginning, from the very moment it started. I'm the one to blame here. You didn't have to do that. You didn't have to make such a mess. I'm not mad, though. A man I once worked for told me the most talented artists are the most volatile, the most difficult to work with. He said you have to admire the fight and passion in them instead of resenting it, that it's what makes them different, makes them great."

"I want to be great. Do you want to be great?" she whispers, turning slowly as if asking permission to move, and I loosen my grip to allow her, nodding when she can see my face.

"How can we be sure this is what we're supposed to do?" she asks. "You never told me. Hazel ruined everything."

"The river will show you, and we will leave this town, Ama. I know a place. We will have a studio, professional equipment. We can make our music. We have to hurry. Hazel is weak and it is dark, and she was so jealous of you—so jealous she screamed!—but she'll come for us. The moment she's discovered, we will be on borrowed time."

Ama steps closer to me, her lips and her tongue inches from my face. She hesitantly brushes her pinkie up and down my fingers. "I've defended you, protected you from the very beginning, when no one else would, Michael. I took on your case, I took on the DA and an unfriendly jury. I took a *bullet* for you. Didn't you ever wonder why? It's because *you* are great, and greatness always runs on borrowed time."

I peer in her eyes, gray as the river, and for the first time I wonder if I am staring at Fate herself.

H
A
Z
E
L

I CRAWL DOWN A DARK, CRAMPED TUBE, MY HANDS AND KNEES SLIPPING in what feels like a slick of damp moss. There is a light ahead, faint and small, and with the roar of my breathing echoing in front and chasing me from behind, I feel like I might be hit by a train. I realize I'm waiting for the blare of a whistle, for the sudden, undeniable moment when I am caught with no way out.

The ring of light becomes bigger, grayer, and as I draw closer, I can tell it is covered by some kind of vent. I struggle forth on sore knees, hands slapping, shoulders burning, the chain from my wrists dragging between my legs. The end of the tunnel is finally within reach. I hold my breath and listen, but the factory is silent. I wriggle my feet in front of me, draw my knees to my chest, and kick. The sound of the bang ricochets on the other side in the lofty room, and the thin metal web is now dented. I kick it again and again, and finally one side gives way and the grate falls open like a door.

I had imagined myself bursting through, tumbling to freedom, but I hang back behind the lip and slowly peer out. Through the darkness, the abandoned factory comes into grainy, two-dimensional focus. The wall ahead of me is lined with full-length metal lockers, covered in a film of dust. Bill's locker is number 4, I remember, where there will be a spare set of keys to his house and, under a false floor he installed, a revolver. When the alarm went off that day, he and everyone else had to leave everything behind. They never let the employees back in to retrieve their belongings. Each of these lockers is like a time capsule. For many, like a grave. The factory may not have killed them straight out, but over time, it came back to collect one by one. It's about damn time it helped save a life instead.

I slide out of the hole, jumping as the length of chain connecting the shackles on my wrists strikes the edge of the vent. I'm sure I've been discovered, but I am alone. I creep across the floor and pop open his locker. A rough textured jacket is hung on a hook and a knit beanie is on the top shelf. I shake out his hat and pull it on. The air is cold, and I realize I don't even know what season it is, only that it is night and that I am free. I am not safe, however. I kneel at the foot of his locker and press on the corners of the false floor one by one. The back left corner feels nearly spongy under my finger, and I hear a click. I press harder, and the metal plate lifts, revealing the outline of a short-barreled revolver. When I pick it up, it will be the first time I've ever held a gun.

In my mind, I make a list of what Bill taught me: right hand on the handle, left hand supporting underneath, slight bend in your knees, and a bend in the elbow—*Don't straight-arm it, Hazel. Cock the hammer. Bring the gun to your eye, not your eye to the gun. Exhale, steady, trigger.*

I am reaching for the gun when the faint wail of a far-off siren dispels the hush of black and solitude. I stand and move toward a broken window. The siren is louder and joined by a second, and a third. Fractured blue light paints the tops of trees. They're coming here.

They're coming here.

I nearly laugh, shout, leap. I grab a boot from another locker and break out the remaining glass. All I have to do is drop through the window and run toward the light and I will be free and safe.

But for how long?

If they don't catch Michael, he will come for me again. How will I close my eyes? How will I leave my house, my room? Will I ever be able to exist in a space alone again, if I know he can reach it? I am rooted to the dusty floor, watching in silence as the squad cars pull up on the other side of the chain link fence, sirens blaring, lights flashing. I have no idea how they knew where to come, only what Ama said, that a detective and my father were on their way. She must have let herself get caught by Michael the first time on purpose. But the way she fell to the concrete, the panic in her eyes when she told me to run . . . I don't think she meant to get caught again.

They won't find her, not with their lights and their shouts and their dogs and their slow steps. Michael will go to the river, if he's not already there, and he'll be swept out of sight. He'll either kill that woman, or he'll take her with him. My neck burns with the memory of a tightening wire, and suddenly I can't swallow. He won't kill her. He'll just make her wish she wanted to die.

I could run to the police, tell them everything, try to explain what he will do, but it will be slow. They'll want me to sit, to be evaluated, to rest. They'll want me to show them the bunker, when instead we should be running anywhere else. They won't let me hunt him. They will sit me in the back of a cop car or an ambulance, and they will leave me alone and go out into the woods and chase a shadow in the dark.

I go back to Bill's locker and pluck the gun from the floor. Then I move back to the window and study the length of the fence in the flickering light. Before Michael took me, I probably could've scaled it. Now, my arms already ache from crawling the length of the tunnel, my wrists burn where the shackles have rubbed off skin in new places, and my hands are barely strong enough to grip the gun. Near the end of visibility, I see a panel of chain curled away from the right-hand corner. If I can squeeze through the corner of a dog crate, that opening should be a walk in the park.

I toe out of my shoes, too loose to run in, and store them in Bill's locker. I can't help feeling as though I'm leaving another marker in this room—another grave. I stand by the window, waiting, and the second the lights on top of the cars go dark, I slip out of the factory and sprint to the break in the fence.

MARTIN

By the time they reached the factory, Captain and every unit on the payroll were gathered near the perimeter fence. Ama's name flooded the air like cicadas on a summer night, rhythmic and constant. Flashlight beams swept over dead grass. Ama's location had finally popped up when he'd been standing in Janie Walton's driveway, a blinking, little red dot on the barebones map. At the sight of it, Martin had damn near thrown the old woman into the car. Eddie had been right—Ama was headed to the factory.

Martin had used the rest of the drive to fill Eddie in on the true identity of Jonathon Walks. And now that they were here, Martin was losing faith. Captain and every uniform in the county had beaten him to the factory by nearly twenty minutes and had yet to report finding anything. Worse, Ama's little red dot had disappeared off the map before they'd reached the end of Janie Walton's road.

"You're absolutely sure this is where the signal was coming from before it dropped?" Martin asked Eddie.

"Yes. She was right here. On the north side of the factory, maybe off the back of the building by a quarter of a mile."

Martin leaned in to instruct Mrs. Walton to stay where she was, but she was already out of the car. Her face turned up at the night sky, and she sampled the air.

"This place still smells exactly the same," she said. "Don't waste your time searching the factory. Michael would never go inside."

"I don't mean any offense, ma'am, but right now I don't think any of us can predict what Michael would or wouldn't do," Martin argued, struggling for patience.

"I'm telling you, he won't be in there. If he knows you're looking for him, if he knows he's being chased, he won't be in there. He'll be out there," she said, and pointed her finger away from the building and into the woods. Martin stared at her, wondering how she knew where to point.

"The factory isn't the only thing I can smell," she said, as if she'd read his mind, and she turned her eyes upon him. "Can't you smell the river?"

"Her location was here, not the river. Let's check where the map showed her to be, then we'll go into the woods." Martin peered into the dark. Chasing a perp through alleys and down city streets was one thing. Combing these woods was going to be a completely different monster.

"We got something!" a voice called in the dark.

Martin bolted across the field. Stanton was shining a light down what looked to be an open sewer lid just inside the tree line. There was a square hole in the ground, six feet deep and sealed with brick. Two doors were cut into it. The larger door almost looked like the hatch to a spacecraft, and the other was a small, square metal door, which stood open, a combination lock cast off to the side.

Martin climbed down. There were scuffs in the dust on the floor, and Martin saw what looked like a smear of blood on a lower rung of the ladder and another on the doorframe. He shone his light beyond the opening, revealing a tunnel, three feet in diameter.

Stanton dropped down beside Martin and tested the bigger door, which didn't budge.

"Do we have anything to blast it open?" Stanton called up to Captain, who stared down at them from above.

"Don't bother," Martin chimed in. "This reads like they left, not like they're holed up in there. If Michael had Ama here, he'd have been sure to secure the way in." He spotlighted the edge of the ground-level lid, revealing tiny keyholes on both sides. "It locks. They're not here."

"What about the other open door?" Captain asked.

Martin returned his focus to the tunnel. The track was straight and level as far as he could see. He climbed the first couple of rungs of the ladder so he could follow the trajectory aboveground. Assuming it stayed straight, the tunnel led right back to the factory.

He relayed his findings to the captain.

"Stanton, check it out," Captain ordered. Stanton crouched to enter the tunnel.

"Someone went that way, but I don't think it was Michael," Martin cautioned, Janie Walton's advice echoing in his mind.

"Got it," Stanton replied, and disappeared.

Martin surfaced. Eddie approached the hole, hope and fear and hesitancy pulling at his features.

"She's not down there." Martin wiped the grime and disappointment from his face. "Where's Mrs. Walton?"

Eddie turned back in the direction they'd come. Several other officers dotted the grass, but she was not among them.

"Come on." Martin touched Eddie's elbow, swinging his gaze back and forth. He reached under his coat to withdraw a gun and then produced a second one and handed it to Eddie. "Do not shoot unless I tell you to."

Eddie's phone chimed, and he glanced at it. "It's back!" he nearly shouted.

"Where?" Martin stared at the screen. The little red dot flashed beside Cold River. "Refresh the location every thirty seconds," Martin instructed. "Can you run?"

"Today, I can," Eddie said, and they sprinted into Tarson Woods.

A
M
A

MICHAEL STOOD AT HER BACK, AND THE RIVERBANK CRUMBLED AT HER feet as he again told her the story of the river and how it made him clean . . . how it made him invincible. She'd heard it all in pieces before, but she let him talk. The river was barely a half mile from the factory, if that. Hazel had gotten out. Martin—if all went well—should have her location. She just needed to borrow as much time as she could.

A flash of movement to her left nearly made her look up, but if she looked, so would Michael. He had repeatedly said he wouldn't push her, that it had to be her choice, but Ama wasn't sure he would keep that promise if the police appeared.

She must have tensed, because Michael stopped talking and she felt his attention swing left.

"I think I saw someone," she whispered, following his gaze. She heard a rustle in the leaves but didn't see any flashlights. "Maybe it was a deer," she said.

"Probably. Let's move upstream a bit, just in case," Michael said, his hand skimming her waist, guiding her to the right, protecting her from venturing too close to the edge. Ama noticed they were moving uphill. The fall would be farther.

"You're scared," Michael said.

"It's a long way down."

"It is. But at the bottom is freedom. If you invite Death to eat at your table and Fate intercepts the invitation, you'll have nothing to fear for the rest of your life, because you will know, beyond all doubt, that Lady Fate has you in her hand."

Or that I was a college swimmer and set a record for the two-hundred-meter butterfly.

Ama stayed at that pool in her head. When she jumped, she would pretend she was diving in for a race; the shock of cold water would be just like the training pool at a five o'clock practice, the ache of a one-mile swim during summer conditioning. That grit had been what made her successful in her career and maybe a little tough to understand.

That grit, she decided, would be enough.

MICHAEL

AMA SMELLS LIKE THE RIVER. THE HEM OF HER LONG DRESS BILLOWS against my legs, and her hair dances on a gust of wind. Even standing still, she is movement, water, Lady Fate herself.

I can feel her turning over pieces of her life in her head, probably looking for a sign. I remember how it felt, standing at this spot, looking into the water, cold and scared. Then the moment came when I knew I would survive, and it will come for her, too.

At her sides, her fingers curl and uncurl. Her weight shifts back to front, and I remember the same show of nervousness she'd displayed in the courtroom before they read the verdict. Now she will be on trial, the river her judge and jury, and I am her defender. The symmetry is beautiful, perfection.

Beyond her, something flickers in the trees, and I straighten with attention.

"Okay," she says. She must not have seen it. I feel her lean away from me, weight gathering on the balls of her feet, her dress blowing backward. Hesitation bleats inside me, and I want to reach for her, to tell her to wait, but I cannot interfere, not if she has chosen now to jump.

From behind, there is a scuffle of leaves and twigs. A ray of light sweeps the bank, and I realize the flicker I saw earlier wasn't something moving over here but weak light catching on the boughs of trees lining the opposite bank.

We've been discovered.

Ama drops to a crouch, and her face appears over her shoulder. I move to shield her from view, but with the distraction and sudden pressure of a closing window, she may need more—she may need me to jump first.

Two flashlights glare at us through the dark, and I recognize the shape of one man: Eddie Stevens's stilted gait as he jogs up the crest of the hill, wheezing and puffing. Hazel sent them; that jealous little bitch sent them.

"Michael, stop! Hands up! Ama, stay down!" another man's voice shouts. I look down at Ama. Tears streak her face. She nods up at me. "Michael, step away from Ama, or I will shoot you! Michael!"

"The river will set us free," I say, preparing to push off. Maybe this is the way it was meant to be—I was always meant to jump a third time. Maybe my mother was wrong—pushing me into the water didn't count.

One last time, one last jump, and we can begin.

HAZEL

I RACE ALONG THE BANK OF THE RIVER, MY GAZE TRAINED UPWARD ON the beam of light swinging across the ledge above, and I hear a man shout. Ama is kneeling on the bank. Michael looks down at the river, leaning out. He's going to jump. If he hits the water, they'll never catch him.

He lurches forward a step. I lift the gun, bend my knees, and keep my arms bent, too, and peer over the barrel of the gun.

I'll keep both eyes open, Bill, I promise.

Suddenly I am grateful I used the dark of that hole to imagine shooting Michael one hundred million times.

His arms fly up, his body completely exposed. I train the sight on him dead center. Ama's hand claws at a pant leg, but she won't stop him.

Exhale.

Steady.

Trigger.

MICHAEL

BANG.

A bullet tears through my back, and pain crashes through me, a wave across a beach, and nausea floods behind it.

BANG.

I hit the water, and the cold snatches the pain and my breath and my doubt, and I relax. The river will carry me. I can only hope Ama jumped, that she chose this path and that I won't need to come back and show her the way.

E
D
D
I
E

THE BLAST OF GUNFIRE ROOTED EDDIE TO WHERE HE STOOD, AND IN his mind's eye, he relived the night he shot Ama. In front of him, Ama covered her head and neck with her arms. She pressed her forehead to the damp earth and screamed. Martin hustled to her side. He crouched beside her, wrapping one hand around her back and training his flashlight down on the water with the other.

"Eddie!"

Martin's voice snapped Eddie out of his daze and propelled him forward, his gun trained ahead, ready to fire at whoever was shooting at them from the other side. He wondered if it was Michael's mother, if she'd come to the river first to protect her son one last time.

His feet were lead-heavy as he reached the edge and shone his light down.

"Hazel! It's Hazel!" Martin said, but Eddie barely heard him. All his senses converged on the tender face peering up at him from the river, at her wrists shackled at her front, age in her eyes and a gun in her hands. Tears poured from his eyes, and his heart pounded in his chest. Eddie heard Martin radio for help.

"Hazel!" Eddie said her name over and over and over, praying she wouldn't vanish, that she wasn't a ghost in these woods or a figment of fatigue and darkness.

"Daddy," she whimpered as she tried to climb up the bank. She slid down, her limbs folding like the legs of a newborn fawn.

"Wait!" Eddie cried. "You wait right there. I know the way, Hazel. I'm coming to you, baby. I'm coming."

MICHAEL

Chapter 86 | 7:55 PM, December 9, 2006 | Tarson, Georgia

I ALLOW THE RIVER TO TUMBLE ME, KNOWING THE COLD WILL SLOW THE bleeding and my heart and will reduce inflammation. Fate always brings me here when I need to heal.

I surface when my lungs demand oxygen, only allowing my nose and mouth to emerge, and then slide under again, riding the current down. It will become shallow a ways ahead for just a stretch, and then it plunges to an unknown depth, the water ten degrees colder in that section of the river, how Cold River came to have its name. I close my eyes and sail, listening to the underwater percussion.

The current accelerates, announcing the shallows. Weakness sets in. If not for the river, I would probably be dead. My head pounds with pressure, and the sensation of static on a TV screen marbles my vision. I allow my whole body to surface and float, embracing Fate, trusting her method, her timing. Ama was ready, I decide. She jumped. I know she did. She'll meet me in the river.

The water turns cold again, and I know the deep is coming, then after it the bend near my childhood backyard and into a desolate stretch of forest between towns, and I will be free. Isn't your life supposed to flash in front of your eyes when Fate shines her light?

I bump into something too soft to be a stone, too warm to be a tree, and my eyes open. A woman's silhouette peers down, backlit by the moon. Her hands touch my face; then she threads her fingers through mine. The skin is not smooth like Ama's, the knuckles knobby, fingers longer and spindly. A pianist's hands.

Mother's face comes into focus for just a moment. Her lips move, but I can't hear her. I wonder if she's jealous, if she's proud. For the first time in a long time, she doesn't look angry. She squeezes her eyes shut, and I think she might cry. In the light of the moon, I see silver glint on her wrist. It's the bracelet my father bought her with the first paycheck from the factory. I remember how pink and angry she became upon seeing it, calling it a waste. Later that night I caught her admiring the way it looked on her wrist, smiling down at it, cradling my father's face in her hands and kissing him on the mouth.

Her hand releases mine, moves to my throat, cups my face, and I am eight years old again, basking in the glow of a mother who does not hate me. Then she pushes me under.

I try to stand and slap at her, but my feet can't gain a hold. My legs buckle each time I try to bear weight, and my arms are weak with cold and blood loss. Something bites into my neck. She's fastened a metal cord around my throat and now she's towing me downstream, to the deep where she cannot stand.

M
A
R
T
I
N

MARTIN STOOD ON THE LEDGE OVERLOOKING COLD RIVER. ABOVE him, morning sunlight filtered weak and pale through naked branches. Below, divers disappeared under the surface of the black water. He breathed out hard, his breath a puff of vapor in front of his face.

Captain finished a conversation with the head of the dive team and made his way toward Martin, his hands shoved in his pockets and a cigarette dangling from the corner of his mouth.

"Don't be disappointed if they don't find Michael," Captain said.

Martin spun his phone in his hand. He knew he should be celebrating. Hazel and Ama would both spend tonight in their own beds. But he also doubted either one would sleep, that either one would feel completely free of Michael Walton until *he* was the one locked in a cage—or a coffin.

Martin's phone buzzed with an incoming call, and Ama's name flashed on the screen.

"Speak of the devil," he muttered to himself. Captain raised an eyebrow.

"Hey," Martin said into the phone.

"Have they found him yet?" she asked. Martin could practically feel her glaring.

"They just started," he answered.

She was silent on the other end for two seconds. Three. "There's a walking stick he carried. It has piano keys carved down the side."

"I know the one. We found it. It's bagged and tagged in evidence. GBI is taking over the case," he added.

"Get it back," she said.

"The case or the stick?" Martin asked, and pressed his fingers against his throbbing forehead.

"The stick."

"You know I can't do that," Martin responded quietly.

"I need it, Martin," she said, her voice breaking.

"You don't want that in your house, Ama. God knows what he's done with it."

"If you don't find him, that stick will be the best way to tell if *he's* found *me* again," she explained.

"How do you figure?"

"If he sneaks into my house or my office and the stick is there, he would have to take it, Martin. And if it's gone, I'll know he's back."

"Ama, we'll find him," Martin said.

"You don't know Michael like I do," Ama whispered, and hung up.

Martin stared at the ground, his hands squeezed into fists and planted on his sides. He needed to sleep for a week. He needed to drink or eat something besides coffee. He needed a damn body.

"You shouldn't make promises you can't keep," Captain advised, regarding him from his peripheral vision. "I'm not saying Michael isn't down there. With how many bone fragments we found in that bunker, I'd bet my fishing boat there's at least one body in this river somewhere. Divers are just going to have a tough time finding it."

Martin realized Captain was attempting to console him. "Why's that?" he asked.

"The river is about thirty-five feet deep here, but the floor has a crevasse vein cut in it about four feet across at its widest points, and only the devil himself knows how deep that goes. They'll do what they can, but it's going to be slow going." Captain dropped his cigarette to the damp earth and stomped it out with the toe of his shoe.

Martin leaned against a tree and watched for nearly an hour as divers surfaced, taking breaks or changing gear, and then sunk back down into the dark water. Each time they surfaced with no signal to the retrieval boat, the squeeze of pressure clenched harder. He tried to slow his mind, to calm his nerves, to silence the craving for a hit roaring in his blood. He pulled his phone out of his pocket and dialed Stacy's number. She picked up on the second ring.

"What's wrong?" she asked upon answering.

Martin relayed the events of the past forty-eight hours and the revelation about Jonathon Walks and Michael Walton. "We had him cornered on a riverbank. We *had* him, and he jumped," Martin explained, curtaining his mouth with his hand. "They're searching the water now."

"You found the girl. Isn't that the most important part?"

"Ama found her," Martin admitted, and in his mind, he made the commitment to bring her that damn stick no matter who he pissed off to do it.

"You know, Marty, I know this is a rough day, but you sound . . . you sound like yourself. I think the move has been good for you."

"I wanted a fix," he confessed.

"You called me instead," she reasoned. "Call me back if you need to."

"I will," Martin answered. A faint smile crossed his face. "I love you," he said, and immediately wished he hadn't.

"I know you do," she answered quietly, and the line went dead.

Martin pocketed his phone and watched a diver's bubbles rise, breaking the surface of the water. His craving was temporarily alleviated, but his heart was heavy as a stone. All he'd done in the last year was let people down: his ex and Toni, now Eddie, Hazel, and Ama. He needed to move his legs and clear his head, the pressure of this truth too thick to breathe through while standing still. Maybe he'd go buy a Sunday copy of the *AJC* and amuse himself with the fact that news of Ama's kamikaze stunt had no doubt bumped Esther Kim's article off the front page. He took one last glance at the water in spite of himself. The diver who'd just emerged pulled out his mouthpiece and waved.

"We got something!"

Martin stared down at the gray, lifeless faces of Michael and Janie Walton as a GBI forensic tech took photograph after photograph of their bodies.

He zeroed in on Michael's neck, where a silver cord looped in a snare around his throat, then ran straight for about a foot before coiling around Janie's wrist, joining them together. Her fingers strangled the metal even in death. The coroner mentioned that it was too early to declare who had drowned who, but Martin recalled the stony resolve on Janie's face during their drive to the factory, how she could smell the river, the way she had disappeared into the woods.

Michael's shirt had a gaping hole, revealing a gunshot wound that exited to the left of his belly button, blood washed clean from the wound and the fabric from a night spent in frigid, moving water. When Martin saw Toni's trademark garnet ring bagged in the evidence collected in the initial sweep of Michael's underground bunker, he'd held it up to the sun, watched the light wink off the stone, wanting to believe Toni knew, wherever her soul was, that he'd never stopped looking, never stopped trying to find who killed her. He'd been unwittingly hunting this man for a year, and even when he knew his name, he never knew his face. He studied Michael now, wondering if there could've been any telltale sign Martin could've spotted had he crossed paths with him when Michael was alive.

"I didn't see the male at first," one of the divers said to Martin. "The female's body had settled across the crevasse and was lodged half under a rock. His body had dropped inside the crack, but the wire kept him from sliding all the way down."

"Stroke of luck," Martin managed to say, leaning back against the lip of the boat as the tech motioned for the coroner to zip the body bags. He watched Michael's profile vanish beneath the black canvas and nearly asked them to reopen it just so he could make sure Michael hadn't disappeared.

They followed the coroner off the boat and to the access road, where the bodies were loaded into the back of a van. Two uniformed personnel slammed the doors shut, and Captain clamped a hand on Martin's shoulder.

"Martin, remember this feeling. Hold on to it like hell. This is over for the Stevenses and for Ama, but there will always be a next one for you."

"So I'm not fired?" Martin asked, only partially joking.

"No. We've got a shelf full of cold cases with your name on it, when you're ready. There will be an office door with your name on it, too."

"Tomorrow," Martin answered. "This is the kind of news I want to deliver in person."

He headed for his car, his mind already inside Eddie and Hazel's home, no longer silent, no longer plagued with empty places where Hazel should be.

H
A
Z
E
L

DAD PULLS THE VAN INTO THE LOT AT THE TARSON WOODS TRAILHEAD. It's empty except for Ama. She's leaning against a silver car, her arms folded across her chest, her eyes all shadows. My palms break out in a clammy sweat, and my throat threatens to draw shut.

"You called Ama?" I manage to ask.

Dad nods. "You two fought your way out of those woods together. If you really got it in your mind to go back in there, I thought she might be able to help see you through," he says. "But we don't have to go one step on that path, Hazel. We can turn around right now and you don't ever have to come back here."

"I do," I whisper. I'm leaving Tarson for Savannah College of Art and Design come August, and if I don't face these woods, I am afraid I'll bring them with me no matter how far I go. And I've tried. Oh, I have tried. Twice now, I've made it as far as where the concrete gives way to earth, but I shook with such a force, blown back from it as if by a rogue gust of wind only I could feel, and both times I turned, head down, and somehow made it back to the van on wobbling legs.

"Michael's not out there, Hazel," Dad says.

I nod.

We climb out of the car. Ama strides toward us. Even though the spring afternoon is warm and the air still, I swear I see her shiver.

"Thank you for coming," Dad says to her.

"Thanks for calling," she replies. "This is something I need to face, too."

"You haven't been back here?" I ask.

"Fuck no."

She stares into the woods, and I am mystified by this. Ama Chaplin, the angel in a white dress who came through Michael's door and would see it stand open long enough to slide me through, is rocked back on her heels, goose bumps covering her arms, her body stiff as if she is bracing against the same frigid wind I feel every time my mind travels this path, every time I breathe air that tastes like it tumbled across the surface of Cold River on its way to me.

"Are you ready?" she asks.

"No," I say. We shuffle toward the path anyway, side by side, my dad a few steps behind.

Ama stops where the concrete turns to dirt. I glance at her face. She's glaring up the trail.

"I can go first," my father says.

"We got this," Ama says. My legs are lead, my feet cement blocks, and it is everything I can do to not turn around.

"I need you to go first," I whisper.

"You don't," she says. We stand in silence. I can feel Dad shifting, wanting to whisk me back to the car, back to our home, to cook dinner and put on my favorite movie and offer to add a blanket or take one away, making sure I am neither too warm nor too cold at fifteen-minute intervals.

"Without you, I would still be out there," I whisper. This truth has haunted me, as present as a shadow in every room.

"Maybe," she says. "Without you, I would still be out there." She looks at me. "But we're not out there. And those are not Michael's woods. This is not Michael's trail. We were not Michael's fate, and he was not ours. That's not how it works. Only one thing had to go right for Michael to take us—he had to not get caught. About nine million things had to go right for us to survive him. So if there is such thing as Fate, you tell me whose side Fate was on."

"So why haven't you come back here?" I ask.

"Because this is still the last place on earth I'd choose to be."

I nearly smile. I keep my eyes on her taut face, witnessing her blatant reluctance somehow making it easier to define my own, and I step with one foot onto the dirt.

It is only dirt.

Not quicksand or a trapdoor. Not the center of a snare or the trigger point of a landmine.

"How far do you want to go?" she asks.

"I want to make it one step past the place where Michael took me. One step."

"Okay," she says. "We'll follow you."

We enter the woods. The trees seem taller, the air still. Even from this distance I swear I can hear the river. I breathe out slow and count as I've been taught to do when my pulse rockets.

Dad's uneven strides are a comfort in my ear. I know the sound like I know my own hands. Ama treads so lightly I'm not convinced she's there until I peek over my shoulder to see her. Her stare is fixed beyond me, and her lips are pressed into a line.

The trail turns on a series of switchbacks climbing the first big hill. Sweat beads on my hairline. The exertion feels good, and every few seconds I realize I'm just thinking about my breathing, the trail, my pace, and I am the girl who could run this six-mile hike in under fifty minutes, not reduced to the headline of the girl who survived a year with Michael Jeffery Walton. Then I see the scars on my swinging arms and I am back in the bunker, cold and hungry and terrified and silent. That girl still lives inside me, still wakes up gasping for breath when dreams of black water haunt my sleep.

We reach the bend in the path, and I remember seeing Michael come through the trees and start the other way down the path. My legs demand to move faster, and I start running down the hill. Ama keeps pace, stride for stride. My dad's footfalls come heavy and quick. The trees blur, the dirt feels like a wet sandbank under my shoes, and each breath feels like it's made of shards of glass. My lungs could be on that wall, my vocal cords strung across them. I run harder, legs and arms burning, air whipping past me.

I remember exactly which two trees we had stopped beside when Michael pretended to see a turtle in the leaves. I'd bent down for a better look, then felt a blow on the back of my head, a crunch reverberating in my skull, and when I woke, I would not see the sun again for a year.

I see the two trees now, unchanged, still leaning away from each other in a haphazard V. I slow to a stop in front of them and stare up at the sky. Light winks down through the canopy of the forest. Ama stops beside me. Dad catches up, one arm swinging in front of him, the other hand pressed into his side.

"What happened to Michael's walking stick?" I ask as my breathing slows.

Ama lets out an uncharacteristic bark of laughter.

"What's so funny?"

"That damn stick." She walks in a circle, her chin tilted skyward, her hands on her hips. "I asked Martin for it before we knew Michael was dead. Once his body was found, I fantasized about all the ways I could get rid of it—burn it, bury it, throw it in the river. But they all seemed too . . . meaningful."

"So what did you do?"

"Put it out with the trash," she answers. "Michael doesn't get one minute more of my life."

I draw a line in the dirt with my toe, nodding. "This is where Michael took me." Standing here, I understand why. It's mostly downhill from here to the bunker, for anyone willing to hike off the trail, and not many people come out this far. I step over the line with both feet.

"Okay," I say. I'm not exactly sure what I'm feeling, but it's a stirring of something, or maybe it's the stirring of nothing at all, but I find myself still glad to feel it.

"Okay?" Dad holds himself up with his hands on his knees, one eye open, sweat pouring down his face, dripping from his chin.

"Let's go home."

Ama glances up the trail. "My line in the sand is a little farther from here," she says. "And actually, I think I want to finish this run one last time."

"Do you want company?" I ask. I feel Dad's stare on my cheek.

"No." She slides her Walkman along her waistband and pulls earbuds out of her jacket pocket. "You got me this far," she says. "I think I can go the rest of the way on my own." Then she jogs down the next hill at a relaxed pace and disappears around a bend.

Dad and I walk back to the car.

"Should we wait for Ama?" Dad asks.

"No." I stare into the trees. "She'll be okay," I say.

We pull out of the lot. Dad glances at me every few seconds. I roll down my window and stick my hand out, feeling it slice through the air. Then I turn the knob for the stereo. A song comes through the speakers. I watch my fingers ride the wind, feel the music as it fills the car, imagine Ama running up the trail, reclaiming it stride by stride.

The singer reaches the chorus, one I know by heart. I close my eyes, and I hum along.

Acknowledgments

I'VE OFTEN HEARD THAT AS AN AUTHOR I SHOULD WRITE WHAT I KNOW. In the case of this story, I (thankfully) first had a lot to learn. Thank you Katelyn DeRogatis and Jason Lovell for answering all my questions, no matter how minor the details or unnerving the subject matter. Thank you to my husband for helping me bust through the walls of the dead ends I'd written myself into. You're better at it than you think. To all three of you: I am grateful not only for all of your expertise but also for your support. Another person's curiosity is like a breath of pure oxygen on an open flame, and when that fire becomes too small to cast warmth, people like you are who keep it burning long enough to catch the next piece of kindling.

Thank you to Christina Kaye for making me believe the draft I sent you could really be something, for teaching me and guiding me, and for shining your light every step of the way. To Shayne Leighton, a creative force of nature, who is, by turns, both the storm and the captain of the ship, and the kindest person I know.

My deepest gratitude to a brilliant editor, Katie McGuire, for your vision, your encouragement, and your love of these characters. And to an extraordinary agent, Rosie Jonker, who has quite literally changed my life and become a champion of my dream. It feels like we're nearing a finish line as I type this, and in a way we are, but I realize and I hope—desperately hope—that this is also just the beginning.